The Werewolf Thief

- Book 1 of the Divinity Stone Series -

Steven Wombell

First edition paperback and hardcovers were produced in 2021

Edited by Angela Brown
Book design by Thea Magerand

978-0-6453793-0-3 (e-book)
978-0-6453793-1-0 (paperback)
978-0-6453793-2-7 (hardcover)

www.stevenwombell.com

To Sonia Wombell (my dearest mother), who inspired and nurtured my creativity and my love for fantasy and science fiction. She always encouraged and supported me, no matter how long my endeavours took or how crazy they seemed. Unfortunately, my mum was diagnosed with Alzheimer's six years ago and slowly, steadily regressed over the years. Alzheimer's is a terrible disease, with no cure, that affects our friends, family, and loved ones. It leaves a feeling of hopelessness, as there is nothing, we can do except watch them deteriorate and eventually die. This is what happened to my mother, who passed away in July 2021. That is why I would like to donate 20% of the proceeds made from this novel towards Alzheimer's research. Hopefully this will help find a cure and stop this dreadful disease from affecting the people we love.

Map of South-Western Kalmeer

Chapter 1

A large, dense forest surrounded the campsite. It had been a harsh winter, and the tall snow-covered trees stretched up like skeletal fingers reaching towards the heavens. It was early evening; the campfire's flames dancing as the wood crackled, illuminating the area with flickering shadows. Having already eaten, Darla lay sleeping with a thick fur-lined blanket wrapped around her. Her horse stood nearby, a silent guardian, content while he munched on some oats. His name was Midnight, due to his pitch-black coat. To Darla he was more than just a horse, however; he was her best friend, a loyal companion.

Etched into the tree next to Midnight was an elaborate glowing symbol. The same symbol was inscribed into other trees, in a pattern circling the campsite. The symbols were invisible to the naked eye but had revealed themselves due to the ring Darla wore on her left hand. The symbol indicated a Brotherhood hideout, a hidden encampment protected by a mirage spell—one that completely masked any occupants, enabling them to avoid detection. To gain access all you needed to do was say the password. It was an added measure of security. Darla knew all the passwords for every campsite location, but such was the privilege when you were an elite Brotherhood assassin.

The Brotherhood was a vast network with spies, operatives, and members encompassing every corner of Kalmeer like an intricate spider web. They had their fingers in every pie; their influence infiltrating every town, royal court, and guild like the tentacles of a giant octopus enveloping the world. Being so extensive, they constantly had messages, letters, contracts, documentation and intelligence in transit. For long-distance communication they utilised their gnome-designed ships and zeppelins. It was rumoured the high councillor even had his own magical orb that he used for communication. The identities of the recipients of these messages, however, was a complete mystery.

For the most part, the Brotherhood used their rookery of ravens to send and receive communications. The large birds were highly intelligent and had been trained by the rook master since they were chicks. Many of them could speak, and even though they were mischievous, they were also extremely sociable. The ravens could fly great distances, gliding on the wind currents and resting periodically. As black as midnight, they also blended into the night sky and were oblivious to prying eyes. They were the perfect messengers.

The Brotherhood had a monopoly on business dealings, both criminal and legitimate. Some people had tried to branch out, to compete, only to find themselves warned, quite brutally. Those that ignored it, soon found themselves with their throats slit or floating face down in a river. The only competition that existed was the Shadow Hand, five vampires that operated in secret. The Brotherhood had tried to recruit them, only to be rejected. With their egos diminished and their noses put out of joint, they'd sent a dozen operatives to try to neutralise the threat. A gift-wrapped box had arrived days later with a note, a small pouch of gold, and the operatives' heads. The note read, "Thanks for the feast. We'll settle for a partnership. The gold is a present. Send some A-class jobs our way and we'll give you a commission." Far from stupid, the Shadow Hand had come up with a compromise, one that benefited both parties, one the Brotherhood begrudgingly accepted. It was better than having them as thorns in their side. The Brotherhood was patient, though, and the time would come when they'd end their partnership and destroy the Shadow Hand like they had all their rivals.

Darla's eyes flickered as she tossed and turned, restless as she dreamt, reminiscing about the past. It was the same nightmare, plaguing her subconscious and haunting her. Moaning, she flicked off her fur lined blanket. Accustomed to these episodes, Midnight quietly trotted over then bit down, grabbing the edge of the blanket, and pulled it back over her. Darla mumbled something incoherently, tossing her head as she relived her terrifying past, that fateful night fresh in her mind.

The manor was a hive of activity, with people visiting from every nation within Kalmeer. A celebration was taking place; it was her father's birthday or maybe her mother's—she couldn't remember. All the guest rooms were full, the house in chaos. Darla even had to share her bedroom, although she didn't mind sharing it with Lance, her guardian and best friend. He was like an older brother, loyal and protective. The other guest in her room, though, was a baby, the youngest of the princes of Sethanon. His older brothers were sleeping two doors down in one of the guest rooms.

Even from the second story, she heard the ruckus, the laughter, and raised voices of the partygoers. The bard played a jaunty tune while the jester mingled, prancing from group to group and entertaining them with jokes, tricks, and acrobatics. Darla and Lance had tried to sleep but couldn't, and it was now well past their bedtime. Unfazed by the noise, the drooling baby was fast asleep on a pile of pillows.

Darla lay in her four-poster bed, its lace curtains enclosing her. Lance sat next to her, leaning against a pile of pillows. A massive fur-lined blanket covered them. She was twelve and Lance fifteen, but their parents trusted them explicitly. Leaning on one of her elbows, her head resting on her hand, Darla listened intently, captivated by one of Lance's stories. She giggled as he scrunched up his face and spoke in a funny voice. His tales were always amusing, making her smile and laugh.

Rolling onto her side, hugging the corner of her blanket, Darla smiled at the cherished memory. Everything had been so simple back then—a time when she'd had no responsibilities and not a care in the world. Then everything changed. She moaned as the dream continued. *Lance didn't even get to finish his story. Concerned, they looked towards the door as shrieks erupted from downstairs.*

Darla frowned as her dream seemed to skip. Some fragments were missing, blocked out, and she couldn't remember them. As more and more came back to her, she gradually put the pieces together. She couldn't remember jumping out of bed or running down the hallway; her mind was blank, devoid of the memory. Part of her wished she was devoid of the entire experience, as it was something no twelve-year-old girl should have to endure. Even now, years later, she often questioned herself, wondering what might have happened if she had stayed in her room, had never witnessed the horrors. The answer was simple: she would have been killed along with everyone else.

The blanket became a tangled mess as she continued to dream, tossing in her sleep. *She ran down the staircase, taking them two at a time, Lance following close behind. Without even thinking, she had grabbed the baby and held it close to her chest with one hand. In her other hand she held her dagger. She couldn't see her parents —something was wrong, very wrong. A pack of werewolves had*

4

stormed inside the manor, their mission to kill the nobility. Beside them, fighting, were dwarves, humans, gnomes, vampires, sandrigar, elves and gorkin.

The sandrigar were a desert people that were barbaric. They were a huge, muscly race that were dark skinned and excellent fighters. The Brotherhood poison master was sandrigar. A huge man that had a booming voice and often told stories about his homeland. He had claimed to have been stung by one of the giant scorpions that they rode. When Darla had questioned why he wasn't dead, he had explained that all sandrigar were given small doses of poison to drink from infancy. Over the years they developed an immunity. Darla had scoffed, disbelieving him until he had shown her the scar on his dark brown skin. She had laughed, embarrassed, and apologised even though inwardly she still had doubts. Since then, Darla had always wanted to visit their desert land and see the giant scorpions that they rode into battle.

The gorkin were a fierce race, horrid in appearance, a crossbreed between orcs and goblins. They were outcasts, shunned by their races and banished, so they had travelled across the sea and settled in the wastelands. That was a century ago, and what had started out as a group of outcasts, a small settlement, was now a small empire. Living on the borders of multiple kingdoms, they had proven to be ferocious and cunning adversaries, formidable opponents for their werewolf, vampire, and dwarven neighbours.

The fanatics created chaos, sowing seeds of discord and distrust amongst the races. They were zealous, their eyes wild. They yelled out the name of their leader, whom they worshipped, as if it were a mantra that gave them strength and purpose, urging them on to victory or death. It was as if they were muted, though; Darla couldn't hear the name, no matter how much she tried. She looked around frantically. The polished wooden floor of the dining room was now stained red with pools of blood. Mangled bodies and limbs littered the space—a massacre had taken place.

The guards stood steadfast, rallying a defence as they barricaded themselves. Armed with swords, axes and other melee weapons, they stood with their shields held in front of them, a protective wall against the onslaught. A man and a woman pushed forward, barging past the guards. Lance's parents, people Darla considered family, ran towards Lance and her and grabbed hold of them. They took the baby from Darla and shielded them with their bodies, trying to protect them, as they guided them towards safety. Three guards flanked them, providing a shield-like wall, and slashing at any fanatics who came close. One of them collapsed, his leg hacked off, and a gap opened. It was through this gap that Darla spied her parents lying dead on the floor.

Their bodies were shredded, mangled, and lying in a pool of blood. It was a memory etched into her brain, one she'd never forget. *The werewolves' leader was hovering over her parents, plucking something off her father's corpse. He was a beast, huge and imposing, with her father's thick white-gold necklace dangling from his clawed hand. Attached to the end of it was a large white stone with swirls of grey; it looked like a mini moon. Darla instantly recognized it as their family heirloom.*

She screamed, tearing herself away and running to her parents. She was hysterical, unable to see clearly due to the tears. There was no thought, no rational logic for her actions. Standing next to her mother and father, she snatched the chain from the beast. It was hers, a reminder of her parents, her birthright. Growling, the werewolf swiped; the blow was swift and powerful, aimed straight at Darla's head.

She ducked, narrowly missing it. If it had connected, it would have cleaved half her head off. With a flash of metal, she swung her dagger in retaliation. The blade was razor-sharp and made of silver. It sliced through the werewolf's fingers, severing them off. With a spray of blood, two fingers dropped to the floor and the werewolf howled. Glaring at her, his lips raised, he snarled. All she had done was piss him off. She was about to die.

* * *

Like a flash, he pounced on her, his jaws wide-open, ready to rip her throat out. She tried to dodge but wasn't quick enough. His teeth sank into her shoulder, clamping down and tearing through flesh and muscle. Falling backwards, bowled over by the impact, she screamed. Darla cried out in her sleep, and her hand unconsciously went to her shoulder, a shoulder that bore a horrific scar. It was a constant reminder and identified her as the monster she was. She kept it hidden, allowing only a few select people to know about it. With a little whimper, she slid her hand back to her side and continued dreaming.

Gripping her dagger tightly, she plunged it into the side of the werewolf's head. The beast yanked its head back, blood dripping from his mouth and streaming down Darla's chest. He pulled the dagger free and, with a deep rumbling growl, tossed it to the ground. Slowly Darla scrambled back. The werewolf was unstoppable, and she was now defenceless. She clambered further backwards but stopped abruptly when she bumped into a corpse. Terrifying, with hate-filled eyes, the monstrous werewolf leapt forward... and Darla woke up, sitting bolt upright, shaking, gasping for breath.

Her breathing ragged and heavy, she found herself fidgeting with her ring, a habit she often resorted to after nightmares like this. For some reason she found it comforting and reassuring. The ring had once been a solid band made of white gold and intricately engraved with wolf heads. In between each wolf head had been a tiny red ruby. It had been dazzling, unique, a symbol of her lineage. It was also sentimental, the only thing she had to remind her of her parents, her family. Now, though, her parents were nothing more than a faded, distant memory, and the once-beautiful ring was now just a plain band.

Ten years had passed since that eventful night. Somehow Darla had survived the ordeal, but she didn't know how. Her brain had either blocked out the trauma, protecting her, providing her with a natural coping mechanism, or magic had been used, Darla suspected both and she planned on getting to the bottom of it. Finding out why? The Brotherhood had become her family, adopting her and training her in spy work, thievery, and assassination. They had changed her identity, claiming it was to protect her until her amnesia restored itself, until her memories returned. The memories had started to come back, mainly in dreams like these. It was upsetting and frustrating, leaving her confused and with unanswered questions. She wanted to know her identity, to embrace her heritage and the destiny that lay before her.

In the early days after the massacre, Darla had been introduced to Jocelyne and Vexlan, a young couple in the Brotherhood. They immediately bonded, becoming fast friends. Jocelyne had heard what had happened at the manor and had comforted Darla, giving her a hug, protecting her in a warm, loving embrace. She had then immediately gotten to work, focusing on the ring with purpose and determination. Jocelyne cast an intricate deception spell on it, masking its appearance. She was an expert when it came to illusionary magic, a skill that made her an exceptional assassin. The Brotherhood's high lord also had instructed her to come up with extremely specific catch words. The two words would negate the spell, revealing the ring for what it was. Jocelyne had sworn a vow of secrecy and held on to the secret, even though it broke her heart to do so. She had to believe Darla eventually would remember and say the words when the time was right, the words being her true name.

Vexlan—or Vex, as he preferred to be called—was Jocelyne's loving partner and a rogue, a jack-of-all-trades with a multitude of talents. While Jocelyne had immersed herself in her magic, he had orchestrated a new identity for Darla in the form of a detailed dossier, including a family background, place of birth, and of course a tragedy that had brought her into the fold of the Brotherhood. The information provided the perfect cover, especially if anyone decided to investigate. Only a select few people would know Darla's true identity. The high lord was putting every precaution in place.

* * *

Sitting on the sofa in Vex's workshop, Darla studied the dossier, flicking through the pages and committing every detail to memory. Finished, she threw it into the fireplace. The pages had erupted in flames and quickly turned to ash, erasing the evidence and safeguarding her identity. Her name was forgotten, at least for now, until the day arrived when it would rise again like a phoenix from the ashes. For the last decade, her name had been Darla, but only her friends called her that. Everyone else called her by her alias, "Flow." Even to this day, she still got the giggles over the irony of the name, the fact that it was an anadrome, "wolf" spelled backwards. It depicted exactly what she was…a werewolf.

Vex then brewed a dark-blue potion that smelled like rotten eggs. It tasted just as bad, nearly making Darla vomit. Within moments her hair changed colour from mahogany brown to crimson red. It eventually would change back after a couple of months, or so he said. Darla chuckled at the memory as she tied her long wavy hair into a ponytail. The brown had come back, but not completely, with red streaks running throughout her hair. Embarrassed, Vex had apologised profusely; he was a perfectionist and hated making mistakes. He hypothesized that her lycanthropy had affected the potion. Darla didn't mind, though. She liked the look; it suited her.

Next to her blanket lay two leather sheaths that housed her long-bladed daggers. She picked them up and strapped one to each thigh. The blades were finely honed, made of high-quality silver, and imbued with magical runes. Although they had cost a small fortune, they already had proven to be worth the price. An assassin always needed reliable weapons. Ones that would help her win the battles ahead.

She was on a mission to save as many diamonds as she could, the equivalent of ten thousand gold coins. It was an outrageous amount, but she had no choice. Since she couldn't remember—her memory being fragmented and devoid of certain events—the Brotherhood had revealed what had happened to Lance and his parents. They had escaped with the gorkin contingent and had been put into slavery. All these years, they'd been alive and safe, but how long could that last? Darla needed to buy their freedom.

Diamonds were the gorkins' form of currency, and the larger or rarer the diamond, all the better. They had no use for gold, copper, or silver coins, which definitely limited their trade partners. The merchants they dealt with tended to be unscrupulous, dealing illegitimately in rare merchandise, black market goods, and slaves, which suited the nefarious gorkins perfectly. Darla had been taking on as many contracts as possible, saving and storing. She was close —she only needed a couple more contracts. Her friends were alive, which drove her and gave her the motivation and hope she needed.

With trembling hands, she grabbed her canteen and took a long drink of water. The nightmare was still fresh in her mind, real and unrelenting. Darla heard a neigh behind her and turned at the sound. Midnight was almost invisible, a shadow in the night. She reached out and patted her faithful horse affectionately. He nudged her hand and she laughed, tossing him an apple, which he crunched on happily. "I'll be back soon," she said, walking away. Midnight merely snickered as if to say, *Yeah, right*. Shaking her head, Darla jogged down the dirt trail, towards the open field and the castle beyond it: her destination. The huge wooden rampart, lit up by torches and patrolled by elven guards, loomed in the distance.

As she ran, she scraped against a branch, snapping it as it hit her shoulder. "Crap," she cursed as she noticed one of her satchels. The branch had torn the strap slightly, leaving it frayed and tattered. She had been distracted, thinking about the dream. She shook her head, clearing it. She needed to focus; she had a job to do: a rare green diamond to steal.

The diamond belonged to King Therondal of the elven empire and was priceless—the elves considered it an artefact, spiritual and divine. An elven lord by the name of Kye Dellavenor had stolen it. Why someone would do this and bring the wrath of the elven empire down upon him, Darla had no idea. King Therondal and his son, Prince Velander had summoned the royal councillors to a closed-door meeting, allowing only a selected few to attend. The archbishop had represented the church, while the general and Prince Velander's captain had represented the military. The captain was completely loyal to Velander and was his second in command. He was also known by another title though, that of Prince Jerrick, Velander's cousin and second in line to the throne. This was the only reason he was privileged enough to have a seat on the council. Messages had been sent out, assembling all the banner lords, and raising an army.

The king had a duplicate of all his lord's banners displayed in his throne room. The banner was a representation of the lords and the house that they represented. To have it displayed was considered an honour and a privilege. It showed your fealty to the king. Dellavenor had disgraced the king, shamed himself and his house and because of that the king had burnt his banner. Because of this he was now considered an outcast and a traitor to the elvish nation.

They were now camped within a two day's march north of Lord Dellavenor's castle. The prince, along with two of the banner lords, had ridden ahead with a contingent of troops, besieging the entrance and trapping the occupants inside. All Lord Dellavenor could hope for now was to be killed fighting on the battlefield, because if he were captured, his fate would be far worse than death.

Lord Thace Aldronin, Kye's younger cousin, had hired Darla to steal the diamond. He'd approached the king with the idea after hearing about the theft, proposing to minimise bloodshed and the casualties of war. While in the process of summoning his banner lords, the king had reluctantly agreed, giving the young lord two weeks, the time it would take for his army to assemble and reach Dellavenor's castle. This time restriction didn't faze Darla; it merely made things more interesting, more of a challenge. It also allowed her to set an outrageous price due to the complication. The young lord didn't mind; he could easily afford it. By hiring Darla to retrieve the diamond, he hoped to restore honour to his family name and gain favour with the king, something that was priceless in his eyes.

Without realising it, the prince and the two banner lords had helped Darla out. Their presence was enough to panic Lord Dellavenor. Most of his guards were stationed near the front of the castle, focused on the invading force. It made her job a lot easier. Darla was approaching the castle from the side; even from her position, she saw the numerous campfires that illuminated the large green tents, dozens of siege engines, and the patrolling sentries. There was no drinking, singing, or gambling; the elves were disciplined, all business. The scouts Lord Dellavenor had sent out had been captured and tortured, their heads now impaled on pikes just outside the camp. Darla noticed their eyes had been gorged out—a clear message regarding what would happen to those within the castle.

She entered the meadow, the long grass waving gently in the night breeze. Commando crawling, she slowly made her way towards the castle. As she neared it, she saw the area had been cleared of grass, with a thick metal grate sticking out of the ground like a beacon. It led to the sewer tunnels, one of which ran directly under the castle. According to the blueprints, it was a maintenance entrance, but to Darla it was an option for escape, a last resort, one she hoped she wouldn't have to use.

Upon receiving the assignment, she had made a request, sending the message by raven. Within a day, the Brotherhood had supplied her with blueprints of the castle, the nearby mines, the sewer network, the security system for the vault; a map of the area; and even the updated duty roster. She'd planned the infiltration accordingly. As she crawled along, navigating the perimeter, sticking to the grass, she heard a noise that sent a chill down her spine. It had come from the grate, from a nightmare that lurked within the tunnels. "Fucking great," she muttered. "Ghouls!"

Many guards were walking the rampart, double the number there should have been. They were on high alert, sporadically stopping to scan their surroundings. The king's army was still a couple of days away, which meant somehow they had been warned of her contract, of a plan to steal the diamond. This complicated things slightly. Creeping forward, hidden by the grass, Darla approached the massive stone wall that connected to one of the guard towers, a cylindrical structure that rose to the heavens. Darla counted seven guard towers in total. The centre of the front wall consisted of a huge gate tower with an adjoining barracks. Most of the guards were situated there, fortifying the castle and preparing for the inevitable.

The castle had been built out of stone and wood that was fused together. The technique not only added a camouflaged and natural look to the structure, but it also strengthened the blocks, reinforcing them so the castle was nearly impenetrable. It was unusual, but somehow the elves had made it work. For Darla, the wall would be easy to climb, and the tower would provide her with the perfect vantage point. Focusing on her lycanthropy, she transformed, enhancing her strength, dexterity, and senses. Her eyes became a bestial yellow; her muscles grew, elongating and strengthening; and her long, feminine nails turned razor sharp and hard as steel.

Darla was a rarity amongst the werewolves, as she could control her transformation. She categorised the process into four stages: human, half transformation (going through the initial stages of lycanthropy but maintaining a human form), werewolf (completing a full transformation but maintaining her humanity), and the bestial werewolf (giving in to the bloodlust; the primal, feral nature). She was currently in stage two, in a half-transformation state, maintaining her human appearance while enhancing her abilities.

Her claws digging in, embedding themselves in the stone, she began her accent of the middle tower. Hand over hand, bracing her feet in the grooves, she climbed like a spider up the wall. As she neared the top, the wind buffeted her slightly, flapping her cloak. There were two guards nearby, her keen hearing picking out the sounds of their greaves and determining their exact positions. She waited patiently, hanging motionless, listening as their footsteps echoed on the stone. As they neared each other, she sprang up, a wraith in the night.

Wrapping her arms around one of the guard's heads and her legs around the other, she twisted and broke their necks. Freeing herself, she landed in a crouch. With a smile, she grabbed the powerful recurve bow that had clattered to the floor. Unstrapping the quiver, she slung it over her shoulder. Now came the fun part. For someone as proficient as her, it would be like shooting fish in a barrel. If anything, the elves knew archery; they knew how to design the perfect bow, and this bow had been expertly made. First, Darla needed to take care of the guards at the adjacent tower and the back towers. Drawing an arrow, she nocked it and aimed. With a twang, she fired.

She'd aimed high, sending the arrow rocketing up, before it swooped down like a bird of prey. It hit a guard in the chest, dropping him instantly. The other guard turned, alerted by the noise, but fluidly, with only a slight adjustment, Darla nocked, drew, and fired. She'd even allowed for the couple of cautious steps the guard had taken as he investigated the noise. The only warning was the rustling, whistling noise the arrow made. He looked up, as out of nowhere the arrow pierced his helmet and embedded itself into his forehead.

Now for the back towers. After turning around, Darla nocked and waited. The string was taut, the arrow at full draw and aimed accordingly. She timed it perfectly, allowing for the movement of the guards and the wind velocity. The arrow arced gently, zooming at a phenomenal speed towards its target. The guards were near each other, bored, talking, laughing when the arrow punctured through the first guard's throat before hitting the second guard in the chest. It punctured his armour, piercing his heart and killing him instantly. It was a double kill, perfectly executed.

* * *

The next tower was the closest and was directly opposite her. Darla heard the ruckus, the chuckling, the carrying on. The guards were having their own little party in the tower, and from what she could see, there were at least four of them. This complicated things. Two of them were clutching a medium size barrel they had punctured two holes into. Holding it above their heads, they drank from the steady streams that poured out. All the while, their comrades were laughing and egging them on. The liquid was beige, and Darla recognised it immediately. It was elven spiced liqueur, rich, sweet, potent, and highly flammable. It gave her an idea.

After tearing a piece of cloth off one of the dead guards, she wrapped it tightly around the arrowhead. She nocked the arrow then touched it to a nearby torch, igniting the cloth. Squinting slightly, she drew the string back and carefully aimed. Even with the short distance, it was a difficult shot; it needed to be perfect, precise. With a twang, she fired. The flaming head flickered and danced as it soared through the air. Flying through the arched window, it hit the wooden barrel dead centre, cracking it...and *boom*!

Darla grinned. Although the elven castle design was superior and advanced in many ways, she had just found a way to use it to her advantage. The reinforced stone strengthened the walls and towers, but it also helped to contain and muffle the explosion. It was just big enough to incapacitate the guards. The blast was muffled, the noise dampened, drawing a limited amount of attention. The guards on the opposing walkways ran towards the tower, alarmed, their swords drawn. Darla had accounted for this. In rapid succession, she drew two arrows and fired. Her aiming was impeccable, both arrows hitting the guards in the head and toppling them over the wall.

The last tower was the farthest. The wood of the bow groaned slightly as Darla pulled the string taut. She aimed high and, with another twang, let the arrow fly. It sped towards the heavens before gravity took hold and it descended, plummeting towards its target. It hit one of the guards in the helmet, clanging as it penetrated the metal and sending him toppling over the tower's edge. Concerned, his comrade rushed over, leaned over the side, and peered into the darkness beyond. Darla's next arrow slammed into his shoulder, and screaming, he toppled over as well. Darla cursed; the alarm had been raised. Two guards from each adjoining wall ran to investigate. A large bell was situated just inside the tower, the brass reflecting from the lantern light through the arched tower window. She had to kill them before they reached it and sounded the alarm.

Darla drew again and aimed, tracking the first guard's movement. She fired, the arrow soaring down, slamming into the guard and propelling him over the wall. She nocked, swivelled, and fired again, felling a guard on the opposite wall. Swivelling again, she fired, hitting the third guard in the leg, but she merely wounded him. Fluid, a blur, she fired again. The guard fell face-first onto the walkway. One guard to go. The remaining guard raced towards the bell. Darla fired and missed, the arrow soaring harmlessly over the wall. "Fuck," she mumbled before taking a deep breath and nocking another arrow. She drew, held her breath, aimed, and fired. The guard reached the bell, his hand grabbing the chain. The arrow flew through the window, slamming into his chest. Coughing up a mouthful of blood, he collapsed next to the bell.

Now for the guards on the remaining two walls. Beads of sweat rolled down Darla's forehead when she realised she was running out of arrows. Three arrows and four guards. Taking another deep breath, she drew and fired; the arrow soared before gliding down in a graceful arc. The guard had stopped, leaning slightly as he peered over the wall at the meadow. The arrow slammed into him, piercing his throat, and sending him toppling over the wall. Two arrows left. Nocking another arrow, Darla aimed at the other guard, who had reached the far end of the wall. Although it made for a difficult shot, she was more than capable. Using her enhanced strength, she drew the string back, the bow bending to accommodate. With a loud twang, she sent the arrow spiralling towards its target. It flew, gliding effortlessly, before plunging into the guard's chest. He collapsed in a heap on the walkway next to the tower.

* * *

One arrow left. After positioning herself at the edge, she nocked and drew. It was an easy shot, but she couldn't afford to miss. The guard had stopped next to the wall. His pants were slightly down, and one of his hands was on his crotch; he was pissing over the wall. Darla heard his contented sigh from where she stood. Taking another deep breath, she nocked and drew, holding the arrow in position. She released, sending the arrow spiralling forward, just as the guard turned and started to pull his pants up. The arrow thudded into him, piercing through his unarmoured throat.

He toppled backwards, falling into the courtyard below. Darla cursed, watching as the guard landed on top of some rosebushes. Branches snapped loudly, spraying petals and leaves across the courtyard path. She waited as the remaining guard came out from his position, taking a few cautious steps away from the tower. She quietly set the bow and quiver case down; they had done their job. With a slight hiss, she drew a dagger from its sheath and leapt off the tower. Her knees slammed into the guard's back, and with a thrust she stabbed her dagger into the side of his neck. The guard toppled forward with Darla landing on top of him. After wiping her dagger on his tunic, she knelt at the edge of the walkway. From her vantage point, she spotted her target, the captain of the guard. Another guard was with him, and they chatted casually as they patrolled the perimeter of the castle. Slowly, carefully, sticking to the shadows, Darla crept down the staircase to the courtyard below.

* * *

Chapter 2

A shadow concealed by the darkness, she ran across the wide-open area. Guided by the lanterns, she kept an eye on the patrol. The captain and his companion were inattentive, joking and chatting. She increased her pace to a sprint and quickly ducked behind a bush. She heard the crunch of footfalls a moment before someone else rounded the corner: another patrol. "I need to take a piss," the guard told his companion before veering off the path and walking straight towards the bush Darla was crouched behind.

She held her breath as the guard stopped right in front of her. After unstrapping his pants, he flopped out his penis and began to take a piss. The steady stream of urine sprayed onto the leaves and pooled at her feet. It reeked, and Darla held her breath, trying not to gag. "Hurry up," his buddy yelled. The guard at the bush turned and pointed a clenched fist at his friend. Smiling, he then raised his middle finger in a silent "Fuck you." He was still pissing, though, and without even realising it, he sprayed urine all over Darla's sleeve.

Cursing, Darla silently moved her arm away, trying desperately not to make a sound. Stealth was the key; she needed to remain undetected. The corner of her sleeve caught on a branch...and *snap*! Startled, the guard turned, his pissing stopping abruptly. "What the...", he gasped as Darla sprang up in a flash. Her right palm shot up, slamming the guard under the chin and jolting his head so forcefully that it broke his neck. In a flicker, her other hand snaked forward and sent her dagger spiralling through the air. It slammed straight through the second guard's eye with a meaty thud.

"That's what you get for pissing on me." She smirked as she dumped the man's body behind a bush. After retrieving her dagger, she cleaned the blade on the second guard's tunic before hiding his corpse behind a nearby tree. Her feet pounding silently across the grass, she quickly beelined for the armoury, keeping to the shadows as she weaved between trees and bushes. She needed to make sure she kept a good distance between herself and the captain; her plan depended on it.

The armoury was in a large alcove, with the kitchen and dining area on the other side. A well-maintained garden decorated the area in between, offering a picturesque view. It also provided Darla with ample cover. She leapt from the grass onto the pavement and, crouching, crept silently towards the armoury door. The paved tiles were adorned with an intricate design of leaves and flowers. It was a beautiful, artistic design, but Darla didn't have time to admire it; she had work to do. She had a matter of minutes before the captain reached the armoury.

She held a long, thin-bladed dagger in one hand while the other carried a pick. At the door she got to work, jamming her dagger into the keyhole. She then inserted the pick and, concentrating, lifted the pins. She was rewarded with a soft click, followed shortly after by another. Two picks down, two to go. The captain and his companion were approaching the alcove. With her keen hearing, Darla could hear them from a mile away.

She fumbled with the pick, trying to shut out the resonating clanking noise of the guards' boots. She didn't have long; judging from the sound, they were nearing the corner of the path. A click sounded, the third pin lifting into place. One to go. "Damn it, Hal. Can you smell that roasted pheasant? I'm starving." It was the captain's friend; Darla heard him as if he were standing next to her. The aroma wafting out of the windows was mouthwatering; it provided a moment's distraction and gave Darla a few precious extra seconds.

"How about you go grab us something to eat? I'll continue our patrol," the other guard said. Darla's stomach was grumbling. The roasted bird, cooked with herbs, smelled delicious. There was a crunch of pebbles as the guard detoured from the path, hurrying across a small garden trail towards the kitchen.

Fortunately, Hal was the one who took over the patrol. He was the captain, her target, the one with the keys. He waited briefly, watching his friend, before continuing. He whistled softly as he neared the corner, a bawdy little tune called "The Mistress." Darla concentrated, gently manoeuvring the pick. The captain was nearly upon her, looming near the corner, illuminated by the torchlight. A click sounded, and with a gentle pull of the handle, the door opened, squeaking slightly. She slid inside, into the cover of darkness, just as Hal rounded the corner.

The bait had been set. "Who's there?" Hal called out. The sound of his footsteps slowed as he cautiously approached the door. Darla had purposely left it ajar, wanting to draw his attention. He pried the door open farther with the tip of his jaghuer, a weapon of elvish design, resembling a double-bladed curved sword. The door opened with a creak, and Hal entered the darkness, stepping across the threshold into the armoury.

His keen elvish vision enabled him to see in the darkness, making out the crates and the neatly stacked weapons, shields, recurve bows, and armour. Barrels of feathered arrows had been set against the wall, their labels depicting the various kinds of arrows within. He only had a moment to gasp as he noticed a silhouette step out from behind the door. Darla punched the side of his head, the blow powerful and deadly. It crunched his steel helmet, dislocating his jaw and fracturing his skull. Hal's legs wobbled, his eyes flickered, and his jaghuer clattered to the tiled floor. A moment later, he collapsed, landing on the ground face-first, unconscious and dying.

"Hal, are you all right?" It was the other guard, who had heard the commotion and was approaching cautiously. His steps had slowed, and his sword was drawn. He was carrying a neat little package in his other hand, a thick sandwich for the captain. He had already eaten most of his, discarding the remnants when he noticed something was wrong. Approaching the doorway, he saw his prone friend and rushed forward. He was so focused on his comrade that he didn't see the large crate that came flying towards him out of the darkness.

The crate hit him full force in the chest, shattering and spraying leather strips in all directions. The strips were of assorted sizes and shapes, used for quivers, shields, armour, sheaths, and scabbards. The guard flew backwards, hitting the doorframe with a thud. Somehow, he managed to keep his footing and staggered forward, blinded momentarily as the debris fell to the floor.

Darla picked up one of the elven star shields and threw it like a discus. The shield was medium size, golden in colour, and star shaped, with each point honed to a razor's edge. The design enabled a trained soldier not only to trap, deflect, and disarm their opponent, but also to use the shield as a weapon. The guard didn't even see it coming. The shield sliced through his neck, decapitating him, before embedding itself in the door. A spray of blood erupted from his neck like a fountain as his head spiralled through the air before landing with a clunk and rolling into the garden.

Darla casually walked to the doorway, her boots squelching in the blood. She pried the sandwich from the guard's outstretched hand. She was starving, and aside from a splatter of blood on the crust, it was perfectly edible. "No need to let this go to waste," she said, taking a bite. She chewed slowly, savouring the taste, then swallowed and took another bite. The sandwich consisted of two thick, warm, freshly baked pieces of bread and was filled with roasted pheasant, lettuce, tomato, and a spicy creamy sauce. It was absolutely divine! Darla took another couple of quick bites, devouring half the sandwich. She rewrapped the other half in the cloth and put it in one of her satchels.

Grabbing hold of their legs, she hid the two corpses behind some crates and closed the door as quietly as possible. Although the armoury was pitch-black, it didn't take long for her bestial eyes to adjust. She walked over to Hal's body and retrieved her prize, the ring of keys strapped to his belt. The captain was methodical, with most of the keys engraved and neatly labelled. This helped her considerably. Quickly walking past the racks, the keys jingling softly, she headed towards a door at the far end of the room. It was almost time for the change of shift, and the captain's disappearance would be noticeable. Time was of the essence now. She unlocked the door with a soft click then opened it, barely making a sound. Before her was a short staircase that led to another door leading into the barracks; this second door was ajar and spilling a sliver of light onto the staircase.

The wooden steps creaked slightly as Darla ascended. Even before reaching the door, she heard a variety of sounds coming from within the barracks: snoring, the clanking of mugs, the clinking of coins, laughter, and drunken, rowdy voices. Based on the sounds, she pictured the layout in her mind. Seven guards—no, eight—on either side of the door, their beds in rows. Another six guards were seated at a gambling table at the back of the room. The captain's quarters were situated halfway along the left-hand side. The captain, due to his rank, had his own quarters, a room adjoining the barracks. This room was her objective; from there she would get the code then proceed to the vault. Twelve metres of sneaking without being seen or heard—a piece of cake.

Peering in, Darla allowed a moment for her eyes to adjust. She then snuck through the door in a crouch and quietly closed it. An arm suddenly flung out, nearly smacking her in the face. She froze, startled. A mumble sounded, followed by snoring. Darla inched her way around the outstretched arm and snuck forward, past the first bed, then the second. She stopped when she heard creaking. One of the guards was getting up. "Mylar, it's time to get up. It's nearly time for our duty." Mylar grunted in reply, throwing the covers off, the sheet and blankets cascading over the side in a tangled mess. Holding on to the frame, Darla slid under the bed and cursed under her breath. This delay was costing her valuable time.

The two large wooden doors at the entrance of the barracks opened as two guards came in from their patrol. "Deal me in," one of them said, walking over to the gaming table. Beyond the doors was a large wooden staircase that led to the training grounds and a massive courtyard. The remaining entrance to the barracks consisted of a large oak door situated slightly down from the gaming table. It led to the castle's extravagant main hall.

She lay there in the darkness while the guards fumbled with their clothes, getting dressed. They then retrieved their armour from the trunk at the foot of their beds. The mattress creaked as Mylar sat down to tie his boots. "Crap!" he exclaimed, standing up. "Where's my sword?"

"You put it under your bed you, oaf. Come on. We still have time for a round of cards." Mylar reached under the bed, searching blindly for his sword, which lay right next to Darla. She grabbed it and quietly pushed it towards him. Probing, his hand touched it then pulled it out. Darla waited for a moment as he ran to catch up with his friend before she rolled across the floor to the other bed. She froze, stopping momentarily as the large oak door opened.

The guards stood at attention, knocking the table in the process. Wine and ale splashed across it, the only sound being the clatter of the goblets and mugs. Lord Kye Dellavenor stood in the entranceway. "Where is Captain Hal?"

"Still out on patrol, my lord. I'll get him for you." One of the guards threw down his cards and dashed off, almost knocking the double doors off their hinges as he hurried to find Hal. Darla cursed silently. She didn't have long; things definitely weren't going to plan.

"Inform the Captain that I'll be waiting for him in his chambers." Not waiting for an answer, Dellavenor walked briskly through the barracks to the captain's door before reaching into his pocket and withdrawing his own set of keys. He unlocked the door then walked in and closed it behind himself. She heard a faint click as Dellavenor locked it behind himself.

"Fucking Dellavenor. He's obsessed with that stone. I swear to God, he's going to get us all killed." The conversation was coming from the gaming table. The guards had sat down and had continued playing.

"What you need to do, Izail, is keep your damn mouth shut!" one of the guards replied. "If the lord hears you talking like that, he'll personally feed you to the ghouls."

"From what I hear, Dellavenor keeps the stone near him. He doesn't even keep the cursed thing in the vault," another guard chirped in. "Anyway, rumour has it he plans on using the secret tunnels to escape with the stone. By the time the king gets here, the castle will be empty, and we'll be long gone."

* * *

"As long as there's no fucking ghouls in the tunnels," Izail muttered, gulping down some wine.

After making sure the coast was clear, Darla rolled under the last bed and crawled out from underneath it. Blending into the shadows and keeping an eye on the guards at the gaming table, she crept towards the captain's quarters. It was about time she introduced herself properly to the Lord Dellavenor.

Darla had noticed the key the lord had used and easily found its twin on the key ring. Inserting the key, she twisted and was rewarded with a faint click. Taking the key out, she held the ring clenched in her fist, with the large key sticking out in between her index and middle finger. As she anxiously watched the gaming table, her free hand snuck forward and grabbed hold of the door handle. Laughing, shouting crude remarks, the guards were caught up in their game, oblivious to her presence. Darla turned the handle and leapt into the room.

"Cap—" It was all Lord Dellavenor had time to say before Darla's fist slammed forward, stabbing him in the eye with the key. She pulled her arm back, and with a squelchy pop, the eyeball came out, speared on the end of the key. As the lord threw his hands to his bloodied face and screamed, Darla slammed the door shut. She already could hear the guards charging forward. After pulling the eyeball off the key and tossing it to the floor, she inserted the key and locked the door. Slamming her fist on the bow of the key, she snapped it off, leaving a jagged piece of the key still in the lock, then put the key ring in her pocket. This would buy her a bit of extra time.

"You bitch! Guards!" Dellavenor screamed, reaching for his dagger. His left hand was covered in blood, trying to stem the flow as he held it over his eye socket. Darla sprang forward, sweeping her leg around. There was a hiss, a scraping of leather as the lord's dagger came free. Her leg moved fluidly, lightning quick, her foot arcing across from his blinded side. Her boot crashed into the side of his head, and he flew into the opposing wall, smashing into it, before collapsing in a heap, unconscious. She had taken heed of the guards' conversation and, in an instant, revised her plan; she searched Dellavenor thoroughly, looking for the diamond, but there was nothing.

The captain's room was sparse, consisting of a bed in the corner, a small bookcase, a desk, a chair, and a trunk. A fireplace was situated next to the far wall, crackling away, keeping the room warm and cosy. Darla walked over to the desk and rummaged through it. She snatched up a parchment, looked at it, and quickly discarded it. She picked up another piece, followed by another, and discarded those. The guards were thumping on the door, trying to break it down. Frustrated, she shut the drawer and gritted her teeth. Where was the code to the damn vault?

Looking around the room, she noticed two daggers stuck in the wall, each one pinning up a piece of parchment. Shards of wood flew off the door as the guards hacked at it with axes; they would be in in a matter of moments. She studied the pieces of parchment. One was a guard roster, while the other depicted a series of coloured buttons with a number written on each one. A sequence of numbers, the order in which the buttons needed to be pushed—it was the code! She ripped it off the wall and stuffed it into her pocket.

Wood cracked. Darla heard booted feet charging forward. Two guards collided with the door with a thud, ramming it with their shoulders. It exploded, spraying debris across the room, and the two guards toppled forward. Other guards clambered over them, and Darla ran, sliding across the desk and swinging out of the open window.

Her clawed hands dug into the stone, sending dust and pebbles cascading to the ground. Finding purchase, like a spider, she scrambled diagonally across the wall. Her destination was an open window twelve metres away, its curtains fluttering in the night breeze. It was Lord Dellavenor's bedchambers. From there Darla would go down the short corridor to the vault.

The sophisticated vault security system had been designed with gnomish ingenuity. Dwarves had built the walls, which consisted of thick stone, sturdy and impenetrable. It made breaking into the vault an almost impossible feat. For some maybe, but not for Darla—for her it was merely a challenge. She had two obstacles to overcome; the code would help her with the first.

Darla climbed through the window and took everything in. The room was spacious, clean, and organised. The red carpet was soft, and flames flickered in the small fireplace. Next to the hearth was a large wooden chair lathered with pillows; a book rested on top of one of them. A four-poster bed stood in the centre, with two large wooden dressers on either side. A huge wooden wardrobe was situated against the opposite wall; built into one of its doors was a large mirror. Opposite the wardrobe, Darla saw a portrait of Lord Dellavenor. *What a vain, self-righteous prick*, she thought. On the other side of the wardrobe was the door. Against the far wall stood a wooden mannequin decorated with the lord's armour; on either side hung his sword and shield. Fortunately, there weren't many places to hide the gem, which was just as well because Darla was rapidly running out of time. The question was where to start.

Pillows were strewn across the carpet, and the book now lay open and discarded. The bedding had been ripped off; the mattress cut open. One of the wardrobe doors was open, and Darla's arms were flying back and forth, littering the carpet with clothes. She was about to open the next door when Dellavenor shouted, "She's making her way to the vault, you idiots. Quickly!" Well, it looked like the lord had awoken from his slumber, and boy, was he pissed. She had stabbed him in the eye, though, so she couldn't really blame him. Ignoring the door, she walked up to the painting and giggled. *Now you're going to have to add a patch to this,* she thought. She unhooked the portrait and threw it on the floor, revealing a hidden niche—a niche with a large green diamond in it.

After grabbing the diamond, Darla froze, staggering as it emitted power, radiating with swirls of blue and red. She wobbled, almost collapsing. Righting herself, she peered at the diamond, at the silhouette that seemed to appear, disappear, and dance within the radiant swirls. A voice sounded in her head, calling to her, pleading, trying to mislead her. The voice was consistent, rising in volume, growing into an overwhelming noise. Her head felt like it would explode as it repeated two words over and over: *Free me!* This was no ordinary diamond; it was magical, an artefact of immense power.

It was no wonder the lord wanted it. Darla stuffed it into her satchel, grabbed the wooden chair, and dragged it across the carpet towards the door. After swinging it open, she entered the hallway. Ornamental shields and banners decorated the wall. Halfway down the hallway was another door, this one leading to the landing of the main hall. As the chair scraped across the wooden floorboards, Darla heard the booted feet of Dellavenor and his guards clambering up the two staircases leading to the landing. They were nearly upon her. The chair was awkward, her muscles straining as she pulled it along. She reached the door just as a guard began to open it. She grabbed the handle and slammed the door shut, then wedged the chair under the handle, jamming the door and locking it in place.

Slamming and smashing sounds commenced as the guards rammed the door then took to it with axes. Above the clamour, a hysterical Dellavenor could be heard shouting and threatening. This would buy Darla some time, but not long. At the far end of the hallway stood another door, this one leading to the vault. Three rows of one-centimetre holes ran in a vertical pattern along the far wall. It was part of the security system, with each hole housing a poisonous dart. If Darla punched in the wrong button sequence, she'd activate the spring-loaded dart shooters and would be riddled with darts.

Reaching the vault door, she fumbled with the ring, desperately searching for the right key. She couldn't find it, which meant it had to be one of the four unlabelled keys. After choosing one, she inserted it into the lock. Nothing; it wouldn't even turn. *Crap, wrong key*, she thought. *Time's running out.* She pulled the key out of the lock, almost snapping it in the process, and quickly inserted another. Carefully she tried to turn it, but this one was a dud too. *Shit! Two more to choose from.* Fumbling, Darla almost dropped the ring. Taking a deep breath, she grabbed hold of an ornate brass key and inserted it. She turned it, and with a loud click, the door unlocked.

She opened the door to reveal the first part of the vault's security system. Ten large wooden poles ran across the doorway horizontally, barring her way. On the wall next to the door was a keypad with six coloured buttons. After unsheathing her dagger, Darla pulled the code out of her pocket and pinned it just above the keypad. She then grabbed hold of the handle on the opposite side of the door. Her grip tightened, and the handle bent slightly. Now for the moment of truth. Taking a deep breath, she punched the buttons. After pushing the last one, she knew something was wrong—the poles weren't retracting. A moment before numerous clicks sounded, she leapt into the air and flung herself around to the other side of the door. Multiple thuds resounded as the door shielded her, the darts embedding themselves into the thick wood. She had punched in the incorrect code. There was only one explanation: the code had been changed.

Shouts erupted as the door was mostly shattered, the only thing blocking them being the chair. "Fuck it," Darla muttered, stepping back around and facing the poles, which barred her way. Taking a step back, she leaned against the wall. Concentrating and gritting her teeth against the pain—a pain that was both excruciating and exhilarating—she tapped further into her lycanthropy. The bones and muscles in her legs, back, and arms grew longer and thicker, strengthening. She stopped just as abruptly as she started. If she continued, she'd bring on a full transformation. "Shit, this is going to hurt," she said, springing forward. She tucked into herself and used her shoulder and upper back as a battering ram.

Six of the wooden poles splintered into shards as Darla flew into the vault. She extended her body, reaching out with her arms, her fingers outstretched. As she touched the large square tile beneath her feet, she used it to springboard, flinging herself forward through the air. A second after she touched it, the tile vanished, flipping down and revealing a dark chute. This was the second part of the vault's security system.

The chute led to the sewer system, a network of tunnels that ran throughout Kalmeer. These tunnels were connected to smaller pipes that transferred the waste matter to a factory. Through the ingenuity of gnomish science, the waste was then converted into fertiliser. It was supposed to be the best in the world, with farmers, vineyard owners, and even head gardeners who worked for the nobility raving about it.

Unfortunately, during the construction of the waste tunnels, the workers had accidently dug into a catacomb that consisted of an underground city, a labyrinth of tunnels infested with ghouls. Workers had been killed, and a gate was quickly installed, blocking off the catacomb entrance. As a precaution, the grates leading into the sewer sections were locked and reinforced. It was rumoured that the gate had been destroyed and ghouls now roamed the sewer tunnels. This part of the security device took advantage of that—thieves would fall down the chute and trap themselves in the sewers, leaving them to the fate of the ghouls.

Darla spread her legs slightly and landed with her feet planted on either side of another tile. It quickly vanished, flipping down like the previous one. She wobbled slightly, but keeping her feet braced, she regained her balance and looked straight ahead. A large green emerald stood right in front of her, glistening, radiant, in the shape of a diamond. It had to be worth a fortune but was nothing compared to what she held in her satchel. Quickly she realized it was a decoy, a replica of what she already had. She was greedy, though. She would either keep it or use it to further her own agenda.

The emerald was on a pedestal, the centre piece of the vault. It was surrounded by open chests full of gems, coins, and jewellery. An ornate short sword caught her attention, almost as though it were calling out to her. She knew the value of things and what she could get for them; it was an important part of her profession. Her eyes scanned, taking everything in, and as quick as an arrow her hand snaked out, grabbing gems and jewellery. She considered this a bonus, a reward in addition to the commission she was getting for the contract. She quickly stuffed everything into her spare satchel. Suddenly the chair shattered; the elves had broken through. She heard them running down the corridor.

Darla stretched forward, her feet sliding on the tiled floor, and grabbed the short sword. It was a compulsion; she snatched it against her own volition, as if she were compelled to. The scabbard was made of the finest leather and engraved with intricate runes. The hilt was as black as obsidian and shaped in the design of two interwoven wolves. Inserted in the hilt was a purple gem that was radiating and shimmering. The gem was speaking to her, an angelic voice resonating in her head, bonding her, linking her to the sword. It was intoxicating. Shaking her head, gasping for breath, Darla cleared her mind and regained control of herself. After hooking the scabbard over her shoulder, she grabbed the emerald off the pedestal and immediately noticed the discrepancy. It was minor, almost unrecognisable, but to Darla it stood out plain as day. The emerald was slightly lighter in colour. She was just about to add it to her satchel, as Dellavenor and his guards reached the door.

"Halt!" one of the guards yelled, an officer, judging from the looks of him. Darla froze, smirking as she held the emerald. Shoving it into her almost-full spare satchel, she turned her head slowly to look at the men. Two arrows were aimed directly at her head. Kill shots, and at this range they wouldn't miss. She was trapped.

* * *

Dellavenor laughed and ordered the guards to lower their bows. "You have failed, thief. The emerald you hold is indeed worth a fortune, but it's nothing compared to the artefact I possess. The artefact I will be rewarded for. I will be given immortality once I give this to my master."

"Your master?" Darla questioned, confused.

"Malgorath, the Prince of Demons. Our master, the one we serve." A memory flashed through Darla's mind, making her wobble slightly. The name, she remembered, was the same name the fanatics had been screaming. Was this demon prince the one responsible for orchestrating her parents' deaths? It was as if another piece of the puzzle had slotted into place. Why now, though? Then she remembered the gem; her father had owned a similar artefact. The Prince of Demons had to be collecting them, but why? All Darla knew was that she needed to keep this artefact away from Malgorath at all costs.

Dellavenor shrugged. "On second thought, shoot her; the ghouls need feeding." The two guards raised their recurve bows, the strings taut, the arrowheads glistening and pointed straight at her.

It was Darla's turn to laugh. "If you kill me and feed me to the ghouls, you'll miss your chance at becoming immortal."

"Why's that?" Dellavenor demanded, his tone arrogant.

"Because I have this." With that, she reached into her satchel and brought out the emerald's twin.

"*No!*" Dellavenor screamed, stepping onto the tiles. He knew the pattern, knew which tiles to step on.

Smirking at him from beneath her hood, Darla brought her legs together and vanished, sliding down the chute.

Malgorath jolted as the image flashed through his head. The Divinity Stone had been activated. But how? To activate it, one needed the blood of a divine. He scowled. This was both good and bad. This thief could potentially threaten his plan but could also prove to be his salvation. He wouldn't have to rely on his own blood anymore. If the thief were captured, Malgorath could drain the thief's blood, harness it to activate the portal and summon his brethren. Then there would be no more need for secrecy; he could reveal his true form and conquer Aragoth.

He had been in this world for an eternity now. Summoned by a noble arch mage an eon ago, he had been ripped from his hellish existence, a dimension between worlds, and thrust into Aragoth. Initially he had been outraged, insulted that this inferior being—a mere human —could summon him. A demon prince! This human had not only summoned him but also had managed to contain him. Then he realized how: the mage wore an amulet, a powerful magical relic; and embedded into it was a divinity stone. How the mage had managed to possess one of the divinity stones was a mystery to Malgorath. One he intended to unravel.

Each divinity stone was imbued with the soul of a fallen, an angel-demon hybrid that had embraced and harnessed both light and dark magic. They were considered abominations, a threat to their world. There had been ten of them, as far as he knew, and each had been hunted down like the monsters they were. The divinity stones had been locked away, sealed with both angelic and demonic blood. This was to ensure that neither angel nor demons could access them. Yet somehow, they had gone missing. It was a mystery. Each side blamed the other, and a never-ending war erupted in their world.

* * *

The mage was good, powerful even, but he had overestimated his power. The containment field was weak, flawed, not nearly strong enough to hold Malgorath, who had obliterated the field, shattering it and freeing himself from its restraints. There were repercussions, though.

Uncontained, Malgorath immediately began to flicker and became incorporeal. This world couldn't sustain angels and demons, not without a host. He had just enough time to unleash his power and kill the mage, smothering and enveloping him with his demonic essence. Screaming, the mage transformed into a lich, a powerful undead mage, the first of Malgorath's minions. When he died, though, a rune that was inscribed on the mage's forearm activated, glowing a bright blue. And just like that, the lich vanished.

Frustrated, Malgorath was left standing alone by two giant oak trees that were gnarled, bent, and engraved with runes. The runes were natural and had formed over centuries. The two trees had joined together, their branches interweaving and creating a giant archway. Even in his incorporeal form, Malgorath could sense the power here —this was a place of magic. He also knew this magic could be harnessed and channelled, enhancing one's ability. Combining it with the power of a divinity stone, the mage had been able to create a portal and contain a demon. The complexity of the spell and the amount of magic used had been phenomenal. If Malgorath were able to obtain all the divinity stones, the possibilities were endless.

As Malgorath was in a spiritual state, his abilities were limited, but he was still able to' manipulate and deceive the various races. He whispered, planting thoughts and images, sowing discord and distrust, playing on their fragile emotions. Alliances were forged, enemies created, and wars were fought. Whether it was political, religious, or ideological, battles were waged, and there was continual conflict, with some races surviving while others were decimated. Malgorath created heroes, geniuses, and even prophets, while others were deemed tyrants, evil and insane. Fanatical groups were created, small armies that worshipped him. He was in his element, all the while manipulating things to further his agenda. Although everyone had a purpose, they were nothing more than pawns for him to control and play with.

It had taken Malgorath centuries, and he had been patient, waiting for the right host to come along. Like a parasite, hungry and craving, he possessed a young human prince, devouring his soul and taking the body for his own. That was years ago; now that the prince had grown into a young man, Malgorath was able to use the full potential of his power. Along the way, he had planted seeds, infecting people with his essence, controlling them but letting his essence lay dormant—ticking time bombs for him to activate when the time was right.

He had suspected something was wrong when he sensed Hal dying. He felt the life-force slowly ebbing from the captain. The activation of the divinity stone had confirmed it. Losing the divinity stone wasn't an option; Lord Dellavenor had failed him, so now it was time for him to take matters into his own hands. Concentrating, he activated the essence within the dying captain. "Go, Jaydrath, my Hunter Demon, and retrieve my divinity stone," he said, as he continued walking down the corridor leading to his bedroom. He passed by a window and looked into the courtyard of the Everthorn family castle situated in Sethanon.

Hal's eyes opened wide, and he screamed; his body felt like it was on fire. His skin hardened, turning a bluish-grey, and he began to morph. His body grew lanky, his arms longer, his leg muscles broader and stronger. Elongating, his jaw transformed into a muzzle as his teeth became sharpened fangs. Glossing over, his eyes became pitch-black, and his nails grew into claws. He had become a demonic monster, a predator. Like all demons, he had a natural affinity towards magic, magic he felt coursing through his body.

Growling, he bounded forward on all fours, running up the stairs and shattering the barracks door. Continuing, his claws scraping the wooden floor, he sprinted into the main hall and leapt up the stairs four at a time. After barging through the landing doorway, he bowled over two guards.

"Hal?" Dellavenor questioned, looking at him not in fear but in awe.

"Hal is dead. I am Jaydrath," he replied.

"Our master has evolved you," Dellavenor said zealously. "But why, Malgorath? Why am I not worthy?"

Jaydrath didn't have time for this; he leapt forward, knocking over one of the guards and, with a snap, clamped his teeth over the throat of the other. He landed nimbly on one of the safe tiles. As he shook the guard's head, the neck snapped as the guard flopped around like a play toy. He then tossed the corpse down a nearby chute. After leaping over the remaining tiles, he dived headfirst through a chute. The same chute Darla had disappeared down moments before. It was time to hunt down his prey.

Chapter 3

Darla landed with a small, squelchy splash and, wrinkling her nose, cringed at the smell. It was times like this that she regretted having heightened senses. She detected faeces, urine, vomit, rotting food, and something else----- decay and death. The diamond was radiating again, swirling blue and red, illuminating the tunnel with an eerie glow. She put it back in her satchel and carefully did it up. The strap bore the weight; it was taut but wasn't ripping any further. She would have to be careful, though.

The strap was already worn from overuse, and then it had gotten snagged on a branch, fraying it even more. Getting a new satchel was long overdue, and with the money she made from this job, she planned to get a new one, a fancy one with hidden compartments. First, though, she needed to get out of the sewers. She had memorised this region's sewer network and had left Midnight near one of the grates. This had been her backup plan, an alternate means of escape, one she'd hoped she wouldn't have to use. Things hadn't gone as planned, though, and here she was.

Drawing one of her daggers and gripping it tightly, she crept forward, her golden bestial eyes allowing her to navigate her way through the darkness. Darla cursed; as quietly as she tried to walk, her padded boots still made a soft crunching sound as she crossed the small rocks and the litter of bones, a graveyard of her predecessors, of the thieves who had been trapped and condemned.

A scraping came from a nearby chute. A moment later a corpse dropped out, the guard's armour clanking as it hit the rocks. She knelt for a closer look. The guard's neck had been snapped. What had done this? A rumbling sounded, followed by an echoing growl that reverberated down another chute.

Darla sheathed her dagger as she spied a thick gold ring and a pouch of coins next to the corpse. Greedily, she grabbed them and stuffed them into her bulging satchel. Why shouldn't she benefit? The guard no longer had any need for them. In his pocket she found a carefully wrapped package. Something sweet, judging from the smell of it. After unwrapping it, she found a thick biscuit, full of spices, nuts, and raisins. It looked scrumptious! She was about to take a bite when her company arrived, exiting the chute and landing before her.

"You should have run, thief!" the beast snarled.

Darla stuffed the biscuit into her back pocket. "What? And miss the opportunity of looting this corpse you so generously provided for me?" The monster was lanky and had powerful legs built for speed and stamina. He had a muzzle like a wolf, teeth that dripped blood, and elongated arms ending in sharp claws. Darla took in his bluish-grey skin, his tattered clothes, and the remnants of his armour hanging loosely from his body. What gave her the shivers, though, was his soulless black eyes, which stared at her hungrily. "Captain?" she said, suddenly recognising him. Hal had transformed into something ungodly, something inhuman.

"The captain is dead, I am Jaydrath, first of the Hunter Demons. I have been sent to retrieve the divinity stone for my master. Now give it to me."

Darla opened both satchels and rifled through her pockets, including the hidden ones in her cloak. Looking puzzled, she shook her head. "Ah, now I remember. Here it is," she said, giving the demon the middle finger. Jaydrath leapt forward. Damn, he was fast. With a hiss, Darla drew her short sword, and the demon came to a screeching halt. She saw the fear in his eyes, which were fixed on the weapon. Slowly and cautiously, he backed away, afraid of the sword. But why? Could it actually kill a demon?

She was about to charge forward when she felt a chill in the air. Her breath frosted as her hackles rose, alarming her to the threat. "I'll take the stone from your corpse, thief," Jaydrath spat. The air around her grew even colder, and she felt a tingling in the air, a sensation she recognised immediately: Jaydrath was using magic.

With a natural, gentle flow, Jaydrath drew the magic forth. Darla leapt backward then dodged and weaved as razor-sharp frozen stalagmites erupted from the tunnel floor. Her arm snaked out, and the short sword sliced through a nearby stalagmite. After grabbing it with her other hand, she threw it like a spear, aiming it at Jaydrath's chest. It spiralled through the air, spraying water droplets in its wake. In a flash, she drew one of her daggers and sent it twirling through the air, following like a silent shadow behind the stalagmite.

In a heartbeat, Jaydrath had a shield up. It consisted of condensed air, thick and swirling at a phenomenal speed. The shield was practically invisible, but with Darla's bestial vision, she saw the shimmering air. It glistened and sparkled as the stalagmite crashed into it, shattering into tiny diamond-like shards. Jaydrath grimaced, staggering slightly as the shield wavered, absorbing the impact and weakening. The stalagmite had obliterated into a cloud of ice shards that blanketed and hid the dagger. The enchanted dagger easily pierced through the shield, catching Jaydrath by surprise as it cut through his rib cage and embedded itself in his chest.

He screamed. He had never felt anything like this—it burned with excruciating pain. The dagger had been perfectly aimed, slicing through his ribs and puncturing his heart. It was a killing blow; a mortal would have died instantly. Grabbing hold of the hilt, Jaydrath gently pulled the dagger free. The blade ground against bone, and blackish blood sprayed across his torso and the ground. His magic —his essence— was the only thing that had saved him, keeping his heart beating. As he pulled the dagger free, the wound rapidly knitted closed.

Howling with rage, he unleashed his magic. He already felt drained, weakened, as he hadn't allowed himself enough time for his host body to heal and for his demonic magic to replenish, to get up to full capacity. He now only had a minute amount of essence remaining. Icy spikes shot out of the stalagmites, impaling everything in their path. Darla somersaulted, leaping onto the wall, dodging, and evading the deadly onslaught. Once again, she had harnessed her lycanthropy, focusing on lengthening her body and strengthening her claws. Dust and pebbles fell to the ground, a gentle shower as her claws found purchase, sinking deep and embedding themselves into the wall. A scurrying rat caught her attention, screeching as it was impaled.

Her breath frosted as a chill went through her, giving her goose bumps. The wall was beginning to take on a glistening sheen. It was freezing, and she had nowhere to go. She tried to retract her claws, but it was too late—they were stuck, frozen in the rock. Gritting her teeth, she pulled, but it was useless. She was about to try to pry herself free with the short sword when she saw something sparkling out of the corner of her eye. Jaydrath stood there spinning her dagger on the tip of his finger. He smirked then threw it. Darla was a sitting duck.

Her timing and precision were perfect, effortless. It was as if the sword guided her, as if she were linked to it. She raised the sword, then angled it and struck the dagger's handle. It spiralled upward, implanting itself into the frozen wall above her hand. She was rewarded with a loud reverberating crack. Now all she needed was a distraction. A moment later, she saw it glistening before her: a stalagmite with icy spikes branching off it.

Darla sheathed her sword, and unhooking it from her shoulder, dropped it to the ground. One after another, her belt, pouches, daggers, satchels, and boots fell in a heap on the floor, as she awkwardly undressed herself. Unclasping her fur lined cloak, she let it drop as it too joined the pile of discarded items. Items that she had no intention of ruining. Confused, Jaydrath watched the proceedings, captivated, unsure what to do. What the hell was she up to? "Do you plan on giving up mortal? Shame, I was hoping for more of a challenge," he smirked, smug and contrite. "Don't worry I will grant you a quick death."

Darla smiled wickedly. "I was about to say the same thing to you." *Giving up,* she thought, laughing inwardly at the thought. It was the furthest from the truth, she refused to give up, it wasn't in her nature. She was just preparing herself for what was about to come next. Concentrating, using her willpower to keep the mental barriers in place, to keep her humanity and reign in the primal urges. She let go. The surge was like a torrent as she tapped into the full extent of her lycanthropy. The transformation was a painful process, but it was a pain Darla had grown accustomed to. She welcomed it and embraced it.

She rarely turned into a werewolf, only doing it in private, secluded areas. Only a few people knew about it as well, the last thing she wanted was to draw attention to herself. The transformation also ruined her clothes. She had lost count of the number of outfits that had been shredded and destroyed. The outfit she currently wore had been designed using a fur lined elastic material, it had been expensive and would hopefully withstand her transformation. It was the moment of truth; she was about to find out.

Her hands and feet grew longer and broader, reshaping and changing their appearance. Darla grit her teeth as her bones lengthened, strengthening along with her muscles. Her jaw elongated, her teeth growing bigger, her canines becoming longer and sharper. Teeth ideal for biting, tearing, and ripping apart her victims. Her ears were next, growing and becoming long and pointy. Claws that were already partly established, elongated to their full extent, becoming razor sharp, weapons for maiming and killing. Finally, it was her hair, mahogany and red streaked hair that grew at an alarming rate becoming thick, course, reddish brown fur. Reaching out, she grabbed hold of the stalagmite just below the spikes and let out a low menacing growl.

She dug in her claws and the ice cracked, the stalagmite coming away in her hand. Her fingers instantly felt numb, followed by her entire hand, the coldness seeping through her glove. Throwing her arm forward, she sent the stalagmite spinning and spiralling through the air. Jaydrath was surprised and baffled. This mortal had just transformed into a monster that almost resembled a demon. Was she kindred? The huge piece of ice rocketed in front of him, missing him completely before crashing into the opposing wall. What was this woman up to?

Darla waited patiently. As the stalagmite hit the wall with a thunderous crash, she reacted. Her muscles strained as she yanked. Rubble and dust cascaded around her, and then with an almighty crack, a huge chunk of rock came free. Tumbling backwards, her purchase gone, she bent her knees and, using the wall, pushed herself backwards with her feet. As she soared over the deadly stalagmites, she aimed and threw, retracting her claws and hurling the massive chunk of rock towards her target.

* * *

The ice from the stalagmite had shattered into thousands of particles that created an icy cloud, blinding Jaydrath. He barely had time to blink before the rock smashed into his head with the force of a battering ram.

Darla scratched her thigh on one of the spikes and landed awkwardly. Her pants were torn, and blood trickled in a steady stream down her leg. There were a few other tears, but overall, it had withstood her transformation. At this rate, she'd need to buy herself a whole new outfit. Standing up shakily, she watched as the massive rock collided with the demon's head, almost cleaving it right off. She was proud of her handiwork; everything had gone according to plan.

Jaydrath's skin was shredded, blood spraying from his body. His muscles were torn, and with a loud, sharp crack, his neck snapped in two. His head flopped to the side, hanging limply at a strange angle. Although he was almost decapitated, somehow he was still standing. Darla couldn't believe it. With a guttural roar she bounded forward, her claws slashing, ripping into the demon. Torn off, the demon's arms flew to the back of the tunnel, yet he remained standing. Her claws were a blur, ferociously shredding Jaydrath's torso to pieces. Stomach, intestines and bone fragments, littered the ground in front of her. She refused to bite the demon. She hadn't developed a taste for demon blood—yet!

The demon fell, a bloodied mess at her feet. Satisfied, she slowly walked back. Transforming back, she redressed and collected her belongings. She picked up the discarded biscuit, wiping off the dirt. Transformations and fighting always made her hungry. Raising it to her mouth, she prepared to take a bite, stopping as she heard a noise. Turning, she watched as the demon rapidly regenerated, knitting itself back together. Was this demon truly immortal? What would it take to kill him? Not waiting to find out, she shoved the biscuit into a pocket, turned and ran.

* * *

Jaydrath was as still as a statue. He was severely wounded and paralysed with an emotion he'd never experienced before: fear. Although he was practically immortal, this was the closest he'd ever come to dying. The only thing keeping him alive was his miniscule piece of magical essence. He had lost the divinity stone, for now at least. He had underestimated this woman, this mortal, this monster. This was his mistake; next time, he vowed, he would be better prepared. Right now, however, Jaydrath needed to heal. Lying there, he closed his eyes. Being a demon, he possessed phenomenal regenerative powers. It would only take a matter of moments for him to heal. Although there were other creatures in these tunnels, he was safe for now, barricaded behind the shelter of his stalagmites.

Darla slowed down, her heart racing. There was no sign of pursuit. Proceeding through the tunnel, taking it slow, she listened for any sounds. She picked up a noise to her left, something scurrying along the side of the tunnel. Slowly she lowered her hand, wrapping her fingers around the hilt of her of her long-bladed dagger. It came out of the sheath with barely a sound. Her arm lashed out, and—*crunch* —she stabbed something, pinning it to the tunnel floor. She pried it free and looked at the rat's corpse, its blood dripping down her blade. Rats—she hated rats, the little vermin they were.

Darla had been walking for about ten minutes, navigating the tunnels, when she came upon something sticking out of the waste that flowed through the sewer. Whatever it was, it was a writhing mass covered in rats. They squeaked as she neared, then scuttled off down the tunnel. She grabbed hold and pulled out the object: the remnants of a human skeleton. The legs had been ripped off, along with the bottom half of the jaw. Huge claw marks could be seen along the broken ribs, and a broken piece of claw was embedded in the skull. Ghouls! Hopefully this one was long gone.

She progressed farther into the sewer network, turning left, right, then left again. This place was a labyrinth, a maze of tunnels someone could easily get lost in. If it hadn't been for her photographic memory, she would have been in deep trouble. She walked along, trudging through the filth. She glanced at the blueprints of the sewer system the Brotherhood had given her and estimated she had about ten minutes to go. Her stomach grumbled. Even though she had eaten half of the captain's sandwich, she was starving.

She reached into her back pocket and pulled out the thick biscuit. She took a bite as she rounded the corner, chewing slowly and savouring the flavours. It was just what she needed. She bit into some of the nuts...and *crunch*. Darla froze midstep, her eyes wide, her heart pounding. A seven-foot creature stood before her, a monster from nightmares. A ghoul. Attracted by the sound of the crunch, it turned its head abruptly.

The ghoul had just bitten a rat in half and was chewing it with a sickening crunching sound. It tossed the remains as its head turned this way and that. Ghouls were blind, having milky white orbs for eyes. These eyes were overly sensitive to light; it was their only weakness. Humans and elves had taken advantage of this, hunting them, carrying torches and lanterns, then attacking the ghouls while they were vulnerable. Ghouls were intelligent creatures, though, and had adapted to their blindness; their survival depended on it. Many of them started wearing blindfolds and full covering helmets that covered their eyes. Some even went so far as to sew their eyes shut. The hunters soon became the hunted.

Due to their blindness, ghouls relied on their other senses to hunt their prey. These senses were extraordinary, developed from a lifetime of living underground—the reason for their pale grey skin. While the ghoul was turning its head, it not only was listening, but it also was trying to pick up Darla's scent. It slowly stepped towards her, its long tongue flicking out as it raised its hand and licked some blood off it. The ghoul's teeth were long and razor sharp, capable of chewing flesh, muscle, and bone. Assassins always joked that the best way to dispose of a body was to feed it to a ghoul; the remains would be unidentifiable.

* * *

The ghoul's claws were long, retractable, curved, and just as sharp as their teeth. They were made of bone, making them both strong and durable. Darla watched as the ghoul's claws, each one the size of a dagger blade, slowly extended from its hands. The ghoul would prove to be a challenge, as it was the ultimate predator. Darla's muscles tensed as she stood motionless, watching, waiting, anticipating what the ghoul would do. To transform again would be noisy and taxing on her body. She needed time to recover.

With her nail, Darla pried a nut free from the biscuit and flicked it at the left-hand tunnel wall. The nut struck the wall like a bullet and shattered, spraying tiny shards. The ghoul reacted instantly, bolting to the left in a blur. Darla was already on the move, leaping towards the right side of the tunnel and catapulting over the ghoul. She landed in a run, spraying filth in her wake.

Darla sprinted, taking even breaths, her body in a rhythm as her feet pounded through the waste. The ghoul was close behind her; she could sense it and hear it grunting and scraping. The ghoul wasn't restricted to running through the waste; it bounded on all fours along the tunnel wall, its claws digging in and giving it the necessary purchase. It would catch up to in a matter of moments, she had to do something.

As she turned a corner, she suddenly realised she still had the biscuit in her hand. An idea came to mind, one that hopefully would distract the ghoul. She needed something heavier, though, and then she spotted it: a discarded shield with half a gauntleted arm still attached. She quickly picked it up, bending down and grabbing the arm as she ran past. She took one last bite of the biscuit. *What a waste*, she thought.

Darla shoved the rest of biscuit into the gauntleted hand and, breaking the fingers, clamped the biscuit firmly into it. As she passed the next side tunnel, she leapt into the air, throwing the shield like a discus. It twirled, shooting down the side tunnel like a rocket. Meanwhile, Darla flew forward and landed silently at the side of the tunnel. The shield clanged into the side of the tunnel, ricocheted, and landed in the waste. Standing motionless, Darla watched and waited.

The ghoul slowed and retracted its claws. It took a hesitant step into the sludge and stood at the junction. Turning its head, it listened and sniffed the air. With one final sniff, it slowly walked down the side tunnel. Darla couldn't believe her luck; the decoy had worked—although it wouldn't fool the ghoul for long. She took a cautious step, followed by another, silently edging her way farther down the tunnel. She wanted to put as much distance between her and the ghoul as possible. Another five minutes of running, and she'd reach the grate. Her foot edged forward another step and lost purchase. She slipped, arms flailing, but quickly righted herself. Regaining her balance, she sighed, knowing how close she had come to falling face-first into the waste.

Carefully she continued, slowly turning her head and risking a glance back. It had only been a couple of minutes, but it had seemed like an eternity. There was no sign of the ghoul; it obviously was still distracted. Making her was through the sludge was a gruelling process; she had only managed to edge her way three metres farther along. She quietly groaned, moving her foot to take another step, when she heard an unearthly wailing shriek. Darla gasped, lost her footing, and began to fall. She put out her hands to brace herself and landed on all fours with a splash. She quickly got up, grimacing. She was covered in faeces and God knows what else. "Fuck," she muttered. Fortunately, however, the path was now clear, and she raced once again down the tunnel.

Another shriek sounded behind her, reverberating—the ghoul was right behind her. She heard its claws scrape against the wall, gaining purchase as pebbles rained into the putrid sludge. A moment later multiple shrieks sounded, farther away but echoing down the tunnel from multiple locations. Other ghouls were answering the call of the first. They were not only communicating to each other but also hunting and stalking her. The ghoul shrieked again, the sound once again coming from behind her but closer this time. She had put a little distance between her and the creature but not much. The ghoul was in its element and was gaining on her once again. Five minutes to go! Five long fucking minutes.

Darla skidded around the corner, her feet pounding, spraying up waste behind her. The shrieks sounded again. She was impressed; the ghouls were herding her. The only reason she was still alive was because she had the blueprints of the tunnels. Amongst the shrieking, she detected another sound. A shriek, but different, higher in pitch, more like a scream. It was out of fear, distress, and panic, and it was getting louder. She reached a T junction and turned abruptly, skidding in the sludge. Four minutes left!

A pile of bones lay ahead of her—other unfortunate victims of the ghouls. Part of it caught her attention. Two broken femurs stuck out like jagged spikes, with a thick rounded skull sticking up between them. Darla surmised it was a dwarven skull, thicker and smaller than a human skull, due to their stature. The jaw was open wide, as if in an eternal, silent scream. Darla immediately got an idea.

She leapt into the air, somersaulting between the femurs. As she passed between them, she grabbed hold of the skull, snapping it off at the spine. After she landed, she immediately leapt back into the air, spinning as she did so. Soaring through the air and facing the oncoming ghoul, she pulled back her arm, aimed, and threw the skull. Completing the spin, she landed in a run and continued sprinting down the tunnel. Three more minutes!

The skull soared through the air like a missile and hit the ghoul square in the head with a loud crack. The creature stopped abruptly, dead in its tracks. Its powerful claws held its appendages firmly to the wall as it stood frozen, shocked, its body wobbling. Then it toppled sideways. Darla was oblivious to the outcome as she ran, her heart pounding, but smiled slightly as she heard the loud splash behind her. It bought her a little bit of time; hopefully that would be all she needed. The ghoul groggily got up out of the waste, shaking its head, stunned momentarily. It then shrieked and continued its pursuit. Darla heard the ghoul, its claws scraping the ground as it rounded the corner. Answering shrieks sounded, echoing, some closer, some farther away. The ghouls were closing in on her. Two minutes to go!

After sliding around another corner, she headed towards a huge open chamber, a junction branching off to multiple tunnels. This was her destination; according to the blueprints, this was the maintenance entrance she had passed earlier. The tunnel was long, but her goal was in sight. One minute to go—she was nearly there! A stream of moonlight illuminated the area, revealing something large moving in the distance, splashing amongst the sludge. A loud roaring screech resounded. Whatever it was, it was panicked and scared. But why? Darla didn't want to find out. A side tunnel loomed before her, a detour. Her mind went into overdrive, calculating a new route in a matter of seconds. The next exit was a couple of minutes away, and the ghoul was closing in. *Crap!* Her muscles aching, Darla put on a burst of speed.

She skidded as she turned the corner. Another seven-foot-tall ghoul loomed before her. She leapt to the left side of the tunnel and sprang off. Extended, her left leg swung round, her boot smashing into the side of the ghoul's head and sending it toppling like a fallen tree. It collapsed sideways, slamming into the tunnel wall. Debris splashed into the waste. Darla landed on the right side of the tunnel, facing the way she had come. Sprinting back, she turned the corner and headed towards the chamber. She had no choice; the alternate route was no longer an option. She'd also lost the brief lead she'd had and now had two ghouls chasing her.

As she ran, she drew the short sword from its sheath. The runes along the blade glowed, intensifying to a bright blue. It illuminated the tunnel with a radiant blue light that announced her presence and attracted more ghouls as she entered the chamber. Six ghouls were situated around the outskirts of the chamber, circling their prey, stalking, tormenting, and coordinating their attacks—attacks that had injured the creature chained in the middle of the chamber.

It was a large serpentine creature with a scaled reptilian head. Its long-barbed tail was thrashing wildly. Numerous scratches and bite marks could be seen, wounds the ghouls clearly had inflicted. It stood on two powerful, muscular legs that were situated just below its elegant, mighty wings. Darla couldn't believe it. They had chained up a wyvern. She suspected Dellavenor's elves had done it, it was his land after all. Darla felt sick to her stomach,

Judging from its size and its colouring, the wyvern was a juvenile male. This answered the question of how the local ghouls had managed to survive: the elves had been feeding them. As the elves were supposed to be nature loving, this was both hypocritical and barbaric. The wyvern tried to rear up but was restricted by the chains. It looked at Darla with both fear and hope.

As she walked farther into the chamber, her boots crunched. The ghoul's heads turned, as she drew their attention and pinpointed her location. It couldn't be helped; the chamber was littered with bones of varying shapes and sizes. Animal, creature, and human bones all mingled together. It was a graveyard, a feeding ground for the ghouls. The chamber branched off in six locations, its numerous tunnels providing easy access for the ghouls. High above was the large grate, the bars thick and sturdy. It was padlocked shut, making it impossible for Darla to escape. She had thought this was a maintenance entrance; how wrong she had been.

Her keen hearing picked up a faint but distinct scraping sound behind her: the two ghouls pursuing her, creeping stealthily along the wall. The scraping suddenly stopped, and Darla reacted instantly; the sword was in sync with her thoughts and movements. She could almost sense the ghouls' positions. Cautious, one of them had stayed at the tunnel's entrance. The other one had been bold, using its momentum to leap at her at lightning speed.

Tucking her legs, Darla somersaulted backwards through the air. As she flew overhead, spinning through the air, her arm swung out at the precise moment. The blade sang as she slashed it across, slicing through bone and muscle and decapitating the ghoul. She landed in a crouch, the ghoul's corpse landing, crashing to the ground behind her. Its head rolled, stopping near the wyvern, who snorted at it decisively. Gingerly it picked it up in its mouth and spat it at one of the ghouls; apparently even wyverns were fussy about what they ate. The head shot forward like a bullet, slamming into the ghoul's chest and making it stagger backwards. With a thud it dropped at the ghoul's feet.

All the attacks on the wyvern had ceased as the ghouls' attention turned to Darla. Somehow, even blinded, they could sense the sword, the power it emitted. They stood by the edge of the chamber, wary of the weapon she wielded. The ghoul who'd been struck was taller, broader, and a darker grey than the others. It knelt and picked up the head. Holding it firmly in both hands, it lifted it to its face and sniffed it a couple of times. Its long tongue snaked out, licking it, tasting the blood, identifying it.

This ghoul seemed intelligent, cunning, and held authority. It demonstrated there was a hierarchy amongst the ghoul civilization, a system of ranking and authority. Maybe the ghoul that attacked her had been hoping to claim the kill and gain the accreditation and honour that would come along with it. It had failed, and the ghoul leader now held its head in his hands. Darla had painted a bullseye on her forehead, proven to the ghouls that she was a greater threat. In pure rage, the high-ranking ghoul tossed the head to the ground and shrieked, commanding the other ghouls to attack. Within moments the tunnels were echoing, ear-piercing shrieks coming from every direction.

* * *

Asserting its authority, the high-ranking ghoul stomped in the sludge, spraying faeces everywhere. Immediately, every ghoul in the chamber followed suit. The high-ranking ghoul then screeched out a deep, rhythmic tune. A war chant—Darla had heard about various races that used this practice, like the orcs and the barbarian tribes, both of whom put themselves into a frenzied, violent state. There was nothing she could do except watch as the ghouls took on a heightened, bloodlust-fuelled disposition.

All fear of the legendary weapon had vanished, replaced by an unsatiable berserker rage. "Oh, fuck," Darla said, backing up and bumping into the wyvern. Lying there helpless, its chain rattling, the creature watched the ghouls. Darla and the wyvern were allies, at least for now. Shrieking as one, the ghouls charged forward. "Let's even the odds, shall we?" she mumbled. She lifted her sword, the blade glistening in the moonlight, and brought it crashing down straight at the wyvern.

The thick chain snapped. With a clatter, it fell off the wyvern to the ground. Lifting itself onto its powerful legs, the wyvern roared defiantly. Darla rolled as a ghoul swiped at her, its claws narrowly missing. Springing up behind it, she rammed her sword through the back of its neck. The radiating, bright-blue blade erupted through the other side.

When she pulled the blade free, the corpse fell face-first into the waste. Sensing an attack, Darla spun, her eyes scanning the chamber, but nothing seemed out of place. Then she spotted the movement, the moonlight illuminating figures against the wall—two ghouls were descending upon her. They had climbed the wall and were now leaping off to attack her from above. A bold tactic she hadn't anticipated. As she raised her sword, something whipped forward—large, menacing, and in a blur of speed. The ghouls vanished, flying at lightning speed as the wyvern's tail smacked into them and sent them careening into the far wall. Darla heard multiple bones break as the two corpses, along with a pile of debris, crashed to the ground.

* * *

The wyvern's long neck whipped out, its head darting forward, and with a crunch, it bit another ghoul in half. After crunching on it a couple of times, making sure it was dead, it hurled it across the chamber. Only three ghouls remaining. Suddenly Darla heard a scratching noise that seemed to come from everywhere: the sound of claws rapidly extending and retracting, claws that enabled the ghouls to bound quickly across the tunnel walls. "Fuck me," Darla said, scanning the tunnels, her keen vision picking up the movement. Three, five, seven—no, twelve—more ghouls. The reinforcements were about to arrive.

The ghouls were pouring through every tunnel except the one Darla had come from. That one remained eerily silent. "You've got to be shitting me," she muttered as she felt the icy chill emitted from the tunnel's entrance, a chill she had experienced only minutes before. A chill emanating from something far worse than the ghouls.

* * *

Chapter 4

As a thick mist flowed into the chamber, Darla immediately recognised the silhouette cloaked within it. *Jaydrath!* The demon smiled as he emerged from the mist. "Why won't you just die?" she said with a sigh. She raised her short sword, which glowed brightly in response to the demon's presence.

"Because I am a demon. I am immortal." With his demonic pride, he refused to admit he had come very close to dying.

"Well, you can't blame a girl for trying." Darla smirked as she watched two ghouls emerge from a neighbouring tunnel. They crawled silently along the wall towards the demon, making the most of Darla's distraction. Next to her, the wyvern swished its tail back and forth. The creature was silent, watchful; like the ghouls, it was biding its time, waiting for an opportunity.

"Give me the divinity stone *now*!" Jaydrath roared, his patience gone. "You cannot evade me. I am linked to the stone. I will track it for an eternity."

"I won't let you give it to Malgorath," Darla replied calmly, gripping the short sword. The weapon reassured her, gave her hope.

"Then I will take—" Jaydrath didn't get time to finish as the ghouls pounced, springing off the wall with shrieks. It was the only warning he received. The demon, however, seemed unfazed. With a slight turn of his head, he acknowledged the ghouls before returning his attention to Darla. The ghouls were fast, their claws glistening in the moonlight—they were so fast, in fact, that Darla could barely track them. The demon was faster, though. His hands shot out, grabbing one of them by the wrist and the other one around the throat. The effect was instantaneous. Sparkling ice creeped across their bodies like a spider web. Within moments they were frozen solid, nothing but two statues.

The ghouls' leader roared a bellow of unbridled rage. The rest of the ghouls growled in response, low and menacing. They remained submissive, though, refusing to attack—it was all bravado, an empty threat. Jaydrath turned his attention back to Darla. The ghouls were nothing to him; they were feral, primal, an inferior race. "Now give me the Divinity St—" Jaydrath didn't get to finish that sentence either, as something smashed through the two frozen ghouls, shattering them and hitting him with the force of a battering ram. Thrown off his feet, the demon found himself impaled on the razor-sharp tip of the wyvern's tail; the creature had seen an opportunity and taken it.

Jaydrath clung to the wyvern's tail, trying to free himself as the thing swished back and forth. He appeared to be desperately trying to freeze the wyvern, but something was terribly wrong. With a tremendous thud, the beast slammed the demon into the grate. The grate rattled, buckling and denting as the wyvern smashed Jaydrath against it repeatedly. His body was battered, bruised, and broken. Regardless of his injuries, he was still generating an icy-cold temperature; Darla saw it shimmer off him in waves.

She smiled as the realisation came to her. The wyvern inhabited this land and had thrived in the frozen tundra of the dwarven kingdom for centuries. It was only natural that during that time they had evolved and developed an affinity for—and an immunity to—the cold. The wyvern was impervious to the demon's attacks.

Throughout the ordeal (as entertaining as it was), Darla kept an eye on the ghouls. They were wary, waiting to see how things played out. It wouldn't be long, however, before they returned their attention back to her.

The grate, the chain, and its foundations were frozen, the icy crystals shimmering in the moonlight. Debris and dirt rained down as other parts of the ceiling began to freeze. Darla's heart sank as a sickening cracking sound reverberated throughout the chamber. Like a giant spider web, cracks appeared across the ceiling. "Oh, fuck!" she shouted.

The demon was free, no longer impaled, hanging by one arm from the frozen grate. Severely injured, his grip failed, and he plummeted to the cavern floor. With a flap of its powerful wings, the wyvern took flight, hovering, dodging as rocks cascaded around them. Keeping the blueprints in mind, she quickly looked around and got her bearings. Picturing each of the escape routes, she quickly calculated the best option. Darla groaned, of course, it had to be behind the ghoul leader.

The wyvern roared and Darla turned to face it. Looking straight at her, the beast nodded as if to say, "Thank you" and "Goodbye." Darla returned the gesture. "Farewell, my friend," she said, then turned and ran straight at the ghouls' leader. Half a dozen ghouls stood between her and the entrance to the sewer. More ghouls emerged from neighbouring tunnels, scurrying across the walls. Within moments they'd join their brethren and bolster their numbers.

The one thing in Darla's favour was that the ghouls were wary of the hovering wyvern. The wyvern dodged a small boulder, landed near Darla, and tucked in its wings, encompassing and shielding her. A moment later, the large frozen grate fell and landed on the demon. The impact made it shatter, sending fragments shooting through the cavern.

Darla heard multiple thuds, but the wyvern's wings held firm, protecting her. Unlike its dragon cousins, the wyvern had wings that consisted of tough, flexible membranes that were hard as steel and could withstand the harsh elements. "Thank you," Darla whispered. With a roar, a final goodbye, the wyvern leapt through the grate opening and soared into the night.

She couldn't blame the wyvern for leaving; it had been captured, tortured, and just wanted its freedom. "Just fucking great," Darla muttered, turning to face the ghouls. There were now ten ghouls standing between her and the entrance, blockading it and making escape nearly impossible. To make matters worse, every ghoul had refocussed their attention on her. Shrieking, with their claws bared, they closed in from all directions. She was surrounded.

The ceiling shook from a sudden explosion as a ball of sizzling energy flew through the grate opening. Her ears ringing, her body wobbling, Darla fought to retain her equilibrium. With their heightened hearing, the ghouls were in just as bad shape. Some were even rocking on the ground in a foetal position, with their hands over their ears and screaming in agony. Looking up, Darla saw the wyvern open its mouth and launch another lightning ball. Confined in the cavern, the beast had been unable to use this deadly attack, but now that it had the necessary range, it was able to exact its revenge. Darla quickly covered her ears, protecting herself as the sizzling ball of energy rocketed towards the ground. It struck with deadly efficiency, exploding and sending debris and dirt raining down.

A large chunk of rock fell, followed by another. One of the ghouls wasn't quick enough and was crushed by a boulder, leaving nothing but a pool of blood oozing out from underneath. The rest of the ghouls quickly dove for cover as more rocks crashed down. Rocks were coming down everywhere, along with dirt and dust. The roof was caving in. *We're about to be buried alive!* Darla thought, panicking.

She sprinted forward, dodging rocks, and running towards the entrance. A mountain of dirt rained down in front of her like a giant waterfall. Closing her eyes, she braced herself. She had no choice but to run through it. Only the top half of the tunnel entrance was now exposed—she had to hurry.

Another explosion, the concussion almost rocking her off her feet. Steadying herself, Darla leapt into the air and dove into the long, narrow gap. She narrowly missed one ghoul and was heading straight towards another. Raising her short sword, she brought it crashing down on its head. Her blade easily sliced through its body, cleaving it down the middle. As the ghoul toppled backwards, she pulled the short sword free. Landing in a crouch, she then swept her sword across. The blade whistled through the air, slicing through the ghoul's kneecap. The creature toppled like a fallen tree.

Darla raised her short sword for the killing blow, but halted, hesitant. Although blind, the ghoul was staring straight at her—it knew exactly where she was. "Well, what are you waiting for? Kill me!" What the fuck! Had the ghoul just spoken to her? This ghoul wasn't feral at all; it actually showed signs of intelligence. A noise caught Darla's attention: the scraping of rocks. The ghouls' leader and another ghoul were crawling through the entrance tunnel, hunting her down.

As the gap narrowed further, Darla looked back and saw more ghouls scurrying behind them. "I only kill when I have to, ghoul," she said, withdrawing the short sword and sprinting down the tunnel. A moment later, a rumbling sounded as the cavern finally caved in. Running in a steady rhythm, Darla navigated the tunnel, not daring to look back again to see how many of the ghouls pursued her.

She created a mental picture of the sewer's layout and used it to navigate; she couldn't afford to make a mistake—to do so would mean certain death. She had about a kilometre to go; from her calculations, the exit should bring her up near her campsite. She heard the ghouls behind her, their scraping a constant noise, faint but getting louder. Although she couldn't determine how many there were, it didn't matter—they were closing in.

She turned a corner abruptly, skidding in the sludge, and noticed a grate in the distance, slivers of moonlight illuminating this section of the tunnel. It was a beacon of hope, of survival. Hanging from the concrete frame was part of an iron ladder. Half of it had snapped off, leaving the ends sharp and jagged. The other half had long been buried amidst the waste. Her goal in sight, she increased her speed.

Darla sprinted forward, ran up the wall, and bounded off, leaping towards the ladder. Grabbing hold of the top rung with her hands, she braced herself, planting her feet firmly on the bottom rung. The broken ladder consisted of six rungs, and she quickly climbed up, hooked her feet around the fourth rung, and wedged her knees underneath the second for extra support. This put her in an uncomfortable kneeling position, but there was no other choice. It was better than being pulled off the ladder by ghouls. She let go of the top rung and hung there.

She reached for her belt and pulled out her pick. Each grate was sealed with a large iron padlock to keep the ghouls from getting out. As Darla was an assassin and a thief, locks were one of her specialties. A shadow emerged from the darkness as a ghoul appeared, walking slowly and sniffing the air—it hadn't detected her yet. With her free hand, Darla slowly drew the long-bladed dagger from its sheath. Arching, she leaned back, and the satchels slid, dangling precariously as she prepared to pick the lock. Suddenly she heard the frayed strap snap, the two pieces flying in different directions. All Darla could do was watch horrified as the precious satchel containing the Divinity Stone began to fall.

She shot her arm out, desperately reaching for the pack and dropping the pick in the process. Her one and only pick. Her hand clamped shut, but the satchel was just out of reach and continued to fall—only to stop abruptly, swinging in midair, with Darla firmly clutching one of the frayed strap ends. She watched the pick twirling, sparkling in the moonlight as it fell past the satchel. *Crap!* That wasn't the worst of it, though—the pick then hit the ghoul on the forehead before flicking off and falling into the waste with a tiny splash. The ghoul's head instantly shot up.

Her position had been compromised. The ghoul crouched and looked up at her with its eerie, blank, milky-white eyes. Darla was motionless. She knew the ghoul couldn't see her, but somehow it sensed her and knew her position. How could it sense her, though? Then, with a daunting realisation, it came to her—it wasn't her that it sensed, but the swinging satchel. It sensed the movement. Darla quickly began to pull the satchel up just as the ghoul pounced, leaping high into the air.

Its clawed hand swung across, narrowly missing the satchel and grabbing hold of the other end of the strap. Darla winced as her arm was jerked down with the sudden extra weight. She gasped, horrified, as she heard the satchel rip. The Divinity Stone poked through, shining in the moonlight. As the satchel swung back and forth, the ladder groaned as the metal bent from the strain. Darla's ankles and knees were faring no better, as they were the only thing supporting her. Ignoring the pain, she concentrated on the task at hand.

Slowly the ghoul tried to climb up the long dangling strap. Another rip—now about a third of the Divinity Stone was showing. The ghoul seemed to sense it, or perhaps the power it emitted, and letting go, reached up with one clawed hand. "No, you don't," Darla said, her muscles straining as she yanked the satchel up. The ghoul's hand swayed as the strap swung. Another tear and even more of the Divinity Stone revealed itself. After steadying itself, the ghoul once again reached for the stone; it was nearly within its grasp. Swinging her other hand across, slashing with her dagger, Darla sliced through the strap and the ghoul fell. One of its claws scraped against the Divinity Stone before it crashed to the ground. Arms flailing, it landed in the waste.

Darla firmly tied the two pieces of strap around her thigh, securing the satchel. She had saved the Divinity Stone but lost her pick in the process. How would she open the grate now? Looking down, she saw the pick sparkling in the moonlight, floating in the waste right next to the ghoul. "I don't suppose you could pass me that little sparkly thing?" she said. The ghoul replied with a deep guttural sound, its equivalent of a "Fuck you." A loud growl sounded, and the ghouls' leader emerged from the shadows. The pick floated right smack between the two creatures. Darla was well and truly screwed.

The ghouls' leader was an intimidating figure to behold—eight feet tall, broad and muscly, with enormous talon-like claws. The first ghoul knelt in the waste with its head bowed as it submitted to its leader. The leader said something, a bark, a guttural noise, and instantly the subordinate pointed its clawed hand towards Darla. The leader snorted, and raising its head, bared its formidable teeth, growling at Darla. Roaring loudly, it communicated to the other ghouls, informing them of their prey's location. It kneeled, tensing its powerful leg muscles, then pounced, leaping forward in a blur of speed, and grabbed hold of the bottom rung of the ladder.

* * *

Darla quickly sheathed her dagger and firmly grabbed the top rung with both hands. She then unhooked her feet and lifted her knees to her chest. The ladder shook as the ghoul reached for the next rung. Darla waited patiently until it pulled itself up. When it did, her legs shot down, planting the heels of her boots into the ghoul's forehead. A loud crack resounded, and the ghoul fell, taking three rungs of the ladder with it.

Darla was left dangling, as her feet dropped away and hung precariously. A brief snicker sounded from the insubordinate ghoul as its superior quickly picked himself up from the waste. It brushed some faeces off its face indignantly and started barking commands. Darla had just humiliated the leader, and in doing so, she had just made herself ghoul enemy number one.

One, two—no, five—ghouls emerged from the darkness, quickly converging on her. Two of them were survivors from the collapsed cavern, while the other three had come from elsewhere, answering the summons. Seven ghouls, and she was dangling here helplessly. Barking further commands in the same guttural language, the ghouls' leader pointed towards Darla. Without question, the six ghouls went to either side of the tunnel. Digging in their claws, they then began to scale the tunnel wall. "Talking about being well and truly fucked," Darla murmured.

Lowering herself, she grabbed the second rung, then the third. Picking the lock was no longer an option she would have to use brute force. Scratching, digging their claws in, the ghouls steadily climbed the walls. Darla began to swing backwards and forwards, gaining momentum. The ladder wobbled slightly as she swung back, her feet touching the ceiling. As she swung forward, she bent her knees in and kicked the grate. Nothing!

Darla swung back again. The ghouls had clawed their way up the wall and had cautiously dug their claws in, finding purchase on the rocky ceiling. She threw herself forward, putting force and power into it. Springing her legs out, she kicked the grate again. It banged, rising slightly before landing back down with a thump. Small rocks tumbled into the waste as the ghouls slowly proceeded across the ceiling. Darla straightened out and swung again, her feet scraping the ceiling. More pebbles tumbled as the ghouls clawed their way closer. They were close to the grate, about an arm's length away. Darla swung forward and kicked.

The grate finally swung up, the lock cracking and flying off. Darla dashed upwards, pushed the grate free, and climbed out. She scrambled forward and slammed the grate down just as a clawed hand reached up. The ghoul retracted its claws as its fingers reached up through the grate, enabling it to firmly grab the iron bars. Its other hand, along with its feet, were embedded firmly in the ceiling. It pushed the grate, raising it slightly, only for Darla to slam it back down. She needed to relock the grate, but the lock lay about a metre away at the edge of some tall grass.

The second ghoul's face appeared, snarling at her as it assisted, pushing on the grate from below. Grunting, straining, Darla held the grate firmly down. One by one, the other four ghouls appeared, aiding their brethren by taking positions on either side of the grate. The grate was gradually rising, and try as she might, pushing with every ounce she had, Darla couldn't keep it closed. Even though they were only using one hand each, they were working cohesively as a team. Looking from below, watching eagerly, their leader smiled. Darla was about to be overpowered, and he knew it.

Suddenly something stood next to Darla, its shadow looming over her. It reared up high into the air then came crashing down with its powerful hooved feet. A sickening crack sounded as a horse's hooves landed on two of the ghoul's fingers, mangling them and shattering bones. The ghouls howled, letting go of the grate, their hands limp and useless. Darla looked up into the satisfied face of Midnight, her trusty companion.

* * *

Three of the remaining four ghouls retreated, enabling Darla to slam the grate down. Even the feral ghouls weren't stupid, choosing the option of self-preservation. One continued the onslaught, though, sticking two fingers through the holes in the grate just as Midnight nimbly sidestepped away. Its claws were extended, razor-sharp bone knives that could easily maim her horse. It tried again, but the horse already had danced away, snickering happily, enjoying this little game. Darla drew the short sword and waited patiently. She wasn't about to stand by and watch her horse get injured. Midnight snorted, tormenting the ghoul as he planted two hooves firmly on the grate.

The ghoul roared as it pretended to shove two fingers through before quickly withdrawing them. It was evaluating the horse, and the horse had responded, rearing slightly in the air. Midnight's predictability provided the ghoul with an opportunity, allowing it to concentrate, listen, and anticipate where the horse would land. With an evil grin, it shoved all ten of its deadly clawed fingers through the grate just as Midnight was about to land.

Darla's arm lashed out. The blade of the short sword glowed, the runes illuminating it with a bright-blue radiance. In a quick sweep, the blade cleaved through all ten fingers. Midnight landed, crashing onto the grate and the bloodied stumps. The ghoul howled; the pain so excruciating that it retracted its claws in its feet. Without any purchase, it fell backwards landing with a splash in the waste below. Midnight turned his head and snorted decisively at Darla as if to say, *I knew what I was doing. I was handling the situation. You worry too much!* Darla smiled and patted him under the chin. "Yeah, well it's my job to worry. Deal with it!"

Midnight blissfully rolled his head from side to side. He loved being patted, especially under the chin. He stomped once again on the grate and stood firmly, enabling Darla to dart across and retrieve the padlock. Looking at her, Midnight shook his head and snorted as if to say, *This wasn't the smartest of escape plans. I could have told you there were ghouls down there.* Biting her tongue, Darla merely rolled her eyes. This damn horse was as stubborn as she was and always had to have the last word.

The shackle of the padlock was bent, the locking mechanism broken. Given time, it could be fixed, but time was one thing Darla didn't have. She inserted the shackle through the adjoining iron holes of the grate and gave Midnight the command. He stomped upon the shackle, bending it slightly. "Again, boy," she said, firmly holding the padlock. The horse stomped again, and then a third time, bending the shackle and hooking it around. The grate was secure.

Standing, Darla smiled and lifted her foot to put it in the stirrup. "Okay, boy. Let's go get paid." Midnight shook his head, snorted decisively, and sidestepped away. His disgusted look said everything. *I don't think so. You smell like shit, worse than the ghouls. Don't expect to ride me until you've had a bath.* "Do you see a tub around here?" Darla said with a smirk. "As soon as we get to the inn, I'll have a nice soapy bath. I'll even buy you some apples." She lifted her foot, and the horse sidestepped out of the way again, nickering and shaking his head. *When we get there, I want grooming and...a whole bag of apples.* "Fine," Darla said, finally putting her foot in the stirrup and swinging herself onto Midnight's back.

They set off at a steady pace, having two days of hard riding ahead of them. Their destination was a small inn called the Kitty Fox, located in the town of Greybak on the border of the Blackrock Kingdom, an arid wasteland of snow and mountains, otherwise known as the dwarven homeland. Being on the border, it was the perfect place for Darla to meet her benefactor, Lord Thace Aldronin. It meant their meeting would be private, secure, with no elvish interference.

Darla rode hard, galloping through the forest. Her keen vision and the moonlight enabled her to navigate the path easily. They stopped at dawn, just as the sun began its ascent over the distant mountains. It provided them with a brief rest and time for them to quickly eat something before they continued. The day was dreary and cold; instinctively Darla wrapped her fur-lined cloak around her. It looked like it might snow soon, which was good because the snow would help hide her tracks.

Squinting, she looked back through the fog at the way she had come. Although she couldn't see anyone, she sensed Dellavenor and his minions. Closing her eyes, enhancing her other senses, she heard them about ten kilometres behind her, by her estimation. Dellavenor was crazy and fanatical, and with the situation Darla had put him in, he was desperate too. Like her, he and the other elves must have travelled throughout the night. "Shit!" Darla exclaimed as she mounted Midnight and urged him forward. The aspect of having a brief rest was quickly forgotten as she focused on putting as much distance as possible between her and her pursuers.

From the intel Darla had received, Dellavenor had around two hundred troops garrisoned at the castle. Half of them were unaccounted for, abandoned and left behind. He had probably taken an elite force consisting of his best soldiers and deceived those left behind, promising he would get reinforcements. That was pure speculation, though; perhaps they had volunteered to stay; Darla didn't know. Either way, they had been sacrificed and left to die.

She trotted for a while before galloping once again, stopping twice for short breaks. It was late afternoon, and the temperature was dropping. She huddled within the confines of her cloak. She was craving a hot coffee and a warm meal, but as much as she wanted these luxuries, she avoided making a campfire. The elves had no idea where she was, and she refused to provide a beacon for them. She laughed at the irony—usually she was an apex predator, and now she was the hunted. She needed to get to the border and fast. She still had about a day of hard riding, and she was exhausted.

The hours were strenuous, with Darla constantly listening for any sign of the elves. She couldn't hear anything, however, and there was no sign of them. Perhaps she had evaded them? No, she didn't want to give herself false hope. She yawned, her eyes drooping, the events of the last day and a half catching up and taking hold. She hadn't slept and was utterly exhausted. She could doze in the saddle, though, just for a little while. Her eyes closed, and within moments she was asleep, rocking gently and snoring softly.

Midnight trotted off the path towards a nearby stream. He stopped near the bank and, rearing up onto his two front legs, threw Darla into the air. She flew, her arms and legs flailing, before landing headfirst into the icy water. She emerged, splashing and gasping. Her eyes were wide, and she was shivering. Her eyes then narrowed as she looked at Midnight, who let out a snicker. *Well, you needed a bath*, he seemed to say. "Yeah, well, so do you," Darla replied, splashing him playfully.

She dived under the water as some fish darted by. Clutching the dagger, she whipped her hand forward. She emerged from the water shortly after with two fish speared. She was exhausted, and there was still no sign of the elves; this riverbank was as good a place as any to make camp. She started a fire and hung her wet clothes between two nearby trees to dry. This might give away her position, but thanks to Midnight she had no choice. Even with the wash, her clothes still smelled awful, as if the sewer waste had absorbed into the fabric. They'd have to do for now, but when she got to Greybak, where she was meeting her benefactor, the first thing she would to do was burn them and buy some new clothes.

A rustling beyond the trees had Darla turning, sword in hand. Midnight neighed nervously, sensing something as well. After wrapping her fur-lined blanket around her naked body, she stood up. Cautiously, without making a sound, she proceeded forward. With the glowing runes of the short sword illuminating the way before her, she slowly weaved her way between the trees and bushes. The trees thinned out, and she entered a small clearing. The wyvern lay there curled up, sleeping. Next to it sat the remains of its meal—a few deer, from the looks of it. There wasn't much left, just some antlers and bones. As Darla stood there, captivated by the sight, the wyvern's eyes suddenly opened, looking straight at her.

Unfazed by her presence, it snorted in greeting. "Hello, my friend," Darla said, lowering her sword. "I'm glad you're okay." She didn't know whether it understood her, but it seemed the right thing to say. The wyvern grunted in reply. "Goodnight," she said, and turned around to head back to the campsite.

Midnight snorted in surprise, as if to ask, *Why didn't the wyvern eat you?* Darla patted him affectionately. "The wyvern already ate," she replied. "I don't think it's a threat." Midnight snorted decisively as if to say, *Maybe it wants us for dessert.* Darla merely shook her head, yet as she walked back to the campfire, she couldn't help but wonder whether there was some truth to this.

The wood crackled as the fire flickered and danced. Darla finished the fish and tossed the scraps in the fire. She had given Midnight some oats, and now he was grazing happily by a tree. "Wake me in a couple of hours," she said, lying wrapped in her blanket, cosy and content. He gave a flick of his head, followed by a half-hearted neigh, and returned to his grazing. Watching the fire was almost hypnotising, lulling her and wrapping her in the warmth of its embrace. Within minutes her eyes were drifting shut, exhaustion grabbing hold as she fell into a restless sleep.

* * *

Chapter 5

It wasn't the wet lick that woke her, as annoying and gross as that was; rather, it was the snapping of a branch. She sat bolt upright, fully awake, her blanket wrapped around her. The fire had gone out a while ago and was now just a pile of ash. She berated herself for sleeping, even for a little while, and allowing Dellavenor to catch up. Aware of the danger they were in, Midnight silently nudged her. As quietly as possible, Darla stood up, threw on her clothes, and secured the blanket to her saddle. Grabbing hold of the reins, she put her foot in the stirrup and...*creak*! "She's over there," one of the elves shouted.

"Crap!" Darla said, quickly mounting Midnight. Anxious, he neighed a warning. An animal erupted from the bushes. Darla reacted instantly, lashing out with her boot and kicking the shadow cat in the head. The shadow cats were what the elves used for hunting. They were deep black, lean, agile, and only slightly smaller than a dire wolf. This explained how the elves had managed to track her. Dazed by the blow, the shadow cat shook its head.

Darla nudged Midnight's flanks, urging him forward, and galloped from the campsite. Eventually they entered the forest and weaved amongst the trees. She heard Dellavenor barking orders; he sounded livid, desperate to retrieve the Divinity Stone. Multiple twangs resounded, and Darla ducked, leaning forward. An arrow flew overhead, and with a thud another one embedded itself in the tree next to her. Low feline growls could be heard behind her as more shadow cats appeared and gave chase. The elves were close behind, following the cats, crashing through the forest in hot pursuit.

Everything was a blur as the wind whistled through the trees. Midnight's hooves pounded, spraying up dirt and snow. Darla spotted movement out of the corner of her eye, and then whatever it was disappeared. One of the elves was in her blind spot. Hearing the wood of the recurve bow stretching, she steered Midnight to the side. The horse reacted instantly, swerving, using a massive pine tree as cover. The twang sounded—it was a near-miss, the arrow hitting the tree and spraying bark across her face.

The elf already had nocked and redrawn, preparing for another shot. Elves had earnt the reputation of being the best arches in the world. Darla was in trouble. Again, she swerved. The trees whirled by, providing her with cover. Occasionally there was a brief gap, but the elf was being patient, biding his time and waiting for the right opportunity. Galloping past an outstretched branch, Darla reached out and snapped it off. The branch was sharp, jagged, and covered with fascicles and needle-like leaves. It wasn't perfect, but it would have to do.

As the elf emerged, shadowing Darla's movements, Midnight jumped over a high bush and sprayed up a shower of leaves. He was blinded momentarily, the leaves obscuring his vision. A moment later he was in the clear, and as the leaves floated back to the ground behind him, he drew the string back tautly, aimed, and took the shot. Darla heard the humming sound the arrow made and judged its position. She then swung the branch, its sharp leaves swatting the arrow in mid-flight and deflecting it. The arrow skimmed across her shoulder, slicing through her tunic and drawing blood. In the blink of an eye, the elf already had reached for another arrow and nocked it.

Darla didn't give him time to take the shot, instead hurling the branch like a spear. It struck the elf, knocking him off the horse. The road was just ahead; she saw it amongst the treeline. She would be in the clear, able to use Midnight's speed and endurance, but she'd also be out in the open with nothing to shield her. She would be a sitting duck.

A series of growls sounded, along with the thundering of hooves. The elf's companions were nearly upon her. As he picked himself up out of the snow, Darla pulled on the reins, altering their course. Midnight skidded, spraying up snow as they abruptly changed direction and continued galloping through the forest. It was time to take a short cut, her destination only forty metres away.

Although the detour was perilous, it was a gambit she was willing to take. She veered, weaving between the trees, the thundering of the elves close behind them. Bark sprayed around her as four arrows embedded themselves in a tree. Swerving around it and galloping past the last of the trees, she entered a small clearing of tall grass. Thirty metres to go. She pushed her heels into Midnight's flanks, urging him forward.

The elves entered the clearing, their horses spraying up dirt and grass. Twenty metres to go. They drew back their strings, pulling them taut, the razor-sharp arrowheads sparkling in the morning sun. Ten metres to go. They aimed. Five metres to go. They fired, the volley of arrows soaring forth…but hitting nothing but air as Darla and Midnight disappeared over the edge.

The slope was a steep decline, almost a cliff face, treacherous and suicidal if not for Midnight. He was a rare breed of horse, extremely intelligent and trained in all conditions, environments, and terrains. He had been bred for speed and stamina and knew how to pace himself, how to navigate and manoeuvre the decline. Skidding, trotting, sliding as if it were some kind of dance, he proceeded down the steep slope. Behind them, twenty of the elves had followed Darla but were unable to stop in time and plummeted over the edge. Their horses let out cries of anguish and fear, as they maimed themselves crashing into one another. The elves and their horses were mangled in an avalanche of death.

Darla clung desperately to Midnight, trusting him explicitly, watching as he dodged and weaved while the enemy rolled and flew past them. He skidded past the corpse of a horse stuck on a rock and proceeded onto the snowy plain. The worst was over. The decline had eased off into a gentle slope, blanketed with snow and full of winter flowers. Nudging his flanks, Darla urged him into a canter and made her way towards the Galthezamer Bridge.

It was bitterly cold in the plains. The wind howled, freezing Darla to her core. She wrapped her fur-lined cloak tightly around her as they approached the Galthezamer Bridge. The structure was made of thick stone slabs and had been there for centuries, spanning across the icy, raging sea below. The Duegart Sea was treacherous and home to some of the most feared marine life in the world. Although the bridge was worn in parts, it had stood the test of time, withstanding wars and the harsh elements. A testament to dwarven architecture, the bridge signified the border between the two kingdoms and was technically neutral territory between the dwarven and elvish kingdoms.

Darla had about thirty miles to go, across a barren, snow-covered plain. In the distance, she could see the battlement outlining the small coastal town of Greybak, her destination. Above the walls, streams of smoke rose from the chimneys like fluffy marshmallows, a beacon leading her to her destination. It was a teasing reminder of the long, arduous journey she had ahead of her.

The quaint inn where she was meeting her benefactor was run by a rotund dwarf and his wife. The town was popular, a frequent stopover for travellers coming to and from the Blackrock Kingdom, home of the dwarves. Greybak backed into the Bloodgar Mountains but was surrounded by an open, treacherous snowy plain, A plain that was vast and had brought many a weary traveller to their death. The town was renowned for its trading and fishing, with the large, flat, triangular dygar fish in abundance.

They were extremely fast, ferocious, and had a barbed tail and three rows of spiky teeth. They were also extremely tasty and highly sought after. It was a dangerous business, though, because the dygar were also the favourite food of the crocark. Tales had been told in many an inn about crocark that had even attacked fishing boats. Darla, however, didn't put much stock in these old wives' tales,

Not only were the dygar fish tasty, but its poisoned barb also possessed hallucinogenic properties. This made for an extremely profitable enterprise for the town, as the Brotherhood paid a fortune for the poison. Although the area was bitterly cold all year round, it was also picturesque with the snow, pine trees, and the mountains looming in the background.

The town was heavily fortified with thick stone walls and dwarven soldiers constantly patrolling it. This was due to the constant attacks by bandits, snow giants, and gar. The latter were fierce monsters that resembled bears, except they were much bigger. Their thick white fur enabled them to blend into the landscape and camouflage themselves. They were said to have retractable claws as long as a dagger, tusks protruding out of the side of their head, and needle-like teeth. Whether the rumours were true, Darla didn't know; not many people survived an encounter with a gar. She was safe for the moment, though. From what she'd heard, the gar inhabited the mountains and rarely came out onto the plains.

Midnight's hooves clomped through the snow as he cantered along. The layer of snow was thin on the bridge, making it ideal for travelling across. The snowy plains on the other side would be another story. They were exhausted and even though they were somewhat near their destination, it still seemed like it would take an eternity to get there. Upon arriving, Darla would hand over the Divinity Stone to her benefactor so he could return it to the King Therondal. She would get paid, buy some supplies, have a hot meal and a steaming-hot bath and have a good night sleep in a comfortable bed. The following morning, they would begin the long trek home.

Darla heard the rumbling growl before she saw it. Its thick white fur made it hard to distinguish against the snow, but as it bounded along on all fours, it sprayed snow high into the air behind it. Its mouth was wide-open, its golden eyes gleaming. Two large bony tusks protruded out of the sides of the monster's head, ending in a sharp point—tusks used for goring its prey. It was a gar, but why had it ventured this far east? It was unheard of.

Darla wasn't about to stop and ask. She kicked Midnight in the sides, putting the horse into a gallop. Clumps of snow flung up behind them as the horse gained speed. He trusted Darla, obeyed her every command without hesitation, and knew (or more to the point, hoped) she wasn't about to play chicken with this monstrosity. Darla had a plan, though, even if it was a gamble. From her vantage point in the saddle, she had spotted something earlier. The gar bore down on them, charging towards them, rapidly getting closer.

Darla pulled on the reins, angling Midnight towards a huge stone slab at the side of the bridge. The stone had risen and shifted over time, as the slabs around it eroded, cracked, and crumbled. It was covered with a thin layer of snow, forming a large ramp. A ramp that Darla intended to use. Midnight galloped towards the ramp as the huge gar altered its course, charging at it from the opposite direction.

Darla nudged Midnight's flanks, gaining speed and momentum. The gar thundered forward, a juggernaut of reckoning and destruction. Midnight's hooves hit the ramp, and he bounded up it a moment before the gar crashed into it. Snow and fragments of stone sprayed through the air as the ramp shattered and collapsed. Midnight already had leapt high into the air, flying through the debris and over the gar. He landed behind it and continued galloping, as the gar roared in frustration, shook its head, and turning around ran after the fleeing horse.

Midnight had gained a couple of metres on the gar and continued to extend his lead as he galloped across the bridge. They reached the end, slowing considerably, Midnight reduced to a struggling canter. The plains were thick with snow, and they still had twenty-nine miles to go. The gar, however, sprinted onto the plains, spraying up snow and accelerating. Midnight snorted in fear, and Darla knew, without looking back, that the gar was rapidly gaining on them.

To her left, she noticed something else charging towards her. *What the hell?* she thought, and then she heard the fierce battle cries. Cries that would put the fear of God into most enemies, cries radiating from the dwarven warriors riding towards her. Their dire wolves sprinted effortlessly across the snow. They were the size of a ponies, larger and bulkier than normal wolves. Like the gar, they were covered in thick white fur, enabling them to blend into the landscape. They were intelligent, agile, and the preferred mount of the dwarven warriors.

The dwarven captain waved his arm forward, a command that was instantly obeyed. Four of the dwarves raised their heavy crossbows and, with simultaneous thrums, let their bolts fly. The bolt tips were jagged, specially designed to bore into and penetrate the thick hide of the gar. As they flew, they made a high-pitched whistling sound, before thumping, tearing, and burying themselves into the beast.

The gar roared in defiance and, changing course, charged at the attackers. Another command was issued, and the two dwarves either side of the captain nudged their mounts and sped ahead. The gar thundered forward with its head down, charging, ready to tear into the dire wolves. Out of immediate danger, Darla slowed Midnight to a trot and watched, riveted.

The gar was stronger and far superior, but where the dire wolves lacked strength, they made up for it with speed and agility. In a one-on-one melee, a dire wolf wouldn't stand a chance, but as a cohesive, coordinated pack, they were devastating. With mounted dwarven warriors added to the equation, they were unstoppable. Darla watched as the two dwarves whistled a command. Instantaneously the dire wolves changed course, darting to the side. Their dwarven riders hung sideways in their saddles and, with a swipe of their battle-axes, slashed across the gar's front legs.

The gar toppled forward headfirst, its front legs crumpling in midstride. The dwarven captain's dire wolf continued to sprint towards the gar, the captain nimbly lifting himself up and standing upon its back. The dire wolf knew exactly what to do, rearing up onto its front legs a metre from the injured gar and catapulting its rider forward. The captain flew through the air, jammed his battle spear into the back of the gar's neck, and landed on the creature's back. Leaning forward and putting his weight onto the spear, he then rammed it in farther. The gar died instantly, collapsing onto the bloodstained snow.

After freeing the spear and cleaning it with some snow, the captain remounted his dire wolf. Resuming formation, the dwarves bounded forward, approaching Darla's position. Uneasy and unsure, Midnight nickered at the oncoming dire wolves, but Darla patted him reassuringly. "Greetings, Captain," she said. "Thank you for your assistance."

The dwarven captain huffed. "The name is Rygar, milady. What business do you have in the Blackrock Kingdom?"

Straight to the point, Darla thought. "I have business with Lord Thace Aldronin at the Kitty Fox."

The captain nodded before sniffing disdainfully. He looked around, trying to pinpoint the obnoxious smell. Darla hid in her cloak, pulling her hood down to hide her embarrassment. She wanted nothing more than to burn her clothes and have a hot bath.

They rode in silence, the dwarven squad escorting Darla to the Kitty Fox Inn in Greybak. Eventually a set of large wooden gates creaked open, allowing them entry into the town's courtyard. Dwarven soldiers, dressed in thick coats, could be seen walking along the bulwark. The gates slammed shut, and a thick wooden plank was slid across to bar it. Although it was solely for protection, Darla felt like she'd been trapped. The captain pointed to a three-story building that had a sign with a red-and-black fox above the semicircular double doors. "Me and my men are heading to the barracks. Good luck with your dealings, milady," Rygar said with a nod of his head.

Next to the inn stood a spacious stable, while on the other side was the barracks. A separate stable was situated next to the barracks for the dire wolves. The adjacent road curved around, leading down to the harbour and docks. Small but stocky townhouses lined the street, while a large market square stood in the middle of town. The market was a hive of activity consisting of a variety of workshops, food carts, stores, and stalls. Greybak was a prosperous town, vibrant with life. Darla led Midnight towards the stables and paid the stable hand a little extra to brush and feed her horse.

* * *

She then decided to stretch her legs and explore the town. Her benefactor could wait. At sunset, she returned with two bags of supplies, some new clothes, a couple of trinkets and a bag of apples. She even had managed to offload a few of the gems and pieces of jewellery she had stolen. Every town had someone who dealt in black-market and stolen merchandise—you just had to know where to look. As Darla walked back towards the inn, she spotted the wyvern flying in lazy circles in the sky. Standing on the street corner and watching it, she wondered whether there was some truth to what Midnight had thought, whether it was stalking them. After circling for a while, it flew off, disappearing beyond the mountain range.

The inn was bustling with activity, the patrons drinking merrily and enjoying the bard's music. A mixture of patrons frequented the Kitty Fox, most of them consisting of locals, but a few being hunters, merchants, and sailors. A huge fire pit stood in in the centre of the room, with two large deer skewered and roasting over the flames. The ceiling above the pit was funnelled, the end leading to a large chimney that bellowed out most of the smoke. The inn was popular, and it was easy to see why: the innkeeper!

The innkeeper was easy to spot, being a full-bellied, boisterous dwarf with long braided black hair and a matching beard. He moved from table to table, serving drinks and talking to patrons in an easygoing manner. Darla instantly liked him. She stood by the doorway and waited patiently, her eyes roaming the room. In the corner, about two metres from her, was a somewhat small dire wolf lying on a fur mat and chewing on a bone. Unlike the other dire wolves, this one was dark grey. Beautifully coloured and rare, this wolf would have been the runt of a litter, an outcast. Its golden eyes watched her while it chewed, curious and alert.

Darla headed to the counter. With a bang, a woman came out of the kitchen backwards, using her ample buttocks to swing open the double doors. She miraculously carried four plates of food, two nestled on her arms and the remaining two in her hands. She looked Darla up and down and hmphed. *Obnoxious*, Darla thought, but smiled nonetheless. Her mouth watered. The woman must be a damn good cook; the venison pie smelled divine. With a clatter, the woman put the plates on the counter, drawing her husband's attention. He patted the customer he was speaking to on the shoulder and, with a sigh, walked over to the counter. "I'll be with you in a minute," he told Darla apologetically.

He delivered the plates two at a time then hobbled towards her. "Greetings, milady. I am Gustus, the proprietor of this humble establishment. I take it you have met my wife Kimber and our dire wolf Wraith. Welcome to the Kitty Fox." The dire wolf growled and stood up.

"Greetings, Gustus. This is a fine establishment you have. My name is Flow and—"

"Oh, don't worry about Wraith," Kimber said, interrupting and leaning on the counter. "He's a big softy, unless he sees you as a threat. Then he'll rip your throat out." She had a glint in her eye, daring Darla to stand her ground.

Voluptuous and a bitch, Darla thought. *A bitch who needs to be put in her place.*

"No! Sit, boy!" Gustus commanded sternly, pointing his finger. The dire wolf ignored him and growled again. Staring at Darla, it slowly walked towards her.

"Wraith!" Gustus shouted. Darla held out her hand, halting Gustus, letting him know everything was under control.

"It's okay," she said, smirking at Kimber. Kneeling, she looked the dire wolf in the eyes, staring at him with her own bestial yellow eyes. Eyes that were hidden behind her hood, eyes only Wraith could see.

The dire wolf growled again, and Darla replied with an assertive growl in return, showing her dominance. Slowly she held out her hand. The dire wolf opened his mouth...and licked it affectionately. "Who's a good boy? You're beautiful, aren't you?" Wraith nuzzled her hand, and she patted the top of his head. The dire wolf had recognised her for what she was, and a battle of wills had ensued. Now they were fast friends, kindred spirits.

"By the gods!" Gustus said, shocked, "He's never done that to anyone before. Looks like you've made a real friend." Grumbling, Kimber shook her head and walked back into the kitchen. Gustus rolled his eyes. "I'm sorry about that. Kimber gets a little moody at times. That's why she tends to stay in the kitchen; she's very passionate about her cooking."

Darla smiled. Obviously, out of the two, Gustus was the people person. "It shows. The venison pie looks and smells wonderful."

"I'll make sure to pass that compliment on to her. Anyway, my dear, what may I do for you?"

"I'd like a room for the night and some venison pie, if there's any left." Her stomach grumbled loudly; she was starving.

Gustus nodded. "I'll have a large serving brought to you right away."

"Also, I've heard a rumour that you serve the best spiced ale in all of Blackrock Kingdom."

Gustus laughed, his belly jiggling. "Well, I personally think it's absolutely delightful, but I'll let you be the judge of that."

Darla reached into a pouch and pulled out three gold coins—a substantial sum—and placed them in his hand. "I also require some information. I have business with Lord Thace Aldronin."

* * *

"He's sitting over there." He pointed a stubby finger towards the far end of the room. "Shall I bring your meal to his table?"

"No. Please send it to my room."

"For this generous sum, milady, you will have the best room in the inn," Gustus said with a wink. "I will bring you your key in a moment. Would you like me to take your bags up to your room?"

"Thank you. That would be greatly appreciated."

Gustus grabbed the bags at her feet then hobbled up the staircase. Darla casually walked towards Lord Aldronin. He was shorter than most elves and had a slightly broader nose. Half a dozen guards sat with him, dressed in chainmail armour. Over their armour they wore a green surcoat emblazoned with Lord Aldronin's house emblem of a black fox.

Darla had never met the lord. He had organised the contract through the Brotherhood, who had then referred Darla for the job and sent her the contract via raven. Although some operatives preferred face-to-face meetings, Darla liked her privacy and needed to be secretive; her life depended on it. She only met her benefactors when it came to concluding the contract, and even then, she used her alias and kept her features hidden. They never knew her name or identity. Darla adjusted her large hood, ensuring her face was kept in shadow. Some strands of her long reddish-brown hair escaped, flinging out from within its confines and cascading down to her ample breasts.

As Darla approached the lord, her eyes took in everything, including the unwanted attention her benefactor had attracted. Attention that was now also drawn to her. A group of a dozen men sat two tables across from them, eating, drinking, and enjoying the night's festivities. It was subtle, unobvious to the untrained eye, but Darla knew what to look for.

* * *

Two of them were paying keen attention, spying on Lord Aldronin over the tips of their mugs. One of them was an older, grizzled half elf wearing an eye patch. Two thick scars ran from each side of the patch—discernible scars that identified him for who he was: Brigg Letoth, otherwise known as Brigg the Butcher. He had been a specialist in King Therondal's army, but as he was a half elf, the king had seen him as expendable. The king had sent him on a mission that meant certain death, but what he hadn't counted on was the fact that Brigg was an unstoppable killing machine. Rumour had it he had gone rogue, leaving the army and becoming a bandit. He had earnt himself quite the reputation and, in the process, had drawn the Brotherhood's attention. Darla had heard a contract had been put out to infiltrate the bandit group; Brigg's bandits would either be incorporated into the Brotherhood's fold or eliminated.

Caught out, noticing Darla, Brigg quickly turned his attention, speaking to the big man next to him. He laughed at an obvious joke, slapping the mountain of a man on the shoulder and spilling some ale on the table. The other bandit continued to observe her from under the hood of his cloak. Darla's keen vision could still make out his features, though. The man was unshaven, with midnight-black strands of hair sticking out from the folds of his hood. She took in his partially obscured shimmering blue eyes—eyes a lady could easily get lost in. It unnerved Darla slightly that he was staring boldly back. As he lifted his mug to take a drink, she noticed the two ornate gold rings he wore on his left hand; both were old and worn but in excellent condition. They were polished and well looked after; clearly they meant the world to him and possibly depicted who he was.

Oddly, she vaguely recognised both rings. One resembled those worn by high-ranking members of the Brotherhood, a ranking with which she was unfamiliar. The other ring was a unique design of a large triangle, maybe a mountain, with two inverted triangles on either side of it. The ring was both a mystery and familiar to her, something she remembered from her past but couldn't place. The man lowered his mug and gave an indistinct nod in her direction, an acknowledgement, a discreet greeting. It was as if he knew who she was…or what she was. Was he friend or foe? That was yet to be decided.

Darla shrugged and continued to Lord Aldronin's table. Perhaps it was only a coincidence that Brigg was here. She was tired, being overly cautious; maybe there was nothing to worry about, but the hairs on the back of her neck had risen. She had learnt long ago to pay attention to her instincts; they often forewarned of danger and had kept her alive so far.

"Greetings, my lord. My name is Flow. You requested my services through the Brotherhood. I have the item you requested."

The elven lord looked her up and down and sniffed disdainfully. "By the seven gods, you smell like shit, woman." Luckily the lord couldn't clearly see her face; if he had, he would have seen her blush in embarrassment and her jaw clench.

Darla took a deep breath, calming herself before speaking. But even then, she couldn't keep the anger out of her voice. "You're paying me to get you the gem, not to smell nice and look pretty."
Aldronin nodded to one of his guards, who promptly placed two bulging pouches on the table. Darla cringed—the lord was being far from discreet. She slipped her satchel off her shoulder and casually dropped it onto the chair next to her. Quick as lightning, her hand snaked out and snatched the pouches off the table.

Judging from the weight of the pouches, Lord Aldronin had paid her handsomely, even more than the job was worth. It always paid to check, though. Opening the first pouch, she saw an array of silver coins, with a few gold coins sparkling within. The second pouch radiated in sparkling colours. It consisted of an assortment of small and medium diamonds. She had requested diamonds as her form of payment, and the lord had been more than happy to oblige.

* * *

She had been tempted to trade the Divinity Stone for the lives of Lance and his family; it would have more than covered the payment for their release from slavery. Reluctantly, however, she had decided against it. She was too honourable, and the Divinity Stone was far too dangerous. She had a code of ethics and a reputation to uphold. These diamonds would definitely help with her cause, though. Two more contracts, and she should have more than enough to pay for her friends' release. Darla noticed Brigg and his companion out of the corner of her eye, as she hooked the pouches to her belt. They were spying on the lord and whispering in hushed tones. Realising their mistake, they quickly turned away. So much for their presence being nothing; something was afoot.

The guard nearest to her reached out, took her satchel, and passed it to his lord. Aldronin examined the contents. "The king will be pleased. You have done well." Suddenly the inn door burst open, letting in the chilly air. The flames of the fire pit flickered briefly. Aldronin's face paled. "My cousin used a large green emerald as a decoy. How do I know this isn't it?" he quietly said, raising the hood of his cloak, covering his face in shadow.

Darla was annoyed; she was a professional and wasn't used to being questioned. She opened her other satchel and revealed the real emerald it in all its glory. It radiated and sparkled in the firelight. "The emerald is slightly lighter in colour. Thank you for confirming this, milady," he said, nodding. How in the seven hells did he know this? She was about to ask him when his guards quickly wrapped their cloaks around themselves, hiding their emblem, their identity.

"That is mine. You will give me back the Divinity Stone now, thief." Darla instantly recognised the voice from the doorway. It belonged to Aldronin's cousin, Lord Dellavenor. He and his men had finally caught up to her. She had been played.

"You bastard," she said, slowly putting the emerald back in her satchel.

"You are expendable thief," Aldronin smirked, arrogantly. "I am not."

The one-eyed lord stood there with a dozen soldiers, their weapons drawn. But Darla wasn't about to go quietly. Reaching behind her shoulder, she drew her short sword.

"Give me the Divinity Stone now, and I will grant you a swift, merciful death. Refuse and I will slowly flay the skin off you. Either way the Divinity Stone will be mine."

"This woman is a guest and is under my protection," Gustus barked, pulling out a hefty, studded hammer from behind the bar. "Leave now, elf!"

"I am an elven lord, innkeeper, and you will do well to remember that!" Dellavenor shouted, spittle spraying from his mouth. Rising to his feet, his hackles raised, Wraith growled menacingly. The elves looked nervous. Two of them covered Dellavenor, aiming their crossbows at the dire wolf.

"Your rank means nothing here. These are dwarven lands," Rygar said, sliding off his stool. Darla hadn't even noticed him there. He reached behind his shoulder and drew forth a broad-bladed sword. "Now piss off. You've interrupted my dinner."

"I will once you hand over the thief," Dellavenor said through gritted teeth.

Rygar pondered, stroking his beard. "Um...no! Now fuck off before I shove my sword up your pompous arse."

"Don't threaten *me*, little man. I have eighty elves at my disposal. Tomorrow morning, I will charge across the plains and—" He stopped in midsentence as Rygar burst into laughter. Gustus followed suit, his big belly jiggling. This aggravated the elven lord even more. The dwarves were laughing at him, having a joke at his expense.

Rygar's laughter stopped abruptly. "I'll look forward to it, elf lord," he said seriously. "You won't even see our dire wolves coming! And after we've reaped you like a harvest, I'll order my sergeant to charge in with his squad and finish off your rabble." He raised his other hand; gripped tightly in it was an ancient conical white horn that had been passed down from captain to captain over the centuries. He lifted it to his lips and blew, the deep rumbling sound resonating for miles. It was a summons, Darla realized, a call to arms.

The inn was dead quiet as everyone watched the confrontation. Due to their numbers, the elves seemed to have the upper hand, but not for long. Darla heard a chorus of booted feet pounding in the snow. They roared a battle cry as they charged towards the inn. Dwarves weren't renown for being stealthy by any means; it wasn't in their nature. The elves turned, all except Dellavenor, who stood staring at Darla with unadulterated hatred. He was fanatical and had nothing to lose, and that made him dangerous. The dwarves were unarmoured, dressed in long, thick fur overcoats with the emblem of the dire wolf printed on it. It was the insignia of their king, and they wore it proudly.

They formed a semicircle around the elves, surrounding them with no chance of escape. There were at least two dozen of them. Contemplating the situation, Dellavenor ground his teeth then gave a brief nod to one of his men. The elf pressed his trigger and sent a bolt soaring through the inn, aimed directly at Darla. Her body moved, sliding sideways as she slashed with the sword. The manoeuvre wasn't of her volition; she had no control as she acted, guided by the sword. The sword glowed briefly as it slashed the crossbow bolt in half and deflected it harmlessly to the floor. Gasps of awe echoed around the inn. A few patrons even clapped and cheered, infuriating the elven lord.

* * *

Soundlessly Rygar charged forward and slashed. The powerful stroke easily sliced through the elf's light armour and cleaved off his leg. A moment later, he toppled forward, his crossbow clattering to the ground. Rygar then brought his sword crashing down on the fallen elf's head. "This is your last warning, elf lord," he said in a low, menacing tone. "You have no regard for your men, and you're beginning to piss me off. Leave now, before I decide to kill you."

Looking down at the bloodied elven corpse, Dellavenor addressed Darla. "You win this round, thief, but the next one will be mine. I will take the Divinity Stone and you will die." He turned his back to her and walked out of the inn, his soldiers following.

"Escort these elves out of Greybak!" Rygar ordered his sergeant. "If you know what's good for you," he called after Dellavenor, "you'll cross the bridge, reenter the elven lands, and never come back." He smiled devilishly. "If I see you again, I won't be so pleasant." He slammed the door closed as his men surrounded the elves and began to escort them towards the gates. The entertainment over, the patrons resumed their festivities.

Blushing, Gustus waddled towards Darla, a large bronze key in his outstretched hand. "I'm sorry for the disruption, milady…"

"I am at fault. Please forgive me, Gustus. Lord Dellavenor is a fanatic, unpredictable and dangerous. He—"

Gustus stopped her in midsentence and, with a wave of his hand, dismissed the apology. "No harm done. The situation was taken care of. Anyway, here is your key. Go up the stairs. Your room is the second on the left. I'll bring your dinner in a moment."

He turned away, ready to depart, but Darla stopped him. "Gustus, who are those people over there?" she asked, gesturing with her head.

* * *

Gustus looked in the direction she indicated and ran his hand through his beard. "The half elf introduced himself as a merchant. The rest might be his guards." Darla nodded her thanks. "I'm sorry I can't really help you. If you want, I can go over and find out more for you."

"No, it's okay, Gustus," she replied, eyeing the group. *Merchant, my arse*, she thought. Brigg was a bandit through and through. He had to be on a job, but if it didn't interfere with hers, she had no quarrel with him.

"You sure? I promise I'll be subtle. You'd be amazed at what people tell an innkeeper."

Darla smiled. "I'm sure you've heard your fair amount of gossip. Thank you for offering, Gustus. Everything is fine. It's probably just my paranoia getting the better of me."

Gustus nodded, patting her arm. "If there's anything else I can do for you, let me know." He walked towards one of the other tables and chatted with another customer. His conversations were always warm, friendly, but brief as he went from one person to the next. His moody wife stood there with a scowl, her arms folded as she waited with two steaming plates on the counter, ready to be served.

Darla turned to Aldronin and lowered her voice. "I would be careful, my lord. This so-called merchant is a notorious bandit. He has been conspicuously watching our proceedings, and I believe you may be in danger."

"Nonsense!" he replied. "I have my guards to protect me. They're more than capable of taking care of that rabble."

Darla kept silent as she nodded farewell to her benefactor. She had given him fare warning, but in his arrogance, he had chosen to ignore it. As she walked away, she had a sudden inkling she'd be coming across the Divinity Stone again.

As she approached the staircase, she passed Rygar at the counter. The captain had just finished his meal, scraping the last bit of venison and gravy off the plate and stuffing it into his mouth. "Superb! Absolutely delicious, Kimber," he said, winking. The innkeeper's wife blushed profusely and retreated into the kitchen. Rygar burst into laughter.

"Greetings, Captain," Darla said. "I thought you'd be eating dinner with your men in the barracks."

The captain finished his mouthful before replying. "The food here is better than what we get in the barracks." He waved his hand, grabbing Gustus's attention, and pushed aside his empty mug. "And the drinks are *far* better," he said with another wink.

Gustus came hobbling over, wiping his hands on his apron.

"What would you like?" Darla asked. "It's my treat. My way of saying thank you for your assistance earlier."

The captain raised his eyebrows as Darla reached into her pouch. "Well, if you're buying, I'll have a glass of Gustus's Fire Brandy."

"Two glasses of your Fire Brandy," Darla said, placing six silver coins in Gustus's palm.

Instead of heading to the bar, Gustus opened a door and went into the back room. Darla thought this a little strange, until he returned a brief time later with a wooden stepladder. He propped it up against the bar, climbed up, and carefully lifted a large bottle off the top shelf. Obviously this drink was a luxury and rarely ordered.

After pulling out two crystal goblets from underneath the bar, Gustus poured each one to the brim. The captain eagerly grabbed his glass and raised it in salute. "To good health," he said before draining a third of the glass. He shook his head and cleared his eyes. "By the gods, that is good stuff."

Darla followed suit and grimaced as she swallowed the potent liquor. Her throat felt like it was on fire for a moment, then soothed, leaving a warm feeling radiating throughout her body.

Impressed, Rygar smiled. "Milady, even though I appreciate the kind gesture, part of me wonders if there's a hidden agenda behind it and you want something." The captain was perceptive and blunt, Darla thought.

"Well, since you mentioned it, I was wondering if you'd kindly escort me back to the bridge tomorrow morning? That of course depends on the situation with Lord Dellavenor. King Therondal wants him flayed, castrated, and beheaded." Rygar cringed. "Well, he did steal the elven Divinity Stone after all."

"A Divinity Stone you then stole yourself."

"Was commissioned to steal," Darla corrected. "And delivered to his cousin, who plans on returning it to the king."

Rygar nodded. "Cunning bastard. He gave our fanatical lord the impression you still had it in your possession. Meanwhile, he slips away unhindered, gains the king's favour, and is considered a hero."

"Yes. Well, apparently I'm expendable. Dellavenor can't afford to wait us out, so hopefully he's hightailed it out of here."

"And if he hasn't?"

"Then I'll need to find alternate transport."

"Well, I do know the captain of *The Bridget*, a nice little fishing boat.

I can organise transport for you easily enough."

"Know the captain? He's your goddamn wife's cousin and your best friend," Gustus interrupted, eavesdropping. Rygar frowned at him and Gustus guffawed. "And a fishing boat, my arse."

Darla looked at him questioningly. "Fine," he admitted, "Jonah's a smuggler. But *The Bridget* is the fastest smuggling skeet in the dwarven kingdom." A skeet was a sleek but also spacious vessel often used by smugglers and blockade runners.

Perfect! Darla thought. "Sounds great," she said. "How much?"

Rygar relaxed and let out a chuckle. "Well, tomorrow is my day off, it's freezing, and I'll either be escorting you or negotiating your passage…and it's such a long walk to the harbour." He looked at her with a twinkle in his eye. He was willing to do it; the question was how much it would cost her.

"How much?" she repeated.

Contemplating, the captain ran his hand through his beard. "A bottle of Fire Brandy."

"Done," Darla said, reaching into her pouch, "payment for booking me passage." She handed two gold coins to Gustus. "A bottle of your Fire Brandy, please."

Gustus raised his eyebrows as he stared at the coins. He quickly pocketed them, pushed aside the stepladder, and reached into a cupboard underneath the bar. A moment later, he pulled out a full stoppered bottle of Fire Brandy and placed it on the counter.

Rygar picked it up, shook his head, and placed it back on the counter. "Keep it just in case all goes well and we're able to escort you," he told Darla.

Smiling, Darla pushed the expensive bottle back towards the captain. "If that's the case, you can consider it a present."

Rygar laughed so hard he nearly fell off his stool. "Damn it, woman. I knew I should have asked for two bottles." He smiled warmly at Darla and held out his hand. Darla grabbed it firmly and shook it. "I'll see you bright and early in the morning. Goodnight, milady." He drained the rest of the Fire Brandy in one gulp. His eyes watered and he shook his head to clear it. After sliding off the stool and clutching his precious prize, he hobbled towards the door.

"Two more bottles of your Fire Brandy, please, Gustus," Darla said, smiling as she handed the innkeeper another four gold coins.

Gustus reached into the cupboard again and pulled out another two full bottles. "Looks like I'd better start brewing some more." With a sigh, he handed them to her. "I only have one more in the cupboard. I wasn't expecting to sell three bottles in one night." He looked at her solemnly, his tone turning suddenly serious. "If you plan on a night of heavy drinking, I'd be careful, lass. That Fire Brandy is potent stuff."

Darla laughed. "Don't worry, Gustus. They're a present for a friend of mine. Like yourself, he owns a quaint inn, but he mixes Fire Brandy with whisky and a few other ingredients and has created his own popular liqueur called Dragon's Breath."

Gustus looked at her in awe. "I've heard of this legendary liqueur. It's said to be the liqueur of the gods because it's so efficacious."

Darla laughed again. "That's one way of describing it." Marek was no scientist, but he had produced a concoction that was truly extraordinary. It was extremely expensive and popular with the richer clientele, being sweet, potent, and exceptionally nice to drink. Along with being extremely flammable, it also had another unique quality. When a cold element was added to it, a chemical reaction occurred, and instead of dowsing it, it increased the heat dramatically. The colder the substance, the more heat.

Darla was the top contender at the Black Raven, the inn where she lived back home. She had won countless amounts of money from people betting against her, with her downing shot after shot of the liqueur with an ice cube bobbing in the middle. Her lycanthropy was the only thing that had saved her, her regenerative abilities healing the damaged tissue and reducing the toxicity levels in her system. For Darla, that was part of the fun, the risk; it made her feel alive.

Gustus stroked his beard as he thought. "I have an offer to propose to you. Next time you stop by here, bring me a bottle of Dragon's Breath. In exchange I'll give you three bottles of Fire Brandy."

Darla considered it. The proposal was good, even profitable. "I'll run the offer by my friend and see what he thinks. No promises, though." She was covering herself, but deep down she could almost guarantee Marek would jump at the offer.

"Fair enough," he replied, shaking her hand.

After nodding farewell to Gustus, Darla grabbed the two bottles and proceeded up the staircase. She unlocked the door and entered a spacious room with its own little fireplace. The space was warm and cosy, with a double bed and a tub of steaming, soapy water in the corner. Her bags had been placed in a neat pile next to the bed. She sat down at the table and ate the venison pie, washing it down with the spiced ale. The pie was delicious, full of chunks of venison, vegetables, a thick gravy, and coated with a crisp, flaky pastry. Content, her hunger satisfied, she stripped off her clothes. After scrunching them up into a torn, stained, putrid pile, she threw them into the blazing hearth.

She stepped into the tub and slowly slid in, the water enveloping her with its warmth. It was scented with lavender and rose petals, the fragrance soothing. It was heavenly. After washing off the layers of filth, she emerged clean and refreshed. Dressed in her new clothes, she then collapsed onto the bed, exhausted. The mattress was as soft as a marshmallow, and a moment after she sank into it, she instantly fell asleep.

The king's army had arrived at dawn, to find Dellavenor's castle already breached and in control of the two banner lords. There had been no legendary battle, only a few minor skirmishes. Most of the soldiers and servants had surrendered, realising that they had been left behind, sacrificed by their lord. Therondal felt sorry for them, they had been abandoned, while Dellavenor had fled, scurrying like a dog with its tail between its legs. He couldn't be lenient though, he had to make an example of them, so he ordered their questioning, torture and execution.

King Therondal had led the army personally, with his second in charge being his son, Prince Velander. The Divinity Stone belonged to the elven nation, it was his responsibility and he had vowed that he would personally recover it. His son had recklessly commandeered two banner lords plus his own company and ridden ahead to besiege the castle. By doing this he had panicked Dellavenor, who had scurried off, using secret underground tunnels to escape. Leaving the banner lords behind, Velander had pursued the traitor, hunting him down. Therondal couldn't help but wonder though whether it was to gain his favour and redeem himself, or whether Velander had his own secret agenda. He had heard the disturbing stories about his son but had dismissed them as blatant lies. Now he began to wonder whether there was some truth to them.

Upon his arrival the two banner lords had relinquished the castle to their king. Who would be granted the castle was yet to be determined? King Therondal had transformed the spacious dining room into his personal war room. The room was now a hive of activity. He currently stood there amongst his banner lords, pacing, anxious for news.

Meanwhile, the captain of Therondal's rangers jogged silently through the forest, trying to catch up with his squad. He had sent them ahead, while he investigated a trail. It had proven to be a waste of time, nothing more than a decoy. Now it was their job to track down Dellavenor and the prince and pave a way for the king's army. He navigated his way past a small crater, a maintenance hatch that had caved in, leaving nothing but a pile of rubble and debris. What had caused such destruction one could only wonder.

The captain had sent his corporal galloping off to rendezvous with Prince Velander's forces. The corporal had been demoted to a simple messenger, an insult to someone of his calibre. The message was simple: Lord Dellavenor must be taken alive so the king could personally judge him and deliver his execution. The captain wondered how the message would be received. Would the prince heed his father's wishes? Or for that matter, would the corporal even come back alive?

The captain pondered these questions as he dodged past some bushes and jogged along the outskirts of the crater. If he hadn't been distracted and had stopped to look, he would have noticed a bluish-grey hand erupt out of the dirt, clawing at the rubble, slowly and methodically digging its way out. In the dark, cold tomb, he had rested and gradually rejuvenated, healing himself back to full strength. Now it was time to escape, recover the Divinity Stone, and exact his revenge.

* * *

Chapter 6

The capital city of Sethanon was the bastion of the human empire. The crown of the Hiberathian Kingdom, it was a vibrant, beautiful city, bustling and full of activity. Ruled over for centuries by the Everthorn royal family, the city had expanded and flourished. Sethanon was tiered into levels, with each level representing a class of people. The areas were all cordoned off with walls and gates. Guards patrolled the sections day and night, watchful and alert, protecting and serving. Not that it mattered anymore.

Sethanon was no stranger to crime, wars, and brutality. It was also rumoured that the city had been built upon the ruins of an ancient civilization. It had overcome historic tragedies and prospered. The city was a true testament to humanity, courage, strength, hope, and unity.

* * *

Over the last ten years, things had changed, though. People had started to become disheartened. An evil presence inhabited the city, infesting it and haunting the residents within. The guards were useless against the monsters that had been reported, those that were apparently roaming the city. Even the Everthorns were powerless to save their people, but that was because they were burdened. Burdened with the responsibility, the fact that the root of the evil came from within their family.

Prince Zane was the youngest natural son in the Everthorn family, his older brother Prince Jace being the heir to the throne. Their younger brother Stryxen had been adopted by King Erithen and Queen Raylene at the age of one after his parents had been brutally murdered. Technically he had been their cousin, but now he was their brother and a prince of the realm. Now Stryxen was twelve, nearly a teenager. And just like any teenager, he had the mood swings and attitude to go with it.

"This is horse shit," Stryxen screamed, frustrated and slamming down his pencil. His tutor hobbled to her desk, giving him his space; she was used to the young prince's tantrums. "Why do I have to do my grammar and writing while my brothers get to study magic?"

"You'll join us when you're old enough, *little* brother," Zane replied. He was shit stirring, he knew exactly how his younger brother would react and was prepared for it. He mumbled an incantation immediately after finishing his sentence. Stryxen hurled the pencil, sending it spinning through the air. His aim was true, the pencil directed at Zane's face. It froze in midair half a metre from him. "Good throw, Stryxen. You'll need to do better than that, though."

Varyn Kabel looked at them sternly. He was of the Magici Order, which consisted of people born with a natural magical ability, a gene that enabled them to use magic. They were intensively trained in the disciplines their ability was strongest in, receiving a vigorous education in the reading, writing, principles, foundations, and casting of magic. Kabel's rank was Varyn, which was extremely high, and as such he only answered to the king. Along with other duties, he oversaw the prince's magical education. In the king's opinion, there was no better teacher. This was because Kabel was an expert in six of the magical disciplines and could easily teach the remaining two. The ninth discipline, dark magic, had been banned, with all artefacts, scrolls, and tomes relating to it having been destroyed. The reason behind this decision had been its evil and destructive nature, for it consisted of spirit, death, blood, and demonic magic.

"Enough, the both of you!" Kabel yelled. He peered through his large wire-rimmed glasses at the floating pencil. "Nicely done, Zane, but if you stir your brother up like that again, I'll turn you into a rabbit for a week. Now get back to your studies. Zane, Jace, I'll be evaluating both of you when you come back from your holiday." Grumbling, he returned to his work, his black feathered quill making sharp precise lines and intricate curves. Finishing the scroll, he placed his quill next to the inkpot.

Zane was studying hard to become a battlemage, a master in five of the eight disciplines, and had a long way to go. The magic had manifested six years ago, when he was in his teens. He had been tested and had scored extremely high. Apparently, he possessed a natural aptitude for magic, which placed him in a unique category, as most magic users studied one or occasionally two disciplines. His older brother Jace was a wild mage, which was extremely rare. He didn't have to speak incantations; the magic just flowed through him. According to the ancient scriptures, the last wild mage had existed centuries ago. It was rumoured that master wild mages could merge spells together, even those from various disciplines. This enabled them to create their own unique spells no other mage could cast.

Jace smiled warmly at Stryxen. He was calm and levelheaded, the mediator between the brothers and a natural leader. "Your time will come. Just give it time. When you're older, you'll have responsibilities and burdens. On top of this, you'll have to fit in rigorous weapons training and copious amounts of intense study. You've seen how much studying Zane has to do. You need to be patient and enjoy your childhood for what it is."

"Childhood," Stryxen shrieked, angered even more. It had been the wrong thing for Jace to say, especially considering the mood he was in. "I am fed up...ahhh." Jace raised his hand and Stryxen levitated, hovering above his chair. With a swipe of his other hand, Kabel's feathered quill rose into the air and flew towards Stryxen, flittering near his head. Eyes wide, Stryxen looked at the feather. "Don't you dare," he squealed, knowing what was coming.

"Dare?" Jace smirked, a glint in his eye.

"No!" Stryxen screamed as the quill shot forward and the feather brushed the back of his neck. He laughed so hard that tears streamed down his face. His body convulsed, flailing as though he were a puppet. "Stop it!" he screamed, trying to catch his breath. "I'll wet myself."

"You'd better stop, Jace, and put him down," Zane said, chuckling. "If he wets himself, you'll be the one mopping it up."

With a devilish grin, Jace lowered his younger brother back to his seat.

Glaring at them, Kabel hmphed. "I see it is pointless to continue studying. This lesson is over. You're dismissed, Jace, Zane." He glanced at the tutor, who nodded. "You might as well go too, Stryxen." Although he wasn't impressed with their antics, overall the lesson had been productive. Smiling, Jace and Stryxen ran for the door, leaving their workspaces a mess.

Zane stayed behind; he wanted to talk to Kabel. "I'll catch up in a minute," he yelled as the door slammed shut behind them. Thanks to

Jace's stunt, the tension had eased, and Stryxen was back to his playful, easygoing self. Jace always knew how to handle things. The laughter had also felt good, adding some normalisation to their day. It was a pleasant change from the bleakness, distrust, and sleepless nights that seemed to be embedded into the fabric of their lives.

Malgorath had decimated their lives, haunting their dreams and leaving them doubting themselves and the reality they lived in. He had possessed one of them, but the question was who? The demon laughed cruelly as he manipulated things, sowing seeds of distrust and thriving on the misery and hopelessness he caused. Both Zane and Jace had found a way to silence the demon's call by intoxicating themselves to a certain point with alcohol. Whenever they drank, it was as if the demon was put to sleep, giving them a moment's respite. Was it a ruse, though? Was Malgorath giving them this false hope? They didn't know whether it was a hope worth clinging to.

A fortnight ago, something nightmarish had occurred. It had been late at night, and Stryxen had screamed, a piercing wail of fright... and of pain. After clambering out of bed, Zane had swung open his bedroom door. Two doors down, Jace had done the same, standing with his sword in a shaking hand. Even though they could defend themselves, they were afraid; they would have been stupid not to have been. Stryxen ran down the hallway in his pyjamas, blood dripping from his arm. Something was chasing him, something that resembled their mother. The creature was demonic, humanoid in appearance, but with soulless, black eyes greyish skin and deadly, daggerlike claws. Horrifyingly, it was wearing the queen's clothes.

Jace ran to Zane's room and quickly ushered Stryxen in. He slammed the door shut as Zane sprinted to his bedside table to grab his key ring. Jace was leaning against the door, barring it as something twisted the handle from the other side. "Quickly!" Jace screamed. The keys rattled on the brass ring as Zane sorted through it with trembling hands. Fumbling, he tried to insert the key. Wrong one. Rattling, he grabbed another key, inserted it, and turned. *Click*! A wave of relief passed through him as the door locked.

* * *

A brief silence ensued, and then the door shook on its hinges with relentless pounding. The three of them stood huddled together, comforting and fortifying one another. Perhaps it was the adrenaline, but Zane was spurred into action and recited a shield incantation, an extra level of protection. He stopped in mid incantation, however, when suddenly the pounding stopped, leaving an eerie silence in the room.

The following morning, their mother denied it was her, but they had both seen her, and there was the physical proof, the scratches on Stryxen's arm. They didn't know what to believe. Was their mother the dreaded Malgorath or perhaps one of his minions? Either way, something needed to be done, and Zane took it upon himself to orchestrate it. That's why as much as it broke his heart, as much as he loved his mother, he was organising a contract to have her killed. He needed to be strong, brave, to protect his family, and no one else seemed to have the courage to do it.

"Have you got any more books on dark magic?" he whispered to Kabel. Technically it was illegal, but Kabel had taught him some dark magic. Zane always had been intrigued by it, suspecting the forbidden discipline was merely misunderstood. A kindred spirit, Kabel shared the same passion and had managed to squander away a couple of dark magic books. Kabel had been part of the family for years, known the princes since they were children, and was aware of the demon, of their family situation.

Dark magic was the key; Zane just knew it, but the spells he had learnt had been rudimentary. He needed to be challenged, to learn more powerful spells. Spells he could master, providing him with the means to fight the demon and save his brothers…hopefully before it was too late.

Grunting, Kabel walked over to a small chest. It was locked with a combination spell only he knew. His fingers a blur, twisting and interlocking with each other, he made a magical sign. Technically it was eight signs combined to form one powerful sign, a key to unlock the chest. He lifted the lid with a slight creak and pulled out two old books. After wiping off a thick layer of dust, he handed them to Zane. "Take these. Read them while you're on holiday. Just make sure you keep them well hidden." He knew it was a stupid thing to say—of course Zane would keep them hidden; he had as much to lose as the Varyn did.

"I won't be going on holiday. I need to study for the exam and read these," Zane said, flicking through the pages.

"Hogwash. You're excelling with your studies, and you can either secretly take those with you or read them when you get back. The holiday will do you some good!"

Groaning, Zane closed the book and frowned. Even though the spells were unfamiliar to him, they seemed basic, intermediate at best. "I need more powerful spells." He cringed, knowing how it sounded, knowing it was the wrong thing to say, but he was desperate.

"Well give them back then!" Kabel barked. "This magic is forbidden. I could be banned from the order, putting my neck out and doing this for you. You're nothing but an ungrateful retch!" He sighed. "I know you're desperate, and I know your plight, but the only book that would contain that kind of magic is the *Val'Markyl*. Its spells are ancient and are even beyond my comprehension. And as you well know, both parts are lost, their location a mystery, except for the rumour that one of the halves is in the dwarven lands."

The Val'Markyl was an ancient, legendary tome, otherwise known as the *Divinity Tome*. It had two parts: the first containing angelic spells, the second containing demonic ones. It was said to have been written by one of the most powerful magici Aragoth had ever known, Baligorn Val'Markyl. Zane doubted that, though, because

depending on which stories you believed, the *Val'Markyl* predated
the magician's other tomes. Another rumour had it that the book had
belonged to a group of divine beings but had ended up in
Val'Markyl's possession. That's where the story started to get hazy.
Had Val'Markyl been given the tome, or had he stolen it? Val'Markyl
had written other powerful tomes; there was no question about that.
Those were rare volumes containing ancient spells and incantations,
but they still paled in comparison to the *Divinity Tome*. Like the
Val'Markyl, though, the other tomes had been lost during the ages.
Zane had vowed to get the *Val'Markyl* and *Divinity Tomes* at any
cost.

"Have you contacted Kyrene about the tome?" Kabel asked.

"Yes. She's looking into it. Gamel sent out an expedition team to
investigate a couple of sites." A dwarven baroness, Kyrene was a
close friend Zane had grown up with. She was quite an attractive
dwarf and, like Zane, had a magical aptitude. It was something that
bonded them, something they loved and were passionate about.
Kyrene's ability wasn't nearly as strong as Zane's, though; whereas
Kyrene studied hard, persevering and sometimes struggling, Zane
grasped things easily, mastering complex spells in little to no time.
They both, however, had a thirst for power and dark magic. They
had spent many nights drinking wine while discussing various
aspects of magic. They were extremely close, and at one point
Kyrene's husband Gamel had been very jealous. Over time, though,
he had learnt to accept their friendship.

Zane had been tempted to flirt with Kyrene, to stir things up. He
hadn't, though. It would have been too weird; Kyrene was like the
sister he'd never had. When Kabel had discovered a few possible
locations of the *Val'Markyl*, Zane had contacted Kyrene through a
magical orb. The orb was a device that allowed the user to
communicate with anyone holding its twin. Zane had acquired two
sets of orbs and had given Kyrene the twin of one of the sets. When
he contacted her and explained the situation, she had been more
than happy to help. The question was whether she would want to

keep the tome for herself or whether she would sell it to Zane.

Feeling embarrassed and a bit reprimanded, Zane clutched the books, hiding them under the folds of his jacket, and apologized to Kabel. He appreciated everything the Varyn had done and knew he was only trying to help him. He rushed out and hurried to his bedroom. Two guards stood at attention and raised their fist to their chest in salute. "My prince," one of them said. while the other hurriedly opened the door for him. They were part of Zane's personal guard, loyal and obedient to him alone. Upon reaching seventeen, both he and Jace had been deemed adults, young men responsible enough to oversee their own guards.

"Sergeant, I am not to be disturbed," Zane replied, crossing the threshold of his bedroom. The door closed behind him with a gentle click, leaving Zane to his solitude. Walking over to his bookcase, he couldn't help but admire his collection. Some volumes were rare, limited editions, their leather-bound jackets worn from age. Others were newer, stories written by some of his favourite authors, ones he read purely for enjoyment. He knelt and pried the backing off a section of the bottom shelf, revealing a hidden compartment. After pulling the two forbidden books out of his cloak, he carefully placed them in the compartment and replaced the backing. He dreaded to think of the consequences if he was caught with them. The privilege of his royal status wouldn't save him because even kings were answerable to the Magici Order.

Hearing laughter, Zane walked to the window and smiled. In the courtyard below, Stryxen and Jace were sparring. Their wooden swords clanked together as Jace easily deflected his younger brother's wild strokes. "Kick his arse, Stryxen," he yelled.

"What do you think I'm trying to do?" Stryxen shouted back.

The boy was terribly outmatched, as his older brother was an expert swordsman. Smiling, Jace dodged the incoming stroke, pivoting out of the way and gently tapping Stryxen on the buttocks. Fuming, Stryxen turned and swung wildly, only to lose his balance and fall face-first into the dirt. Jace began to laugh until he noticed his younger brother convulsing, crying on the ground.

Worried, he bent over and put a reassuring hand on Stryxen's shoulder. Hidden just a moment before, his younger brother's wooden sword snaked out and smacked Jace's shin. Zane heard the sound from where he was and winced. He could see the pain Jace was in from his expression. Although his mouth was clamped shut as he bit back the pain, his eyes said it all. His shin guard would have absorbed the brunt of the blow, but he would be walking away with a whopping bruise.

"You should be prepared for anything and never let your guard down," Stryxen said, smiling. The tears were gone, part of an elaborate act.

Jace smiled and burst into laughter. "Well, I definitely won't be underestimating you again," he replied, grabbing hold of Stryxen's outstretched hand and helping him to his feet. "How about we go inside and grab something to eat?"

"Sounds good. I'm famished!" He tossed the practice sword to Jace and ran off towards the kitchen.

"I'll come down and join you," Zane called out.

Jace nodded his confirmation and went to put the wooden swords back on the stand. Zane bit his lip and walked towards the door. He needed to tell them he wouldn't be going on holiday, but he was struggling to find a way to broach the subject. Jace wouldn't buy the excuse that he needed to prepare for their upcoming exam. Both brothers were excelling and would pass the exam easily. He needed to think of another excuse, but what?

* * *

Pondering, Zane walked down the curved stairway to the ground floor, Jace's laughter could be heard echoing from the kitchen. "What's for lunch?" he called out as he walked down the short hallway. The French doors swung as he entered the kitchen and joined his brothers at the large wooden table.

"Boring old soup," Stryxen mumbled, scowling and clearly disappointed. He sat with his arms folded. The table was usually where the servants ate but was also used by the cooks, who loaded a multitude of dishes upon it when the boys' parents held banquets. Occasionally the three brothers used it, having a quick meal between classes.

A serving girl bought over three bowls of chunky chicken soup. Stryxen dug into his, slurping it in great big mouthfuls. *So much for it being boring old soup*, Zane thought. He suddenly pitied the kitchen staff. He and Jace had been the same when they were Stryxen's age: teenagers with hormones and attitude.

Smiling nervously, the serving girl set Zane's bowl down before hurrying back to help her mother with the cooking. Jace smirked before taking a mouthful. He knew the serving girl fancied her brother, but Zane was yet to act on it. Smiling, Zane scooped up a large piece of chicken and put it in his mouth. The girl's name was Millie, or was it Marge? No, he was pretty sure it was Millie. He really should take more notice of people's names, he chided himself. She was in her late teens, attractive, curvy, and had perky, medium-size breasts. Breasts that were half revealed with her low-cut bodice. He definitely wanted to bed her. It looked like forfeiting the family holiday would have its advantages.

"Can we go horseback riding after lunch?" Stryxen said through a half-chewed mouthful of chicken. They had been so busy with their chores, studies, and other responsibilities that they hadn't had time to take their younger brother riding. *It's been at least a month*, Zane thought.

* * *

He looked at Jace, who nodded. "Why not?" he replied. "We've got the afternoon free." It was a rarity, but the two older brothers had some free time on their hands. This also gave Zane an idea, and he wasn't one to look a gift horse in the mouth. He'd come up with the perfect excuse to stay home. Finishing his soup, he smiled and handed Millie his bowl.

"I'll meet you by the stables. I'm going to get my jacket," he said, leaving the table, his chair scraping the floor. Both his brothers had already got their jackets prior to going out for sword practice. Jace's was neatly hung over the back of his chair, while Stryxen's lay on the floor by his feet. Zane exited through the French doors and hurried upstairs to his room. The brown jacket he chose was made of fine leather, with a thick furry inner coating. It would keep him warm and provide him with protection.

Outside, Zane's boots crunched as he walked along the gravel path and joined his brothers. His breath frosted as he wrapped his arms around himself and shivered. "Whose idea was this again?" he muttered. The three stable hands guided nine horses out, the princes' horses and six for their guard escort. This came with being a prince; even though they would only be riding in the nearby fields, they had to have an escort. It was the king's order and was unnegotiable.

Zane grabbed the reins and gave his horse an affectionate pat. Neighing, the horse nuzzled him. The mare was a beautiful grey and had been suitably named "Storm" after the grey clouds that formed when a storm was brewing. After putting his foot in the stirrup and grabbing the saddle, he hauled himself up and mounted his horse. One of the guards assisted Stryxen, while Jace nimbly mounted his own horse. The captain of the guards called out, and with a creak, the small northern gate opened. It was a private gate used exclusively by the royal family and enabled them to enter the meadows of Sethanon.

* * *

The horses galloped through the field, its riders leaning forward, clinging to the reins. Stryxen screamed out of pure exhilaration, and Zane's horse took the lead. While Jace's horse was a purebred, a warhorse of extremely high calibre, Stryxen's was a young colt, a follower. Where Jace's mare possessed strength and stamina, Zane's made up for in speed. Close behind the three of them were the six guards. Prince Zane looked behind him; he had a marginal lead, and now was as good a time as any. He slowed the horse, mumbled a few words, and subtly performed some gestures with his hand. It was a summoning spell he had learnt from one of the books on dark magic. A dark smoky trail leapt from his hand and hit the ground. A moment later, a large black-and-white snake materialised in front of them, rearing up, fangs bared and hissing menacingly.

Startled and panicking, Zane's horse reared up onto its back legs. The prince flew from the saddle as he was thrown backwards, flailing in the air before landing awkwardly on the grassy meadow. He lay there, his leg and ribs bruised, his foot broken and sticking out at a sickening angle. His horse bolted to the left as the snake slithered towards him. Zane cringed as he prepared for the inevitable, closing his eyes as the snake struck, its fangs sinking into his leg.

The riders reigned in cautiously around Zane and his horse. Jace leapt to the ground and ran towards his brother. "No!" Zane shouted, waving him away. He didn't know whether it was the command, the urgency in his voice, or his worried expression, but Jace froze in midstep and was as still as a statue. "Here you go, my liege," one of the guards shouted, throwing Jace his sword. Jace, however, couldn't see the snake in the tall grass. On top of his horse, though, the guard had a vantage point.

The sword landed beside Jace, spraying up the light covering of snow near his feet and embedding itself in the ground. The soft thud attracted the snake's attention. Slithering forward, it hissed at the newcomer, then reared up, ready to strike again. Jace was motionless, except for his hand, which edged towards the sword's handle. In a blur of speed, he gripped it, pulled the sword free, and swiped. The razor-sharp blade sliced through the tall grass and cut off the snake's head. "Zane! Are you okay?" he shouted.

"I am now. But the damn thing bit me." He moaned. "And I think I broke my ankle when I fell."

Jace took charge, pointing to two soldiers and ordering them to ride back and get Kabel and a cart. The two men saluted and galloped back towards the northern gate. Another soldier trotted forward on his horse, grabbed Storm's reins, and led the horse back to the group.

Jace shot his brother a quizzical look. "That was a radrawg. They don't usually emerge until spring. It's too cold for them this time of year." Zane merely shrugged. He could tell Jace knew something was up, but he kept quiet. "Well, it looks like you won't be able to join us on holiday. It's a shame. Rylan and Gareth were hoping to introduce you to one of the local vintner's daughters. Looks like I'll have to sleep with her instead." He winked and laughed heartily at his brother. And just like that, Jace was back to his usual jovial self. Zane felt a little remorse at having to deceive him, but he had a good reason.

They didn't have to wait long until a cart came rumbling through the field, driven by Varyn Kabel. Being part of the Magici, Kabel had been additionally trained as a scholar, healer, and an alchemist. The cart rumbled to a stop before them. "Broken foot, huh?" he said, assessing Zane with a quick glance. He motioned for two of the guards to lift the prince into the back of the cart.

"And this bit him," Jace said, holding up the headless snake.

"What? That's an adult radrawg. They should be in hibernation. What the hell is it doing out at this time of year?" The Varyn looked baffled. "Toss it into the cart. I'll need to make a potion immediately." He was already deep in thought, compiling a mental list of ingredients he needed to scrounge up. Even though the radrawg was a large aggressive snake, Kabel, like Zane, knew it was only moderately venomous, unlike its distant cousin the blue wavyl, which had blue and black stripes and was highly venomous.

Kabel turned abruptly to the two soldiers who were carefully trying to carry the prince. "By the seven gods!" he shouted, "Move your arses, men. If the prince dies, it will be your heads on the chopping block."

The soldiers quickened their pace, dumping the prince unceremoniously into the back of the cart. Zane held back a scream as his foot hit the edge of the cart. Before he could say anything, the cart lurched off, heading back to the castle.

As the cart barrelled along, Kabel turned around in his seat, a greenish-blue potion in hand. "Take this, my boy. It will help with the pain."

Zane grabbed the bottle, almost dropping it as the cart went over a bump. After unstoppering it, he drained it in one gulp. The liquid was thick, sweet, and pleasant to drink—a nice change from most of Kabel's potions. Within moments Zane felt its effects, his whole body going numb. His eyelids felt heavy, and soon he was fast asleep.

* * *

Chapter 7

In his room at the palace, Zane woke up periodically, remembering being carried up the staircase and placed in bed, seeing his mother cry, and being forced to drink another potion. With a start, he woke up again, moaning and slightly groggy. His mouth was dry and had a bitter aftertaste. Once again, he remembered the potion that had been forced down his throat and attributed it to that. From his bedside table he grabbed a glass of water and gulped it down in three quick swallows. Relieved, the bitterness gone, he looked out the window. The sun was setting; he had slept most of the afternoon. Judging from the aromas wafting up from the kitchen, it was nearly dinnertime.

He tried to get comfortable but found it difficult because of his broken foot. The bone had been reset, and his foot was heavily bandaged. On top of this, a pillow had been tied around it for protection and support. Although he was sore and exhausted, he was alive. The poison had dissipated from his system; the bitter-tasting potion had obviously been an antidote. He closed his eyes and said a few words. Magic radiated throughout his body, tingling and healing him. The achiness eased; the bruising disappeared; the bones mended; and the torn muscles knitted together. For all intents and purposes, he was fully healed; still, he needed to continue this ruse.

He grabbed a book that sat next to his empty glass. It was a novel based on historical heroes. As enthusiastic as he was about magic, he wanted a break from it. Lying back, he began to read. Engrossed in the story, he flicked through the pages. Zane didn't know how much time had passed. It hadn't seemed like long, but the sun had set some time ago. As he put his bookmark in, a knock came at the door. "Enter," he called out, placing the novel back on the bedside table.

Millie entered, carrying a tray with his dinner and a goblet of wine. She stopped at his table and hesitated. It was large and ornate, accommodating four cushioned chairs. Zane often ate there, in addition to entertaining. Circumstances had changed, though. "Would you like your dinner in bed, my prince?" she said.

He nodded politely—it made sense, especially with his "broken" foot. After handing him the tray, Millie fluffed up his pillow as he awkwardly shuffled into a sitting position. On the plate was a slice of boar-and-mushroom pie, mashed potatoes, and steamed vegetables. Comfort food, the meal was one of his favourites. The pie was rich and flavoursome, with a crisp pastry and a thick gravy that he mixed with the potato. After scraping the plate clean, he placed the tray on the bedside table. Millie would collect it later.

"Captain," he shouted, then waited until the door creaked open.

* * *

The captain stood silent, peering in, waiting for his prince's command. Although Brenan was the captain of Zane's personal guard, he was also one of his closest friends; they'd grown up together. While Brenan was on duty, though, Zane addressed him by his title.

"I'm retiring for the evening. I'm not to be disturbed." There was a slight incline of Brenan's head as he acknowledged the order and closed the door. Zane pulled back the covers, climbed out of bed, and crept towards the nearest wall. Hanging from it was a large two-hundred-year-old painting of the war between the Allied Forces and the Jardoshian Empire. It had taken the combined effort of the human, dwarven and elven kingdoms to defeat the empire. The painting was Zane's favourite; he loved the colours and the details the artist had incorporated, capturing the battle in all its bloody glory. He carefully grabbed each side, tilted the painting slightly, and was rewarded with a click.

The castle had numerous interconnected secret passages, all which Zane had memorised. They were used as escape routes and enabled people to discreetly traverse from one area of the castle to another, but Zane used them for another reason. Stretching out his hand, he mumbled a series of words. A ball of bright light manifested above, hovering, illuminating the tunnel's interior. After stepping across the threshold, he clicked the wall back into place and began his journey into the deep, dark depths, of the bowels of the castle.

The tunnels were dark, cold, and dusty. Zane immediately regretted not bringing his jacket. With the ball providing an eerie glow, he navigated the passages, which twisted this way and that and had numerous sets of stairs going up and down. He finally reached an open arch with a spiralling, sloping stone staircase. He made his way down it, humming a tune while his booted feet echoed on the steps. After a couple of minutes, he reached his destination: a large wooden door with metal strips across it.

* * *

The ancient door was covered in black runes that could only be activated with dark magic. Zane drew his dagger and lightly sliced his finger. He then muttered an incantation while tracing his blood along one of the runes. When his finger completed the outline, the rune glowed blue. Zane moved to the next rune and repeated the process, infusing it with his blood, with dark magic. Each rune had to be completed in a particular order. After he traced the last rune, the entire door radiated with a blue light. The metal strips spiralled outwards, unlocking it.

Zane entered his laboratory, his magical sanctuary. A few months ago, he had chanced upon it while exploring the tunnels. He remembered the first time he had come across it. He had instantly recognised the runes, identifying them as symbols of dark magic. It had taken him some experimentation, but eventually he had worked out how to unlock the door. He couldn't help feeling that it was destiny— that this sanctuary was meant to be his.

The room had been left in pristine condition. Magical lamps had been positioned strategically throughout the space, providing constant unlimited lighting that enabled Zane to explore at his leisure. The furniture was sturdy, hand crafted, and expensive— ancient furniture that had stood the test of time. The amount of dust indicated the sanctuary hadn't been used in a while. Zane had no idea who the sanctuary had originally belonged to or why it had been abandoned, but it didn't matter; it was his now.

He hadn't wanted to get his hopes up, but he couldn't help it. The sanctuary was ancient and forgotten. Could it be one of the resting places of the *Val'Markyl*? Dusty floor-to-ceiling bookcases lined an entire wall. They overflowed with scrolls, tomes, and journals—a wealth of knowledge; the question was where to start. After Zane mumbled an incantation, a white sheet of light flashed across the room, instantly removing the layers of dust.

He headed to the first bookcase and examined the titles. The tomes were beyond old, the leather jackets worn. Zane was an avid reader, especially when it came to magic, but it would take him years to read all this. He searched frantically in the vain hope that one of the parts of the sacred *Val'Markyl* was here. Hell, even one of Val'Markyl's other tomes would suffice. But he found nothing.

Sure, there was a wealth of knowledge here, just not what he was after. Was it too much to hope for? Obviously! Cursing, he hurled a journal at a nearby tapestry, an intricately detailed picture of a battlemage riding a dragon. The journal struck the top corner of the tapestry, causing it to flicker. "Now what do we have here?" Zane said, intrigued.

He stepped towards the tapestry and reached his hand out gingerly. The tapestry, Zane quickly realized, was an elaborate illusion and had been put in place to safeguard something. It still flickered, the illusion wavering as he reached past it, his hand disappearing beyond the barrier. He fumbled around for an instant before grabbing hold of something. Carefully he pulled it out.

Wiping the dust off with trembling hands, he stared gobsmacked at the tome before him. His voice was barely a whisper as he read the title aloud, the letters engraved in intricate silver writing. It was the first part of the *Val'Markyl*, the angelic tome. He needed to tell Kabel! He rushed towards the door but stopped midstride, thinking things through. Whether it was the right or wrong decision, Zane didn't know, but he decided to keep his discovery a secret, at least for now. He moved to a comfortable, cushioned chair and lost himself, captivated as he read the tome, studying its details and working it out on his own.

A scraping sound brought him out of his reverie. He looked at the tapestry, the resting place of the book. His efforts to work out the angelic tome had been fruitless. As enlightening as it had been, it had only added to his frustration. The dark magic was a catalyst, a foundation for both angelic and demonic magic. He needed its powerful foundational spells—spells that would combine with divine magic. What spell books contained those kinds of spells were a mystery to him though. He had hoped that Kabel's books would contain them, but even that avenue had been unfruitful.

Heavy footsteps thudded towards him, and a shadow loomed over him. Turning, Zane nodded in greeting. A ghoul stopped dead in his tracks and stood before him. Eight feet tall, broad, and well muscled, he towered over Zane. One of his arms was covered in chain mail that had been surgically attached.

Attached to the chain mail were thick metal plates with iron spikes sticking out of them. The ghoul's arm had been transformed into a devastating weapon. Like his arm, the rest of his body had been enhanced. Thick steel armour covered the ghoul's body, moulded to his flesh. Most humans would have struggled with the heavy material, but the ghoul wore it like a second skin, unencumbered by its bulk. Zane had transformed the beast into a lethal killing machine.

"Master," the ghoul said, lowering himself to all fours, a sign of respect and subjugation. The ghoul was an abomination, an outcast amongst the other ghouls. Zane had modified him using a combination of science and magic. As a result, the ghoul was stronger, faster, and more intelligent than other ghouls. More important, though, he was completely loyal and obedient to Zane, who had named the ghoul Scourge.

After locating his sanctuary, Zane soon realized the room was in the castle's catacombs, which were infested with ghouls. The sanctuary was protected with an invisible, radiating barrier, defending it from unwanted visitors. Curious and observant, Zane often watched the ghouls through the shield. Some even attacked the shield, trying to get to him. They were feral, with no regard for the injuries they sustained. Scourge had been different, though. He seemed familiar with the shield and obviously had served the sanctuary's previous master. Chuckling, Zane remembered the surprise and shock he'd felt when the ghoul had approached the barrier, mumbled a word, then entered. Surprise and shock? Hell, no, he had been scared shitless and had every right to be. Everyone in their right mind would be intimidated by Scourge.

Zane had quickly formed a bond with the ghoul and even went so far to consider him a friend. Through talking with Scourge, he had learnt a great deal about the ghouls' history, hierarchy, and dynamics. Over the past couple of months, Zane also had managed to read some detailed journals regarding ghouls, written by an arch mage named Fabias. Zane had never heard of him before, but he suspected the mage had used an alias to hide his identity. Fabius had been meticulous with his research into ghouls and had given Zane the motivation to further his research and create a ghoul army that was loyal to him and at his disposal—an army he could use against Malgorath.

"Have you done as I've asked, Scourge?" The ghoul nodded enthusiastically. He had given him explicit instructions to collect some of his feral brethren for him to experiment on. Zane reached into his jacket pocket and pulled out a large brown block. Chocolate! He smiled, giving it to Scourge, rewarding him for his good service. The ghoul took the chocolate enthusiastically and devoured it. Scourge had quite the sweet tooth! Zane looked over and saw the two ghouls he had chained to a large bench. The chains were lined with magic-infused runes that made them nearly impossible to break. These ghouls were shorter than Scourge and quite leaner. Both lay on the bench, limp and unconscious.

Zane picked up a spell book and one of Fabius's journals from his desk and flicked through them. The spell book was one that Fabius had left amongst his journals. It was obviously important, but whether it held the key or not was yet to be seen. Fabius had documented an experiment he had done, and Zane was now trying to perfect it, to cure the ghouls' feral, primitive nature. Apparently, centuries ago the ghoulish race had been sophisticated, evolved and civilized, but somehow they had digressed, becoming beastly and wild. As with Scourge's transformation, the procedure involved a combination of science and magic. The equipment was laid out neatly on a bench next to him; it was time to get to work.

Zane had been at it for hours. He threw the spell book across the room. The bench was covered in blood and the ghouls were dead. The experiment had failed...again. With a sweep of his arm, he sent the journal sliding across the bloodied bench and onto the floor. He shouted in frustration. What was he missing? He was close—he knew it—but some detail was eluding him.

Scourge had been easy because he was born with a special gene that made him smarter and more sophisticated than the other ghouls. Was his genetic makeup the key? How could Zane replicate his traits without killing Scourge in the process? There had to be a way to alter the genetic makeup of the ghouls. Determined, he vowed to keep persevering.

"Dispose of the corpses, Scourge. I have something I need to do. I'll visit you again soon." Disposing of them was easy enough, as the ghouls would eat anything, even their own kind. Scourge nodded, understanding. Zane bid his friend good night as he walked towards the door.
"Goodnight, master," the ghoul replied.

Zane closed the door behind him, the runes locking it in place as he walked up the staircase. Muttering, contemplating things, he navigated his way back through the maze of tunnels, guided by the glowing ball of light, which hovered above his hand. He was so caught up in his thoughts, however, that he almost missed a turn. He had so much on his mind: the conundrum involving the ghouls, as well as the letter he was about to compose. He knew he had to do it, but it was about his mother, someone he dearly loved. He was conflicted, partly feeling obliged and partly reneging. Was there another way, a compromise? Then, as he reached the secret wall, it came to him. Smiling, relieved, he flicked a switch, and the wall swung out to reveal his bedroom.

He heard a gasp, and with a clatter, Millie dropped the tray, plate and goblet. "I'm sorry, my prince. You startled me. I didn't see you there." The wall had silently clicked back into place, and although startled, Millie showed no indication that she knew what he'd been up to. "Should you be out of bed, my prince?"

"Probably not, Millie, but I needed to stretch my legs." It was a guess, a gamble, but it paid off. He was rewarded with a smile.

"I can't believe you know my name." Looking slightly embarrassed, she blushed, then knelt and picked up the silver tray. The plate and goblet lay shattered on the floor, a colourful combination of ceramic and crystal shards.

"Don't worry about the mess," Zane said. "I'll clean it up."

"Thank you, my prince. I'm so sorry." She looked nervous, worried. Zane knew her mother would scold her and take the cost of the items out of her meagre pay.

He smiled reassuringly. "Don't worry, Millie. I'll explain everything to your mum and take full responsibility for this."

Even though she was clearly relieved, there was still a brief, awkward silence. She looked anxious, fumbling for something to say. Zane thought it was cute. "I love that painting," she said, motioning towards it. "I admire it every time I come in here. It's one of my favourites."

"It's magnificent, isn't it? A masterpiece. Like you, Millie, I admire art. This painting is also one of my favourites, although I've gotten quite used to it. Feel free to look at it whenever you like."

She gasped, taken aback. "Don't keep it there on my account. Why not swap it for something different, something you can truly admire?"

Zane smirked. "There's no need. I've got you to admire." Blushing, flustered, Millie began to walk away. "So you're going to deprive me of that as well?" he asked, stopping her in her tracks.

"I need to return to the kitchen," she mumbled nervously. "I have duties there."

"Fine. I have work I need to do anyway. Return in an hour and bring a flask of wine and two goblets. I'd like your company this evening."

Even with her hair hanging down hiding her rosy cheeks, Zane could still see her smiling. "As you wish, my prince," she said, turning to leave.

Trying to hide his smirk, Brenan, standing in the hallway, nodded at Zane and closed the door behind her. Zane took a seat at his desk then dipped the quill in the inkpot and began writing. He had a contract to propose to a woman named Flow, one of the deadliest assassins in the Brotherhood. She came highly recommended, and considering the contract he had in mind, she was perfect.

Stopping for a moment, he thought of what to write and how to word it. "Perfect," he said, pleased with himself. He continued writing, his instructions explicit. The orders were to observe the queen and only kill her if necessary. He still had his doubts and didn't want to believe his mother was a demon. The assassin would spy on the royal family as they travelled back from their holiday, intercepting them enroute. It was a compromise, the best he could do, and one with which he was happy.

He signed his name and rolled up the letter. He then picked up his lead stamp and placed it firmly in the hot wax and pressed it to the parchment. The red wax quickly cooled, forming a circular seal. A picture of a flying gryphon was outlined within the wax, the royal Sethanon emblem. A knock came at the door. Zane put the contract in his desk drawer and mumbled an incantation, locking it. "Enter," he said, scraping the chair against the floor as he hopped up. Millie entered, carrying a tray with a flask of deep red, sweet wine, one of his favourites. Also on the tray were two crystal goblets.

Brenan nodded at Zane. "I'll make sure you're not disturbed," he said, closing the door and locking it. With slightly shaking hands, Millie put the tray on the table. Zane grabbed the flask and poured them each a goblet of wine. After they both took one, they stood there silently, looking into each other's eyes, unsure what to say. As Millie began to take a sip, Zane broke the silence. "To an enjoyable evening and very pleasant company." He covered his smile by raising his goblet and taking a sip.

He took two more small sips, then drained the goblet. The fruity wine was meant to be savoured, but Zane didn't care. He put his goblet on the table, and Millie followed suit. "Would you like me to refill your goblet?" she asked, reaching for the flask. Zane stopped her, gently grabbing her hand. *Fuck it*, he thought, and pulling her towards him, he kissed her deeply and passionately. Her arms wrapped around his shoulders as they entangled themselves in an ardent embrace. When the kiss ended, Millie pulled away and began to undo the lace ties of her bodice. The wine forgotten, Zane grabbed her hand and led her to the bed. He was about to have a very enjoyable evening.

* * *

Chapter 8

Hearing noises, Darla had woken with a start. She had always been a light sleeper; it came with her profession. She felt exhausted and achy, she had a headache and thought she was going to vomit. All she wanted to do was sleep. *The elves are disillusioned*, she thought, *thinking I still have the Divinity Stone*. She was tempted to give them the green emerald and send a note along with it explaining who had Dellavenor's precious stone. Let the damn elves sort it out amongst themselves; she had done her job. Now she just wanted to rest and be left alone in goddamn peace. Cringing, she moaned, knowing full well that wasn't going to happen. She had insulted them, taken what was theirs and now they wanted her dead.

She had heard them clambering up the side of the building, using the beams, as well as the cracks in the stone blocks. They had pried the lock on the window to her room and the window in the room adjacent. With soft clicks, three of them had quietly entered each room. They had done it stealthily, with minimal noise, but Darla had heard them, and she was ready.

The curtain masked her presence. She waited quietly and patiently, before spinning into a reverse roundhouse kick. It was a powerful, lethal manoeuvre, well timed and perfectly executed. The kick connected, her boot slamming into the side of an elf's head, spinning it around and snapping his neck. A second elf turned, crossbow in hand, but Darla was already on the move, a wraith in the night. She leapt forward with her knee outstretched into a deadly battering ram. A battering ram that shattered the crossbow and slammed into the elf's chest.

As the elf's ribs cracked, Darla followed through with four consecutive punches. Powerful, fast, and precise, they connected, rocking the elf's head back and forth. He flew backwards, unconscious, before crashing into the side of the tub and falling in. Water splashed onto the floor as the elf lay there with his legs hanging out. Darla left him submerged and slowly drowning.

A scream erupted from the room next door as a woman was cut down by the elves. "Please don't. I'll give you anything." It was the man who'd been sleeping with her, old and rich, begging for his life. The clink of coins sounded as he threw a pouch at them. A moment later there was a gurgled cry as they slit his throat. They didn't care for his riches; they only had one goal in mind: killing Darla. The distraction cost her, as the third elf's curved dagger slashed across. She dodged it just in time, the blade slicing through a few strands of her hair. It had been a narrow miss.

A loud rumbling growl sounded, followed by shouting. Darla recognised Gustus's voice. More elves had broken in downstairs. Gustus whistled, the sound short and sharp. It was an order, a command to attack. Screams sounded, piercing and horrifying. Darla could almost picture the ferocious dire wolf ripping the elves apart. From the sounds of it, Gustus had the situation well in hand. She almost felt sorry for the elves...almost.

The stairs creaked, alerting her to the presence of more elves, bounding up the stairs two at a time. The third elf slashed again, but Darla deflected it with her own dagger. Wanting to finish this quickly, she went on the attack, feinting with her dagger and sweeping with her leg. The kick buckled the elf's knee, dropping him into a kneeling position. She then swung her leg around and hooked it around his neck. Holding it firmly, she rolled backwards, flipping him and snapping his neck in two.

Thump! Thump! Thump! Darla heard the elves outside her room, their booted feet running down the corridor. "Fuck this," she snarled, reaching over her shoulder and drawing the short sword. The handle turned, but the door was locked and bolted from the inside. It shook with repeated whacks as it was kicked, rammed, and finally hacked at. Darla positioned herself next to the door just as a blade erupted through the wood with a shower of splinters. It wouldn't be long now. Weapons at the ready, she leaned against the wall and waited.

The door swung open, dangling precariously off its remaining hinge. The other one was connected to a shard of wood and lay broken and bent. Darla was hidden for the moment, the door blocking the elves' view. She waited as one of the elves stepped across the threshold. His sword appeared, held protectively in front of him. It disappeared as he turned, searching the room. Another cautious step, and his boot and leg came into view.

Coming out of nowhere, Darla's leg swept around and tripped him. The elf stumbled forward and toppled like a fallen tree. As his head came into view, she swung, her short sword slicing through the elf's neck and decapitating him. The corpse fell with a meaty thud, spraying blood in a crimson pool across the floor.

* * *

The elf's companion stepped forward but was hindered by the corpse. He swung his laghesh at her, but it skimmed past her, grazing the door and sending a chunk of it spiralling away. An elvish-designed weapon that had been adopted by mercenaries and assassins, the laghesh was a cross between a short sword and a sickle. He swung again. With a backhanded swing, Darla caught the blade and deflected it upwards. In a blur, her other hand shot forward, stabbing him in the vulnerable part of his armour. The long-bladed dagger pierced his arm pit, slicing through muscle and bone, before finally puncturing his heart.

After pulling her dagger free, she knelt and wiped the blade on the elf's tunic. She then sheathed the short sword and walked down the dimly lit corridor. The lanterns weren't modern and switch based like the new gnomish-designed ones. They were of an older elvish design, beautiful and intricate, with a moonstone and shutter technology. They were fiddly, but no problem for Darla. Reaching up, she extinguished the two lanterns. The corridor became pitch-black, an environment she was used to, a setting she wanted.

As her boots were padded, her footsteps were silent, barely making a sound. The adjacent bedroom door opened, flooding the corridor with light. Darla stopped and waited patiently, standing against the wall, melting into the darkness. The first elf stepped forward, his shadow distorted, silhouetted against the far wall. Darla waited until he entered the corridor. It would take a moment for the elf's eyes to adjust, and she took advantage of that, lashing out, her leg a nearly invisible blur. Her foot hit the elf in the back of the neck, snapping it and propelling him face-first into the wall. He fell backwards, limp, dead, just as a second elf cautiously stepped forward.

His sword slashed blindly from the doorway, probing the darkness. Hesitantly he stepped forward, the wooden floorboards creaking. Darla could now see his gloved hand gripping his sword tightly. She waited once again. His breathing was rapid as he scanned the darkness, searching for any sign of her. Another cautious step and his arm emerged, susceptible, providing her with an easy target. Leaping forward, her knee raised, she rammed the elf's arm into the doorframe. The wooden frame cracked and the elf's arm shattered. His sword clattered to the floor, his fingers limp and useless, unable to hold it.

As Darla landed, she twisted, throwing her shoulder forward and using all the force and power she could muster. Her arm extended as her hand snapped forward in a lethal punch. Grabbing the hilt of her dagger, her fist slammed under the elf's nose, breaking it and pushing the bone and cartilage segments into his brain. The elf died instantly.

A twang sounded and a crossbow bolt spiralled towards her. Darla was immediately on the move. With her free hand, she dug her fingers inside the top of the dead elf's leather armour. Spinning the limp corpse to the left, she used it as a shield. The bolt hit it with a thud, puncturing the elf's chest and narrowly missing Darla's arm. Continuing the spin as if she were dancing, she positioned herself with her back to the crossbowman. She then dropped backwards into a roll, pulling the corpse with her and using her feet to catapult it.

The elf had been in the process of recocking his crossbow when the flailing corpse hit him in the chest, bowling him over. The crossbow clattered to the floor as the elf landed with a crash, pinned by the corpse, weaponless, helpless as Darla approached him. "I want you to deliver a message to your lord," she said smirking, as she skilfully twirled her dagger.

"Fuck you," he replied, spitting at her and lunging for his crossbow. Darla's dagger flew, spinning through the air. The elf's gloved fingers reached for the smooth handle when...*thwack*! The elf screamed as the dagger pierced his hand, pinning it to the wooden floor.

* * *

Flailing wildly, he tried to get free. Finally, he grabbed hold of his comrade's armour with his free hand and threw the corpse off him. He was hyperventilating, and his pupils were dilated, his eyes wild. He reached into his belt and grabbed hold of a handle wrapped in leather twine; with a screech of metal on leather, he drew forth his laghesh. Screaming, maniacal, he raised it above his head and brought it crashing down. The curved, razor-sharp edge easily cut through his wrist, leaving a bloody stump. He had severed an artery and was losing blood rapidly. Groggily he lifted himself unsteadily to his feet. "Now it's your turn, bitch," he roared, glaring at Darla.

Blood gushed from his stump, pooling on the floor. He was dying but acted as though he were oblivious to the pain. Eyes glazed, he charged forward, slashing at Darla. She needed to deal with this quickly before he bled out; she needed him alive so she could send a message. Easily catching the blade and deflecting it upwards, she extended his arm. She then swung her other arm across, her fist clenched, and brought it crashing down, shattering his elbow.

Not a word or a whimper, just the sound of the laghesh crashing to the floor. The elf's arm hung limply and at an obscure angle. He was unarmed and crippled, but Darla wasn't done with him yet. With a short, sharp kick, she shattered his kneecap. The elf dropped to one knee, and Darla grabbed him by the hair and threw him headfirst, sliding across the floor.

Instinctively the elf stretched out his arms, trying to brace himself. He bowled into the grille of the hearth, bending the frame and landing on top of it as it fell into the fireplace. Ash and embers flew into the air. His stump was cauterised instantly, sending the reeking smell of burnt flesh wafting throughout the room. The left side of his face was also burnt, branded with the bright red pattern of the grille. It would leave a horrific scar, Darla thought. Grabbing hold, she pulled him out by his legs. He glared at her, clenching his teeth, refusing to scream. She had tortured him enough; now it was time for him to deliver her message. She dragged him to the wall as he flailed and lashed out, trying to kick her with his good leg, the one she was holding. "Stand up!" she yelled, pulling him up by the scruff of the neck. Holding him there, she smiled as he struggled to support himself.

His pain was only physical, not mental. His eyes revealed pure rage, undying hatred. Darla could tell, as she'd seen it often enough. The elf was resilient, defiant, and unbroken. She hadn't tortured him to break his spirit, though—the torture, the injuries were part of her message. Now it was time for the written part, the icing on the cake.

She cut the straps of his dark leather armour and let it drop to the floor. Starting from the bottom, she then slowly sliced open his white tunic, the cold tip of her blade gently touching his skin. She leaned in close, seductively. "Deliver this message to your lord," she whispered. "Tell him if I ever see him again, I'll pluck out his other eye and feed it to him." With delicate precision, she then engraved her final message on his chest with her blade. The elf gritted his teeth, biting through the pain. It simply read, "Fuck you." By the end of it, his entire torso was bloodied. Opening his mouth wide, the elf screamed.

Darla stepped back to admire her handiwork. She nodded, satisfied, then kicked the elf square in the chest. The wall shattered as he crashed through it. A cloud of fragments and debris flew outwards, along with the flailing elf. Screaming, he toppled two stories before landing with a squelchy thud, the layer of snow covering the pavement being the only thing breaking his fall. The snow was quickly stained red, leaving a trail as he crawled through it. The snow and freezing-cold temperature would hinder the elf's progress, but Darla didn't care; eventually her message would get to Lord Dellavenor.

The inn was once again quiet; the elves had been taken care of. "I'm going back to bed," Darla said to no one, yawning. Slowly she sauntered back to her room and collapsed onto the bed. After wrapping the thick blankets around her, she fell fast asleep.

* * *

Zane stirred, opening his eyes. He and Millie had been asleep for hours, exhausted after their rigorous sexual activities. The sheet and blanket were a tangled mess, their naked bodies lying amongst it. He was cold, thirsty, and felt peckish—he had a craving for something sweet. Carefully he pulled his arm free from under the pillow and Millie's neck. When she stirred, mumbling and waking up, he kissed her gently on the mouth. "I'm sorry for waking you. I'm going down to the kitchen to get something to eat and drink. Would you like anything?"

Millie grinned. "Why get something to eat when you can have me?"

Zane laughed. This woman was a damn nymphomaniac; he loved it. "Maybe after I've had some dessert, my dear."

"Okay, you stay here, and I'll get us some pie and make us some hot chocolate to go with it." She couldn't help herself. It had been ingrained into her; she clearly felt it was her duty to serve. Sliding out of bed, she shivered. "It's freezing. While I'm gone, can you stock up the fire?" The fire had died down to a small flame amongst a pile of charcoal and embers; a dim glow was all that remained.

As Zane nodded, he admired her erect nipples, a product of the cold. He couldn't help himself as his gaze lingered on the rest of her beautiful naked body. Her long chestnut coloured hair was normally neatly tied up, but it now cascaded down her back in waves, wild and free. Grabbing a hair tie off the nightstand, she deftly tied it into a ponytail. Noticing Zane watching she smiled wickedly, her dimples showing, Zane had an inkling of what she was about to do. Seductively, she flaunted her body, teasing him, before grabbing his fur-lined gown and wrapping it around herself.

* * *

Shivering, Zane gingerly climbed out of bed. The room was absolutely frigid—winter was setting in. Kissing her, he tied the cord to the gown. "Can I borrow these as well?" she asked. Not waiting for an answer, she slipped her feet into his warm fur-lined slippers. "I'll be back soon." Giggling, she opened the bedroom door and left him standing there naked and cold.

"I'll escort you miss," Brenan said, closing the door and following her down the hallway.

Zane headed to the fireplace and picked up a small log, which he then placed on the pile of embers. Ash and sparks flew up as the log ignited. He put two more on for good measure, and within moments a fire was ablaze, crackling as the flames danced within the hearth. The warmth and heat were immediate as a radiant glow filled the room.

Even with the warmth of the fire, Zane felt a cold chill: a feeling of foreboding, evil, and death. He had goose bumps that tingled with magic—magic that alerted him, enabling him to sense the supernatural presence within the room. His mind racing, he whispered an incantation and turned, his arms outstretched. Bright white energy flickered from his fingertips. It resembled lightning, except for its sparkling, radiant quality, which identified it as angelic magic. A shadow loomed before him, ethereal, blurring between large and small. Turning, it looked at him with red glowing eyes before walking towards his desk. Unfazed, it seemed to consider him irrelevant. Turning its head back, completely ignoring him, it continued about its business.

One of the desk drawers slid open, even though it had been locked, sealed with dark magic. "Malgorath," Zane whispered, a mixture of emotions surging through him. The demon looked at him, reacting to its name and confirming his suspicions. It held the contract he had written in its clawed hand. Grinning wickedly, Malgorath revealed his razor-sharp teeth. Fear unlike Zane had ever known coursed through him. He closed his eyes and took a deep breath. When he opened them, he felt calm and controlled. The lightning surged forward from both hands, merging, creating a devastating form of pure angelic energy. The energy crackled as it zigzagged, shooting forward towards the demon. The lightning lit up the room with a blinding light, illuminating the demon and enabling Zane to see him in his true demonic form.

Then everything was as dark as midnight. Zane woke, startled and confused. He was lying in bed, and Millie stood before him. She held a plate with a large slice of apple and raspberry pie. It was topped with a large dollop of whipped cream. "I thought we could share," she said, handing him a dessert fork. Two steaming mugs of hot chocolate had been placed on the bedside table, the aroma of dark chocolate wafting throughout the room. Zane felt groggy and bewildered. Had it all been just a dream? The fire was blazing, though, the wood crackling as warmth radiated throughout the room. He looked quickly towards his desk and saw a scorch mark behind it on the wall. The angelic bolt—it had to have been real.

"Was anyone else in here when you came?" he asked, looking around frantically.

"No." Millie giggled and raised her eyebrows jokingly. "Why? Did you have another woman in here while I was gone?" She knelt and looked under the bed. "Come out, come out wherever you are." She laughed again. "I'm sure the guard wouldn't have let me in if someone else had been in here. Mind you, he did look bored and half asleep."

"No one else is here," Zane replied with a half smile, and grabbed the plate. "Sit down and join me."

Millie almost leapt onto the bed. She bounced on the mattress as she manoeuvred herself and snuggled next to him. She could tell he was shaken and something was wrong, and although concerned, she didn't question him further. Hopefully her company would bring him out of his worried state.

They laughed as their forks battled for the last bite of pie. Blocking her fork and scooping it up, Zane won, only for Millie to lean forward and steal it from his fork. Huffing, he put down his fork, leaned forward and kissed her.

The kiss started off soft and gentle but soon became passionate as Millie inserted her tongue. Like snakes, their arms wrapped themselves around each other's bodies. Zane had no idea how it happened, but somehow the gown ended up in a crumpled heap on the floor. Admiring Millie's curvaceous body once again, he didn't complain. Lying on his back, he fondled her breasts while she straddled him. Inserting his erect cock deep inside her, they fucked and all thoughts of Malgorath were long forgotten.

A couple of hours later, Zane smiled as he pulled the rumpled fur blanket over their bodies. They were both sweaty and exhausted. Kissing her neck gently, he wrapped his arm around her and rested his hand on her breast. As he snuggled next to her, she soon fell into a deep sleep, snoring softly. Turning his head slightly, Zane looked towards his desk and the scorch mark on the wall. The sex had provided him with a momentary distraction, but now he found himself thinking about the demon again. For several hours, he lay awake questioning his sanity and wondering whether the beast he had seen was actually Malgorath.

* * *

Chapter 9

When Darla woke up, the fire in the hearth had been reduced to embers, and the faint light of the rising sun could be seen outside the window. She wrapped her thick cloak around her and exited the room. Shivering, she yawned as she walked down the creaky wooden stairs. She'd barely had any sleep, but hopefully the opportunity would present itself throughout the day. Somehow, though, she doubted she'd be so lucky.

As she stepped into the dining room, she smelled the rich aroma of coffee. Kimber was in a foul mood, grumbling as she cleaned. The floor was stained red, the blood having soaked into the floorboards. Getting it out now was a futile task. "'Good morning," Darla said politely. Kimber's only reply was a curse and another grumble.

* * *

Gustus was clattering in the kitchen. With a bang, the double doors opened, and he emerged carrying a huge pot of steaming coffee. "Damn it, woman. Leave the floor alone," he said, shaking his head. He smiled at Darla and grabbed a large mug off the counter. "I told her the bloodstains would be impossible to get out, but she's as stubborn as an ox, and there's no reasoning with her." Darla tried to hide the smirk creeping onto her face. She had thought the exact same thing, but out of her better judgment she'd decided to keep her mouth shut.

"Anyway," Gustus said, filling the mug two thirds of the way with steaming coffee. "I think the bloodstains add character to the inn." He added a bit of spiced brandy to the coffee, looked at Darla, and added some more. Finally, he added a dollop of honey and topped the drink with fresh cream. "You look like you could definitely use this," he said, handing her the mug.

Wrapping her gloved hands around the mug, Darla longingly took a sip. Gustus reached behind the counter and brought forth a large plate of cinnamon buns, still warm from the oven, with maple icing dripping down the sides. "Breakfast," he said, offering her one. Darla grabbed a bun and licked the sticky, sweet icing off her fingers.

"This is her fault," Kimber muttered, glaring at them, "and here you are offering her coffee and goddamn breakfast."

Darla heard a creaking on the stairs, faint, but loud enough for her keen hearing.

Gustus merely laughed. "Well, technically it's Wraith's mess." He turned to Darla. "As you probably know, some of your elvish friends decided to pay us a visit last night. I killed one of them with my trusty hammer, and Wraith tore into three of them, ripping them apart, as you can see. To my, shame though, two of them managed to get past us and run upstairs." Gustus patted his big belly. "I'm not as young as I use to be, I'm afraid." He was apologetic, blamed himself. Another creak sounded, soft but distinct.

Darla shrugged, wiping some icing off her chin. "I took care of them, as well as the other six who came through the windows.

Gustus looked at her bewildered. "Impressive. You managed to kill eight elvish soldiers, assassins at that. There's definitely more to you than meets the eye." More creaking, louder this time, multiple boot steps, slow, steady, and quiet. Whoever was here was eavesdropping, sneaking down the stairs and waiting for the right opportunity to emerge. Darla knew exactly who it was.

She smirked as she took another bite, savouring the taste before speaking. "Unfortunately, they did manage to kill two of your guests and cause some damage to your rooms."

Kimber stopped scrubbing and threw the brush in the bucket. Soapy water splashed onto the floor. "That's just fucking great. And who's going to pay for the damage?" she yelled. Pointing at Darla accusingly, she continued to rant. Darla just stood there and continued eating.

Smiling, Darla looking directly at the staircase. "I'm sure Lord Aldronin will be more than happy to generously compensate you for any damages." And with that the young lord finished his descent, stumbling as he stepped into the light of the dining room. His guards silently followed him, emerging a moment later.

"And why exactly would I do that?" he spat, angry and defensive. "This is your fault, your mess. You clean it up!"

"My fault?" Darla laughed. Her eyes were steely, and her tone became deadly serious. "You're the one who contracted me, hid like a coward, then put me in the firing line. If you don't pay up, I'll personally beat the living shit out of you and deliver your arse to your one-eyed cousin." The guards subtly reached under their cloaks, ready to draw. Darla smiled at them wickedly. "I killed a squad of elves last night. Do you really want me to add to the body count?"

Backing down, halting his guards, Aldronin nodded, easing the tension. Grinding his teeth, he unhooked a pouch and counted out a dozen gold coins. "Please consider this compensation for any damages, good innkeeper."

Smiling, Gustus quickly pocketed the coins. "Would you and your men like some breakfast and coffee?"

Aldronin's only reply was a brief nod and a grunt as he pulled out another six silver coins. Without a word he handed them over and walked away, following his men to a table.

"I like her," Kimber said, nodding in approval as she took the bucket into the kitchen. Darla stood there perplexed. One minute she was being abused, and then suddenly she was Kimber's new best friend. By the gods, that woman was a strange one.

The front door swung open with a bang, startling everyone. Frigid air swept in like icy death as Rygar stepped across the threshold. After closing the door, he opened his thick fur coat and shook the snow to the floor. "By the seven hells, its' freezing out there," he said, walking over to Gustus and Darla. "Those fucking pointy-eared bastards scaled the wall and killed six of my guards last night," he said as Gustus handed him a mug of coffee. He glimpsed the bloodstained floor. "Looks like you had company last night. I'm sorry—I should have killed them when I had the chance. Chopped them up and fed them to the dire wolves."

"By the gods, Rygar," Gustus huffed, "it's not your damn fault. Stop blaming yourself. They're sneaky, stealthy bastards, them elves. They weren't counting on our lovely young lady here, though."

Beaming with pride, he motioned to Darla "She killed eight of them all by herself." Carrying the pot of coffee, he hobbled to the elves' table.

"Well, seven of them," Darla corrected. "I tortured one of them and sent him back with a message to his lord."

"Even tortured, the damn elf won't talk," Rygar spat.

"He doesn't need to talk," Darla said with a smirk. "I engraved the message on his skin." Rygar grinned wickedly, nodding in approval. Darla finished her coffee and handed the mug back to Gustus. He placed it casually on the counter and held out the plate of cinnamon buns. Darla smiled, helping herself to another one.

Rygar scowled. "I went out on patrol early this morning. The damn elves are camped out on the other side of the bridge. I was tempted to charge across and shove my battle spear up the lord's arse, but fortunately my sergeant held me back and stopped me from starting a war."

"Looks like it's by boat then." Darla sighed; she hated travelling by boat. She took a bite of her cinnamon bun. *So delicious!* she thought.

Rygar nodded. "I've already spoken to Jonah. Your passage has been paid for. *The Bridget* is awaiting your arrival. He's transporting some goods to Balgleen and is happy to drop you off there. You'll evade the elves and be able to make your way unhindered."

"Thank you," Darla said. "I'll go get Midnight organised and meet you out front." She pulled out some silver coins from her purse and handed them to Gustus. "For breakfast," she said, and began to walk away. Gustus hastily stopped her, reaching out his arm and barring her way. In his hand he held another mug of coffee.

* * *

"No need to trouble yourself, lass," he said, handing her the mug. "The stable boy has already got your horse ready, and your parcels have been packed and secured. Sit and relax." He brought forth another steaming mug. Rygar took it gratefully and nodded his thanks. Turning around, Gustus opened one of the doors and shouted into the kitchen. "Honey, I've made you a coffee."

"But what about my guards and me?" Aldronin said urgently, walking towards them. The elves' elongated ears gave them exceptional hearing, and the lord obviously had been eavesdropping on the conversation. He stood before them looking anxious and despondent. "We can't travel via the bridge. If my cousin catches us, we'll suffer a fate far worse than death." It was true—Aldronin was in dire need of assistance. He was out of options, and Rygar knew it; Darla could tell from the slight smirk creeping forward and the twinkle in his eyes. She sat down with her coffee, took a long sip, and leaned back, ready to enjoy the show. Kimber emerged a moment later, gave her husband a kiss on the cheek, and sipped her own coffee.

Looking slightly uncomfortable and embarrassed, Rygar stroked his beard. "Well, it never hurts to ask, but I don't like your chances. You see, a couple of months ago, Jonah visited the elves at Casedail. All he wanted to do was some honest trade—see what he could get for his spices, furs, and gems. They weren't interested in any of his goods, though. All they wanted was his pet dire wolf. It's a beautiful looking animal, its colouring magnificent.

"Jonah was flattered and even offered to breed the wolf and sell them some of the pups. But they weren't interested in that. They wanted to roast the wolf over a fire and eat it. He managed to escape with only minor injuries, but the experience left him with a deep hatred towards elves." Rygar shrugged as if to apologise. "I'm sorry. I can try to talk to him, but if he agrees, your passage will be costly. The choice is yours, elf lord."

* * *

Gripping his hair, Aldronin stormed off, cursing. Darla took another sip of coffee and peered at Rygar out of the corner of her eye. "I thought the elves at Casedail were peaceful folk? They're a religious community. Their town is situated around a temple, and they worship Zadene, the goddess of nature. They love animals."

"I know," Rygar said with a wicked grin, taking a sip of his own coffee. "They doted upon his dire wolf. It was fed better than he was." Darla laughed. "I may have embellished the story a little, but it goes to show the elven lord is totally ignorant of his distant cousins. And besides, he deserved it, especially considering that he played you, used you as a scapegoat."

"You're right—he does deserve it," she replied, bending down and giving the dwarf a gentle kiss on the cheek. "Thank you."

"Anytime," he mumbled, blushing slightly.

"So, are you going to tell him the truth?"

Another wicked, cheeky grin. "No! I'm going to finish my coffee and let them squirm for a while." The dwarf was enjoying this way too much. Humming, Kimber proceeded past them carrying the elves' breakfast, a tray laden with cinnamon buns. As she passed, Rygar's hand shot out, snatching two buns off the tray. Turning, she shot the captain a stern look. In response, he smiled charmingly and winked at her. "Come now, Kimber. They're elves. They don't eat much anyway."

Darla giggled and handed Kimber a silver coin. "For Rygar's breakfast." Nodding, the woman accepted the payment and continued towards the elves' table. Rygar already had perched himself on a chair, his stubby legs crossed and resting on the edge of the table. He held his coffee in one hand and the cinnamon bun in the other. "If I'd known you were going to pay for breakfast, I would have grabbed more of these," he said cheekily, taking a huge bite out of the bun.

Darla sat next to him and downed more of her coffee. Its aroma was intoxicating, its warmth comforting and soothing. The brandy spiced it up, giving it some extra kick. It was just what she needed. They sat, relaxing, talking casually and laughing at the elves' expense. It was only a brief break, five minutes if that, but it was still a pleasant change of pace.

True to his word, the stable boy had fed and saddled Midnight and packed her belongings. Darla gave the young man two silver coins for his efforts. Even though he received a regular income from Gustus, this was a bonus—his broad grin said it all. Rygar followed out a moment later, his thick coat buttoned up and protecting him from the cold. The elves followed him, with Lord Aldronin imploring Rygar and trying to negotiate a price. The dwarven captain was in his element, lapping it up like a cat who had got the cream. The elves had no bargaining power, leaving Rygar the opportunity to dictate whatever price he wanted. Darla shook her head as Rygar laughed, winking at her as he walked past and took the lead. Darla followed close behind with Midnight clip-clopping loudly on the cobble road.

As early as it was, the town already was bustling with activity. Darla was amazed. Dwarves worked hard; there was no question about that. They believed in getting a full day's work in—starting early and finishing late. Even though a few were grumpy, most were polite, giving a warm greeting as they walked past. It wasn't long before they reached the harbour, rich and overpowering with its fishy, salty smell. The dark, icy cold water splashed, buffeting the supports, a constant reminder that the Duegart Sea was treacherous at the best of times. The harbour was a flurry of activity, with markets at the forefront, swarming people who chattered ceaselessly, their voices a constant buzz.

Some of the fishermen were bringing their boats in, while others were already in the process of offloading their catches. "I could never be a fisherman," Rygar said, shaking his head. "I prefer to keep my feet on solid ground. Some of them even go out at midnight. Apparently, that's when the best fishing is, or so they say. Fuck that—I'd rather be snuggled up in bed with a good woman."

Darla watched as fishermen hefted their crates and baskets, the fresh fish flopping and wriggling within. They dumped them onto the piers, ready for the crew hands, who'd then load them onto carts or carry them to the market. She looked at Rygar and smiled mischievously. "I'm sure some of the fisherman's wives would happily oblige." Embarrassed, he turned his head and silently looked at the ground. "What? Rygar, you haven't!"

"Hey, I have to take what I can get," he muttered, leading them onto a pier. Even though the piers were sturdy and well maintained, they were a maze of twists and turns. This one consisted of a raised central platform with ramps leading down to a series of piers that branched and overlapped like the tentacles of an octopus. Knowing exactly where to go, Rygar navigated the thoroughfare easily. Numerous ships were moored, and Darla often found herself traversing around cargo and discarded nets.

Waving, hurrying them along, Rygar led them to the end of the farthest pier. Moored, with the gangplank lowered, they approached a sleek-looking smuggling ship. "This is Jonah," he said, pointing to a roguish, red-haired dwarf on the foredeck. He had his beard braided and his long unkempt hair tied back in a ponytail. The dwarven captain gave an extravagant bow, and that's when Darla noticed that in place of his left hand, Jonah had a steel hook. After hooking it over a nearby rope, he used it like a flying fox and swung down towards the deck. He then unhooked himself partway and landed nimbly next to the gangplank.

"Rygar failed to tell me how attractive my guest would be," Jonah said, looking her over, his blue eyes sparkling mischievously.

Cringing, Darla glanced at Rygar and raised her eyebrows.

* * *

"And if I'd known how sickeningly flirtatious you would be," Rygar replied, "I would have hired a boat and rowed her myself."

"The woman wants to arrive in one piece, Rygar, not sink to the bottom of the sea. Don't worry—she'll arrive safely. I'll even keep her warm at night and let you know how she beds."

"Try it, Captain, and I'll cut off that little cock of yours and feed it to the fish," Darla replied.

Frowning, Jonah looked angry. A moment later, he broke into a broad grin, and the two dwarven captains burst into laughter. "I can see why you like her, Rygar. Come aboard, milady. Welcome to *The Bridget*." He waved Darla forward, and she cautiously led Midnight onto the gangplank. "Settle in. Make yourself at home and join my other guests."

"Other guests?" Rygar asked with a lift of his brows. With a loud clank, Midnight gingerly stepped off the gangplank onto the deck of the ship. It was then that Darla saw the other so-called guests. Even wearing cloaks, with their hoods down and their faces covered in shadow, Brigg and his men stuck out like sore thumbs.

"Lead your horse up the stairs. There's a spot near the netting at the back of the ship. And I've set up a bunk for you in a spare room next to mine." Jonah said with a glint in his eyes.

"Thank you for the generous offer," Darla replied sweetly, "but I'd like to rough it and stay with my horse." Jonah nodded, accepting her decision.

As she led Midnight forward, she noticed Brigg's mysterious companion. Yet again his midnight-black hair was covering one of his eyes, with a few wispy strands sticking out from under his hood. He acknowledged her with a brief nod then subtly waved her towards the back of the ship; the gesture went unnoticed by his comrades. The Brotherhood had incorporated such a signal, a warning that something was about to happen. Was it purely a coincidence or did he work for the Brotherhood? Opting for the side of caution, Darla heeded the warning. She nodded back and gave a two-fingered flick of her hood. It was the Brotherhood's response, her acknowledgement of the message.

With a clip-clop, Darla guided Midnight towards the stairs. "This is for you," said a gangly unshaven man, handing her a flask. Darla turned to look at the stranger approaching her. "My name is Callum. I'm the chief of the ship, Jonah's right hand, so to speak. I overheard you tell Jonah you'd be roughing it, so I thought you might like this." Darla looked at the flask questioningly. "It's called Krakens Kiss. It's a spiced rum," he continued. "It'll ward off the chill and help you sleep." Darla noticed the bead of sweat rolling down his neck; he looked nervous.

"So, who are these elves with you, Rygar? More customers?" Jonah asked. Darla turned, distracted, wondering if the captain would allow them aboard.

"Yes, if you have room. They're happy to be dropped off in Balgleen, like the lady." From there they can easily make their way to the elven king."

"Really?" Distinguishing Aldronin as their leader, he directed his response to him.

"Yes, if it's not too much trouble," Aldronin replied, jingling a pouch. "I'll gladly pay you for your trouble."

Jonah stroked his chin, contemplating. "You did tell them the story, Rygar? My history with the elves at Casedail?" Darla shook her head, giggling to herself. The two friends were playing the elves, swindling them for as much as they could. They obviously had done this before. Nodding her thanks, she took the flask from Callum and continued up the stairs towards the rear of the ship. In her wake, she heard Aldronin screeching, pleading to come aboard. Little did he know the elves' boarding was guaranteed. The question was how much coinage it would cost him.

She pulled out two apples, handed one to Midnight, and patted him affectionately. He chomped the fruit in half, spraying juice everywhere. Grabbing the two rolled-up blankets strapped to her saddle, she untied one and wrapped it around herself. The harbour was unprotected, and the wind coming off the ocean was bitterly cold. Sitting down, she opened the flask and in one gulp drained its contents. The amber liquid was smooth, laced with cinnamon and other spices. Even though it initially warmed her, it still left her feeling cold, freezing in fact. Using the other blanket as a pillow, she leaned back against the railing. It was uncomfortable, and the short sword pressed into her back, but she didn't mind; she'd had worse. And besides, she was on her way back to the Black Raven Inn. It was home, she'd be surrounded by people she loved and sleeping in a nice warm, cosy bed.

The blue-eyed bandit, as Darla liked to call him, didn't even turn his head. He just stared at the elves who were now boarding the ship from the gangplank. His left hand dropped to his side and quickly made a flurry of signals. The Brotherhood's codes were based on the sign language deaf people used, which they had modified to their own needs. It confirmed Darla's suspicions that this bandit indeed worked for the Brotherhood. The first couple of signals represented words, followed by a series of letters. It was an introduction, a greeting to her: "My name is Rayze."

Normally, protocol would have dictated she identify herself as well, but she didn't for two reasons. First, she didn't want to draw attention to herself and possibly blow Rayze's cover, and second, she wanted Rayze to stew, to wonder who she was. The bandits were being jovial, laughing, joking, and introducing themselves to the elves. Darla knew they'd wait until they were on the open sea; it would be a while before they made their move.

She tossed the other apple, and Midnight caught it in midair, chomping into it. A roar sounded from above. It was the wyvern, flying around casually, gliding through the air, and circling them. After finishing the apple, Midnight gave a snort as if to say, *I told you so*. Darla hmphed. "He doesn't want to eat us," she replied. She couldn't help but question herself though, wondering whether the wyvern was biding its time, waiting to attack the ship.

Adjusting her blanket, she got comfortable and closed her eyes. She felt sleepy, exhausted, the events of the last couple of days catching up with her. They would be home in a couple of days, depending on the speed of the ship, the wind conditions and the weather. Then Midnight could have some well-deserved rest and relaxation. Hell, they deserved it! As she dozed off, an excruciating headache and stomach pains came over her. Curling up in a ball, she cried out; she'd never felt anything like this. Her last thought was that she was going to die. Then she fell unconscious.

Chapter 10

Zane woke to find it was late morning. He was tired, having had a restless night, tossing, turning, and plagued with nightmares. Millie had disappeared early in the morning, leaving quietly to work in the kitchen. The only reason he had awoken was due to the banging and clattering of the servants as they packed clothing chests, supplies, and gifts onto the royal carriage. It wasn't all the servants' fault though; the guards that would be escorting the royal party were making just as much noise.

His family would be heading off for two weeks on a much-needed holiday, visiting family friends in Belgreth. The town was smaller than Sethanon but was well known for its farms and vineyards. His father's favourite wine came from Belgreth. Zane had suggested they take an extra cart with them so they could restock the cellar. He readjusted his pillow and grabbed the novel from his bedside table. It was pointless to try to get back to sleep.

The door opened, and his mother walked over and kissed him on the cheek. Even in her early forties, Queen Raylene was strikingly beautiful. Unlike his father, who had started to get streaks of grey, Raylene's long brown hair was lush and full bodied. Today she wore it in an intricate bun with a series of diamond-embedded pins holding it together. As she turned, the gems sparkled in the morning sun. "How's my boy, doing? You gave us such a fright." Zane closed the book and smiled warmly at his mother.

Her handmaidens stood in the hallway, giggling. One of them, a cute little brunette, waved at Zane and winked at him. The two handmaidens were to stay behind, allowing for a small entourage for Zane. While the queen was away, they would be working for the castle matron, assisting Zane, and performing chores around the castle. Zane knew the brunette fancied him, and he had every intention of sleeping with her, but now that he had fucked Millie, it complicated things. He was a prince, though, and could sleep with whomever he chose. On the other hand, he didn't want to upset Millie, even though he wasn't committed to her. This proved to be quite the dilemma.

A muffled clanking sounded from the carpeted hallway. The two handmaidens parted, and Prince Jace entered the room, dressed in his heavy armour. "Good to see you're feeling better, brother. I hear you had some company last night?" The queen looked questioningly at her eldest son. "Oh, you didn't know, Mum? Zane bedded Millie, the serving girl, last night. Well...I'm fairly sure it was Millie from the sound of her voice. All I could hear was, 'Oh, Zane, insert that small cock of yours inside me again.'" Zane threw a pillow at him, half-heartedly, in jest. Jace dodged it easily, laughing at his brother's expense. Unfortunately, he wasn't able to dodge the clip around the ear he received from their mother.

* * *

Queen Raylene then turned her fury on Zane. "I thought you were supposed to be resting, getting better. Obviously, you aren't as sick as I thought you were!"

"Mother, it's my leg that's injured. Not my cock."

"Obviously," she said with a humph and stormed out. After exiting the room, she gave her handmaidens some last-minute instructions and walked down the hallway towards the stairs. Although his mum was angry, he didn't blame Jace. It was nothing but brotherly banter, and he often gave as good as he got. His family would be gone for two weeks, just enough time for the queen to get over her grudge. But then again, she was really pissed. All would hopefully be forgiven by the time they got back.

Jace noticed the book lying on the bed and couldn't help himself. Smirking, he motioned towards it. "Are you doing some research on how to please Millie?"

Zane couldn't help but laugh. "Well, at least I know how to read. Let me know when you're past reading picture books."

"There's nothing wrong with picture books," Jace said defensively, "especially when they have pictures of naked women in them." Zane laughed, but Jace knew his brother, could tell it was forced. "What's wrong?" He looked concerned. All the joking was put aside.

"Nothing." Zane shook his head, dismissing it.

"I know something's wrong! I'm not leaving until you tell me."

"Okay, okay. I had a visit from Malgorath last night." His voice was barely a whisper. "I'm questioning my sanity, Jace. I don't know what's real anymore. Initially I thought it was just a dream, a fragment of my imagination, but then I noticed that." He pointed to the scorch mark on the wall. "I cast a bolt of pure an..." He stopped himself abruptly; Jace didn't know he studied angelic magic, and he didn't want to disclose it yet. "Energy. It left that scorch mark. Doesn't that indicate it was real, that it wasn't a dream?"

Jace chuckled. "You made that mark years ago. You were boasting about mastering elemental magic and incanted a spell, created a lightning bolt, and nearly blew up your bedroom. Mum and Dad were beside themselves, but I almost wet myself from laughing so hard." He chuckled, picturing the memory.

Zane didn't know whether Malgorath was playing games with him, manipulating his inner thoughts. This demon was like a puppet master, pulling his strings and leaving him questioning his sanity. He tried to dismiss it from his mind, because to think about it would cause him to spiral down into the deep dark recesses of depression, which even he would struggle to get out of.

He was confused; he had no memory of making that mark when he was a child. Had he simply forgotten it or was the entire story fabricated? "You're right," he said. "Thanks, Jace. I'd forgotten about that. Must have been just a bad dream." He feigned a smile, even a giggle, trying to reassure his brother. He couldn't help wondering whether his beloved brother was lying to him, whether he was actually Malgorath in disguise. He no longer knew who he could rely on or trust. A single tear rolled down his cheek. He loved Jace, enjoyed the playful banter, the close relationship they shared. Was it all a sham, though, a deceitful act?

"Prince Jace!" It was the ranger commander shouting for him, his booming voice easily heard through the open window. The rangers were the king's elite guard unit and were accompanying them on the holiday. Jace walked over to the window and acknowledged the commander.

"I'd better go. They're ready to leave, and you know how antsy Dad gets." He leaned down and gave his brother a fierce hug. Zane noticed the cheeky grin and the glint in his brother's eyes. "Try not to impregnate, Millie. Mum's not quite ready to be a grandmother yet."

"Heed your own advice, brother, and try not to impregnate too many country girls." Jace laughed. "Be safe and have a good holiday. I'll see you in a couple of weeks." They clasped arms in a brotherly farewell. Jace walked towards the door, his armour clanking.

"Get well! We'll be back soon, Zane," King Erithen shouted from the courtyard. Zane slid out of bed, headed to the window, and waved down to him and the entourage; his father wasn't one for long goodbyes. The horses' iron shod hooves clopped on the gravel, Prince Jace and the guards leading the royal convoy. The carriage and supply wagons followed close behind, their wheels clanking as they grinded their way forward.

Frustrated and bored, Zane sighed. He had plenty of things to do but lacked the motivation. After flopping onto his bed, he picked up his novel and read some more. A couple of hours passed, but he didn't even notice. It was quiet, peaceful, and he was engrossed in the book. After reading the last page, he closed it with a thump. "Now what to do," he muttered, climbing out of bed and putting the book back on the shelf.

Searching through the titles, he looked for another book to read. "Dark magic," he mused as he knelt. As he pried open the compartment, a musical ringing sounded, startling him and causing him to knock his hand on the wood. Grinding his teeth, he rubbed his sore hand and stood up. The ringing originated from an orb Zane had on his bookshelf. He used it as a bookend, as it was solid and sturdy. It emitted a blue glow that was steadily growing in intensity. He opened his door and addressed the guards in the hallway. "I am not to be disturbed under any circumstance."

One of the guards saluted. "As you command, my prince," he

replied, closing the door. Zane went back to his bookshelf and held the orb in front of his face. It was one half of the communication device he and Kyrene used. Zane hadn't heard from her in a while. Why would she be contacting him now? Had she actually acquired the demonic part of the *Val'Markyl*? Would he be able to complete the tome? There was only one way to find out. His hands shook slightly as he said a few words. The blue glow subsided, replaced with Kyrene's beautiful face. She was wearing her long black hair tied back in either a ponytail or a bun, Zane couldn't tell. She smiled as she saw him, her green eyes gleaming, highlighted by a pair of gold rimmed glasses.

"You took your sweet time." she said.

"Sorry, Kyrene. I was otherwise engaged." His hand was sore, and he'd have one hell of a bruise. He wasn't in the mood for her games, not today.

She looked concerned, like she could tell something was wrong. "Are you okay?"

"I'm fine. I just injured myself because I'm a klutz." He laughed, lightening the mood. "To what do I owe the pleasure?"

"The expedition team has returned. Unfortunately, it was a bust. I'm sorry, Zane." She smiled, trying to be positive. "On a brighter note, we've discovered the location of a magical sanctuary. Dark-magic runes are sealing the door, so it might take some time for us to get in. It's an exceptionally good sign, though, and it sounds promising."

"Thanks for the update." Zane felt despondent and depressed. It had been a slim chance at best, too good to be true. "I'll keep my fingers crossed. Hopefully we'll uncover it on the next expedition."

"Hopefully." She paused for moment then asked, "So is there anyone in your life at the moment?"

* * *

A knock came at the door. Talk about perfect timing. "Sorry, Kyrene. I have to go. Take care and we'll talk soon." She opened her mouth to say something, but Zane ended the connection and put the magical orb back in place. Leaning back down, he pulled out the two books on dark magic Kabel had given him. As he carefully replaced the backing on the compartment, another knock sounded. "Enter," he called out, carrying the books to his bed.

Smiling sheepishly, Millie entered with a tray. "Your lunch, my prince," she said, placing it on the table. It was a roll, freshly baked and full of chunks of roast beef, sliced tomato and crispy lettuce. Dripping from the top was a generous smothering of seasoned mayonnaise. A roast beef and salad roll. Not his favourite, but boy was he hungry. His stomach grumbled in response. Even though it was rather unappetizing, he devoured it, taking gulping mouthfuls. He washed it down with ale and left the plate and mug on the table for Millie to collect.

He grabbed one of the dark-magic books, then sat on his bed and began to read, silently mouthing the words to a spell and trying to memorise it. He then closed the book, tried to incant it, but failed. Frustrated, he hurled the book against the wall. He was too distracted, thinking about the *Val'Markyl*. It was pointless to try to study now. Exasperated and angry at himself, he grabbed the books and put them back into the secret compartment. "Guards," he called. The door opened with a creak. "Go get Sergeant Bear and Matthias." The sergeant had earnt the nickname of 'Bear' because of his demeanour and his stature. Zane didn't know his real name. He had always known him as the 'Bear'.
"Yes, my prince." One of the guards hurried off, his armour clanking down the hallway. A few minutes later, Zane heard the sergeant and Matthias arguing, wondering why Zane wanted them.

"But we haven't done anything wrong!" Matthias shrieked. The man was beside himself, panicking.

* * *

"Then we have nothing to worry about," the sergeant replied calmly.

A guard opened the door, and the two men crossed the threshold and approached Zane. "You summoned us, my prince?" As calm as he sounded before, the Bear was now sweating and appearing slightly nervous. Ironic, considering the size of the man. Bald and in his late thirties, he was a bear of a man, towering a full head above Zane. An exceptional fighter, he also was intimidating but well respected.

"I've heard that in your downtime you often drink and gamble with the other soldiers?"

"Yes, my prince. That's true, but—"

Zane held up his hand, halting the Bear in midsentence. "Good. I want you to teach me how to play Skirmish." Gambling was a first for him, something he was intrigued by. The sergeant beamed. "Guards, I'd like the two of you to join us as well."

"But we're on duty, my prince," one of them stammered.

Zane smiled. "Your duty is to protect me, correct?" They nodded. "Then protect me while we play cards." Grinning, they entered and closed the door.

"I'll explain the rules," the Bear said. "Matthias, you grab the cards and our purses." Matthias was a lean young man in his early twenties, with unkempt blonde hair. He had proven himself to be an exceptional fighter and a natural leader. Because of this he had just recently been promoted to Corporal. Beaming, he headed towards the door; but as he opened it, the sergeant addressed him again. "And Matthias, I know *exactly* how much is in my purse." Matthias gulped and nodded. Yes, the Bear was definitely intimidating.

* * *

"And Matthias," one of the guards added, "we also know how much *our* purses contain."

As Matthias hurried down the corridor, the sergeant and guards made themselves comfortable at the table. Zane walked over to his desk and muttered an incantation. Opening the drawer, he spied his letter to the Brotherhood. Underneath it was a couple of purses, each one was colour coded to represent which coins went in it. He reached in and pulled out a dark-blue purse, full to the brim with silver coins. He then closed the drawer, locked it, and joined the men at the table.

They all spoke at once, babbling as they tried to explain the rules to Zane. A moment later the door opened, and Matthias entered, juggling four jingling purses and a deck of cards. Standing graciously by the door, being a gentleman, he kept it open as Millie entered. That's where his chivalry stopped, though, as he smirked and ogled her breasts and arse. Embarrassed, she blushed and headed towards the table. Matthias continued to stare as he followed her. Sitting down, joining the group, he handed out the purses and placed the deck of cards in the middle of the table.

Millie sheepishly reached for the empty plate and mug. "I'll definitely have a piece of—" Matthias stopped midsentence as the sergeant kicked him in the shin, a warning for him to shut the hell up. The gesture had been hidden under the table, but Zane heard the loud thump. "What the fuck!" Matthias shouted, glaring at the sergeant. He was completely oblivious, even looked baffled when the sergeant nodded discreetly towards Zane. The big man was far from subtle, though, with the other guards laughing at Matthias's expense. Finally understanding, Matthias turned deathly pale.

"Our dear Millie here is off limits, Matthias. Is that understood?" Zane said, grinning like a dire wolf about to devour its prey. Matthias merely nodded, not daring to say a word. "Now, my dearest, could you please bring us a platter of food, along with some wine and ale?" She nodded, a gesture of both confirmation and thanks.

As she walked towards the door, Matthias finally decided to speak, grovelling and begging forgiveness. "My prince, I'm sorry. If I had known—" he started, flustered and stammering.

Zane interrupted him. "If you had known I was sleeping with her, you wouldn't have been such a blundering idiot. You were just lucky Sergeant Bear decided to save you from further embarrassment." Matthias nodded, refusing to comment. Millie smiled as she walked out the door.

"Yeah, well, in a moment, you'll all be moping like Matthias here because I'm about to win all your money," the sergeant said boldly, reaching for the deck of cards. He shuffled them like a pro, a man who'd had plenty of practise. "Let the games begin," he said, grinning as he rapidly dealt the cards. A quick study, Zane soon learnt the concept and the strategic elements of the game. It was fun and entertaining; he could see why the guards enjoyed it.

To their credit, when Millie returned, the guards were extremely polite. She placed the platter on the side of the table so it wouldn't intrude upon their game. In the middle of the tray sat a large bowl of a spiced sausage dip. Surrounding it was a sliced crusty loaf for dipping. In an instant, hands shot forward, aiming for the platter. While the guards stuffed their faces, talking around mouthfuls of food, Millie proceeded around the table, expertly filling their ale mugs to the brim without spilling a drop. She then sat on Zane's lap and poured him a glass of wine while subtly rubbing her buttocks against his groin. It wasn't long before she felt his hard, erect cock beneath her. After kissing him on the cheek, she then hopped up and left. It was a playful tease and a promise of what would come later.

The men grew increasingly loud. They were in their element, as this was their favourite pastime. They drank, laughed, and joked as one game ended and the next began. It was a revelation, a side of them Zane hadn't seen before, and allowed him to develop a rapport and get to know them on a personal level. They ended up playing a dozen games, some ending in a matter of minutes, while others were exciting and drawn out.

The men finally excused themselves, with Bear and Matthias leaving with most of the winnings. Zane expected they had rigged some of the games, but he was willing to let it go...this time at least. The other two guards repositioned themselves outside his door. It was the end of their shift, so they stood guard and talked quietly while waiting to be relieved. As Zane put his purse away, a knock came at the door. "Enter," he called out, sealing the drawer with its magical wards. Millie entered, smiling, carrying a tray with his dinner.

As he sat back down at the table, she placed a steaming bowl in front of him. Zane looked at it with distain. Stew. He hated stew. "Mum said if you don't eat it, there's no dessert," she said cheekily.

"I thought *you* were the dessert," he replied, pushing the bowl aside. He started to get up, only for Millie to firmly push him back into his seat. She moved the bowl in front of him again.

"Well!" she said. "If that's the case, you'd better eat up." Zane frowned. "Fine. How about I give you some motivation?" Slowly she began to undo her blouse. Zane watched for an instant before picking up the spoon and scooping a mound full of stew into his mouth. He rapidly chewed and swallowed before shovelling more into his mouth. He had to admit, tonight's stew wasn't half bad.

He left the bowl empty—hell, he even wiped up the gravy with a slice of bread. After gulping down the ale, he slammed the mug on the table and headed to the bed. Millie already lay under the covers, naked. She pulled back the blanket, inviting him to join her.

Zane woke with a start. Someone was banging on the door. He

climbed out of bed, put on his robe, and looked out the window. The stars sparkled, the bright moonlight illuminating the courtyard. Eleven guards waited below, mounted on their horses, which were neighing, eager to get going. One of the guards held the reigns of the captain's horse, the man who was now knocking at his bedroom door. "My prince?" Brenan called out.

Zane walked back to the bed and leaned over it. The captain knocked at the door again. Gently Zane traced a symbol on Millie's forehead and mumbled an incantation. Magic surged forth, and the symbol glowed briefly as it took effect, encompassing her and putting her into a coma-like sleep. "Enter," Zane called out, walking towards his desk.

Brenan walked in. He wore pitch-black plate armour without an identifying insignia on the surcoat. The armour had been fashioned discreetly for this very purpose so the guards couldn't be traced back to Zane. It was a mission of absolute secrecy. Strapped across his back were two ornate swords, their leather-bound handles sticking up above his shoulders. The man was an excellent fighter, proficient in dual wielding. Zane smiled warmly at his close friend.

"Sorry for the delay, Brenan. I had my hands full." Brenan looked at Millie and raised his eyebrows questioningly. "Ah, don't worry. She'll be completely oblivious to our business."

"So you used magic on her, Zane," he said, dismissing her and walking towards his prince. Being such a close friend, he was the only one who could get away with addressing him by his name. Gingerly Zane pulled out the letter he had written to the Brotherhood. It looked fine, untampered and still sealed. Again, he began to question things. Shaking his head, clearing it, he handed the contract to Brenan, the only man he trusted with such a document.

Because of the time restrictions and the secrecy behind the contract,

Zane had insisted on casting a portal. The group would arrive in Hemlock, stay overnight and then head out in the morning. Their destination was the Black Raven Inn, where the Brotherhood operative named Flow lived. Most people organised their contracts through the Brotherhood, but Zane had decided to go straight to the source. It was an unorthodox approach, but not unheard of. There was a chance that Flow would reject the contract, but he doubted it. He was offering an exuberant amount, one that she couldn't refuse.

Brenan put the letter in a satchel attached to his belt. "We can always ride, my prince. I wouldn't want to take you away from your vigorous activities." The captain grinned cheekily. Besides his brother Jace, Brenan was the only one who could get away with saying something like that.

Smirking, Zane rolled his eyes. "Don't worry, my friend. I plan on returning to my sexual activities after I cast the portal." With a laugh, he patted his friend on the shoulder. It was pure banter, as casting the portal would exhaust him; after casting it, he had every intention of snuggling up with Millie and sleeping.

"We'll head out first thing in the morning," Brenan said as they descended the staircase. "We'll leave early and travel through the forest. We should arrive at the Black Raven Inn by early tomorrow evening."

Zane nodded; for better or worse, there was no going back now. After opening the door for his prince, Brenan led them into the courtyard. Zane shivered despite his thick fur-lined robe. The sooner he cast the portal, the sooner he could go back indoors to the warmth of Millie and his bed.

He walked to the bucket in the middle of the courtyard. It was filled with blood from the cow that had been butchered earlier. After dipping his hand into the bucket, he drew thick red runes upon the courtyard. They glowed briefly after each one was traced, radiating power and magic. Standing up, Zane incanted the spell. Although his voice was barely a whisper, it carried across the courtyard. Energy emitted from the runes, sizzling, joining together and forming a large, sparkling blue vortex. A portal that would transfer the group directly outside the inn in Hemlock.

The portal had to be a place that the caster could visualise, had visited frequently, and Hemlock was such a place. Zane and his family had travelled there often, usually on holiday but also while his father had been on stately business. Zane staggered back, exhausted, but Brenan was there in an instant, supporting and steadying him. Wearily he nodded his thanks. "Safe travels my, friend." They clasped arms in a warm embrace before Brenan mounted his horse.

"And many wenches." Brenan laughed. It was the standard reply they shared. Nudging his horse's flanks, he urged it forward. The squad followed suit, and the horses' hooves clanked on the gravel as they galloped across the courtyard and entered the portal.

Chapter 11

Waking to the sound of splashing, Darla didn't know how long she had been unconscious. Was it hours or days? Judging by the position of the sun, though, it was early in the morning. Voices could be heard rising and lowering in pitch and volume. Her head throbbed as if she were suffering from a massive hangover, and she felt lethargic and achy. On the bright side, at least she no longer felt like a herd of horses had trampled her. She had to have been poisoned, but why? Darla left her eyes open a fraction, squinting but taking everything in. She controlled her breathing and remained motionless, feigning sleep.

Trying to concentrate, she isolated the conversations and focused on one that caught her attention. Two people were in an intense argument, trying to keep it contained so as not to attract attention. Little did they know that even at this distance Darla could hear every word. "Don't forget we helped you and your mutineers get this ship," Brigg said. So the bandits had helped some of the crew in a mutiny. This confirmed Darla's suspicions; they had wanted her out of the way, but they hadn't counted on her regenerative abilities. She planned to take advantage of the situation.

"And you forget who got you the inside information about Tyrak Gunderson's treasure," a stranger replied. "I still don't know why you wouldn't allow me and my men near the elves Jonah allowed aboard." The man sounded suspicious, suspecting Brigg was up to something. The elves...things were not boding well for them. Were they dead? Did they still have the Divinity Stone?

"I don't have to justify my reasons with you," Brigg snapped.

Darla vaguely recognised the second voice; it belonged to one of the crew. But who? She tried to recall where she had heard it, but her mind was muddled. Frustrated, she continued listening. She had heard stories about the fabled Gunderson treasure, and this conversation piqued her interest. Suddenly a scream sounded from within the ship. "Hopefully your man can get the treasure's location from the captain."

Brigg laughed. "He relishes torturing people. If anyone can get the location, it's him." A brief nod from the crew member and the conversation was over. The bandits finally had made their move. Slowly, so as not to attract attention, Darla slid her hand within the confines of her cloak. She wrapped her fingers around the hilt of one of her daggers and, with a gentle hiss, drew the blade forth. She cursed silently; she would have preferred the short sword. She had grown to like this weapon, but to reach for it would draw too much attention. Another splash, and her attention was drawn to two of the bandits.

She watched as they picked up another body. It was Lord Aldronin, who had been brutally tortured before having his throat cut. He had been stripped of his fancy clothes and all his belongings. This confirmed Darla's suspicions about being poisoned. The bandits had wanted her dead, unable to interfere. Darla cursed; she had tried to warn the lord, and now the bandits had the Divinity Stone. Swinging the corpse back and forth, they unceremoniously threw it overboard.

"Fuck," Darla muttered. This complicated things. She cursed again. Now she would have to steal the Divinity Stone again; she couldn't afford to leave it in Brigg's hands. God knows what he'd do with it. This contract had turned into a complete and utter cluster fuck.

It was only then that Darla's gaze was drawn to the frothing, bubbling water. The water around the ship was stained red, and amongst it, bobbing in the water, were numerous corpses. Darla immediately recognised the elves, all of whom had been stripped of their rich garb. Some of the crew, the ones loyal to the captain, were also amongst the corpses. She also noticed a pile of fur that was stained red, bobbing in the water. Jonas's dire wolf! Darla hoped that she was mistaken, that it was something else, but deep down, she knew she was right.

It was a feeding frenzy. The blood and the corpses had attracted the dygar, drawn to the blood with their extreme sense of smell. She heard them darting in, their powerful jaws tearing, snapping, and crunching on the flesh and bones of the corpses. There wouldn't be much left by the time they finished. Eighteen, nineteen, twenty, she counted, and they were the only ones she could see. God only knew how many there were under the boat or converging on their location. It was a recipe for disaster. "Those fucking morons!" Darla cursed. What were they thinking? They had attracted a school of dygar, and everyone knew dygar could attract larger predatory sharks or worse…a greater white crocark.

As the two bandits picked up another corpse, Darla spied Rayze holding his bloodied sword and staring right at her. The sword was unique, the blade was shiny and black, made from razor-sharp obsidian. "The Nightbringer," Darla mumbled. The sword was magical, an artefact like her short sword. She didn't know how she knew its name, but she did.

"Get a normal sword like mine, Rayze. That weapon of yours is unnatural," one of the bandits shouted. "It's evil as shit and gives me the heebie-jeebies."

"It's not the weapon you should fear," Rayze replied casually, "but the person who wields it." He smiled as the bandit shook his head and walked away. Resting the bloodied sword on his knee, he gave Darla seven quick signals: *Hold for now. Wait and be patient!* He then pulled a rag out of his jacket pocket and wiped down the blade. The rag was already stained with brownish red patches of dried blood from his previous victims. Darla didn't know whether Rayze was an ally or had his own agenda. Even so, he seemed to be helping her, at least for now. After adjusting the sword and bending it over his knee, he polished the edge vigorously. Darla subtly gave a nod, acknowledging the advice. She was happy to wait for now, but if the need arose, she was ready to act at a moment's notice.

Some curses drew Darla's attention; she recognised Jonas's voice instantly. He was battered and bruised, and his wrists were bound tightly behind his back. He was also broken, both physically and mentally. Even though his eyes were squinted from being bruised and swollen, Darla saw the redness in them. He had been crying and grieving for the loss of his crew and his beloved pet dire wolf. They had been butchered, murdered by the bandits. A big, cloaked man stood behind him, pushing him along.

"You traitorous bastard," Jonas said, addressing the man Brigg had been talking to. It was Jonas's second-in-command, Callum. Throwing his head back, Jonas spat a glob of bloodied spittle that shot forward, hitting Callum's face. The spittle slowly dribbled down, as without a word the chief casually wiped it off. He looked at it, smiled, then punched Jonas in the stomach. The dwarf captain doubled over, spitting up more bloodied phlegm. Callum pulled his arm back and punched him again, this time more forcefully. Jonas's knees buckled, but he stood firm, refusing to collapse. With a wicked grin he said, "Is that the best you can do?"

"I'm going to enjoy this," Callum replied, unleashing a flurry of punches in rapid succession.

The big, cloaked man with them chuckled, amused by the exchange. His hands were covered in fresh blood, which was also splattered onto his clothes. He showed no sign of injury, though. Grimly, Darla realised he was one of Jonas's torturers. This man was evil and sadistic, obviously taking great pleasure from torture.

"The only thing he had on him was this stupid, cryptic rhyme," the cloaked man said, confused.

Callum grabbed the parchment from the big man's grasp. "It's torn, you moron. Part of the rhyme is missing. How are we supposed to work out the treasure's location now, you idiot?" he shouted, throwing the parchment back at him. The big man glared at him with pure hatred. As he gritted his teeth and clenched his fists, his eyes darted towards his commander. It was the only thing forcing him to contain his rage.

"What happened, Bane?" Brigg asked. He remained calm and collected, his expression revealing nothing. The big man looked sheepish and hesitant. He was intimidated, genuinely afraid of Brigg and the repercussions that would follow.

"We found this parchment in a secret compartment of one of the captain's boots. As I pulled it out, though, his dire wolf lunged and tore off a chunk. It ate the fucking piece, then sat there smirking, mocking me." Bane grinned wickedly and drew a huge double-sided battle-axe from across his back. "That's why I chopped its fucking head off."

Darla saw red, her muscles tensed, and she clenched her teeth. She breathed deeply, trying to control her rage. The dire wolf was a kindred spirit; its death was needless and unwarranted. The only reason for it was this psychopath's sick pleasure. "I'm going to kill you for this," Darla whispered in a silent vow to herself and whatever gods were listening.

While the men were conversing, Jonas had been untying his restraints covertly. Finally free, he turned on Bane. "I'm going to kill you, you son of a bitch!" he shouted, fuming with rage. He lunged forward, driven by grief and revenge, but his legs betrayed him, giving out as he collapsed to the ground. "You killed my dire wolf," he whimpered.

An executioner ready to do his duty, Bane raised his battle-axe. He looked at Brigg for permission to kill the captain. Darla readied her dagger; she wasn't about to let Jonas die.

You will die as well if you intervene now. Rayze's hands were a blur as he continued the message. *Better to be patient. Wait and then exact your revenge.*

"No!" Brigg shouted. "If anyone should get the honour of killing our defiant captain, it should be the chief." It was a test to see if Callum had the nerve to do the deed himself— whether he had the balls to kill a friend, someone he respected and admired. Biting his lip and contemplating, Callum slowly drew a curved dagger from its sheath.

I can't let him die! Darla messaged back as her hand poked beneath her cloak and gripped the handle of her second dagger. With a gentle, silent hiss she drew it forth.

If you have a death wish, so be it! I can't afford to blow my cover.

* * *

Fuck your cover and your help, Darla thought. *I don't need either of them.* With that she sprang into action. One of her daggers spun through the air with expert accuracy. Callum started to plunge his dagger towards Jonas but stopped suddenly, the dagger slipping from his hand, as with a sickening thud Darla's dagger pierced through his neck. Shocked and confused, he tried to talk but only coughed up blood before toppling forward.

"How is she even alive?" Bane said, gawking at her. "I gave her enough poison to kill two grown men. I watched Callum give her the flask." That confirmed it; she had been poisoned—hell from the sounds of it, she should have been dead.

"Obviously you didn't give her enough," Brigg said sarcastically. "Kill her! Twenty gold coins to the person who brings me her head." *How insulting*, Darla thought. Her head was worth at least fifty gold coins. She drew the short sword from across her back, the runes sparkling a bright blue as three bandits raced towards her.

The swordsman and the axeman reached her first, while the third bandit played it cautiously and took a wide berth. Sticking to the railing, he kept his distance, and drawing his flail, he waited for an opportunity. Another two splashes in quick succession sounded, and with that the last of the corpses had been disposed of. Their job finished, the two bandits drew their weapons and hurried forward, quickly joining their flail-wielding comrade. Five bandits, all driven by desire, incentive, and greed. They had ambition and wanted a piece of the action, but most of all they wanted the twenty-gold-coin reward.

The axeman attacked first, swinging his blade in a wide arc while using his shield to block his body. Darla timed her swing, using the blade of the short sword not only to deflect the heavier weapon but also use the axeman's momentum against him. The man's arm swung in front of the swordsman, blocking him and preventing him from attacking. Ramming his shield, Darla pinned it against his body. Spinning, using it to brace herself, she pivoted to the side and swung. The short sword sliced through flesh and bone, cutting off the axeman's leg off at the knee. Screaming, he toppled onto the deck. Darla turned her attention to the swordsman. The axeman was no longer a problem; he would bleed out soon enough.

Midnight whinnied, warning her. The three bandits had moved, edging farther along the rail, trying to blindside her. Darla shifted position, ensuring the swordsman and the three bandits remained within her line of sight. The swordsman feinted, pretending to lunge and trying to find an opening. Darla saw it coming though; she wasn't so easily fooled. She kept her weapons poised as she waited for her own opportunity.

Movement in her peripheral vision had her turning to face the three bandits. The flail was being twirled, whirling in a blur of speed, but that wasn't what had attracted her attention. It was the monstrous beast behind the three bandits, which had erupted out of the water. The creature was a great white crocark—an adult, judging from its size and colouring. This species was local to the area, having adapted to the harsh, freezing climate. Its distant cousin the black crocark preferred the hotter climate and resided in the tropical parts of the world. Both were renown for being highly intelligent predators. Taking in its enormous fins, as well as its two massive heads, Darla estimated the creature to be at least thirty feet long. Its ability to propel itself out of the water was extraordinary.

Its black-and-white scales glistened in the spray of the water like a multitude of sparkling jewels. The crocark was breathtaking to watch. It opened its massive, elongated jaws, revealing rows of long razor-sharp teeth, demonstrating why it was one of the most feared oceanic predators. Caught between its teeth were dygar remains. It had eaten its entree and now planned to have the boat's passengers for its main course. As it pivoted its heads and turned gracefully in the air, its powerful jaws clamped shut. The elf's flail dropped to the deck, along with his arm. As the crocark's heads pulled away, the bandit was ripped in two. It happened so quickly the bandits—and Darla—didn't see it coming.

As gravity took hold, the crocark began to drop backwards into the ocean. Its twin heads collided with the railing, shattering it and causing the other two bandits to fall overboard. Planting her feet and keeping her balance, Darla went with the rocking as the ship lurched sideways before righting itself. Three of the mutineers weren't so lucky. One was thrown from the crow's nest, while the other two slid across the deck and hit the railing before being flung over the side. There was silence. The crocark could be seen circling the boat, its fin gliding through the water, announcing its presence. It was then that Darla noticed the degree of damage. As well as the shattered railing, there was a large, splintered hole in the deck. On top of that, Darla heard cracking and a steady trickle of water. The ship was slowly sinking.

She turned to face the swordsman while trying to block out the mutineers' screams. The swordsman lunged, but Darla deflected the blow. The swordsman recovered immediately, spinning into a sideways slash. Sparks flew with the scraping of metal against metal as Darla blocked the stroke, halting him before deflecting it. She had been forced onto the defensive, retreating and giving ground with each blow.

The ship was beginning to slant. More cracking sounded, louder now, followed by more trickles of water. The swordsman attacked with an overhead cut, and stepping back, Darla deflected the blade to the side. The deck creaked, cracking slightly, and Darla realised with a sudden certainty that she had backed up towards the hole. She had run out of room and had nowhere to go.

Grinning, the swordsman prepared for the killing blow. He raised his sword but halted in mid-swing. Loud arguing had distracted him, a disagreement involving his comrades. Brigg and three of the crew stood in front of a long, eight-man lifeboat. The three crewmen blocked it, and a heated argument had ensued. Bane stood next to his captain, silent and deadly, Brigg's personal enforcer. With a hiss, two of the crewmen drew their weapons. Things were about to get bloody.

"I'm going to enjoy this," Bane said with a wicked grin. He was like a little boy in a candy store, enjoying killing far too much. It was no wonder Brigg kept him around. Bane reacted immediately, protecting his captain. In a heartbeat, one of the crewman's heads was lobbed clean off. With a flick of his wrist, he then reversed the stroke, angling it down and slicing through the other crewman's arm at the elbow. Blood sprayed across the lifeboat and the deck. The ruckus was settled as the remaining crewmembers promptly exited the wooden lifeboat.

One of them even went as far as to jump over the side into the sea. The man obviously thought his chances were better against the dygar and the crocark. Two of them helped their wounded comrade, dragging him screaming across the deck. Blood dripped over the wooden planks as the two of them held him up and made their way to the other lifeboat. They had tried to staunch the wound by tying a thick piece of cloth around his shoulder, but their friend was weak and still losing blood. They needed to cauterise the wound, but they didn't have either the means or know-how. *He's as good as dead*, Darla thought. Gripping his axe in one hand, Bane helped Brigg into the rocking lifeboat. All the while, Brigg clutched the piece of parchment and the Divinity Stone. Darla rocked unsteadily, almost falling into the gaping hole. In her mind, she heard a desperate call from the Divinity Stone. It was urging her to steal it back, protecting itself.

Thanks to Bane, the bandits had successfully commandeered one of the lifeboats. Rayze was the next to climb aboard. He waved away the big man's assistance then sheathed his sword across his back and agilely climbed into the rocking boat. Five other bandits hurried across the deck, encumbered as they carried a large chest. After placing it at Bane's feet, they quickly climbed in. Two of them grumbled as Brigg passed them an oar, much to Rayze's amusement.

Darla smirked at the swordsman. "Looks like your friends have abandoned you," she sneered.

"They'd never do that, you bitch," the swordsman screamed, but Darla noticed his voice wavered slightly. He was beginning to realise that his comrades only cared about themselves. Darla almost felt sorry for him—that is, until he swung wildly at her, driven by unbridled rage. It was what she wanted; she had goaded him on purpose. As she leaned back precariously over the hole, the broken decking creaked under her weight. The blade passed over her body as she dodged it easily.

Darla sprang with the agility of a cat, righting herself and surprisingly the swordsman. Momentarily shocked, he hadn't had time to recover, and Darla took full advantage of this, as lightning fast she slashed with her sword. The short sword sliced through leather and flesh, severing the man's muscle and tendons. As he was unable to hold it, the sword dropped from his useless hand. It was time to finish this. Stepping forward, Darla drove her dagger through his throat. With a spray of blood, the blade erupted out of the back of his neck. Slumping forward, the swordsman coughed up blood before dropping dead.

Blood dripped from the dagger and the short sword, leaving a spotted trail in Darla's wake as she ran towards the staircase. She watched out of the corner of her eye as Bane carefully lifted the large chest. His muscles tensed and bulged, but although cumbersome, it wasn't overly heavy for him. As the lid flicked open, a sparkling caught Darla's attention: the glitter of gold, jewels, and other merchandise.

The bandits had been busy. While the crewmembers had been prepping and organising the lifeboats, some of them had taken advantage of the situation and plundered the ship. Two of the bandits abandoned their oars and grabbed the side of the chest. Struggling slightly, they carefully placed it between them. Holding the two support ropes, Rayze braced both of his feet against the side of the small boat and grunted, preparing himself for what would come next. Holding onto the sides of the boat, the juggernaut of a man clumsily climbed on board.

Darla sprinted, increasing her pace as she swung onto the staircase and took them two steps at a time. The boat rocked as Bane fought to maintain his balance. Darla leapt down the rest of the steps, hitting the lower deck and breaking the impact by landing in a roll. Then she sprang back onto her feet. With her goal in sight, her feet pounded across the deck as her eyes focused on one thing: the Divinity Stone.

The rocking of the lifeboat subsided as Bane maintained his balance. Stretching his arm out, he reached for the pulley release switch. The small boat lurched unsteadily. "Will you please hurry up?" Rayze asked politely, gritting his teeth as he fought to keep the support ropes as taut as possible. Bane grunted, stretching, his fingers brushing against the switch. It was frustrating; he was just out of reach. He noticed movement: that bitch assassin was closing in; he had to hurry. "Fuck this," he yelled angrily, swinging his axe.

The locking mechanism for the pulley release switch snapped in two. The rope rapidly untwirled, and in an instant, the boat disappeared. Sprinting forward the last few metres, Darla dived and grabbed the course rope. She skidded across the deck, her momentum slowing but also threatening to throw her over the railing. Bracing her feet against the rail, she ground her teeth together and bit back the pain as her shoulders were jarred, almost ripping out of their sockets. The rope became taut, halting abruptly, and very slowly, using her preternatural strength, she began to haul the boat back up.

"Seven hells! Who the fuck is this woman?" asked one of the bandits. Darla didn't know which one, as she didn't recognise the voice. The boat was gently rocking, knocking against the hull as it slowly rose.

* * *

"Bane," Brigg said calmly, an order and a request. Bane swung his axe, slicing through the rope and dropping them to the sea below. With a splash the bandits were drenched, but they remained safely inside the boat. Darla collapsed onto the deck with a thud, the loose, cleanly cut rope in her hands. The bandits had escaped. The ship was lopsided, sinking rapidly, and she was about to die.

This wasn't the way she had expected to die, and although she accepted the cards she'd been dealt, she desperately tried to think of a way out of it. As hard as she tried, though, she couldn't come up with a solution. A tap on her shoulder startled her, disrupting her train of thought. She turned to see Jonas smiling at her. "Thank you for saving me, lass. Now let me return the favour."

Whistling, he led her up the stairs towards the area where she had slept. Midnight whinnied in greeting, and as Darla walked over to pat him, he nuzzled her affectionately. Confused, Darla watched as Jonas lifted a plank of wood to reveal a secret compartment. Leaning inside, he reached down and twisted, opening a small door that revealed a wooden ladder leading into the hold. No wonder Jonas had suggested this location; cunningly he had misled her, and she had unknowingly guarded one of his secrets.

Darla didn't know what she was looking at. It looked mechanical, some kind of contraption. It was like a metal bubble with glass windows, large enough to fit three dwarves. On each side were two large metal cylinders with what looked like a metal flower inside each of them. Its petals were spread out encompassing the inside in a curved, aerodynamic pattern. "This is my pride and joy," Jonah said. "It's called the Big Bubble, my submersible for underwater exploration. I mainly use it for finding sunken treasures and artefacts. I never thought I'd have to use it to escape my own ship." He laughed weakly, an attempt at humour even at this dire time. "There's room enough for both of us, and—"

* * *

Darla interrupted him. "You go. I can't abandon Midnight." Jonas nodded, teary-eyed at leaving her behind but understanding her situation and respecting her decision. They firmly clasped hands. "Until we meet again!" he said before climbing down the ladder and leaving her to her fate. *That'll probably be in the afterlife*, Darla thought. Things were looking grim; the ship was half sunken, and the crocark was circling it. She heard a splash, and the enormous creature suddenly disappeared, submerging underwater.

Jonas entered the Big Bubble and closed the hatch. He climbed into a cushioned seat, strapped himself in and waved at her. Darla didn't see the wave or the tears streaming down Jonas's face. She was too busy scanning the water for the crocark. A moment later, she located the source of the splash. The crewmen had disposed of a body; their one-armed comrade had bled out and now lay face down, floating in a pool of bloodied water. This came as no surprise to Darla; the wound had been fatal.

Then a giant fin emerged, gliding through the water, beelining straight towards the crewmen's boat. The crocark ploughed into the lifeboat with the force of a battering ram. The small boat shattered in half, flinging its occupants into the water. Panicked, they started swimming towards the shore. One by one their bodies vanished below the murky water as the crocark continued its massacre. Meanwhile, the bandits rowed frantically—even Bane looked nervous; one might even say slightly scared. Brigg shouted orders while scanning the water for the crocark. Once again it had disappeared below the water. He didn't have to wait long; wide-eyed, he watched fearfully as the fin re-emerged from the water and headed straight towards them.

Jonas pushed a button, and a moment later, grinding loudly, a hatch on the bottom of the hull opened. Water flooded into the chamber, and the submersible began to sink, the water lapping against its sides. It was then that Darla noticed the absence of the crocark; it had disappeared once again into the murky depths. The bandits looked baffled as they continued rowing towards the shore;

somehow they had survived the ordeal. "Oh, fuck," Darla muttered, cursing as she realised what Jonas had inadvertently done, oblivious of the repercussions. He had not only saved the bandits, but he also had given the crocark a beacon, attracting it to their location.

There was no sign of its giant fin anywhere. Where was it? A humming sounded, soft but growing in intensity, as the petals began to spin, propelling the bubble forward. It slowly moved towards the hatch. The hatch with its murky water leading into the ocean's depths. Murky water with a large shadow lurking within it. A shadow that was growing bigger as it shot upwards towards the hatch's opening. It was the crocark!

Darla looked around for something to stop this massive predator. She spotted the rope tying the sails to the mast, sturdy and thick but lacking any weight. Then she noticed the anchor, hooked on the railing. *Perfect!* Sheathing her sword, she ran over, unhooked the anchor, and began to uncoil the chain. The crocark's formidable tail swished back and forth, propelling it upwards like a giant underwater missile. Holding the heavy anchor like a two-handed weapon, Darla ran towards the hatch. As the crocark neared, it opened its mouths wide. There was only one thing she could do. The crocark was about to tear the bubble apart, its razor-sharp teeth easily able to tear through the steel hull. Its powerful jaws would then crush the submersible. Concentrating, Jonas continued to manoeuvre the Big Bubble, still oblivious to the underwater threat.

A sitting duck, Jonas was closing in on the hatch. Darla dived forward, holding the massive anchor above her head. Rearing up, its mouths opened wide, the crocark erupted with a spray of water just as Darla came crashing down with the anchor. She swung the anchor as hard as she could, straight into one of the crocark's mouths. As the beast bit down, the fluke of the anchor pierced both parts of the crocark's jaw and erupted with a spray of blood. The crocark thrashed wildly, trying to free itself as it dropped backwards into the water. With a screech the submersible halted in its tracks. A shaken

Jonas nodded his thanks; Darla had just saved his life... again.

As the chain quickly unravelled, Darla grabbed hold of it and tried to pull it taut. It whipped back and forth, shattering the planking around the hatch. Holding the chain firmly, Darla dived for cover. Jonas quickly turned the wheel, reversing the submersible. Water sprayed around them. Then the chain went limp, and all was silent. Cracking sounded, and then suddenly the planking snapped and the Big Bubble disappeared.

The chain suddenly went taut and pulled Darla towards the hatch. The crocark was on the move, going after the submersible. Darla tried to brace herself but failed, sliding across the wet planks. It felt like her arms were about to be ripped out of their sockets. She screamed, gritting her teeth, biting through the pain. Shutting out the pain, she tapped into her lycanthropy. It surged through her like a wave, elongating and strengthening her muscles. The crocark was nearly upon the submersible, its tail swishing rapidly, propelling it forward. The Big Bubble moved slowly; although Jonas had cranked it to full speed, it was no match against this sleek, deadly predator. Darla pulled on the chain and watched, horrified, as the crocark's jaws clamped shut...and barely missed.

The crocark thrashed wildly, but it was no use; Darla had halted the creature in its tracks. She watched as the Big Bubble escaped, propelling itself through the water towards the safety of the shore. The chain went loose, dropping to the ground. The crocark had forgone chasing the Big Bubble; Jonas was safe. Instead, it had turned its attention towards something else: her!

Darla let go of the chain and leapt onto the ladder just as the crocark erupted through the bottom of the ship. Water gushed in, drenching her clothes. Holding on tightly, she climbed up the ladder to the deck. The lower deck had sunk and was barely visible below the murky water. The planks were wet with puddles, and within moments the vessel would be completely underwater. The ship lurched, throwing Darla off her feet, as the crocark erupted through the deck. The rear mast fell, narrowly missing her as she scrambled out of the way. Like a fallen tree, the mast crashed to the deck and shattered it.

Darla climbed out from under the sail. She had been lucky, calculating and positioning herself accordingly. She had avoided the mast, positioning herself in such a way that she only got smothered by the sail. Throwing the rope off her, she looked up as Midnight neighed nervously. She was floating on a section of the deck—some partly shattered planks—with a section of the mast lying next to her. Another neigh. Midnight called anxiously to her as he floated away on another section. She had to reach him, had to save her friend. In between them though, gliding menacingly through the water, was the crocark.

The distance was too great; even with her lycanthropy, she wouldn't make it. She had to try, though. Once again tapping into her lycanthropy, Darla harnessed its power and elongated and strengthened her leg muscles. She backed up to the edge and prepared herself. Every second she waited, Midnight floated farther and farther away. Time was of the essence; she had to do this now. "It's okay. I'm coming, boy," she said, sprinting forward. She stopped abruptly as a shadow loomed over her and roared. A roar she recognised.

The wyvern hovered above her, majestic and staring at her with its intelligent eyes. "Will you help me?" she asked, pleading; it was her only chance. The wyvern nodded. Darla was speechless. Did the wyvern understand her? She shook her head, clearing it; she wasn't about to question things. She sprang into action, looping the rope around her arm and cutting it free from the sail. With one end she made a loop and tied a knot, turned it into a lasso. After swinging it over her head, whirling it faster and faster, she let it fly. It soared towards the wyvern, on target, then fell short, splashing in the ocean. Midnight neighed nervously as he drifted farther away.

* * *

"I'm coming, boy," Darla said, kneeling. It was a promise she planned to keep. She quickly pulled the lasso back towards her. Spraying water everywhere, she swung it again. The loop connected, landing limply on the wyvern's foot; the slightest movement would knock it off. With a flap of its mighty wings, the wyvern roared, rising slightly in the sky. The movement helped the loop slide over the wyvern's ankle. Was the wyvern helping her? Surprised, Darla pulled the loop taut, securing it. Holding on tightly, she leapt off the planks just as the giant fin glided past.

Darla swung effortlessly through the air, clinging tightly to the rope, and closed in on Midnight's platform. She was going to make it! Then, with a spray of water, the crocark erupted out of the water. One of its mouths was open wide, while the other was clamped shut with the anchor through it. Part of the chain was still attached to the anchor; where the rest of it was, God only knew. She watched as the razor-sharp teeth rose to meet her. There was nothing she could do —she was committed, swinging straight into its path.

Flapping its wings, the wyvern deviated its course slightly, saving her in the process. Darla took full advantage of the situation, bringing her knees up to her chest, The crocark's head turned, its jaws wide-open as its razor-sharp teeth prepared to bite off her head. Darla felt its breath on her face, smelled what it had eaten. She kicked out with all her might, her boots slamming into its side. Then the crocark's mouth snapped shut.

It missed her by inches, getting nothing but air. The power of her kick had knocked it farther aside. It had not only put her out of harm's way, but it also had positioned the crocark in the firing line of the wyvern. The wyvern opened its mouth and let loose a crackling lightning ball. It was point-blank; it couldn't miss. The lightning ball slammed into the crocark's side, sending sparks of energy radiating across its body. Shocked, it spasmed before crashing back into the water. It wasn't dead, just stunned, providing Darla with a moment's respite.

* * *

She landed on Midnight's platform and gave him an affectionate hug. The wyvern roared, alerting Darla that the crocark had disappeared into the murky depths of the ocean. The beast had seen what the wyvern was capable of and wasn't about to make the same mistake. "Sit, boy!" Darla instructed, as she firmly tied the rope to the railing. "We're about to go for a ride." Sitting, Midnight shook his head and neighed as if to say, *What the hell have you gotten us into now?*

Flapping its wings, the wyvern took off, flying towards the shore. The platform immediately skipped across the water, leaving a trail of spray in its wake. "Hell, yeah!" Darla screamed; she was exuberant, in her element and loving this. A nervous neigh sounded behind her. "It's okay. You'll be fine—" she said, but she didn't get to finish as Midnight gave a more insistent neigh. Concerned, Darla turned around. The crocark had re-emerged, its giant fin gliding through the water behind them...and it was close.

The crocark raised its functional head and opened its mouth. The creature was closing in. Grabbing the rail and leaning across, Darla swerved the platform just as the crocark's jaws snapped shut. Wood shattered as the crocark bit into the corner of the platform. Darla continued to swerve, skipping across the water, weaving from left to the right. The crocark matched them, swerving and sticking to them like glue as it continually altered its course. Raising its head and opening its mouth, it was about to take out a chunk from the middle of the platform, right where Midnight was situated. Its mouth closed, its teeth tearing into...nothing!

Skipping across the water, with a steady stream of spray, the platform gradually increased its lead. Their speed had increased, the wyvern's powerful wings angled back as it entered a wind current. The wyvern dove down, banking up with a flap of its powerful wings as it soared just above the water. Darla saw the crocark's massive tail swish back and forth, propelling it as its fin glided through the water. This was far from over—the crocark was slowly gaining ground, and the race was on.

* * *

The wyvern soared upwards, and the platform slowed. The crocark was rapidly catching up. The wyvern glided, roaring as it soared overhead. The crocark opened its mouth again; it was so close that Darla could see bits of dygar in its teeth. Then the wyvern entered another air current and dived again. The platform increased in speed again. It was as if they were playing a deadly game of cat-and-mouse.

They were approaching the shore, but they had slowed, with the wyvern soaring upwards again. The crocark was almost upon them. It was going to be close! "Up, boy," Darla commanded. Midnight obeyed, standing immediately. They were a team and he trusted her explicitly. Darla untied the rope from the railing and mounted Midnight. After positioning him, she whistled to the wyvern, who responded, turning its head to see what she wanted. Darla pointed, and it nodded its confirmation. The crocark opened its mouth wide.

The wyvern swerved, changing course and rotating the platform. The crocark's mouth snapped shut, narrowly missing them again and tearing another chunk out of the platform. Cracking sounded, starting from the bite mark and spreading like a spider web. The platform was about to tear apart. Darla kicked the stirrups into the side of Midnight, urging him forward.

Midnight soared through the air and landed gracefully on the shore. Behind them the platform shattered, breaking apart to a pile of floating debris. The crocark swam off, disappearing back into the depths of the ocean. Darla was safe and back on dry land. The bandits' lifeboat had been discarded, abandoned in a hurry. She could tell by their footprints that they had fled into the forest. They'd had a decent head start, but Darla had one thing they didn't: a horse.

* * *

Chapter 12

Darla rode through the forest with a blanket wrapped tightly around her. She had briefly stopped and changed into dry garments. Water dripped from her saddlebag, which contained her soaking-wet clothes, leaving a small trail in the snow. The thought of resting and drying them by an open fire had tempted her, but the bandits had enough of a lead; she couldn't afford to stop.

She didn't possess the exceptional tracking skills elven rangers had, but then again, she didn't need to. The bandits had opted for speed instead of stealth, leaving a trail even a blind person could follow. She passed another broken branch and a semi-trampled bush. A roar caught her attention, and she looked up to see the wyvern flying overhead. It had spotted something and was guiding her to it. Darla deviated from the path, and guided by the wyvern, she led Midnight into the forest.

It wasn't long before the trees and brush thinned out and she led Midnight onto Farrew Road. It was one of the major roads within the Quendath Kingdom, leading from the Blood Road and roaming through the elven kingdom, all the way to the Galthezamer Bridge. The road then continued through the snow-covered plain and connected to a large tunnel that weaved through the Bloodgar Mountains before eventually leading to the dwarven capital of Holguard. It was a wide, well-travelled road, but judging from the recent footprints on the snow-covered gravel, the bandits were heading towards the Blood Road. This functioned as a border between the elven and the human kingdoms and led to the Black Raven Inn.

As soon as Darla rounded the corner, she saw the bodies, seven of them scattered across the road. They had been recently killed; their blood still fresh, staining the snow. A moan caught her attention. By the gods, one of them was alive! She dismounted, grabbed the reins, and led Midnight to the survivor. He was a middle-aged man with thinning hair, a well-groomed beard, and expensive clothes. His stomach had been sliced open, and he was desperately trying to hold his entrails inside. His face was deathly white. He was dying a slow agonizing death. "Help me please," he pleaded to her.

Dismounting Midnight and leaving him by the side of the road in the cover of trees, Darla approached the man. He coughed up a copious amount of blood and clearly didn't have long to live. "What happened?" she asked. She had a good idea what happened, but she wanted confirmation.

"Bandits attacked. They stole my cart, the horses, my chest, and my merchandise. They even killed my guards." Darla muttered a curse as the dying man went on. "I overheard them. They were arguing, thought I was dead. They finally agreed, said something about hightailing it to the Black Raven Inn. If you hurry, you and your elvish friends can still catch them." He wheezed, coughing up more blood, and then there was silence. The merchant was dead.

Darla was baffled. What the hell was he talking about? Elves? Was he delirious? Then, with a sickening feeling, she realised. Her hands slid underneath the blanket, reaching for her daggers. She spun, throwing the blanket to the ground, drew the blades in a heartbeat, and halted. Half a dozen elves stood behind her—scouts, judging by their dress. She had been distracted, talking to the merchant, and didn't hear them approach. Three were armed with bows, their arrows nocked and pointed straight at her. The remaining three held swords, standing guard and protecting the archers. On their surcoat was an emblem she recognised all too well: that of Lord Dellavenor!

"We were told you'd be here," the elf who appeared to be their captain said, raising his sword. "That you had massacred a merchant and his guards." He shook his head disdainfully. "All because you wanted to steal from him, like you did from our lord. You stole the merchant's chest, merchandise, cart, even his horses." Darla couldn't believe it; the bandits had sold her out, known she would be following them, and planned it accordingly. It was a masterstroke, perfectly executed. She had underestimated them.

"If I'm responsible for this, Captain, where are the merchant's belongings?" She waved her arms and shrugged for emphasis.

"You probably hid them in the forest before returning to the scene of your crime." The captain looked smug. "Our informant told us as much."

"And if you believe that, you're a fucking moron," Darla replied.

The captain motioned to another elf, one with an ornate horn strapped to his waist. Nodding, the elf raised the horn and put it to his lips. He blew, and a deep rumbling sound echoed throughout the forest. The captain smirked again. "Lord Dellavenor wants the honour of killing you himself. He's going to make you suffer, beg for your life. You'll be lucky—" The captain didn't get to finish his sentence as a lightning ball plummeted down and hit him square in the chest.

The wyvern dived, soaring towards the ground before levelling out and flying over the elves. Crouching, making themselves less of a target, the elven archers tracked the winged beast, their bows following its flight path. Well trained, they wouldn't release an arrow until they had a perfect shot. The archers posed a great threat to the wyvern, their barbed arrows designed for taking down such creatures. Needing to take these archers out quickly, Darla ran straight at the middle swordsman.

Distracted by the wyvern, he didn't see her coming. She leapt into the air and punched the elf in the elbow joint. It was one of the weakest parts of the armour, designed so the elf was protected but also had full flexibility of his arm. The joint shattered, and his arm hung at an obscure angle. As the sword dropped to the ground, Darla followed through with a knee. It connected with the elf's sternum, shattering several ribs, and sending him flying backwards into the archer behind him.

Staggering, the archer released the bowstring, shooting the arrow high into the air. The shot was askew, going wide. Darla landed and immediately let loose with both her daggers, sending them spinning through the air. They hit their targets with meaty thuds. With a clatter of their bows, the archers dropped dead. The remaining archer had recovered and was hastily nocking another arrow. The swordsman who had been protecting him was wheezing badly. Darla surmised that one of his broken ribs had punctured his lung. He wouldn't be fighting again anytime soon, which only left one more immediate threat.

The remaining swordsman charged in. Reaching across her back, she drew the short sword. With a scrape of metal, she deflected the sword to the side then brought up her arm, elbowing the swordsman in the nose. Blood sprayed, splattering his helmet, as with a loud crack his nose broke. Unfazed, continuing the assault, he brought his sword swinging around.

Darla stepped in and grabbed his gauntleted wrist, halting the swing. The swordsman grunted as he desperately tried to cut this woman down. Unrelenting, Darla held it firmly, immobilising his arm. She then brought the short sword swinging across and cut the elf's arm off at the elbow. Following through, she rammed the short sword into his chest. The elf opened his mouth—whether it was to scream or merely say something, Darla didn't know. After a moment of silence, blood trickled out of his mouth, and he fell dead to the ground.

The remaining archer had fired a couple of arrows, purposely missing, guiding the wyvern to a position in the open, a spot that suited him. The bowstring drawn back, aimed precisely, he was about to make the kill shot. With the scraping of bone, Darla pulled the short sword free and hurled it at the archer. His fingers loosened, releasing the bowstring with a twang. The arrow shot forward only to drop short as Darla's sword sliced through the bowstring, snapping it in two. Continuing its trajectory, the short sword then pierced the archer's light leather armour, slamming into his chest and puncturing his heart.

Darla looked up as the wyvern roared and nodded its thanks. Smiling, she waved. "Looks like we have a new friend, Midnight." The horse stared at her and neighed decisively as if to say, *Just fucking great!* Darla laughed as she pulled the short sword free and began to clean it. Not even nicked, the blade was still in perfect condition. Was it due to the enchantments and the ancient, powerful magic with which it was infused? Darla had no idea, but she planned to investigate it.

After sheathing the short sword, she collected her daggers and sighed. The blades were nicked and needed a good polish. That would have to wait, though. She sheathed them and walked back towards Midnight. Whether it was the wyvern's roar or the faint twangs she heard, she didn't know. Regardless, she dived, spraying up snow as she rolled. One after another, arrows shot past her, embedding themselves in the nearby trees with a showering of bark. Lord Dellavenor and his army had arrived.

Crouched, Darla sprinted towards Midnight. More arrows shot past, narrowly missing her. Midnight neighed nervously, pawing at the ground, ready to get going. The elves were advancing, firing in waves. She took cover as more arrows rained down. She was pinned down with nowhere to go. Just then she noticed a group of them branch off; they were trying to outflank her.

More elves emerged from the forest, dressed in mottled browns and greens—camouflage colours to help them blend into the forest. A few to begin with and then more, a large group, organised and disciplined. *Fuck*, she thought; she was surrounded, out of options. Then, without a word, the newcomers raised their bows and fired. Their arrows soared past her, hitting Dellavenor's troops with deadly accuracy.

With a battle cry, more elves emerged from the forest in a thundering blaze of glory: light cavalrymen, riding horses, their barbed lances lowered for their deadly charge. Unlike their archers, they wore the emblem of their house for all the world to see. Darla noticed the highly detailed silver stitching of a dragon, the emblem of the royal elven house. At the lead of the charge, shouting maniacally, was Prince Velander.

The prince had a whole company of elves, elite soldiers, well trained and disciplined. The attack was organised and well executed, leaving Dellavenor's troops in total disarray, floundering and fleeing for their lives. The road and surrounding forest had just become a battle zone, and Darla was caught smack bang in the middle of it. Midnight neighed nervously yet again, but Darla didn't dare run from cover. Instead, she bore witness as Dellavenor's army was massacred. Elves were cut down in sadistic ways, they were maimed, left to suffer in agony, while they slowly died an excruciatingly painful death. Their behaviour, these acts even appalled Darla. There was war and there was bloodlust, but these were atrocities. And worst of all, the prince was committing them.

At the end of it, the battlefield was littered with bodies, and Lord Dellavenor was left standing before the prince. "Where is the Divinity Stone?" the prince roared maniacally, drawing a jagged, curved dagger from his belt. Was it the bloodlust from battle that had caused the prince to behave like this? No, Darla told herself, there was something about the prince, something that scared even her. Slowly, without making a sound, she stood and edged towards her horse. Dellavenor screamed, the sound high pitched, full of fear and agony. Darla refused to stop. She had seen enough. The wyvern was circling above, monitoring, making sure she was okay. "Where is the Divinity Stone?" the prince yelled again.

Grabbing the reigns, she leapt into the stirrup and mounted Midnight. As she mounted, her satchel flew open, revealing the twin to the Divinity Stone. "It's there!" Dellavenor cried, pointing. Turning in the saddle, Darla took everything in: the open satchel, Lord Dellavenor pointing at her and the prince foaming at the mouth like a madman. Two elves stood guard over Dellavenor as the prince mounted his horse, ready to charge, ready to cut Darla down and retrieve the gem.

Darla heard a sizzling sound as the air radiated with energy. She turned Midnight just in time, a moment before the ground between the two groups exploded, spraying snow everywhere. The lightning ball was massive; the wyvern clearly had stored up a huge amount of energy to fire it. Soaring back into the air, the winged beast nodded and smiled at her, gloating, proud of what it had done. Flapping its wings, it then soared down the road, leading the way.

* * *

Darla didn't stop to look at the decimation the wyvern had caused. The cover fire the creature had given had sown confusion amongst the elves, providing her with an opportunity to escape. Midnight didn't need any encouragement; he was off like a shot. As they galloped down Farrew Road, spraying up snow and gravel, she heard the horses behind them giving chase.

She listened to the hoof beats, concentrating, determining how many horses there were. Four—no, five. A small part of the cavalry, and from the sound of it, Prince Velander was among them. Swerving abruptly, she veered off the road onto a thin dirt trail. The elves followed close behind, the prince leading the way as they rode in single file. A couple of arrows buzzed past her, lodging into trees with a spray of bark. As good as the elves were, Darla made herself a near-impossible target. Dodging past trees and leaping over bushes, she led the way, knowing exactly where she was going. Midnight erupted from the tree line into a small grass clearing that ended with a two-metre ridge. Nudging his flanks, Darla urged him into a gallop, and he ran straight off it.

Midnight landed with a skid. Whinnying in exhilaration, he continued at a gallop down the small hill. It was an exercise they'd often performed since he was a foal, one he had mastered and loved doing. The small royal cavalry group followed without hesitation. Prince Velander's horse landed, skidding and righting itself before continuing the pursuit. Two of the other horses landed awkwardly, breaking their front legs and toppling forward. Unable to free themselves, the elven riders were crushed as their horses rolled down the hill in a tangled mess.

Two down. Three to go. Darla huddled down in her saddle; she wasn't out of this yet. Arrows whizzed past from the three remaining riders. They entered the next section of the forest, Darla navigating Midnight slowly between the trees. Dodging between them, they made an impossible target. Darla listened and waited. The elves were right behind her. Midnight turned, dodging a tree, as multiple arrows soared forth, Bark sprayed over Darla as all three arrows thudded into it. At this range she made an easy target. It was all part of her plan, though.

It had been a gamble, but it had paid off. At this range, the temptation had been too much, and the elves had taken the bait. Now they were distracted, nocking more arrows and not paying full attention to their surroundings. Swerving, taking a corner wide, Darla grabbed the end of a large branch. As Midnight charged past, the branch bent back. Darla listened as it groaned in protest, and then she let go.

The branch swung back full force, smashing into two of the riders. They were oblivious to what Darla had done until it was too late. The blow flung the riders from their saddle, leaving them on the ground severely wounded, while their horses frolicked a short distance away. *Four down. One to go.* Of course, it had to be the prince. Somehow, he had evaded the swinging branch and was still relentlessly pursuing her.

Nudging Midnight's flanks, Darla increased her speed. The trees were a blur as she weaved between them. Darla swerved onto a narrow winding trail. As she and Midnight charged down the path, she was unable to lose the prince. He had given up using his bow, though; every time he had tried to shoot, she'd turn a corner, teasing him, constantly eluding him. Instead, he drew his sword, screaming that he would torture her, making her death slow and agonising.

Another corner loomed before them. Darla had one more trick up her sleeve. Nudging Midnight's flanks, she increased her speed again, pushing the horse to his limit. Instead of navigating the corner, though, she rode straight ahead, leaping over the bush ahead of her. Beyond the bush was a ditch, two metres wide and a metre deep. Midnight navigated it easily, landing and kicking up snow. Prince Velander, however, wasn't so lucky, his horse not making the distance and clipping the edge of the ditch. After toppling backwards, the prince nimbly leapt from the saddle and in a blur sheathed his sword and grabbed hold of a tree root. Clinging to it with both hands, he carefully pulled himself up. His horse lay injured, whinnying in pain. Its legs were broken; he would have to put it down.

Prince Velander turned to see Darla watching him He drew his sword and yelled. "Let's settle this now, bitch!" Darla was tempted; she had an opportunity to rid the world of this arrogant, psychopathic asshole. Hell, she was more than tempted, but she restrained herself. Instead, she settled on angering and tormenting the prince. It was petty, but she couldn't help herself.

Looking back one final time, Darla pulling the emerald out of the satchel and held it aloft. "I would happily oblige you," she replied, as she began to canter off, "but I'm currently occupied looking after this."

"I'm going to gut you then strangle you with your own intestines," the prince screamed. Darla smiled then burst out laughing, infuriating him further. She was amused; for an arrogant, psychopathic princeling, his threats were creative.

She still had a fair distance to reach the bandits. By informing Lord Dellavenor and his army about Darla, they had bought themselves some time and increased their lead. However, Darla knew every road, and trail, including some of the secreted ones. She knew the nooks and crannies and short cuts she would take. She knew this area like the back of her hand; the path she was on led to the Black Raven Inn. Finally, she would be going home, but the bandits were hightailing it there and bringing the Divinity Stone with them. The stone was still a mystery to her, but a demon wanted it, which was a good enough reason to keep it the hell away from him. And the bandits were going to take it to her home, along with all the unwanted attention that went with it. Geez, Marek was going to be pissed off!

* * *

Guided by the Divinity Stone, Jaydrath ran through the forest, in a semi-hypnotised state. He heard a constant roaring, mixed with voices and a buzzing sound. Hunter demons were in tune with the Divinity Stone, having a special connection with it that enabled them to track it. There was a downside, though: when he was in this state, he was completely oblivious to everything around him. And it was for that very reason that he ignored the commands of "Halt!" and "Identify yourself!" from the elven ranger squad. Four arrows buzzed through the air as the powerful recurve bows twanged in unison. They were fired with expert precision and at close range, all the arrows slamming into their target with deadly force. The arrows pierced his chest, stomach, and shoulder, toppling him sideways into the nearby bushes.

Four rangers edged forward. The remaining eight had their recurve bows nocked with lethal barbed arrows. They weren't taking any chances. Squelch, squelch, squelch, and the four rangers left a trail of indented boot prints. Squelch, crack, and the rangers froze, looking down at the spider web of cracked ice around them. Stopping had been a mistake. The bushes Jaydrath had fallen into shattered, sending frozen shards of broken branches and leaves rocketing towards them. Instinctively they went to dive, only to find their feet frozen solid.

The shrapnel tore through their armour like tissue paper, embedding itself deep within their bodies. Collapsing, riddled with puncture wounds, three of the elves died instantly. The swordsman who had been farthest from the barrage lay writhing in pain, dying slowly. Jaydrath sat up, bolt upright. He was no longer riddled with arrows. They had frozen solid and shattered, crumbling to dust. Brushing the ice off himself, he stood up and looked at the elves. And boy, was he pissed.

The eight rangers fired with a chorus of twangs. The arrows never reached their target though, instead freezing in midair and shattering with a lift of Jaydrath's hand. They twirled wildly as a blizzard erupted. Each shard then elongated into razor-sharp icicles. Pointing at the elves, the demon sent the icicles shooting forth at a blinding speed. Six elves were impaled multiple times, the icicles tearing easily through their armour. The remaining two managed to dodge the icicles and scurried across the ground, trying to escape.

Holding out his hand, Jaydrath focused. The air sizzled with subzero energy that immediately solidified into ice. Rock-hard ice that lengthened in his hand and moulded itself into a jagged, barbed spear. The two elves scrambled to their feet, panicking as they ran for their lives. Jaydrath weighed the spear in his hand, calculating, and then he hurled it.

The spear sparkled as it soared through the air, shooting in between the trees and bushes and glistening in the sunlight. It flew straight as an arrow and hit with the deadly force of a battering ram. The two elves were thrown off their feet as they were propelled forward, the sharp head easily puncturing their armour. The spear head erupted, tearing through the chest of the first elf before slamming into the back of his comrade. With a loud crack and a spray of bark, the spear then embedded itself into a tree trunk. The two elves died instantly, their limp bodies dangling, pinned to the tree.

"Pesky mortals," Jaydrath cursed. "Don't they realise they can't kill me? All they've done is delay my hunt." He walked over to the carnage he had caused and looked around critically, searching for something. Satisfied, he unclasped one of the elves' cloaks and put it on. With only a couple of holes in it, the cloak was still wearable and in good condition. He didn't need it to ward off the cold—he was impervious to that. He did, however, need a disguise to help him blend in. Whistling, he continued towards the inn, the location that his link was leading him to, the place that he was certain he would find the Divinity Stone.

Chapter 13

Located in a prime position, the Black Raven Inn was a popular destination. It was one of six inns situated throughout Kalmeer, that was not established within a city or town. It was also within commuting distance of three villages and located on the border between the Hiberathian and Quendath Kingdoms. Because of this, it attracted a range of customers, including merchants, tradesmen, adventurers, nobles, messengers, and peasants.

The owner, a man named Marek, had inherited the inn from his father. The inn went back four generations, having been handed down from one son to the next. Prior to inheriting it, however, Marek had adventured throughout the land of Kalmeer and had travelled to exotic lands overseas. Throughout this period of his life, Marek had done everything from mercenary work to smuggling, merchandizing, and thievery. During this time, he also had met a beautiful woman named Angelene. With his roguish charm, he had courted her and eventually married her. A year later, they had a son named Garen. Unfortunately, though, Angelene died during the child's birth. It was at this point Marek returned home, a single parent in need of family support. He learnt the trade of being an innkeeper while his parents helped him raise Garen.

It was late afternoon, and the sun could just be seen above the treetops of the surrounding forest. Marek wiped the sweat from his brow. He had been deep in thought, reminiscing about his past. All of that had happened years ago, when he was young, adventurous, and getting himself into all kinds of mischief. He was older now, wiser, and had settled down. Garen was now a teenager, almost a man. He was also remarried to Jenna, a woman he adored, a woman who supported him and put up with the antics that he and Darla got up to. He laughed. Who was he kidding? He might be older, but he still got up to mischief; some things never changed. Smiling, he raised his axe and hefted it into a mighty swing.

It came crashing down with a crack, splitting the small log in half. Marek collected the two pieces and added them to those already in the large sack. With a contented sigh, he hung the axe back on its hook, lifted the sack, and swung it over his broad shoulders. Marek's muscles bulged as he carried the heavy load into the inn. From the weight, he judged that it should be enough wood for the night. If it wasn't, he'd send Garen out to chop some more. At the moment, Garen was cleaning the stables—a job he enjoyed, due to his love of working with the horses.

When Marek walked inside, he was greeted with a soft humming that grew louder as he neared the kitchen. He opened the door with a slight creak, and the humming abruptly stopped. Jenna stood before him, smiling warmly at him. Even after all this time she was as gorgeous as ever. She had gotten a few strands of grey hair coming through, adding streaks of silver amongst her black hair. In Marek's opinion that added to her beauty. "Stoke up the oven, dear," she said, gesturing towards it. Marek placed the sack next to the oven and threw a dozen pieces of firewood onto the raging fire. Inside the oven was some fresh bread, the crust already starting to turn a golden brown. "And while you're over there, take the bread out and put the apple pies in." Her only reply was a grumble from Marek.

Jenna got back to work, humming another song while she chopped some rabbits Marek and Garen had caught in the morning. She cut the meat with expert precision and placed it a large pot. Next to the pot was a variety of vegetables, ready to mix in and make a nice, rich stock. An hour later, the aroma of Jenna's famous hearty rabbit stew wafted throughout the tavern. The stew was so good that the inn's patrons always wiped their bowls clean.

The stew simmering, Jenna sliced the bread while Marek poured glasses of wine and ale. There were only a few customers this afternoon, but then again, it was usually quiet in the middle of the week. They were lucky enough though to have a bard playing for them this evening. He had arrived earlier that afternoon, and Marek had negotiated for him to perform, giving him a free night's lodging in return. The bard would have to pay for his own meals and drink, though, which was fair enough.

Marek was in the process of pouring a mug of ale when he heard Garen shout for him. Ale spilled over the mug onto the counter, and he cursed. He quickly wiped it up, handed the mug to the patron, and rushed outside, almost colliding with the inn's sign. The sign was dangling, hanging by a single chain, and swinging back and forth. One of the hooks had come loose and now lay at his feet. Marek looked despairingly at the wooden sign; it had faded over the years, and now the black raven on it almost looked a grey colour. It needed a fresh coat of paint, but that was a job for tomorrow.

"What, Va—" Marek shouted, then stopped when he noticed what it was. A large dust cloud was coming down Blood Road. A dust cloud caused by galloping horses, which meant the riders were riding hard.

They were heading away from the elven lands towards the King's Highway.

The King's Highway connected Sethanon to the Blood Road and branched off to smaller towns and villages within the Hiberathian Kingdom. Quen Anathiel, the elvish capital, was situated at one end of the Blood Road, with the other end connecting to Farrew Road. The three major roads connected the three kingdoms, allowing a trade route for the elves, humans, and dwarves.

The riders were coming from either the Quendath or Blackrock Kingdoms, and Marek suspected they were heading towards Sethanon. It was late in the afternoon, and they'd need to stop at the Black Raven for the evening. But why were they in such a hurry? Were they trying to make good time or did they have an alternate agenda?

To reach Sethanon from the Black Raven, it normally took about a week, but one could do it in three to four days with hard riding. Often travellers stopped at the inn on their way to Sethanon, home of the royal family and one of the biggest cities in Kalmeer. Sethanon even rivalled the picturesque, elven forest city of Quen Anathiel and the impregnable, dwarven mountain city of Holguard. It also was the leading city for trade and commerce, thanks to its coastal location and its proximity to the King's Highway. Roads detached from the highway like branches from a tree, a network that led to farms, villages, forts, and cities. Marek stepped down the wooden steps, joining his son, and waited as the riders approached.

The Black Raven was the only tavern located along Blood Road, making it an ideal location for a stopover. The Blood Road was named after the red gravel that formed it, but unlike most roads, this one had a tale to go along with it. A tale Marek thoroughly enjoyed reciting to new and enquiring customers. Being an innkeeper was like being a bard; storytelling and gossip were part of his trade.

* * *

The quiet afternoon was about to get eventful. The horsemen's clothes were covered in dust and dirt from the hard riding they'd endured. Marek sensed their fear, even though they masked it with smiles and joviality as their horses trotted to a stop near where he and Garen stood. The half-elf leader claimed to be a merchant, with his five companions being his mercenary bodyguards. The mercenary part seemed true enough; they were heavily armed and wore cloaks that concealed their armour. The rest of the story was crap, though! Although the leader was articulate and silver-tongued, he was also lying. Marek had a chequered past himself, having done a fair amount of adventuring in his youth. Because of this, he recognised the men for exactly what they were: bandits.

Claiming to be a merchant had been the leader's first mistake, as Marek knew most of the merchants from the elven, dwarven, and human provinces and had dealt with them on numerous occasions. There was the possibility the half elf was a small-time merchant he hadn't come across, but he doubted it. Marek stood by the doorway, contemplating as Garen walked past him, ready to deal with the horses. The half elf looked nervously in the direction from which they had just come. Were they being pursued? Marek masked the grin that was starting to creep forth. He didn't care one way or the other; he just saw this as an opportunity. Smiling warmly, the half elf tossed Garen a small pouch of copper coins. "Put the horses away as quickly as possible, boy, then brush them down and give them some oats and water." Garen smiled, nodding his thanks as the group turned their attention to Marek and walked towards the inn.

Garen was ecstatic. Hefting the pouch and weighing its contents, he estimated he had received the equivalent of about a week's wage—and he knew exactly what he would spend it on. Darla's horse was purebred, well trained, and highly intelligent. The horse, however, had been too intelligent for his own good lately, managing to escape from his stall and break into a neighbouring stall Marek had isolated for one of his mares. The mare had been in heat and was now pregnant. Darla had been furious, berating her horse. Midnight had merely snorted at her as if to say, *Why should you have all the fun?*

* * *

Marek hadn't minded, though, promising Garen the foal. Garen was now in the process of saving for feed and equipment for his new horse. He leapt forward enthusiastically and grabbed the lead horse's reins. Garen, with his great knowledge about horses, had automatically recognised the lead horse due to its dominance over the others. Whistling and talking to it, he led it towards the stables, jogging as the horse cantered alongside him. The three other horses meekly followed them. Marek watched Garen proudly as he led the horses away. The leaders flustering, erratic behaviour had been the leader's second mistake, confirming Marek's suspicions. Without a doubt, these fellows were bandits and were being pursued. There was an opportunity for a tidy profit; Marek was going to enjoy this.

Marek also had an inkling the pursuers were elves, the best trackers in the world. If this were the case, these imbeciles had just led their pursuers to his inn. Marek bit his lip, contemplating his options. This could either prove extremely profitable for him, or it could end very badly. "Welcome to the Black Raven," he said, addressing the leader, a man with an eye patch, long black hair and scarred face. "What may I do for you?"

"We'd like to book a merchant room if one is available," the man said, following Marek into the confines of the inn. Merchant rooms had earned their name because they accommodated merchants and nobles, along with their entourages. The rooms were large, elaborately decorated, and furnished with multiple beds.

"Certainly," Marek said, smiling. he had decided to play along with the subterfuge. He and pulled out a large brass key out of a drawer and placed it on the counter. The leader's hand snaked out, grabbing the key. He fumbled in his pouch and placed eight gold coins on the counter. A generous amount, considering the room only cost half that.

"For your silence innkeeper, and so we are not disturbed."

* * *

Nodding, Marek grabbed the coins and placed them in a belt pouch. "What merchandise do you deal in?" he asked casually.

"Gems!" the bandit leader said abruptly. Taken aback, Marek wondered if he had pushed things too far. Seeing this, the half elf quickly added. "We deal in gems, selling them to various jewellery shops." Marek smiled, releasing his grip on the handle of the small crossbow he had strapped behind the counter. A small hole in the counter allowed him to shoot any troublesome customers. It was one of various security measure he had installed around the inn. He then opened the side door and led his guests into the dining area.

The dining area was quiet, with a few guests casually sitting around, drinking. They were too engaged in their own conversations and drinks to even notice the new arrivals. One person did take notice, though: a cloaked woman isolated from the rest of the patrons, drinking at the bar. She turned and glanced at the newcomers, her green eyes staring at them, taking everything in. A heartbeat later, she turned back, seemingly disinterested. Marek pointed to the top of the staircase. "Go to the end of the hallway and turn right. Your room is the last on the right. Dinner will be served at seven p.m. Would you like me to reserve you a table?"

"No, thank you," the half elf said. "We'll eat in our room tonight. Could you have the lad bring up our meals? To wash it down, we'll have six ales and some bottles of wine."

"Certainly," Marek replied, then suddenly lowered his voice. "It's a shame, though. I was hoping to join you and discuss the prospect of acquiring some of your merchandise."

The bandit leader was clearly surprised. Marek could sense the conflict battling within him, could see it in his eyes. Eventually greed won out. He smiled cunningly and nodded. "In that case, I'll dine with you this evening while my men remain in our room."

* * *

"I'd love to, but being an innkeeper, I don't get the luxury of sitting down to eat. Once dinner service is finished, though, I'll sit with you and have a few drinks, and we can conduct our business."

The bandits' leader thought about it then nodded. "Until then, innkeeper." Silently he turned away from Marek and walked up the stairs, the five mercenaries obediently following him.

Marek waited, listening to the creak of the floorboards, as they walked down the hallway. Once they were out of earshot, he sighed with relief and walked towards the bar and the cloaked, long-haired woman sitting there. The way she was dressed suggested she might be an upper-class citizen or a noble. Her dress was low cut and of fine silk, while her cloak was fur lined and of the latest fashion. To Marek she was an associate, a friend—hell, he even considered her family. And she was dressed like this for a reason.

The woman was voluptuous, having curves in all the right places. She took a sip of wine before slowly turning her head towards Marek. A few strands of her long, wavy reddish-brown hair slid out from the confines of her hood, cascading down to her bosoms. Although her hood cloaked her features in shadow, Marek saw the broad grin illuminating her face. "Shit me, Darla. This is going to be fun *and* profitable," he said, grinning broadly. He slid onto the stool next to her, grabbed a bottle and a glass, and poured himself a drink.

Marek loved Darla—not in a romantic way, though; she was like the sister he'd never had. They knew everything there was to know about each other: his deep dark secrets, even Darla's lycanthropy. The night Darla had told him, he had drunk a bottle of whisky, pondering while he drank. Eventually he had accepted it. He knew Darla would never harm his family—far from it; it was because of her that he still had a family.

One quiet evening, a group of bandits had raided the inn. Times had changed over the years. Bandits had started roaming the land, killing, raping, and stealing, leaving nothing but destruction and misery in their wake. They hadn't counted on Marek and his repertoire of skills, or for that matter that Darla was staying at the inn on that eventful night.

The bandits had the element of surprise, positioning themselves and attacking within moments of entering the inn. Marek was a fighter, but his first concern was for his family. He beckoned to his mother, who quickly ushered Garen up the stairs. His son had been eight at the time. With deadly precision, one of the bandits aimed his crossbow and fired. The bolt soared through the air, embedding itself in his mother's back. Garen had watched in horror as his grandmother collapsed on the staircase, her eyes staring blankly at him. Another crossbowman had aimed, ready to dispatch the boy, when a bolt suddenly pierced his throat. Lightning quick, from years of practice, Marek had cranked the shaft of his repeater crossbow, reloading it in a matter of seconds. He dispatched the second crossbowman just as a bandit cut down his father with a sword.

Jenna had screamed from the kitchen door, and Marek urged her to stay in there. Giving her a quick kiss and closing the door, he calmly discarded his crossbow and grabbed his mace from his belt. The bandit who had killed his father swung his sword, but Marek was faster, crashing his mace down on the man's hand. Bones crunched and the sword dropped in midswing, clattering to the floor. With another swing, Marek brought the weapon crashing down on the bandit's head, caving in his skull.

Darla had dispatched the remaining three bandits. She had moved like a shadow, their weapons unable to touch her. It was like a dance —not only did she dodge their weapons, but she also expertly positioned herself, ready to strike. It was as if she knew their every move and was constantly one step ahead of them. Each strike was perfectly timed and lethal. Her first opponent went down with the long blade of her dagger piercing his throat. She then ran and slid towards her second opponent, parrying his sword and deflecting it with one of her daggers. From a crouching position, she then stabbed him in the gap at the bottom of his leather armour, puncturing his lung. As the man dropped, her last opponent rushed at her and swung his sword wildly. Darla deflected it; raising his arm and ducking under it, she stabbed him in the vulnerable spot of his armpit, her dagger sliding into her opponent's heart.

After the battle, in a stupor, Marek had staggered out back, his son and his wife following him. Grimly he dug two graves while Darla dragged his parent's corpses out. He laid his mother and father to rest and saying a silent prayer alongside Jenna and Garen. They all stood their silently, feeling numb, tears streaming down their faces, comforting one another and mourning their losses. Eventually headstones were added, with his parents' names carved elaborately into the stones. A purple flowered shrub, his mother's favourite, was planted as well. It was sentimental and provided a nice decorative border for the grave sites.

At the time, Darla had been staying at the inn while conducting some business in the area. She had been contracted to rescue a lord's wife who had been naïve, only travelling with a small entourage of guards. The group had been attacked by a well-organised group of bandits. The guards had been brutally killed, and the lord's wife had been kidnapped. Darla had dealt with similar situations before. The bandits had an inside man or woman within the lord's court; it was the only explanation. The job was simple enough: rescue the lord's wife, ideally without having to pay the ransom. The job had turned out to be a complete and utter cluster fuck, but that's a story for another day.

The inn had been the perfect place for her to stay. She had paid for three days' lodging, a short stay—one that ended up being indefinite. Something about the inn, about Marek and his family, had appealed to Darla. They filled a void, something deep down she had been craving. A family! That had been several years ago, and Darla was now like part of the furniture. She owned one of the rooms, having paid for it outright with some of her savings. The Black

Raven was more than just an inn to Darla; it was her home.

Darla had arrived at the inn hours before, racing Midnight and overtaking the bandits. The horse had been bred for both speed and stamina and, like Darla, knew this area well. The bandits had been overconfident, thinking they were in the clear. Darla had travelled all afternoon, sneaking past their camp while the bandits had a late lunch. "Go home, boy," she'd said after they were clear. Midnight flicked his head and neighed, protesting, as if to say, *I'm just as tired as you,* but it went on deaf ears because Darla already had dozed off.

Little did either group know that Prince Velander and his company, consisting of one hundred and fifty elves, were following close behind them. In her haste to escape, Darla had left an obvious trail for them. Unknowingly she was leading Velander to the bandits and to the Black Raven Inn.

Darla had leapt from the saddle, handing the reigns to Garen before running inside. Marek had instantly realised something was wrong but knew better than to question her. Darla needed to think and unwind. When it was time, she would talk to him. After freshening up, she had sat at the bar, confronted Marek, and presented him with the two bottles of Fire Brandy. His broad grin said it all. As she poured herself a drink, she mentioned Gustus's proposal to Marek: three more bottles of the dwarf's Fire Brandy for one bottle of Marek's Dragon's Breath. She watched as Marek contemplated, running his fingers through his goatee. Darla laughed as he slowly nodded. She knew his mannerisms, knew quite well what his answer would be.

The finer details would have to wait, though; they'd had more pressing issues to deal with. Jenna had joined them, and Darla had divulged everything—well, almost everything. She had opted to keep some things to herself. Darla also informed them that the bandits' leader was Brigg the Butcher, a half elf with a nasty reputation throughout the kingdom. After she laid out her plan,

Marek's smile said everything. A few hours later, the bandits arrived, as she knew they would, just like clockwork.

Darla took another sip from her goblet, sighed at Marek, and shook her head slightly. "I'm starting to believe the Divinity Stone is cursed and will end up in Malgorath's hands. We need to stop that from happening. God knows what will happen, but I suspect that his intentions are evil and that nothing good will come of it." The last part was merely a whisper.
Marek looked at her, concerned. "I just know it." He didn't ask how she knew; he just nodded, accepting it.

"Yeah, well," he said, "this situation has provided us with a rare opportunity. A chance to retrieve the Divinity Stone and give it to the elven prince. We'll be in his good graces and be rewarded for our effort."

Darla had briefly described the Divinity Stone and the power it had. She skipped over the part about it communicating with her, dismissing it due to not understanding it herself. "I don't know, Marek," she said. "You didn't see Prince Velander's reaction when he thought I had the Divinity Stone." She drained the last remnants of her glass, contemplating. "The elven prince is just as much a fanatic as Lord Dellavenor. Possibly worse."

Marek looked at Darla sternly. "We can't keep it. I don't want us to get caught up in a war zone."

"That could very well happen anyway. Lord One-Eye is a fanatic, and the prince is just as bad."

"I take it you had something to do with his missing eye?" Marek looked at Darla questioningly, his eyebrows raised. The look she gave him said it all. "Just fucking great! Not only is this lord a fanatic with an army, but he also has a personal grudge against you."

* * *

"I just hope the whole thing doesn't go pear shaped," she said. "I've had enough to drink. I'm going to go up to my room. Could you ask Garen to bring my dinner up? I'll eat there tonight." Marek smiled and gave her a look. She knew that look too well. "What do you need me to do?"

"Well, I've got the vital role of dealing with Brigg, pretending to be an interested buyer and then relieving him of the Divinity Stone."

"Be careful, Marek. Don't underestimate him. He's notoriously ruthless."

"Don't worry Darla. I'll be careful. I've got the easy job though." He grinned wickedly. "You'll be the one taking care of the other bandits."

"Since I'm doing all the work, I think I should get an extra-large serving of apple pie after dinner." Jenna had been working laboriously in the kitchen, and Darla could smell the rich aromas of cinnamon and nutmeg infused with the apple.

Marek hmphed. "Fine."

She reached for the bottle. "Looks like I'm going to need another drink" She filled it to the brim then poured Marek a glass.

"Now we drink and wait until dinner." Marek said, smiling and clinking their glasses together. The inn door suddenly flung open, startling him and causing him to spill some whisky onto the counter. Cursing, he wiped it up with a rag and turned to see eight elves walk into the inn. "Welcome to the Black Raven Inn. I'm Marek, the proprietor of this fine establishment," he said jovially, hopping off the stool and walking towards them. "What may I do for you fine gentlemen?" Two of the elves parted as their leader stepped forward, dragging something on a chain as he grinned maniacally. Curious to know what was on the chain, Marek tried to subtly look past the leader. The other elves quickly blocked his view, however, keeping it hidden.

Their leader was dressed in high-quality leather armour emblazoned with his family's emblem in gold stitching. A jewel-encrusted sword hung from his hip, partly covered by his flowing black cloak. His long black hair had streaks of blue through it A braid hung over each shoulder, while the rest flowed neatly down his back. He walked forward, ostentatious and self-assured. It was the evil glint in his green eyes, though, that made Marek slightly nervous. During his adventuring days, he had seen that glint before: the wild look of a psychopath. "Greetings, inn keep. I am Prince Velander, and we are in pursuit of a low-life scum, a thief who stole something precious to me. My family's Divinity Stone. We have a suspicion this woman is staying at your inn, where she obviously has scurried into hiding."

Darla drained her whisky and took a deep breath. Settling her nerves, she poured herself another drink. Panicking would draw attention to herself. She needed to remain calm, be inconspicuous, just another customer at the inn, oblivious to the prince. Taking a sip, she questioned herself. How had the prince tracked her here? Then, like a slap in the face, it dawned on her. In her haste to overtake the bandits, she hadn't covered her tracks. Normally that wouldn't have been a problem, but she was dealing with elves, the finest trackers in the land. She cursed at her stupidity. Nothing could be done now, though; she and Marek just had to improvise and make the most of this situation.

"I have plenty of women staying at the inn. You can take your pick," Marek said, smiling and draining his glass. "I also have some bandits staying here who have a green Divinity Stone in their possession."

"This woman has my Divinity Stone, innkeeper!" Prince Velander roared. "I saw it with my own two eyes."

* * *

"What? That gorgeous green diamond-shaped stone? You'd better buy it off those bandits. I've already cleared out the area above the fireplace to display it," Jenna said, carrying out a platter of cheese and spicy sausages and placing it on the counter. Darla deposited a couple of silver coins into Jenna's outstretched hand before leaning across and helping herself to the platter.

"You must be mistaken, lady," Prince Velander replied.

"That depends on whether you're referring to that bright-green gem...say, so big," she stated, emphasising the size and shape with her hands.

Prince Velander turned red with anger and embarrassment. Turning abruptly, his back to Marek, he yanked on the chain, pulling whatever it was forward. "You imbecile, you lied to me!' he shouted, spittle flying everywhere. "You got greedy and wanted a reward, and because of this prolonging, you provided the thief with the perfect opportunity to steal it. You told me the woman had it, but she doesn't...and you wouldn't lie to me, would you?" He turned back around and faced Marek again. Whoever was there was still a mystery. The prince laughed, the sound bellowing throughout the inn. The sound of a madman, it scared Marek to his core. "So obviously those bandits stole it from under the thief's pretty nose. He yanked on the chain, pulling it forward, revealing what it was. A man, half naked and shackled. Gasping, Marek paled and wondered whether Darla did indeed have the easier task ahead of her.

Marek initially thought the tortured man was human until he realised what he was looking at. The elf had his long pointy ears sliced, cut into the shape of a humans. His ornate armour had been removed, and his underclothes were torn and ragged. His body was riddled with cuts; parts of his flesh had been sliced off him then charred as the gaping wounds were cauterised. His face was battered and bruised, his one good eye swollen and half shut. Over his other eye he wore a bloodied eye patch. It was Lord Kye Dellavenor, captured, broken, reduced to a prince's pet, a dog on a lead.

Dubious, Prince Velander looked questioningly at Marek. "But how exactly did you come to hear about this? Bandits wouldn't divulge something like this to you." Darla was listening to every word. Marek was playing a dangerous game, one that could be extremely profitable or fatal. Fortunately, her back was to them and they hadn't noticed her yet. Quietly her hands slipped under her cloak, her fingers tightly wrapping around the hilts of her daggers. She was preparing herself. She was ready to fight.

Marek laughed. "I'm an innkeeper, my prince. People divulge things to me. After one drink, they warm up to me; after a bottle, they're willing to tell me their deepest secrets. You'd be amazed at some of the things I've heard'" Ignoring the elven prince, he walked back to the bar and poured himself another drink. He took a sip before continuing. "I've arranged to have drinks and conduct business with the bandit leader this evening. I will get your Divinity Stone back...for a small fee."

Prince Velander smirked. "And why should I pay you when my soldiers can deal with these brigands themselves? I demand you turn them over to me at once!"

Marek took a piece of cheese and a spicy sausage off the nearby platter—a platter Darla had technically paid for. He shoved the cheese into his mouth, took a bite of the sausage, and chewed. "I'm afraid I can't do that, Prince Velander," he said, spraying a piece of sausage onto the floor. The prince looked as if Marek had just slapped him across the face. He glared at Marek furiously, and with a flick of his hand, the eleven guards reached for their weapons. Darla slid her daggers free, ready to attack.

The guards were armed with a variety of weapons and dressed in elven-weave armour—a high-quality armour made from hardened leather. The leather was then interwoven with steel links. It resulted in a reinforced, durable armour that was lightweight and allowed mobility. Due to its design, it resembled a patchwork of browns and greys, and along with their mottled green cloaks. it provided the elves with the perfect camouflage. Marek couldn't blame the bandits for fleeing to the inn; in the forest they wouldn't have stood a chance.

Unfazed by the act of aggression, Marek swallowed, licked the spice off his fingers, and smiled. "You see, my prince, technically the Black Raven is situated on the border of the Hiberathian Kingdom and the Quendath Kingdom. Therefore, if you and your guards attack the bandits within the confines of my inn, you'd be breaking the treaty between kingdoms and possibly start a war."

Darla spoke softly so only Marek could hear. "Well played, Marek. Well played indeed." A sidewards glance and the flicker of a smile was the only acknowledgement she received.

One of the soldiers stepped forward. "The innkeeper is right, my prince. Any aggression on our part could be seen as an act of war."

"I'm well aware of that, Captain." Prince Velander grinded his teeth, his annoyance showing. Darla studied the captain. It was the first time she had seen him up close. He was slightly younger than the prince and was quite muscular for an elf, with emerald-green eyes and long black hair. She had heard about him; an exceptional fighter, he was the prince's shadow, protector, and right-hand man. He was also Velander's cousin, second in line to the throne; his name was Prince Jerrick. "Fine. We'll do it your way, innkeeper. Just make sure you get the Divinity Stone back." Marek nodded and beckoned the elves into the dining area.

"So not only are we going ahead with the plan, but we're also handing the goddamn Divinity Stone over to the elves?" Darla said, draining half her whisky. Marek could tell she was annoyed. Well, more than annoyed—she was downright pissed.

"Unfortunately, their arrival complicates things. Our hands are tied in the matter; we don't have a choice."

"Then I'll just have to steal it off Prince—" She stopped in midsentence, distracted as a dozen hooded figures entered the inn. Taking a sip of her drink, she watched them intently, studying their every move. They were soldiers, wearing heavy black armour with no identifying insignia on their surcoats. They wanted to be discreet and unidentifiable, which automatically indicated to Darla that they were here to see her and that the job would pay well.

"Welcome to the Black Raven," Marek said, sliding off his stool. "What can I do for you?"

A well-muscled man stepped forward. "Greetings. My name is Brenan. I'm looking for the lady who calls herself Flow. I have a contract for her to consider on behalf of my benefactor." Marek pointed with an inclination of his head towards the seat behind him. The man was well-spoken, Darla noticed, indicating he was educated and worked for either a noble or high-ranking lord. By the sound of his booted feet on the floorboards, she also noted he walked with purpose and determination.

"This is for you," Brenan said, handing her a sealed letter.

Even though to the casual observer, it looked like Darla was being blasé, in that instant of grabbing the letter, she took in every detail. She noticed the exceptional-quality parchment, the red wax seal, and the emblem of the flying gryphons. *The royal insignia of Sethanon!* Each royal personage was entitled to their own stamp, but the indentation was strong, indicating it had been made by a young adult male, more than likely one of the princes. It was indeed an important contract; one she couldn't afford to pass up. She carefully tucked the letter into the secret pocket within her cloak and, lifting her glass, returned to the job of drinking.

Brenan looked dumbfounded. "Aren't you going to read it? My benefactor would like your response now," he said with a hint of annoyance.

"I'm currently working on another job. You'll have to wait."

"What job is so important that my benefactor must wait?" Reaching across his shoulder, Brenan grabbed hold of the leather-bound handle of an ornate sword. He had one strapped across each shoulder, indicating to Darla that he was proficient at dual wielding. The threat was evident, his intention clear. Taking another sip and smirking, she casually nodded down. Looking down, Brenan saw the razor-sharp tip of her dagger an inch from his groin. Slowly, his fingers unclenching, he released his grip on his sword. He nodded in admiration, with a newly acquired respect for this assassin. It was no wonder the prince was hiring her services.

"Well, let's see. The job at hand involves stealing a deadly, magical artefact from a deranged elven prince," she replied. "Yep. That about sums it up."

Marek sat back in his seat and sighed. "There are a dozen elves here, Flow," he said, "and that's just inside the inn. God knows how many more are in the surrounding woods? One hundred and fifty? Maybe even two hundred. You're going to get us both killed."

"The elves won't dare attack! If they do, it'll be a declaration of war," Brenan said incredulously, looking from one to the other.

Darla raised her eyebrows. "Seriously? I've already told you Velander is deranged. He doesn't care if he starts a fucking war." Annoyed, she slammed her glass on the counter, splashing whisky across it.

* * *

Brenan looked at her intensely, weighing things. "I can send two riders off to muster soldiers from Fort Targen. I should be able to get two hundred troops here in half a day or so." He was taking the situation seriously. Unfortunately, it would take the two riders three to four hours of hard riding to reach the fort. Well garrisoned, Fort Targen had been established to protect three towns as well as the neighbouring wineries, orchards, and farms.

Darla frowned. It was always good to have backup. The elves would be reluctant to engage so many troops, but by the time they got here, she and Marek would be dead, the inn burned to the ground.

"I'm sorry," Brenan said. "I know it's not ideal, but it's the best I can do. I'll have them set up a base camp in the clearing down the road." He was right, it wasn't ideal, but then again, nothing ever was.

"Send your riders off now. I'll delay things as long as I can," Darla replied with a wicked smile.

Marek looked dubious. "I still think this is too risky, Flow."

"No, it isn't," she replied. "Just leave everything to me."

Marek groaned. "I'm going to need another drink."
Darla gracefully slid off her stool and walked up the staircase. It was time; she needed to get changed. In her room, she reached into her wardrobe and put on the perfect ensemble: black leather leggings that were both comfortable and practical, a light brown leather cuirass which was interwoven with strips of steel, padded boots, fingerless gloves and a ruby red cloak. She strapped her long-bladed daggers to either side of her belt. Finally, she adjusted the leather strap of the short sword, shortening it and strapping it around her waist like a second belt. The short sword hung comfortably next to her dagger. A fighter, a thief, a woman of many talents, Darla was prepared and ready for battle.

* * *

Chapter 14

The elves sat at two tables along the far wall of the inn, speaking softly as they ate their stew and drank their ale. They wore their hoods up, obscuring their identities; Marek had told them to be inconspicuous. Prince Velander held the chain loosely while Lord Dellavenor sat quietly under the table, occasionally being fed food scraps. The prince couldn't help himself, though; his gaze was riveted on the table near the staircase, where Brigg casually sat. Marek had mentioned he was the bandits' leader, the one who possessed the Divinity Stone.

The half elf sat at the table by himself, eating a steaming bowl of hearty rabbit stew and drinking a mug of ale. The stew was exceptional, full of chunks of well-seasoned rabbit and vegetables. A thick piece of freshly baked break accompanied it, which he used to wipe up the rich gravy. The ale was also surprisingly good, and all it had cost him was a mere eight copper coins. As he ate, he watched Marek scurry around talking, laughing, and serving his guests.

When the dinner service finished, Marek wiped his hands on his grotty apron, took it off, and hung it on the hook next to the kitchen door. Smiling, he walked to Brigg and patted him on the shoulder as if he were greeting an old friend. The bandit leader smiled in return, drained the last of his ale, and slammed the empty mug onto the tabletop. With a wave of his hand, he beckoned for Marek to take the seat opposite him.

Marek pulled the chair out and sat down. The bottom of his long coat swung open as he sat, the mace he had hidden scraping slightly against the wooden floor. A lad, well-built and in his teens, strolled over and placed a mug of ale in front of him. Marek smiled, patting his son's shoulder affectionately. Garen had been trained at the inn since boyhood and would one day take over the business. He already was a skilled bartender, more than capable of serving drinks while his father conducted business with Brigg. He also knew exactly what his father was about to do, as Marek had always said, "Telling tales is thirsty work."

"I'll have another ale as well, lad," Brigg said, pulling out three copper coins and placing them in Garen's outstretched hand. Garen nodded and promptly walked back to the bar. "In all my travels, I've never seen red gravel. I gather that's where the Blood Road got its name?" he asked.

Marek took a long sip of his ale then launched into his story. "Two hundred years ago, during the last great war, the Jardoshian Empire, led by orcs, invaded the country of Kalmeer. The orcs attacked the royal city of Sethanon from the south, ravaging the Hiberathian Kingdom. Desperate, the survivors fled north along the Kings Highway." Marek took another large sip. "Now, the Kings Highway was named after King Aldreth, the first of the human kings. King Desron was his grandson, a young adult princeling, made king due to the demise of his father by the orc horde."

Garen returned, and with a clatter, he placed the mug of ale and a platter of cheese and spicy sausages on the table. Brigg looked confused; he hadn't ordered the platter. Garen held up eight fingers, and the man reluctantly gave him eight copper coins. Marek didn't even wait to be asked, picking up a sausage and a piece of cheese and stuffing them into his mouth. He washed it down with a mouthful of ale, sighed contently and continued his tale.

"Sethanon was burning, the crown jewel of the Hiberathian Kingdom lay decimated and in ruin. The guards had been massacred, overrun by the orc onslaught. King Desron had gathered the survivors and fled the city, sending his two remaining scouts ahead in the vain hope to request aide from their dwarven and elven allies. The scouts hadn't returned, though, and he was beginning to lose hope. The king had taken up with the rear guard, protecting the refugees and the slow-moving supply wagons from the constant hounding attacks from the orc-raiding parties. These parties had been sent ahead while the main army progressed slowly behind them. Thanks to Desron and the rear guard, however, these raiding parties failed to return to the army."

Garen returned to the table, carrying two fresh mugs of ale. Brigg had only managed to drink half of his, while somehow, even with all his talking, Marek had drained his mug. Brigg quickly finished his ale and, grinding his teeth, pulled out six copper coins. This was beginning to become an expensive meeting. Marek smiled and waved the coins away. "This one's on the house," he said casually, lifting his mug and draining a quarter of his ale. Lifting his own mug to his lips, the bandit leader nodded his thanks. Marek smiled; things were going perfectly. He just hoped he was buying Darla the time she needed.

* * *

Darla was upstairs in the hallway, her booted feet treading silently on the floorboards. Her boots were padded, designed for stealth and subterfuge, perfect for the occasion at hand. Mind you, with the ruckus coming from the bandits' room, Darla reckoned a squad of guards dressed in full plate mail armour could have snuck up on them. As she approached the door, she heard one of them shout out. "Drink up, Jak. We're about to become rich."

Jak snorted. "Not if those damn elves catch us. It's kind of hard to spend the money if you're dead. You drink if you want, Gyreth, but I sure as hell won't."

Gyreth laughed wholeheartedly. "You worry too much. So what if the elves catch us? We won't have the Divinity Stone on us. Brigg is about to offload it We'll be filthy rich, and the elves won't be able to prove a thing."

"Why do the elves call it a Divinity Stone? It just looks like a huge fucking emerald. What's the difference?" The voice was deep and gruff, belonging to the behemoth named Bane. Darla recognised the voice instantly.

"It *is* a huge emerald, Bane. The elves are just religious zealots; they worship the damn thing," said a fourth voice. Bane grunted, sounding doubtful.

Jak snorted again. "Zealots, Rayze? They're fucking crazy. You weren't there. Froyd went to negotiate a price for the return of this so-called Divinity Stone. Prince Velander raved and ranted, called Froyd a liar and claimed that the thief had it, that he saw it with his own eyes. He then said and I quote "This is what happens to people that lie to me". Then he cut off Froyd's arms—his goddamn arms!"

Jak was on the verge of hysteria. "They tied Froyd to his horse and sent him riding back. The prince is fucking deranged. Once he learns that we are the ones that have the Divinity Stone, what he did to Froyd will seem like a mercy killing compared to what he will do to us. This prince is even scarier than Brigg!"

Bane chuckled, the sound rumbling and loud. "If I were there, I'd have proven that we had the Divinity Stone by shoving the damn thing down his throat and my axe up his arse."

"You're all talk," Jak replied. "You weren't there! Even Brigg paled. He was scared shitless, I tell you."

"That's because Brigg is a pussy."

"I dare you to say that to his face," Jak countered. There was silence, and Jak snorted. "I didn't fucking think so. Like I said, you're all talk."

Taking a decisive step, Darla reached out, grabbed the handle, and twisted. One of the mercenaries belched loudly, masking the sound of the faint click as the door opened. This was met by roars of laughter from his comrades. The mercenaries were complacent, overconfident, seeing no need to even lock their door. A fatal mistake on their part.

Edging the door slightly open with the tip of her boot, Darla wrapped her hands around the two leather-twined handles strapped to her thighs. Steel softly scraped against leather as she drew her daggers. Footsteps sounded behind her. "What da fluck do you fink you're doing?" said one of the bandits. His speech was slurred, barely a whisper, his breath reeking of alcohol. He had just come out of the communal toilet and was now in the process of fumbling with the drawstring of his pants. The pants were slightly wet, and his hands were dripping water on the floor—well, Darla hoped it was water.

* * *

She turned and, with a flick of her wrist, sent one of her daggers hurtling forth. She was on the move as soon as it left her hand and began spiralling through the air, sparkling in the lantern light. The dagger connected with a meaty thud as it pierced the man's hands, pinning them to his body, before stabbing him in the groin. He looked down, speechless and in shock. Just as he started to scream, Darla clamped a hand over his mouth. A muffled cry was all that escaped as Darla pulled the bloodied dagger free and slid it slowly between his ribs, piercing his heart. His eyes went wide, his body limp. Darla gently lowered him to the floor; she'd deal with the body later.

She walked silently back to the bandits' door and opened it with the slightest of creaks. Immediately, as if in response, two chairs scraped against the floorboards, one clattering to the floor. Darla paused, cursing herself as she heard the groaning and creaking of the floorboards, no doubt caused by booted feet walking upon them. She distinguished two distinctive patterns, two separate footfalls. She held her breath in anticipation as the creaking stopped. Listening, her weapons poised, she stood ready to strike.

Silence. No sign of detection. "Will both of you just calm down? Sit back down so we can finish our hand." Darla recognised the voice; it belonged to Rayze. Relaxing slightly, she let out the breath she'd had been holding. She continued to open the door and crept inside the room like a ghost, unseen and unheard.

Before her stood the behemoth of a man, blocking her view. It was Bane, the psychopath, the one she had vowed to kill. His back was to her, concealing her, for the moment at least. In front of him stood a small bald man. "No way, Rayze. Bane's a fucking cheat!" he shouted. The voice belonged to Jak,

"Maybe I am. Maybe I'm not. Either way, what are you going to do about it, little man?" With an evil grin, Jak drew his short sword and, in a blur, sliced the behemoth across the cheek.

"I'm going to enjoy this," Bane responded, blood dripping to the floor. He drew a long, curved, jagged dagger and swung it menacingly at Jak's head. With a scrape of metal, Jak skilfully deflected the blow with his short sword. Darla briefly considered standing back and enjoying the entertainment as the two idiots killed each other. But, then after a moment of contemplating, she decided to intervene. After all, why should they deprive her of all the fun?

After sheathing one of her daggers, she darted forward and leapt high into the air. Her left arm clamped around Bane's left shoulder like a vice while her legs swung up and wrapped around his right shoulder. His huge muscles bulged, and Darla fought to maintain her hold. "This is for Jonas," she growled, yanking and dislocating his shoulders. The big man screamed as his arms went limp. "And this is for killing his dire wolf," she cried, the dagger in her right hand whipping around and slashing his throat. Retribution had been delivered; her vow had been fulfilled.

Blood sprayed forth like a crimson fountain, covering Jak and the surrounding floor. Darla unhooked her legs and, using the momentum, swung them around. She used her vicelike grip to pivot Jak while using the swing to add force to the blow. Jak never saw it coming; he was too busy wiping blood off his face. Darla's foot connected solidly, hitting his throat and crushing his larynx and trachea.

With a choked gasping sound, Jak dropped to the floor, his short sword clattering beside him. Darla let go of Bane's corpse and landed gracefully on her feet. A moment later the behemoth's body landed with a loud thud beside her. The three remaining bandits, shocked and stunned, quickly leapt into action. Their cards were discarded, scattering across the table as they reached for their weapons.

* * *

Two of them leapt from their chairs, sending them toppling to the ground as they scrambled for the heavy crossbows sitting idly on a nearby bed. The remaining bandit, Rayze, sighed dramatically as he casually stood up and drew his sword. He had been prepared, having his sword nearby, resting against the table. The sword was held in a firm grip, the tip pointed, waving offhandedly between them as if he were having some kind of internal conflict.

"What are you waiting for, Rayze?" Gyreth said, bewildered. Darla recognised Gyreth's shrill voice from the bandits' earlier conversation. He was lean and lanky, a weasel of a man. Distracted, he was fumbling with the bolt, trying desperately to load it. His comrade had no such trouble.

The crossbowman stood, almost kneeling as he stabilized his body, steadied his arms, and aimed the crossbow. With a twang, it fired, the bolt aimed directly at Darla's chest. The crossbow was designed for speed and power, providing it with a far greater range compared to its conventional cousin. At short range, such as this, it would be devastating. A normal person would have been impaled by the bolt, but Darla was far from normal. Her lycanthropy granted her with enhancements, abilities most people could only dream about. While most people called it a curse, she called it a gift. She had embraced it, trained herself to utilise these augmentations, even when she wasn't in a transformed state.

Her hearing was one such augmentation, being so acute that it alerted her to the faint click of a trigger being pressed. She was already in the process of diving forward as the twang sounded and the bolt was released. As she dove forward, her left arm snaked out and her wrist flicked forward like a whip, sending the bloodied dagger spiralling towards her target. Curving and tucking in her body, she rolled, but she didn't have to, because at that exact moment, with expert precision, Rayze cut the bolt in half. He then winked at her as the two halves dropped harmlessly to the ground.

* * *

Darla landed gracefully in a crouched position just as the dagger found its target and embedded itself in the crossbowman's chest. As his body fell, Darla gave Rayze a nod of thanks. Although she didn't need his help, she still appreciated it.

"You traitorous bastard. I'll fucking kill you for this!" Gyreth screamed as he cocked his crossbow and aimed with trembling hands. The bolt was aimed straight at Rayze's chest, but the swordsman wasn't fazed; he even lowered his sword slightly and smiled. Folding her arms, Darla turned her attention from one to the other, wondering how this would play out.

"You have one quarrel and two of us. You need to make a choice," Darla said, flashing the man a wolfish grin as she twirled her remaining dagger. Gyreth squeezed the trigger, making his choice and hurtling the bolt towards Rayze. Darla retaliated by flicking her dagger, sending it spiralling through the air. Graceful as a dancer, Rayze pivoted and slashed, and the bolt fell to the floor. He was indeed a master swordsman—either that or he was just showing off; Darla hadn't yet decided. Her dagger hit with pinpoint accuracy, embedding itself in Gyreth's throat and killing him instantly.

"Why did you do that? I wasn't in any danger." Rayze sounded self-assured, even cocky. It was time to deflate his ego.

"Because he made the wrong choice. He saw you as the greater threat," Darla replied with a smirk, walking forward to retrieve her daggers. As she wiped the blood off them, she heard a clinking sound. Rayze had sheathed his sword and hung it across his back. He was now scooping up a handfuls of coins. Carefully, methodically, he started pouring them into an open pouch. When Darla gave him a questioning look, he shrugged. "They won't be needing this anymore," he replied, scooping another handful in. "And besides, I consider it compensation."

* * *

Steven Wombell

"Why is it compensation?" Darla replied. "Wait. Let me guess. It's because I blew your damn cover. Well, fuck you and your cover. There are bigger things at stake."

Rayze was shocked, speechless for a moment, before letting out a hearty laugh. "No. It's actually because your timing sucks. I had an unbeatable hand." He picked up one of the discarded piles and showed her the cards he'd had. Darla whistled. It was indeed a very good hand: he had three of the five dragon cards in the deck, along with a king, two knights, and a bard. After collecting all the cards, he carefully placed the deck in a leather card holder. It was obviously his deck they played with. No wonder he had such a good hand; the deck was probably rigged. The pouch full, he tied it to his belt and placed another empty pouch on the table. "You're right, though. You blew my cover," he said, scooping the last of the coins into the pouch. "The Brotherhood will be pissed."

"What was your mission?" Darla enquired, sheathing her daggers. Besides their shadow talk, it was the first time they'd had a chance to have any semblance of a conversation.

Rayze smiled, his grin cheeky and mischievous. "Initially it was to recruit Brigg's bandit group or eliminate them. The mission was to get Gunderson's treasure at all costs. The bandits had been planning it for weeks. When the Divinity Stone came into play, my mission changed. I don't know what Brigg's intentions were, he wouldn't tell any of us. It was suspected that he had every intention to sell it to the demon prince. Hell, he even ignored my advice and tried to sell it to Velander. If he had, I would have killed them both. Luckily, the elven prince was delusional and completely insane. He was under the impression that you had it." He paused and looked at Darla questioningly She was about to answer when he continued. "It was the giant emerald, the replica of the Divinity Stone. You've misled the prince into thinking that you have it."
Darla nodded confirmation and shrugged. "He was pissing me off."
Rayze laughed. "That's good. It works out well for us because the

Brotherhood has made it a priority to keep the stone out of Malgorath's hands, and—"

"The Brotherhood knows about Malgorath?" Darla interrupted, annoyed.

Rayze nodded. "They've known about the demon for a while. I thought you would have been informed?"

"It obviously slipped their mind," Darla said, grinding her teeth and getting more and more pissed off.

"Hmm...maybe," Rayze replied, contemplating. Darla raised her eyebrows; he either knew something or suspected something. Silently she waited for him to continue. "There's a strong suspicion that the Brotherhood has been compromised, that one of Malgorath's supporters has infiltrated the Brotherhood. It's a grave concern, one that's being investigated." This sounded plausible; Darla had seen Malgorath's influence firsthand, how he was able to beguile and deceive people, manipulating them and turning them into fanatics for his cause. As feasible as this story was, Darla still had her doubts.

Darla was shaken to her core; the Brotherhood had been her home for years. Now it had been compromised. She didn't know who she could trust there anymore? Rayze gently squeezed her shoulder, reassuring her. "Don't worry, we'll find who it is and eliminate them. We can then transfer the Divinity Stone to the Brotherhood and keep it safe." *For how long though*, Darla thought. "First though, your friend Marek needs to get it off Brigg." So, they knew Marek was her friend. That was no surprise, they were the Brotherhood after all. "Then we just need to keep it safe from Velander. After the fiasco with Brigg trying to sell it to him, we hightailed it here. We didn't cover our tracks. We were too busy riding for our lives. He wouldn't have been far behind us.

* * *

"The prince arrived shortly after you did. Our hands are tied. We have to get the stone for him." There was a brief silence before Darla continued. "One way or another." Darla's lips curled as she smiled wickedly from beneath her hood. "Oh, don't worry. I plan on stealing the stone back from the prince."

"We have to, it's imperative." Rayze let out a sigh. "The Brotherhood has intel depicting him as a fanatic and a psychopath. He may not have direct links with Malgorath, but we think that he is crazy enough to think that he can negotiate an alliance and hand over the Divinity Stone."

"I suspected as much." Darla had a gut feeling about Velander, and this confirmed it. "So all we need to do is kill an insane prince, steal the Divinity Stone, and evade an army of elves in the nearby woods. Piece of cake." Darla smiled as she contemplated her options and began to formulate a plan. Rayze looked at her incredulously. "I was being sarcastic." She paused then added, "Still, as ludicrous as it sounds, there is a way we can do it."

Rayze nodded, accepting her lead and assistance. They had a better chance of doing this as a team. "So, what's the plan?"

"Somehow I'll get the prince to his room. I don't know how; I haven't worked out the logistics yet," she replied, the gears turning in her mind.

"Why does it have to be his room?" Rayze asked.

"Because we need somewhere private if I'm going to kill him. Otherwise, I'll draw too much unwanted attention towards Marek and his family. His death could very well start a war." She would be killing a member of one of the royal houses, one of the worst crimes imaginable. She would have to leave the Black Raven, her home. She would have no regrets, though. The last thing she wanted was to put Marek and his family at risk.

* * *

"What about the men's toilet room?" Rayze suggested. "We could make sure it is clear. I could position myself inside the toilet room, hide in one of the cubicles, and wait until he enters. While you're pleasuring him, I'll sneak out and kill him. You could scream, attracting his guards, while I make my escape."

Darla nodded as she contemplated the idea, refining it and adding in details. Rayze listened intently as she rapidly told him her plan in all its intricacy and detail. It was a sound plan! She grinned as a thought came to her. "I take it you'll need a new contract now. Yes?"

"My other option is to start my own bandit gang. I'll do up some flyers, pin them up, and I'll have a group in no time." He was being dramatic and sarcastic. Darla ignored him, explaining what else she had in mind, the new contract that he would have. It was the icing on the cake—Rayze's grin said it all.

Rayze picked up a second pouch and tied the cord shut. "As a show of good faith," he said, handing it to Darla. Nodding her thanks, Darla hooked the pouch to her belt. She had planned to take the pouch anyway, but she was glad it didn't have to be by force. "I also managed to get this off Brigg," he continued, smirking as he handed her a piece of parchment. It was the rhyme they had stolen off Jonas, leading to Tyrak Gunderson's fabled treasure. And sure enough, it had a chunk torn out of it. Darla quickly read it, memorising every word.

> *To find my hidden wealth,*
> *you must use intelligence and stealth.*
> *Enter the forgotten city hidden deep underground.*
> *and search for the symbol that is completely round.*
> *Fear not the creature within the cage.*
> *It guards the tomb of the undead mage.*
> *In the crypt there is a secret...*

Pull it and you...

The bottom corner of the rhyme had been torn off thanks to Jonas's dire wolf. From what Darla could make out, probably only a few words were missing, but they were crucial to revealing the treasure's location. Darla, however, was always up for a challenge. "The treasure is in Sethanon," they both said simultaneously. Raising her eyebrows, Darla looked at Rayze questioningly.

"Sethanon is rumoured to have been built on top of the ruins of an ancient civilization," he said quickly, although Darla knew this already. Apparently Rayze knew his history.

"Then why give me the information? Why not look for it yourself?" she inquired, pocketing the piece of parchment.

"I'm not one for rhymes, and single-handedly facing a creature in a cage or fighting an undead mage is beyond my capabilities. If you find it—"

"That's dragon shit and you know it," Darla finished. There was something he was holding back on and didn't want to divulge, the real reason he didn't want to search for the treasure himself. "And why should I trust you? You did leave me to die on *The Bridget* after all."

Rayze laughed. "I knew you were more than capable of looking after yourself. And here I was thinking you didn't hold a grudge."

"I don't hold a grudge," she replied. "If I did, you'd already be dead." She unsheathed one of her daggers, flipped it casually in the air, and caught the blade between her fingertips. With the handle outstretched, she handed Rayze the dagger. "It might be better if you use this instead of that cumbersome sword of yours." As he inspected it, she turned and started to walk away, the pouch jingling by her side.

* * *

"So, you think you could kill me hey," Rayze said, smirking. "Maybe, maybe not." He shrugged. It wasn't a challenge; it was purely banter. "Depends on whether you use your sword or your claws." He smirked and began to walk away. Darla stood there surprised and speechless. Did he know that she was a werewolf? What else did he secretly know about her? She had so many questions that she wanted to ask him. He opened the door and smiled at her. "Come on. We have a job to do." He looked her up and down. "Let's go and have a drink."

Humming a little tune, he walked out the door. "Now for you, Princeling," Darla mumbled, stepping over the behemoth's corpse and following him down the hallway towards the staircase and the dining area. "I'll be down in a minute. I need to get the emerald," she said, unlocking her bedroom door. Rayze nodded and pulling up his hood, continued down the staircase.

Marek took a long sip of ale before continuing his story. "Frustrated, the Jardoshian general sent two large forces after the humans. The first was a fast-moving light infantry unit consisting of two thousand orcs. The other was a four-hundred strong heavy cavalry unit. Now you see, back then the Mer Danel Mountains blocked off the Kings Highway. It wasn't until twenty years later that, with the dwarves' help, the allied forces extended the highway and established trade routes into the dwarven lands. Because of this, King Desron only had one option: to turn down the Golden Road. The Blood Road was called the Golden Road back then, due to the golden pebbles that made up the road. It was rumoured the road glowed at night, illuminating the way for travellers. The road also was a beacon and a warning, establishing the boundary between the human and elven lands.

"The progress of King Desron and his men was limited, with the humans having to deal with fatigue and exhaustion as well as the burden of the sick and injured slowing them down. With the orcs gaining on them, Desron was forced to make the hardest decision of his life. He and his men emptied some of the wagons and tipped them on their sides, making a crude but effective barricade. The king and the remaining soldiers of the rear guard planned to sacrifice themselves, delaying the orcs for as long as possible and providing the refugees with a chance to escape. Desron drew his sword and waited patiently, watching as the survivors of his kingdom walked off into the distance."

Marek took another sausage and bit it in half. He chewed vigorously, before washing it down with more ale. "Desron didn't have to wait long. A huge dust cloud bellowed from down the road, accompanied by the pounding and roaring of the orc horde. Desron and his soldiers braced themselves, ready for the onslaught, for their inevitable deaths. As the orcs neared, though, a horn sounded, both musical and eerie.

"Arrows soared through the air, emerging from the depths of the forest and raining down on the orcs with deadly accuracy. Only the keenest eye could see the figures standing at the forest's edge, dressed in mottled cloaks of greens, browns, and greys. Cloaks that shimmered, disguising their wearers. Cloaks that belonged to the elven rangers. Armed with their twin curved, long-bladed daggers and their powerful recurve bows, they quickly tore into the orc ranks. Half the orcs charged towards the forest, only to be met by the Elven Vanguard, elite soldiers armed with long, wickedly curved swords."

"A horn sounded, resonating through the mountain range, accompanied by multiple howls. Within moments, huge armoured dire wolves appeared, charging down the mountain slope, carrying dwarven soldiers. Behind them charged the dwarven infantry, their short legs pounding on the gravel as they easily navigated the treacherous mountain terrain. They shouted mighty, fearsome battle cries designed to invoke fear. As Desron and his soldiers charged past the barricade, tears streamed down his face. He had lost hope, thinking his people had been abandoned, left to their fate, but in the direst of moments, his prayers had been answered, and his people had been saved. The elven and dwarven nations had come to their aide and defeated the orcs."

"The Golden Road was littered with bodies from both sides, the beautiful golden gravel stained with blood. From that day on, the name of the road was changed to the Blood Road, a constant reminder of the battle that had been fought upon it." Marek leaned slightly across the table and lowered his voice, adding emphasis to the last part of the tale. "It's also rumoured that while travelling at night, one can hear the cries of the fallen soldiers. Whether it's the ghosts crying and luring travellers to their death, or just the wind blowing through the trees, it remains a mystery. I for one don't want to find out, so I refuse to travel upon the road at night."

Marek drained the last of his ale. "After that, the combined allied forces pushed south, overpowering the orcs and sending them into a full retreat. The orcs sailed back to the Jardoshian Empire with their tails between their legs. It was said the orc general was executed by their emperor for his unforgiving failure."

"Quite a story," Brigg replied, "but I've never really been one for history. I'm more inclined towards business." He hefted a large pouch onto the table and placed it between them. The pouch was slightly open, the Divinity Stone sparkling in the lantern light.

Smiling, trying to hide his surprise, Marek picked up another sausage and ate it slowly, savouring the taste. He needed to delay the proceedings, buy Darla some more time. "I picked up some new spices a month ago when I visited Garedail. My wife requested them for a new sausage recipe, and I must say I think she has a winner. Please help yourself. They're absolutely divine." He gestured towards the plate invitingly before picking up another sausage. "Honey," he shouted, "these sausages are fantastic."

With a creak the kitchen door swung open, and a smiling plump brunette emerged. Jenna raised her eyebrows at her husband as she strolled towards them. "I hope you're not eating them all," she said, picking up two empty bowls from a nearby table.

Marek smiled back. "I can't help that your cooking is wonderful." Jenna hmphed, sighed, and shook her head.

Brigg picked up a sausage and took a small bite. Chewing, he grinned and nodded his approval to Jenna. "I agree with your husband. They're exceptionally nice sausages, milady,"

Jenna smiled, her face aglow, radiating from the compliment bestowed upon her. With a scoop of his hand, Marek picked up the remaining cheese and shoved it into his mouth. He then grabbed the two remaining sausages and took a bite from each of them. Cheeks bulging, he chewed vigorously.

"Please excuse my pig of a husband", Jenna said, taking a swipe at the back of his head. It was a lazy, playful, teasing swing that Marek easily ducked.

"I may be a pig," he mumbled, "but you love me anyway." He swallowed the remaining mouthful, winked, and affectionately put his arm around her waist.

Jenna rolled her eyes. "Sometimes I wonder," she tutted.

"You're a lucky man to have such a wonderful woman," Brigg said, nodding towards Jenna. He was starting to lose his patience. "Such a lady deserves to be spoilt and what better way to spoil her than with this exquisite, beautiful emerald? It's extremely rare and valuable. I'm sure your wife would enjoy it immensely." A gasp escaped Jenna's lips, and even Marek had to admit the Divinity Stone was amazing. It was huge, about fifteen centimetres high, and even though it was green, it sparkled with a myriad of colours in the lantern light. Brigg carefully pushed it deeper into the confines of the pouch and glared at Marek. His lips slowly turned up into a predatory smile. "Now let's discuss a price."

Damn it! Marek thought. *Where the hell is Darla?* "This gem looks far too expensive for me, a humble innkeeper." Marek sighed as he stood. Throughout the conversation, he had noticed Brigg sweating and looking nervous. The man was desperate and needed to quickly offload the Divinity Stone. It was a gamble, one that could easily backfire, but if his suspicions were right, he would be able to acquire it for a very good price, sell it to the prince, and make a healthy profit. Jenna pouted, sulking, playing along and following Marek's lead. Brigg was caught off guard, fumbling for what to say.

"All I can offer you is this, I'm afraid," Marek said, abashed, placing a pouch on the table. The pouch was full to the brim and consisted of mostly copper coins, with a few silver coins hidden amongst them; it was Marek's spare change pouch. The pouches with his gold coins, his accumulated wealth, were locked away in his safe. He had no intention of giving this bandit any of it. The only reason he was offering this pouch was because he wanted to avoid bloodshed.

Brigg opened the pouch and stared at its contents. "Are you purposely trying to insult me? I said gold, not copper. Gold!" he said through clenched teeth.

"Marek, just give this man the gold. I don't care if you have to clear out the safe. I want this emerald. It's absolutely beautiful," Jenna said. Brigg's eyes lit up at the word "safe." How much gold were they talking about? He could be set for life.

* * *

"True, but it's not nearly as beautiful as you, my dear." Marek cuddled her, squeezing her gently, and Jenna couldn't help but blush. He turned to Brigg. "Let me tell you how I met this gorgeous woman."

"Perhaps after we've conducted our business," the half elf replied with an edge of annoyance. He looked around, skittish and beyond frustrated. He was starting to suspect that Marek was up to something, that he was stalling, but why?

Marek blatantly ignored him as he retook his seat. "It will take but a moment. You see, I was out in the forest teaching my son to hunt when we heard a cry of distress. We raced through the—"

"Enough!" Brigg shouted, drawing looks from neighbouring tables. A large broad-bladed dagger appeared in his hand and plunged in the table with a thwack. It was a clear enough warning. "Now get me the gold, innkeeper." He'd had enough of this blabbermouth and his games.

Marek held up his hand in resignation; he had run out of time. His hand slowly disappeared under the table into the confines of his long coat. He sighed. "Go and get the gold from the safe, Jenna."

"Garen!" Jenna yelled. "Go get the gold for your dad. Flow will help you." Garen stood a few feet away, motionless, holding two mugs of ale. Jenna walked up to him and relieved him of the burden and quickly delivered it to the two customers before returning to her husband's side. Marek could more than handle himself, but Jenna wasn't about to let him face this brigand alone. Garen darted up the stairs two at a time. He knew the code; mentioning Flow meant his dad needed help.

"There, you impatient lout. You're getting your gold," Marek said in an icy tone, his fingers wrapping around the leather handle of his mace. "Now for my story. As I was saying, before I was rudely interrupted, my son and I raced through the underbrush, dodging trees, ducking under branches, and leaping over bushes." He picked up the pouch from the table and reattached it to his belt, making sure it jiggled, masking the sound of him unhooking his mace. "Lured by this beautiful woman's screams, we came upon a small clearing. She was desperate, hopelessly outnumbered, surrounded by twenty highly trained, ruthless bandits."

"That is my Divinity Stone!" Prince Velander screamed. Both men turned at the commotion, watching as the prince pushed two people out of the way and drew his sword. Marek cursed at the prince's irrational and impatient behaviour; he was ruining everything. His hopes of reaching a peaceful resolution to this matter had been looking sketchy at best; now they had dissipated in a puff of smoke.

Brigg stood up abruptly, sending his chair toppling backwards to the floor. "You can't touch me, elf," he sneered. He knew exactly where they were and, like Marek, was well versed regarding the treaty between the two kingdoms. He snatched the Divinity Stone off the table and held it aloft in all its glory, goading Velander. "Come and take it off me if you dare, Prince." The bard had stopped playing, and everyone silently watched, riveted, waiting to see how this played out. The only sound was that of Marek's chair as he stood up and revealed his mace.

Seeing an opportunity, Brigg grinned wickedly. Tipping the table and briefly blocking Marek, he grabbed Jenna fiercely and held his sword to her throat. "I'll be leaving now, with the emerald and the wench. Don't follow me!" The message was crystal clear: if they followed or tried to stop him, Jenna was as good as dead. Brigg's one eye darted back and forth as he slowly took a step backwards. He was like a caged animal, desperate and wanting to escape.

Protective and without thinking, Marek took a step forward. With a slight press, the edge of Brigg's blade sliced, creating a small cut, with blood trickling down Jenna's neck. It was a warning as to what would happen if Marek proceeded any further. Prince Velander laughed. "I don't care. Kill the wench." With a scraping of chairs, two of the elven rangers stood up, pointing loaded heavy crossbows at Brigg and Jenna. Grinning maniacally, the prince raised his sword and took a step forward.

"Fuck me," Marek cursed softly, wondering if things could get any worse.

At that moment, Darla appeared, coming down the staircase and entering the dining room. Her midnight, black cloak twirled around her, her hood concealing her features, except for the long wavy hair that cascaded out of it. The bandit leader didn't recognise her until she neared the table. His eyes went wide as he suddenly recalled her from the dwarven inn and the boat. "You—" he began, but his shout was cut short when Marek saw an opportunity; Darla had provided him with the distraction he needed. His mace whipped around and connected with the side of Brigg's head.

Seeing it coming out of the corner of his eye, Brigg had moved, but not fast enough. Instead of caving the side of his head in, the blow was glancing; even so, it created a deep gash. Blood sprayed across his face, obscuring his vision. Blood had been drawn; a fight declared. It was the code of the warrior, an unwritten law.

Prince Velander cursed silently. Sheathing his sword, he held up his hand, ordering the crossbowmen to lower their weapons. Even though he was a sadistic killer, he still respected the warrior's code. Neither he nor his men could get involved. Only Brigg and Marek were allowed to fight.

"Looks like the fight is between you and me, inn keep," Brigg shouted, swinging his sword. Marek raised his mace, blocking the blow with the metal bar. Turning it, he then smashed the spiked metal ball against the blade. The blade shattered, leaving a jagged, broken piece attached to the handle.

Brigg threw it at Marek and lunged for his dagger. He grabbed the handle and pulled the weapon free from the tabletop, only to have Darla's short sword slashing down in a deadly arc through his right wrist, lopping off his hand with a spray of blood. Turning, Brigg slammed the stump through the glass of a nearby lamp and held it in the scorching flame. His quick thinking saved his life as he cauterised the wound, leaving the lingering smell of burnt flesh.

Unarmed and desperate, he lunged for his dagger with his left hand. Marek's mace was already on the move, smashing down onto his outreached hand. Bones crunched, shattering, leaving his hand a bloodied, mangled mess. "Fuck! I'll—" Brigg screamed, his one eye wild and darting, but he was unable to finish the sentence as Marek's mace smashed into the other side of his head.

A meaty crunch sounded as half of Brigg's skull caved in. As if in slow motion, his body slid sideways and hit the floor with a thud. Prince Velander drew his sword with a screech. "The woman interfered. She needs to pay the price," he shouted. The warrior's code had been breached; it specifically stated that once declared, the fight was one on one, with a single weapon of choice and no interference. The price for such a transgression was death.

Marek snickered as he nodded his thanks to Darla. "Normally I would agree with you, Prince, and deal with her myself. But technically the bandit leader broke the code first by reaching for a second weapon."

Seething, the prince grunted his acknowledgement and sheathed his sword. Marek picked up the Divinity Stone and sighed dramatically. "Damn it! I was just getting to the good part of my story too. The exciting part about how I saved Jenna."

Jenna hmphed, raising her eyebrows. She loved him dearly, but sometimes he was unbearable. "How you saved me?" she questioned, "from twenty highly trained, ruthless bandits? There were two bandits, and they were cowardly, uncouth, and disorganised." She laughed. "Hell, I knocked one of them out with a rusty frypan. The remaining one was blubbering and shaking, holding a small rusty dagger before you shot him with your crossbow. The story gets more exaggerated every time you tell it."

Marek briefly looked embarrassed before a smile crept onto his face. "The story grows just as my love for you does, my dear."

"You're intolerable. I'm going to get the mop and bucket. Someone needs to clean up your mess. The body had better be disposed of by the time I get back."

As Jenna sauntered off, Marek turned to find the elven prince standing before them, his hand outstretched. His captain, Prince Jerrick, stood closely by his side, a dutiful protector and bodyguard, his deadly shadow. Marek reluctantly placed the pouch with Divinity Stone in the prince's hand. Smiling, Velander hooked the pouch to his belt, removed a smaller pouch, and tossed it to Marek. The pouch landed on the table, its contents jingling. Nodding his thanks, Marek scooped it up and tucked it away beneath his long coat. Even though the prince was a psychopath, he also was a man of his word.

"Your father will be pleased," Marek said casually. "You'll definitely be in his good graces when you return it to him." He silently pleaded to the gods that Darla had misjudged the prince.

The glint in his eyes said it all. "I won't be returning it to my father. He is weak, living in the past. With my reign, I plan on leading my people into the future."

"Your reign?"

* * *

Velander laughed maniacally. "Yes. Now that I have the Divinity Stone, my father is as good as dead."

"And what do you plan on doing with the stone?" Marek cringed, dreading the answer.

"The demon prince Malgorath wants it. I've learnt this from this low-life minion of his, Lord Dellavenor." He gestured towards the chained elf a few tables away. "I plan to rule Aragoth, using this demon, manipulating him for my own needs. The elvish empire will grow and flourish with the help of our demonic allies, and the nations that oppose us will be destroyed." Marek felt sick; Darla was right—this was worse than what he imagined. And Marek had helped him retrieve the Divinity Stone.

The elven prince turned on his heel and walked away before stopping in midstride. He turned his head to face Marek. "I couldn't help notice that our dear departed bandit leader knew your young lady friend." The statement was followed by a scraping of metal as Prince Jerrick began to draw his sword. He stopped, the sword half drawn, the blade reflecting in the lantern light, as he held the handle in a menacing grip. The threat was evident as he waited patiently for Marek's response.

Prince Jerrick was watching the wrong person. Darla's face was concealed, but her piercing eyes glared at the prince as her hand slid beneath her cloak, grabbing hold of the dagger's handle. It would take a mere second to throw it—the question was whether Jerrick would be quick enough to stop the dagger from killing his liege. Marek laughed, easing the tension, and gave the elvish prince a sly, wolfish smile. "Oh...our dear Flow is a lady of many talents. She entertained our bandit leader in his room earlier." He winked at the prince. "If you know what I mean."

Prince Velander laughed, then looked sternly at Jerrick, who immediately sheathed his sword. It was the laugh of a madman, someone with a zero moral compass. Marek laughed nervously in response, afraid of what he might have gotten Darla into. "Good. Send her to my room, inn keep. I could do with a good fuck." The prince contemplated, having an internal dilemma. "She is human, though. Is she not?" Marek nodded confirmation. "Shame. I don't want to taint my royal cock, have any possibility of half breeds sired and running around. Perhaps I'll just fuck her up the arse instead." Nodding to his captain, he turned around and carried the Divinity Stone back to his table.

"You made me out to be a slut," Darla remarked, raising her eyebrows.

Marek looked a little sheepish. "It was better that than the truth. I'm sorry—I had to say something."

Darla shrugged. "No need to apologise. I plan on using it to my advantage."

Chapter 15

The bard played a merry tune, the patrons thumping their feet and banging their mugs to the song. Some even sang along, not very well, but at least they were enjoying themselves. Forty minutes had passed; the mess had been cleaned up, the situation with Brigg already forgotten. His corpse, along with those of the other bandits, had been tossed into the pig pen out back. The pigs would be having a feast tonight.

Darla bided her time, sitting at the bar, eating a second serving of rabbit stew. It was exceptionally good tonight, she had to admit. After wiping the gravy up with a slice of fresh bread, she washed it down with a goblet of wine. As he poured a mug of ale for another customer, Marek nodded in her direction, indicating he'd refill her goblet in a minute. Darla waited patiently, her green eyes alert, peering from underneath her hood as she took everything in. The man on the stool next to her belched loudly as he slammed his empty mug down. He wore a tattered cloak with a sword strapped across his back. Like Darla, he kept his face well and truly hidden.

Their sole focus was on Prince Velander, on stealing the Divinity Stone without him noticing. The Sethanon royal guards had offered to help, but only if the elves made the first move. It was a diplomatic nightmare. Darla had slipped a special concoction into the prince's goblet half an hour earlier, a mild poison that would cause an excruciating headache, stomach pains, slurred speech, and eventually temporary paralysis. She had been tempted to use a stronger poison but refrained. Even though it would ensure the prince's death, all the stronger poisons left trace elements and distinguishing markers. She couldn't risk it, didn't want to be responsible for an all-out war. Her plan was to isolate the prince, and this was the best way of doing it. Now they just had to wait for it to take effect.

It had been easy, especially with the copious amount of wine the prince had been drinking. The elves were drunk and celebrating their good fortune, the fact that they could now return home. Prince Velander, however, sat by himself with the Divinity Stone on the table in front of him. Two empty bottles lay flat on the table, and a third one had just been opened and served. The wine wasn't cheap either; it was a spiced, sweet-tasting expensive wine Marek kept on his top shelf. No one dared to disturb Velander as he sat there quietly, concocting his scheme for what to do with the Divinity Stone.

Prince Jerrick, who had been privileged enough to enjoy a goblet of wine from the third bottle, had since re-joined his men and sat there worried about Velander's welfare. Unlike his prince, the elvish captain was sober, taking his duty seriously. He hadn't digested much of the poison and should be fine, Darla judged. Jerrick was next in line to the throne, which was a potential problem, one that needed to be dealt with or used to their advantage. She nodded subtly to the hooded man next to her. It was time. Ungracefully he knocked the stool over and winked at Darla from beneath his hood. It was all part of the act. Staggering, he made his way towards the toilet room.

Rayze whistled as he entered the toilet room. He was pleasantly surprised: the floor was made of porcelain tiles, making the room look both luxurious and modern. An elven made latrine was situated against one wall, while the other side consisted of a half dozen cubicles. The cubicles were empty, their polished wooden doors wide-open. Rayze entered the cubicle closest to the dining room and eased the door closed with a slight creak, leaving a gap that was just wide enough for him to peek through.

He drew the long-bladed dagger from its sheath. There was no need to test it; he could already see how sharp it was. Like Darla, he kept his weapons in pristine condition. A patron entered, humming a drunken, boisterous tune. Rayze inched the door open with his free hand while the other one held the dagger, ready to strike. The man was well-built and had a full-length braided beard; judging from his size, he was either a tall dwarf or a half dwarf. Either way, it didn't matter; it was a false alarm. Grumbling and cursing under his breath, Rayze quietly eased the door closed again and went back to waiting. He desperately hoped it wouldn't be much longer, the smell was starting to get to him. Even though the toilet room was luxurious by most standards, it was still a toilet room and reeked of sweat, urine, and faeces.

* * *

At the bar, Marek, smiling, placed a goblet of wine in front of Darla, knowing exactly what she was about to do. She daintily picked it up and took a small sip. The wine was cheap and had a tart taste to it. She grinned wickedly and winked at her friend. She would need a new dress after this, as the stain probably wouldn't come out. Sacrifices had to be made, though, and the wine was perfect for what she had in mind. She took another sip, looking inconspicuous and waited patiently.

With a swipe of his hand, Prince Velander sent one of the empty bottles flying, and it shattered on the floor. He clumsily lifted himself off his seat and, holding on to the edge of the table, staggered slightly. The drug had taken effect. Prince Jerrick leapt to his feet, ready to give aide, but Velander pushed him away a moment before vomiting over his tunic. His eyes were glazed, blinking. Trying to focus, he picked up the satchel with the Divinity Stone, tied it shut, and attached it to his belt. Wobbling, he staggered towards the toilet room.

The elven prince lurched sideways, colliding into a table and mumbling something to the man sitting there. His speech was slurred, indicating that he was drunk; Darla suspected it was a combination of the alcohol and the poison. The man shot to his feet, drawing a dagger in the process. In response Prince Velander fumbled as he tried to draw his sword. Prince Jerrick was there in an instant, his sword drawn with a scraping hiss. He was honour bound, sworn to protect his liege at all costs.

Standing nearby, Marek also reacted, laughing jovially and patting the customer on the shoulder. He had spent years defusing such situations. "It's okay, friend. It was an accident. How about I get you two free mugs of ale as compensation?" It would cost Marek a little initially, put him out of pocket, but if all went as according to plan, he'd be well and truly compensated. Smiling, the stranger nodded and sheathed his dagger.

* * *

Sighing with relief, Prince Jerrick nodded his thanks and, reversing his sword, sheathed it. He was a fighter; killing was his business, not diplomacy. If he had a gold coin for every time he had drawn blood and saved his prince, he would be wealthy beyond his wildest dreams. At least the innkeeper had resolved the situation, had stopped him from starting a war. As he smiled, pondering these thoughts, he was forcibly shoved and went crashing through the table before landing in a heap on the floor. Angry and embarrassed, his eyes full of hatred, he stared at the man who had just humiliated him. His prince! "I nan ducking well flight by thone flights," he slurred, wobbling then continuing to stagger towards the toilet room. Marek ran over to the elven captain and offered him his hand. As he helped him up, he gave Darla a subtle nod.

She sprang into action; it was time to get to work. Darla walked towards a table where a drunk, rotund merchant sat downing liquor with some potential clients. He was new to the inn but had managed to scope out some of the clientele, attracting the attention of some lower-class nobles. Darla didn't know the merchant from a bar of soap, which suited her purposes just fine. He obviously had made a sale, as all of them had a glass of amber liquor in front of them. A specially designed, ornate bottle sat in the middle of the table. Darla recognised it immediately: Dragon's Breath.

The whole table looked perplexed at the audacity of this woman while the merchant merely sat there confused and uncomfortable, smiling awkwardly as Darla laughed, spoke jovially to him, and acted as if they were old friends. All the while, she watched the prince out of the corner of her eye like a predator, waiting for him to get into position.

Prince Velander grabbed one of the wooden columns, supporting himself momentarily before continuing towards the toilets. Darla waited, timing everything perfectly as the prince neared her. Laughing, she stepped backwards and bumped into him. Her goblet flew into the air, the cheap wine splashing over the prince's expensive tunic. "I'm sorry, Your Highness," she apologised, wiping the tunic with her hand, smearing the wine even farther across it. In the process, she managed to tear the tunic. The tunic looked expensive and now it was ruined.

She seductively ran her fingers down his chest to his stomach. Leaning forward, she licked the wine off his chest. In a blur, her free hand darted towards him. Moaning blissfully, the elven prince didn't even notice as she unhooked the satchel from his belt. Part one was accomplished; the Divinity Stone was secure.

Darla's fingers slid down to his groin, feeling him, arousing him. The bulge in his pants showed, and Darla smiled. Slowly, carefully, her other hand slid back and hooked the satchel to the back of her belt. The prince looked at the stairs, his mind ticking over as he weighed things up. Darla could see the conflict in his eyes, he was in complete and utter ecstasy, but like all nobility, he had no patience. His eyes roamed towards the nearby toilets. Darla smiled; she had counted on his impulsiveness, on this reaction. This was exactly where she wanted him to go.

Closing his eyes, Prince Velander let out another blissful moan. Darla stretched and reached across her back to the other side of her belt. Grabbing hold, she unhooked the other satchel and slowly slid her hand back around. The prince was in a state of pure euphoria. She reached towards the prince, keeping the satchel steady. His belt hook was right in front of her; all she needed to do was hook the satchel on. Then the prince's eyes opened, and he stopped moaning. "I need to go to the toilet," he said matter-of-factly. He pulled away abruptly and knocked Darla's hand. Looking down, he saw her holding the satchel. His expression changed, becoming angry and feral. "You bitch!" he shouted, drawing his sword.

Just like that, the circumstances had changed from going perfectly, to going pear shaped All eyes turned to them, engaged with the drama—attention Darla didn't want or need. Grabbing hold of the handle, she started to draw the short sword, only to stop, letting go and covering her ears as a high-pitched whistling sounded.

Darla winced, wobbling on unsteady feet. Everyone else could hear it but seemed relatively unaffected as they looked around, searching for the source. For Darla, though, with her heightened hearing, the pain was excruciating. The whistling intensified, growing to a crescendo, as Darla's knees buckled, and she screamed. The prince took full advantage of the situation, lunging with a swift overhead slash, his blade flickering in the lantern light. All Darla could do was cringe in pain as she stood there unarmed and defenceless.

The sword missed, failing to connect as both combatants were thrown off their feet and crashed to the floor. The explosion was deafening, taking out half of the dining area, including the ceiling and part of the upper floor. A couple of clay tiles fell to the floor, shattering, and it was then that Darla noticed the gaping hole in the roof. The damage was extensive and would take months to repair. Marek would be devastated and well and truly pissed.

An unnatural mist clouded the surrounding area, blocking the view of the outside world from those inside the inn. The vapor was unnaturally cold, even for this time of year. Darla paled and looked on in shock, her keen vision distinguishing a silhouette before anyone else. She immediately recognised the figure slowly emerging from the mist: Jaydrath. The demon had not only survived but also had managed to track her down. Darla wondered whether there was some truth in the things he had said. Whether he was linked to the Divinity Stone, whether he actually was immortal.

Without hesitation, she reached towards her thigh and withdrew her dagger. In one fluid motion, she sent it twirling through the air, her aim flawless. Darla was a perfectionist with a spotless track record; she never missed her target. The dagger halted abruptly, frozen in midair, inches from the demon's face. Then, with a casual wave of his hand, the dagger spun, faster and faster, until it was nothing but a blur. Raising his bony bluish-grey finger, he sent it hurtling towards Darla.

An indistinct, deadly blur, the dagger rocketed towards her. Darla rolled, landing in a crouch as the dagger embedded itself, vibrating, in the wooden column behind her. She stood up slowly, keeping a steady eye on Jaydrath, and heard a crunch. Looking down, she saw shattered glass mixed with an amber liquid. A liquid with a sweet, distinct smell. Dragon's Breath!

Darla scanned the room. The merchant and his clients lay semi-conscious amongst the debris, moaning and wounded. The bottle of Dragon's Breath lay amid the debris, stoppered, covered in dust and unbroken. As she slowly moved towards it, she noticed movement out of the corner of her eye. It was Rayze, sword and dagger in hand, edging his way between the tables, chairs, and detritus. Hearing the ruckus, he had figured everything had gone to shit and had crept out of the men's toilet room.

He made a couple of hand signals, not at her, she realised, but at the two captains, Jerrick and Brenan. The captains then relayed their own signals to the soldiers under their command. They were planning a coordinated attack, thinking that with their superior numbers they could overpower and kill the demon. They were wrong, terribly wrong. Darla didn't warn them, though; she planned to use their distraction to her advantage.

"The Divinity Stone," Jaydrath roared, spying the emerald at the same time as Darla. It had been torn from her grasp with the explosion and now lay a couple of metres away. The pouch lay open with the giant emerald poking out in all its beauty.

"It's mine, demon," Velander shouted, sprinting forward and diving for the stone. He slid across the icy floor; his sword held out in front of him. Skidding from side to side as he tried to control himself, he extended his hand. His timing was perfect! His fingers wrapped around the emerald, plucking it from the satchel. He laughed maniacally as he spun in circles. Then stopped abruptly and screamed in pain.

A razor-sharp icy stalagmite had erupted through the floor, shattering the polished floorboards and impaling the prince's stomach. "I believe that is mine," Jaydrath said, leisurely traipsing over. With a flick of his hand, a column of ice erupted and, like a snake, wrapped around Velander's wrist, trapping it. Slowly the ice constricted, breaking his bones with an earsplitting crack.

Gritting through the pain, the prince somehow still managed to keep the emerald in his grasp. "The Divinity Stone is ours, demon," he said. "It has belonged to the elven royal family for generations."

"Only because it was stolen from our realm!" Jaydrath shouted. "We are kin to the Divinity Stone and have been linked to it for centuries." He grabbed the prince's hand, his touch colder than ice. Velander stubbornly clung to the emerald, refusing to let go. A loud snap sounded as Jaydrath broke multiple fingers and pried the emerald loose.

"What the—?" Jaydrath said, confused. The Divinity Stone was a fake, nothing but a giant emerald. He didn't get a chance to finish the sentence, as multiple arrows and bolts shot forth in a chorus of twangs. Shouting war cries, the two captains charged forth, alongside their troops. Clutching the emerald to his side, Jaydrath raised his free hand, and a wall of ice rose before him.

One after another, the arrows thudded into the ice. It looked like a pin cushion with the multitude of projectiles embedded into it. All the while, Jaydrath remained unharmed. The soldiers slashed and hacked at it, screaming in frustration as they ripped away small chunks of ice. Although they were persistent, the wall was impenetrable. Jaydrath raised his hand, and the cracks disappeared, an untarnished wall appearing again. The demon smiled, relishing the screams, as more stalagmites erupted through the floor.

Elven and human soldiers lay impaled by the stalagmites, their weapons discarded on the floor. The two wounded captains had retreated with the survivors, perplexed and unsure what to do. They had stopped firing their arrows and bolts, opting to conserve them. The projectiles had proven to be useless, as effective as firing a spit ball at the demon. Now the captains and soldiers were on the defensive, just hoping to survive.

"Marek, use the anplam bolts," Darla said, running towards the bottle. Anplam bolts were gnome-designed bolts with an incendiary and explosive ability, igniting anything they hit.

Marek nodded and disappeared to unlock a secret compartment. He returned a moment later with his repeater crossbow. The crossbow was a work of art, crafted by an expert weaponsmith from across the sea. He had acquired it during his travels, and it had cost him a small fortune. The weapon could accommodate four razor-sharp quarrels, and with a twisting of the crank at the end, Marek could quickly reload and fire off all four quarrels in rapid succession. After loading the four broad dark-red tipped bolts, he aimed and prepared to fire, knowing he had to make every shot count.

Darla ran and grabbed the bottle just as Marek fired two bolts with only the slightest movement of the crossbow. The bolts shot through the air, increasing their angle ever so slightly as they neared the target. They hit the ice wall simultaneously, detonating at different sections. The wall exploded into shards of glistening ice, leaving the surprised demon exposed and vulnerable.

Rayze was there in an instant; he had come out of nowhere. He swivelled as gracefully as a dancer and slashed. His stroke was perfect and precise. The demon's hand fell to the floor along with the emerald. It was the perfect distraction for Darla. Running forward with the bottle in hand, she drew her short sword.

* * *

Rayze's dagger, the one Darla had lent him, glistened in the lantern light. Swinging it up, he tried to drive it into the demon's neck, only for Jaydrath to halt it inches away from its target. The demon's bony bluish-grey hand had wrapped around Rayze's in a vise-like grip, and try as he might, Rayze couldn't break it. He tried again, grunting, but couldn't even budge it. Suddenly a sharp pain shot up his arm, and he watched horrified as it began to freeze. He couldn't move it; it was paralysed, frozen solid. Grinding his teeth, he bit back the pain. Then, with a sadistic smile, Jaydrath squeezed and shattered Rayze's wrist and forearm. Eyes wide, Rayze screamed.

In an instant, the bony bluish-grey hand wrapped around his throat like a striking snake, quick and deadly. Rayze felt a numb, burning sensation and found it hard to breathe. He tried to raise the sword but lacked the strength. He gasped for breath; his lungs were on fire, his vision blurry. He was fading fast.

Then, with a bright blue blur, Darla's short sword was there, slicing off Jaydrath's arm at the elbow. The demon howled in pain as Rayze collapsed to his knees, coughing. Darla followed through with her other arm, smashing the bottle against the demon's head. The amber liquid splashed everywhere, covering Jaydrath from head to toe. "Move!" Darla shouted, diving to the ground and rolling to the side.

Rayze didn't hesitate. He crawled across the floor before collapsing in a heap. The demon merely stood there confused, feeling something that he'd never experienced before…a burning sensation. A moment later, a red-tipped bolt shot past him, aimed with perfect precision. With a thud, the bolt struck the demon in the chest, embedding itself and instantly igniting. Ablaze, Jaydrath wailed. The pain was excruciating, and the more he tapped into his power, the worse it got. His magic was reacting to the heat, increasing, accelerating; it was out of control, and he couldn't stop it. The flames flickered brightly then changed colour from their glowing orange red to blue and finally violet. "Stop the pain!" he screamed.

* * *

"As you wish," Darla replied, leaping forward. She took two steps and, with her short sword outstretched, pivoted. The blade sliced through the demon's neck, decapitating him and sending his head rolling across the floor. Jaydrath's lifeless body dropped to the floor with a thud. It was over; the demon was dead. No longer fuelled by the magic, the fire quickly died out, leaving a smouldering black mess on the floor. "Well, that could have gone better," Darla said, smiling weakly and helping Rayze to his feet.

"You think?" he replied, laughing. He winced in pain. "Don't make me laugh. It hurts." They both laughed, and Rayze winced again. With his free hand he picked up the emerald, Jaydrath's hand breaking apart and falling to the floor. Dead and not of this realm, the demon had lost all substance, its body disintegrating before their eyes.

Looking down, she sighed. "Sorry about your arm," she apologised. She felt guilty; she hadn't not been quick enough. The stump had been cauterised, frozen solid. It had started to thaw, revealing the damaged tissue and flesh. He would need a healer, and soon. Rayze held the emerald aloft, admiring its beauty. It was over, for now at least. Darla looked around at the damage and carnage the demon had caused. Her head was turned, looking in the other direction, when she heard the noise: the rattling of a chain and an ear-piercing scream. By the time she reacted, however, it was too late.

Lord Dellavenor, his chain dragging behind him, had approached from behind Rayze, a broad-bladed dagger in hand. His eyes were glazed, focused only on one thing: the emerald. "The Divinity Stone is mine!" he shouted, spittle spraying everywhere. The dagger stabbed repeatedly, in a frenzy, into Rayze's back. Although the leather armour absorbed a significant amount of the force, the wounds were significant. Darla was helpless, the fanatical lord using Rayze as a shield. Groaning, Rayze leaned into her, forcing her to take most of his weight. Darla's sleeve became wet as his blood flowed steadily down his back onto her arm. His knees buckled, and he dropped slightly, leaving the lord open and providing Darla with an opportunity.

"Remember what I promised to do to you?" Darla spat through clenched teeth. Somehow Rayze still managed to hold the emerald in an iron grip.

"I don't care about your useless threats, bitch. I am Malgorath's loyal servant. He will reward me and protect me."

"Let's see him protect you from this," she said, as she drove the short sword through his remaining eye. She jammed it in to the hilt, puncturing his brain and killing him instantly. The blade erupted through the back of his head. "Well, be thankful. At least I didn't pluck out your eye and make you eat it."

"What?" Rayze asked weakly, lowering himself to the floor and sitting next to the corpse. He quickly hid the emerald beneath his cloak.

Darla shrugged. "Oh, nothing. It's just something I promised to do to Dellavenor if he ever fucked with me again." She beckoned to the Sethanon soldiers for help, catching Brenan's attention. The captain was in the process of being bandaged up. He nodded and mouthed, "I'll be there in a minute."

Darla cursed. "If he doesn't hurry up, I'll drag his arse over here myself." She pulled out the short sword with a squelch and wiped the blood and brain matter off with a piece of the dead lord's tunic.

"Don't worry. I'll be fine," Rayze said. "My armour protected me. The wounds look worse than what they actually are." He nodded and waved her away. "Go collect your daggers. I'll be okay, honest." He smiled reassuringly. Shaking her head and sheathing the short sword, Darla walked off to retrieve her daggers.

* * *

She glanced at Rayze as she wiped the blood off her second dagger. Although her weapons had been cleaned, they would have to wait to be properly whetted and polished. She watched, baffled at what he was doing. He was holding the lord's left arm in the air and had his head over it. Was he biting the corpse? What the hell was he up to? Sheathing the dagger, she headed back to him.

"What are you doing?" she asked, harsher than she intended.

Rayze lifted his head, a thick gold bracelet dangling from his mouth. He dropped it into his hand and smiled devilishly. "It was the only way I could undo the clasp," he explained, offering her the bracelet. "After all, to the victor goes the spoils."

"Keep it," Darla replied, smiling and looking at him quizzically. The Brotherhood operative seemed perkier, healthier; something had changed in just the last minute or two.

Rayze shrugged, putting it in his pocket. "You might want to give Prince Jerrick this, though," he said, handing her a gold signet ring engraved with Dellavenor's house insignia. "I believe Dellavenor didn't have an heir, so Jerrick might want to give this ring, along with the lord's holdings and wealth, to another lord." As Darla nodded, Brenan and one of his soldiers walked over.

"The corporal here is a field medic," Brenan said, looking dubious about Rayze's chances at recovery. "I don't know whether your friend will survive; his injuries are grave. The corporal will do what he can though, and then we'll take him to—" He stopped in midsentence, mouth agape, as Rayze casually stood up.

"I don't need a field medic or a healer, just a horse," he said, showing them the emerald beneath his cloak.

Bewildered, Brenan nodded and sauntered off to give some final orders to his men. Two horses were already outside waiting for

Rayze and Brenan. It was part of their plan; Garen had snuck out to get them ready earlier. Darla and Rayze exchanged looks; they both had noticed the field medic's eyes light up upon seeing the emerald. The question was whether it was from pure greed or whether he was one of Malgorath's minions. Only time would tell.

Before walking over to the captain, Rayze embraced Darla, clasping forearms in a fond farewell. Darla watched him go, wondering if they would ever cross paths again. It was then that she noticed the back of his cloak blotched, ripped and a bloody mess. How was he even walking? Darla shook her head, truly puzzled. Rayze was still a mystery to her, one she was determined to get to the bottom of. Curious, she picked up Lord Dellavenor's bloody wrist and noticed a small incision, sliced with expert precision. A cut she could swear hadn't been there earlier.

"I need a drink," she said, walking to the bar. Marek had his arms wrapped around Jenna, comforting her as she sobbed onto his shoulder. Jenna wasn't weak by any means; in fact, she was the strongest woman that Darla knew. Dealing with bandits was one thing but dealing with a demon was something else entirely. She had every right to be scared. Releasing Jenna, Marek quietly walked over and poured them both a whisky. He gave her a weak smile, as he stood there subdued, drinking and contemplating. Darla knew the smile had been forced. He was worried about his family and the inn. About protecting it from the elements and securing it from any unwanted intruders. Then there would be the cost of the repairs, Marek would already be calculating the hefty cost in his head. "I will help out with the cost of the repairs," Darla said quietly.

"Thank you, but no. You have your own problems that you need to take care of." He was referring to buying Lance and his family's freedom.

"And besides, if it wasn't for you the inn would be destroyed and we'd be dead," Jenna said walking up and wrapping her arms around him. It was an argument she undoubtedly wouldn't win, but she had to try. They were family. She was about to say something, when the kitchen door swung open and Garen walked in chomping on a sausage.

He had been smart enough to hide in the stable during the fight, trying to keep the horses calm and staying out of harm's way. He was able to give Darla a nod of confirmation, before being pulled in by his parents and embraced in a fierce hug. Breaking free momentarily, he quickly addressed Darla. "Your friend in the stables is freaking out the horses." He was about to say more when he was grabbed and embraced in another hug. Confused, Darla grabbed her whisky and walked over to Brenan, Rayze and the surviving Sethanon soldiers. It was time to implement the next stage of their plan.

* * *

Chapter 16

Darla approached Brenan with a large whisky in hand. "Have you had a chance to look over my benefactor's letter?" he asked, raising his eyebrows questioningly.

She swirled the liquor in her glass. "I haven't," she replied casually. "I'm afraid I've been too busy stealing a magical artefact and killing a demon."

"A lesser demon." Rayze snickered from between two soldiers. Grinning, he raised his head slightly. Darla gave him a mocking sidelong glance and received a weak laugh in response.

"I stand corrected…a lesser demon," she said. She didn't know how he knew this kind of information.

Brenan laughed. "Well," he said, oohing and aahing for emphasis. "My benefactor also included these to sweeten the deal and try to persuade you." With a jingle and a clunk, he placed two pouches on the bar.

"Why didn't you show me these when you first offered me the contract?" Darla asked.

"Because, as you stated, you were working and I didn't want to distract you," Brenan replied.

A long time ago, Darla had learnt the unique sound each coin and gem made. The first pouch was full of gold coins, but there was another sound mixed in with it, a sound she didn't quite recognise. She had only heard the sound twice before. With a puzzled expression, she looked at the pouch as she tried to remember. It didn't take long for her brain to recall the information, and as soon as she remembered, her mouth opened in a silent gasp.

With slightly shaking hands, she opened the pouch and confirmed her suspicion. She found mostly gold coins but mixed in were dragon coins. These were produced by master alchemists who worked at the Royal Emporium Bank. They were made from a mixture of yellow gold, white gold, and diamond dust and were imprinted with a soaring dragon. These coins were worth a fortune and were only generally used by royalty and wealthier members of the nobility. One of these coins alone was worth a hundred gold coins, and Darla counted at least a dozen of them. It was the most she'd ever been offered for a contract. It was overly generous, which worried her slightly.

Brenan opened the second pouch slowly, teasing her with its contents, which sparkled with a radiant gleam. The pouch was full of glistening medium-size diamonds. With these added diamonds, she would only need one or two contracts, and then she'd have enough to buy her friends' freedom. And along with these dragon coins and the other wealth she had accumulated, she'd be able to retire and live like a queen. She was dubious, though; what kind of assignment would pay her so bountifully?

"My benefactor heard you were after diamonds." Brenan grinned. "I take it this meets your approval?"

The job was questionable, but Darla knew her abilities; there was no job she couldn't do. Although she was wary, she also didn't want to question the offer, especially when the payout was this good.

"I wish you'd stop calling him your benefactor and address him by his title. Maybe, just maybe, you could refer to him as your prince," Darla replied smugly, a glint in her eye. A brief flicker in Brenan's eyes was all the confirmation she needed. "When I picked up the letter, I immediately recognised the royal emblem of Sethanon and, by the indentation of the wax seal, I surmised that one of the princes wrote it."

Brenan was briefly dumbfounded but quickly recovered his composure. "I do hope you aren't using diamonds to deal with those hideous, conniving gorkin. I believe diamonds are their form of currency," he said, changing the subject. Only a handful of people knew the reason Darla expressly needed diamonds, so she figured it was pure speculation on his part.

"I wouldn't dream of it. I'm just a lady who likes sparkly jewels." she lied. She didn't care whether he believed her; what she did with the diamonds was her business. "I accept the contract."

"But you haven't even looked over the details yet." She had surprised him, caught him off guard. It was the way she liked to conduct her business, to be in control and keep her benefactors guessing.

* * *

She shrugged. "The details don't really matter when you're paying this kind of money. Also, I'm sure you'd rather I look over the details in the privacy of my room instead of an inn full of patrons." The inn wasn't full of customers now—most of them had fled for safety—but that was beside the point. The captain nodded, conceding. "After all," she said with a laugh, "what do you expect me to do? Assassinate someone from the royal family or something?" Little did she know that was exactly what the job entailed.

Brenan finished his drink and slammed the glass on the bar. "I'm impressed with your ability and think you're more than suitable for any assignment you're given. You're intelligent, resourceful, and have proven to be a capable fighter. You handled yourself well; it's no wonder why my prince has requested you." And there it was, the confirmation. The soldier next to him sneered. "My sergeant disagrees with me. Feel free to teach him some manners," Brenan said, sounding slightly irritated.

"What about if I just jam my short sword up his arse?" Darla smirked. She could tell the sergeant didn't like her; the feeling was mutual.

He was a beast of a man, a full two heads taller than Darla and bulking in muscle. The sergeant put down his drink, casually took a few steps, and stood before her. He slowly reached across his shoulder and drew forth a wickedly curved battle-axe. "I'd like to see you try you, whiny little bitch," he spat.

Darla broke into an enormous grin. The sergeant whistled—the man wasn't alone; he had allies. Four of them. Two of the soldiers were swordsmen, dressed in heavy chainmail armour, their gauntleted hands gripping the handles of their swords, ready to draw them at a moment's notice. The other two stood dressed in hardened leather armour, which was lighter and more flexible, enabling them to handle the light crossbows they now held, their glistening steel-tipped bolts pointing right at her. Although the single-handed, light crossbows weren't as powerful as their heavy, two-handed counterparts, they would prove just as deadly within the confined space of the inn.

Behind the bar, Marek listened, alert, taking everything in as he served her one of his finer, more expensive wines. He was extremely careful, ensuring he didn't spill a drop as he poured the wine into a crystal goblet. Darla drew her dagger and skilfully spun it between her fingers before placing it on the bar and picking up the goblet. Daintily, she took a sip. The wine was divine—sweet, mixed with a fragrant spice, and exceptionally smooth. She savoured the taste before swallowing. "Oh, but you said I'm just a whiny little bitch. Surely I pose no threat to you and your ruffian friends?"

The sergeant snickered. "And you'll remain a whiny little bitch until you prove yourself to me and my friends." So he wanted her to prove herself, did he? Well, Darla thought, she'd give it to them in spades. Smiling, she raised the goblet to her lips and like some uncouth barbarian, downed the remaining wine in one gulp. She felt dreadful, regretting having to do it, to scull such a beautifully rich and fragrant wine, but it was necessary. She slammed the goblet onto the bar, shattering the crystal base and sending shards flying everywhere.

With the base shattered, the stem of the goblet had become jagged and sharp. Still holding the goblet, she swung her arm forward, striking out with lightning speed and stabbing the crystal stem into the sergeant's unprotected throat. Blood spurted out in a nightmarish fountain as he clutched at his throat and toppled to the floor.

With her free hand, Darla snatched the dagger off the bar then parried as one of the swordsmen lunged at her. A twang sounded, and she grabbed the swordsman by the throat and pulled him in front of her. A loud cling sounded as one of Marek's bolts hit the swordsman's plate armour and fell harmlessly to the floor. The swordsman winced; even though his armour had saved him, the impact would leave a bruise. Following through, Darla then sliced the swordsman across his gauntleted wrist, causing him to drop his sword with a clang.

The second crossbowman had bided his time, waiting for an opportunity. He was about to pull the trigger when he flew backwards as something slammed into his chest. The crossbowman smashed into the wall behind him and fell in a heap. Marek was already in the process of re-cocking his repeater crossbow. The remaining crossbowman fumbled as he also tried to re-cock his crossbow. Marek was proficient with the repeater crossbow, cranking his second bolt into the chamber in half the time. He aimed and fired, hitting him in the chest and sending the crossbowman crashing through a table.

Seeing his fallen allies, the carnage this one woman had caused, the second swordsman hesitated. Staring at him, waiting for him to make the first move, Darla casually hummed as she spun the dagger in her hand. The swordsman's hands were trembling, and he had visibly paled. Slowly, steadily, he sheathed his sword and helped the sergeant to his feet. The sergeant had gone as white as a ghost from the loss of blood and stood on wobbly feet. His meaty hand was still clutching his throat, stemming the blood flow. There was a chance he would survive, maybe.

With a grunt, he beckoned his allies and left the inn. They all had survived but were ashamed, retreating with their tails between their legs. It was then that Darla noticed Brenan and Rayze had gone, slipping out at some point during all the confusion. "Where the fuck is the Divinity Stone?" Prince Jerrick shouted, and it was then, with a cold certainty, that Darla knew exactly why they had left.

Sheathing her dagger, she turned calmly to address the elven captain. "I don't know where the stone is," she replied, shrugging.

* * *

"I'm not in the mood for your games, bitch. I know you've stolen it, so I strongly suggest you give it back," Jerrick shouted, extending his hand.

"Well, Captain—" Darla started before being rudely interrupted.

"Due to Prince Velander's demise, I'm no longer a captain. I am now the heir to the throne. You can address me by my proper title, 'Prince Jerrick,'" he said arrogantly.

"And as you are aware, this inn isn't within elven lands, which means you aren't my prince. Therefore, I will call you Prince Dumbass.'" Darla smirked. This produced a guffaw from Marek, who was busy clearing up some of the mess.

"You would do well not to make an enemy of me, thief."

"Likewise," Darla replied, refusing to back down. "I was nowhere near the damn Divinity Stone or your deranged prince."

"You weren't, but..." Jerrick said, putting the pieces together. "Your friend. Where is he?" He looked around frantically.

"I don't know. I was engaged in a fight, concentrating on other things. I only noticed his absence when the fight was over."

Jerrick was irate as he ordered Garen to gather the remaining elves' horses. The young stable hand yawned before moving towards the door. He halted in his tracks as his father addressed him. "Garen, it's late and you're exhausted. The elves can get their own damn horses." Marek was annoyed; the elven prince had overstepped his bounds. Garen mumbled something resembling "Good night" and trudged towards his bedroom.

"You really should choose better company," Jerrick told Darla before walking briskly towards the door. With a thud and a crack of splintering wood, a dagger slammed into the door, narrowly missing the prince. His hand immediately went to his sword.

"That's the only warning you'll get. Insult my friends again, and prince or not, you'll suffer the consequences," Darla replied in an icy tone.

Taking his hand off his sword, the prince opened the door and silently walked out. With her keen hearing, Darla heard the elves shouting as their horses neighed, frolicked, and even bolted. The elves were desperately trying to saddle and mount them, but they were failing miserably. Finally, after what seemed an eternity, they were ready to give pursuit.

With the elves successfully delayed, Garen came back out laughing, proud of his performance. It had all been part of the ruse. Sighing, they then got to their own daunting task of clearing up the inn. As Marek cleared the debris, Darla carried the corpses out to the pig pen. Although she was both mentally and physically exhausted, she had one last thing to do. Wrapping her cloak tightly around her, she walked along the gravel path towards the stables.

A familiar roar sounded, causing Darla to look up into the night sky, searching and seeking the source. Nothing. Just the moon, the stars, and the red planet Mykroth faintly illuminating the sky. The planet was worshiped by many cultures, and its god was known by many names, the main ones being War, Sacrifice, Chaos, and Hunter. Every century there was a blood moon event, an eclipse where Mykroth aligned with the moon. During these events, some races claimed to be cursed, while others claimed to be blessed. In Darla's opinion, the werewolves were both blessed and cursed. During the event, all their senses and abilities were enhanced, but they also entered a feral, animalistic state, losing all control and resorting to their primal instincts. And the scary thing was, judging from Mykroth's positioning, the next blood moon event was about three months away.

* * *

She unlatched the door and entered the stable to a frenzy of stamping and kicking. The horses in the right-side stalls were going crazy, snorting nervously, their eyes flickering. They were scared, reacting to a threat nearby, a threat other than her. Curious, she walked around to the right side of the barn, her boots crunching on the pebbles. Another low roar sounded, and she peered around the corner. The wyvern lay there, leaning against the stable wall, its eyes staring at her fearful and scared.

It made sense that the wyvern was hiding here in fear. The forest was full of elves, its captors, and it didn't want to risk flying and being seen. Even as deadly and powerful as they were, like their dragon cousins they had been hunted, captured, and even tortured. Due to this, they usually kept to the forested and mountainous regions, avoiding larger settlements. From their experience, those places often spelled danger and death. For the wyvern to be here, it showed how desperate it was.

Darla suspected the wyvern hadn't intervened with the demon because it didn't want to draw any unwanted attention from the elves. "Come on, boy," she said quietly, patting her side and leading the creature away. Walking a short distance down the gravel path, she led the wyvern to the barn. Creeping behind her, looking around anxiously, the wyvern barely made a sound. It treaded softly, leaving next to no imprints. The beast was stealthy, the way it sometimes hunted its prey. Darla was impressed that such a large creature could do this.

The barn was small, consisting of a medium-size cart and rows and rows of sacks of animal feed, which were organised, labelled, and categorised. There was also a huge stack of hay. It wasn't ideal, but it would have to do. Leaping forward, the wyvern tore into the bale, its sharp claws shredding the thick rope around it. Hay sprayed everywhere, a colossal mess raining throughout the barn. The last of the hay flittered down as the wyvern kneaded the pile before him. The creature was making a bed for itself. With a snort it lay down and got comfortable. Closing its eyes, knowing Darla would keep it safe, it fell asleep. The stock of straw was ruined; as it was winter, it would be nearly impossible to order fresh hay unless it was from overseas, in which case it would cost a fortune. Yet again, Marek was going to be well and truly pissed!

With the wyvern taken care of, Darla walked back to the stables. She was deep in thought, wondering how she was going to tell Marek about the hay and the wyvern. The horses were still skittish, even with the wyvern gone, but then again, they always were skittish around Darla. They feared her, could sense what she was. Midnight was the only one that was completely calm around her. He had been specially trained, was used to her idiosyncrasies and her scent, and accepted who and what she was, to a point. Ignoring the other horses, she walked over to Midnight and reached into his stall.

He nuzzled her hand, and she gave him an affectionate pat, and then he neighed cheekily. "Fine," Darla said, succumbing and reaching across to a sack hanging on the side of the stall. He happily munched into the apple she tossed him, spraying juice everywhere. "You're being lazy," she told him. "You know you can reach these yourself." Another neigh, followed by a snicker, as if he were saying, *Why bother when I can get you to do it for me?* Darla shook her head. "You're intolerable," she muttered, walking away. Midnight neighed affectionately behind her, as if to say, *Yeah. I love you too.*

Tapping into her lycanthropy, Darla grabbed hold of the bandit's large wagon and pulled it out. Slowly and steadily, she rolled it to the inn and threw back the hide covering—that of a mamolith; a large, furry, stocky mammal with tusks. The savage barbarian tribes were renown for riding them into battle, while other cultures hunted them for their tusks and hides. Underneath the covering were two large chests and a pile of medium-size obsidian figurines. One of the chests she recognised, the one the bandits had plundered from *The Bridget*.

* * *

Two at a time she carried the figurines inside. There was a dozen of them; it was an impressive collection. Although they had a bit of weight, they were lighter than she'd expected. Shrugging, she dismissed it. Now for the chests. Grabbing the handles, she lifted each of the chests from the cart, carried them inside, and placed them next to the figurines. The one from the boat was closed but unlocked, while the one they'd stolen from the merchant had a steel padlock. She recognised the lock; it had a five-pin tumbler, a complicated and expensive lock that was difficult to pick. She was confident she could do so, but it would have to wait. She had to help Marek secure the inn.

She and Marek tipped the wagon on its side, blocking the gap in the wall to keep any wild animals or undesirables out. Next, they nailed the hide cover and attached it to the ceiling to cover the gaping hole. The two second-story bedrooms would have to be rebuilt, but that was a job for another day.

The place was secure, at least for the time being; the rest of the repairs would have to wait. It would take months to get the inn back up and running. "I'm so sorry, Marek," Darla said, almost in tears. The inn had belonged to his parents and was his legacy, and now it was in ruins. She blamed herself; it had been her plan, and it had backfired.

Marek wrapped his arms around her, comforting her. "Don't you dare blame yourself," he said sternly. "We love you dearly." He gave her a gentle squeeze and laughed. "Besides, now I can do those upgrades I've been wanting to do." Marek had been dreaming of installing a third floor, but he'd never had the time or money.

Jenna came out of the kitchen with a broom and dustpan. "Sorry, honey, but we need all our money just to do the repairs. I'm afraid the extensions will have to remain a dream, at least for a while," she said, matter-of-factly. Marek sighed, looking deflated and depressed. She was just stating the facts, though, as hard as they were to hear.

Darla ignored her, distracted by something else. The two chests—
she had almost forgotten about them.

She had a plan, but it all centred on what the two chests held. She
opened the first one, the one plundered from the ship. It contained
rare silks, a jewelled dagger, a small intricate bronze statue of the god
of the sea, a golden tiara, some golden necklaces, a handful of
antique golden coins, and a small pile of silver coins. There was
definitely some money to be made from it, but only if the market was
there and you had the necessary contacts. She and Marek could do
it, but it would take time and effort.

Darla pulled out a lockpick from her belt. Everything now depended
on this chest. She pried her dagger into the tumbler and got to work
on the first pin. Within seconds she had successfully unlocked the
first two pins. The third one was proving a bit trickier, as though the
pin were jammed. She didn't want to force it, due to the risk of
breaking the pick. Taking a deep breath, she gently eased the pick in
farther and, twisting it slightly, was rewarded with a faint click. Two
pins to go!

The fourth pin was surprisingly easy, automatically clicking into
place. One to go! She inserted the pick farther, taking her time and a
breath, and concentrating on being slow and steady. The pick in
place, she gave it a slight turn and was rewarded with a faint click.
When she carefully turned the dagger point in the lock, the shackle
sprang open, and Darla pried it off the chest.

The lid was stiff, the hinges rusted and partly frozen from the cold.
She opened it with a creak and gasped. "Marek, you'll have more
than enough money for your renovations," she said, beaming.
Marek walked over, Jenna joining him a moment later. Both stood
there with their mouths hanging open. The chest was brimming with
gold and silver coins. "This is for you and Jenna. The coins should
more than cover the cost of your renovations." She smiled, as teary-
eyed, they both embraced her.

* * *

She stepped back and picked up the golden statue. "Sorry. I need to keep this. It belongs to a friend, and I promised I'd return it to him," she said. "You'll have to find buyers for everything else. The golden necklaces I thought Jenna could keep, though; after all, she deserves them for putting up with your antics." She winked at Jenna. "There are also a dozen obsidian figurines here as well." Darla felt good about herself; she was glad her plan had worked out and she was able to help her friends, her family.

Smiling, Marek and Jenna nodded to each other in an unspoken communication. "You keep the obsidian figurines," Marek said. "You've done more than enough for us."

"Thank you." Darla appreciated the gesture but didn't know what she was going to do with them. Perhaps she could sell them? She picked one up and examined it, admiring its exquisite detail. They had to be worth a fortune. Suddenly something caught her attention. A brownish-red mark. She scratched at it, flaking more off and revealing more of the brownish-red substance. She sniffed at it, her heightened senses distinguishing the smell. It was clay mixed with traces of lead to add density and weight to the compound. The figurines had then been painted and polished to resemble obsidian.

"Throw it against the floor," Marek instructed. Lifting the figurine above her head, Darla hesitated. "Look around you. I'm going to have to replace the floor anyway." Smiling, she forcibly threw it straight down. It cracked slightly but withstood the impact. A jingling sound, faint but distinguishable, caught her attention. It was a sound she had heard only once before but had been etched into her brain. She began to hyperventilate. Could it really be? She picked up the figurine and, with shaking hands, threw it at the ground again, shattering the casing into tiny shards. Even though her hunch had been right, she still gasped and looked in awe at the sight before her. Mixed amongst the shards was a large, glistening black diamond.

* * *

The merchant and his so-called guards had been smugglers. Had the bandits known what secret treasure they held, or had it been blind luck? She gave Marek a bashful look. This complicated things; she felt like she had deceived them. Marek smiled warmly at her and giving her a hug, whispered in her ear, "I'm a man of my word, Darla. They're yours. You deserve it."

One by one, she threw the figurines, cracking them open to reveal their hidden treasures. All in all, there were a dozen black diamonds, the equivalent of twelve thousand gold coins. It was more than enough to buy her friends' freedom. Hell, she could retire right now as well, relax, settle down and enjoy herself. But she already had accepted the prince's contract. She had committed herself, and her word meant everything. This would be her final contract, though, and then she was done.

After carefully placed the black diamonds in a sack, she walked over to the bar. She would hide the black diamonds in a secret compartment within her room. It had been an eventful evening, and she was exhausted. Before going to bed, though, she needed to have a nightcap and read the details of the contract, find out exactly what she had agreed to. She grabbed a bottle of whisky and a glass from the bar and proceeded to the staircase, juggling everything as she slowly headed to her room.

Halfway up the stairs, she stopped, realising that in all the drama and excitement, she had forgotten to inform Marek about the hay situation and, more important, the wyvern camped out in his barn. The timing hadn't been right, though, and there was no easy way to broach the subject. Slowly she continued up the staircase, pondering the situation. With all the additional money she had given them, perhaps it wouldn't be such a big deal anyway. And if it was, she'd just make sure the wyvern was gone by the morning and just blame the whole thing on the demon.

Chapter 17

Upon reaching the top of the stairs, Darla placed everything on the small table next to her bedroom door. She retrieved her key, which was securely fastened to a long gold necklace she wore dangling in between her bosoms. The room was near the stairs, on the left-hand side, with a large window that offered a breathtaking view of the adjacent lake and forest. It was very picturesque, but that was only part of the reason she'd purchased this room. The window opened near the back corner of the stables, providing her with an alternate escape route, a necessity in her line of work.

She unlocked the door and opened it a couple of inches. She carefully reached through, her hand tracing up the back of the door until it touched a small metal hook. With nimble fingers she detached the thin, taut rope that was connected to a crossbow with a poisoned bolt. A security measure she had rigged up in case anyone decided to break into her room. It was now second nature to her, a practice that had been ingrained throughout her years with the Brotherhood. She opened the disarmed door fully and entered.

After closing the door, she placed the contract, sack, bottle, and glass on her desk. She then unhooked one of the pouches Brenan had given her, tossed it into the air, and caught it, smiling at the sound of the coins jingling within. She pushed the wardrobe aside, the heavy furniture moving easily due to the sliding mechanism to which it was connected. As it slid, a hidden compartment was revealed within the wall space. Within the compartment was a large oak chest with exquisite engravings all over it. Specially made for her, it had cost a fortune. The key was concealed in a pendant that was connected to her necklace. She carefully opened the pendant, pulled out the key, and inserted it. It turned fluidly, and she was rewarded with multiple clicks. The chest had a three-lock mechanism and was nearly impossible to pick.

She opened the lid and poured the contents of the pouch into its depths. The coins fell like a gold waterfall, clinking as they landed amongst the wealth she'd already accumulated. Within the chest was a mixture of copper, silver, and gold coins, as well as a variety of sparkling gems and jewellery. In a partitioned section were her accumulated diamonds. She added the white diamonds Brenan had given her, along with black diamonds. The chest was half full now, making her a very wealthy woman.

Leaving the chest open, Darla walked back to her desk. With a slight scraping, she pulled out the cushioned chair and sat down. Getting comfortable, she raised her legs and rested her feet on the corner of the desk. She then picked up the letter, carefully broke the wax seal, and unrolled it. The letter was written in black ink, each letter expertly scripted.

Using her heightened senses, Darla focused on the first word.

Before her eyes, the text shimmered and blurred. She wrinkled her nose at the pungent smell that had suddenly appeared, a smell caused by cloaking magic. Her hackles rose as well in a warning.

Using her senses to detect the magic was a trick an old friend—or should she say an ex-lover—had taught her. Their relationship had been doomed from the start, with both having secrets and haunted pasts. The trick, however, had proved useful on many occasions.

Her benefactor had used magic to disguise his letter formations, to manipulate and hide information. Was it just his signature or the entire content of the contract? Although Darla didn't know, she sensed it was dark, powerful magic. It was a powerful illusion, masking the original contents of the letter. The spell made it nearly impossible to reveal the prince's actual handwriting or the original contents of the letter without a dispel magic spell. She knew someone who could cast such a spell; whether she would do it, though, was another question. Slowly she read the letter, taking in every detail.

> *Dear Flow,*
>
> *It has come to my attention that you are one of the best, and therefore I'm willing to pay you a considerable sum for this job. Your targets are currently enroute to Baron Sandrik's estate in Belgreth and will be travelling back in eight days' time. You are to attack them on their return journey, eliminating the royal family and killing whatever guards get in your way. Prince Zane has remained behind in Sethanon and is of no consequence, for now. Good luck with your endeavours, I will be in contact once the contract is completed.*
>
> *Sincerely, M Z*

Fuck! Darla almost screamed; it was just her luck. The contract was time sensitive. She wouldn't have time to go to Sethanon, see her friend. To see if she could dispel the magic and reveal the hidden message within the contract. Darla felt like she was being deceived, she had a bad feeling about this contract. She had accepted it, though, and was honour bound to do it. She would just have to accept the consequences that came with it.

To most people, the *Z* would be prominent, standing out from the signature, but Darla could almost make out four scratch marks. Was it a capital *M*? She couldn't be sure. The rest of the signature was indistinguishable, consisting of elaborate swirls and curves. She smiled as she carefully rolled up the letter; she had learnt a long time ago that letters like these were worth more than any amount of gold. They were blackmail material, ensuring not only her well-being but also those of the people she cared for and loved.

She tucked the letter away in a secret compartment concealed in the lid of the chest. After closing the lid, she locked it with the key, which she then placed within the confines of her pendant. She grabbed the wardrobe handle and carefully pulled the piece of furniture back in place. She had an inch to go when a loud knock at the door startled her, and the wardrobe slammed into the wall, chipping some of the wood. Splinters rained onto the floor. Cursing, she walked towards the door and flung it open, glaring at the person before her.

It was Garen, oblivious to what had just happened, holding a tray with some sweet buns. "I thought you might like these," he said sheepishly.

Darla's expression softened. "I'm sorry. It's not you, Garen. Thank you." She grabbed the tray from his shaking hands. The boy smiled, nodded, and started to walk away. "Could you also ask your dad if I can borrow his repeater crossbow?" she called after him. "I've got a feeling I'm going to need it."

* * *

"No problem," Garen said with a nod.

Darla closed the door and walked over to her desk. Sitting down, she withdrew a map and began to plan a strategy. Deep in thought, she gazed out the window at the stars. She devoured one of the sweet buns and washed it down with a swig of wine before turning her attention back to the night sky. She didn't know how long she'd been thinking when she heard another knock at the door. The bottle was empty, though, with only the dregs remaining. She stumbled to the door and swung it open. No one was there, but on her doorstep was Marek's repeater crossbow and a quiver full of bolts.

"Thank you," Darla said quietly. She placed them alongside her other weapons next to her bed. She had the beginnings of a plan in mind, and if it all went to hell, she'd improvise and get the job done. Darla had to get up early for the long, tiring ride ahead. She climbed into bed and extinguished the lantern and pulled up the thick blankets to ward off the winter chill. The fire in the hearth crackled as the flames danced within, warming the room and lulling her to sleep.

Rayze lay on a makeshift cot. Although it was far from comfortable, he found himself dozing. The ride had seemed to take forever, especially since they rode at a canter. Brenan had spotted two elven scouts positioned by the roadside and were ready to sound the alarm at a moment's notice. Even though the situation was tense, no alarm was raised as they continued towards the base camp.

When they arrived, two medics ushered Rayze into a tent. One applied a thick salve, and the other wrapped bandages around his wounds. He was then given an elixir to ease the pain and help him sleep. He instantly felt the effects of the powerful drug. A lesser man would have fallen unconscious, but Rayze wasn't any normal man. He would sleep in a little while, but right now he wanted to reflect for a while longer. He also needed to feed and soon.

A moment later, a drunken battle priest was brought in, bleeding from the neck. He had been involved in a brawl, killing a soldier by caving his head in with his mace. He had suffered a deep cut in his shoulder and a gash on the side of his neck. When questioned, he laughed, claiming it had been God's will. He was given a sleeping elixir, but it hadn't taken affect yet. He staggered unsteadily towards Rayze and stopped a metre from him, his glazy eyes fixated on his stump. Lurching forward, he then vomited all over it. There was no apology, just drunken arrogance as he said with a smirk, "That's a battle priest's healing elixir. It'll grow your arm right back."

The medic apologised profusely and led the priest to a nearby cot, leaving Rayze surrounded with the putrid smell of beef, carrot, bile, whisky, and rum. "You just wait and see. God has plans for me!" the priest screamed at Rayze before the medic forcibly sat him on the cot. *I don't know about your God, but I certainly have plans for you*, Rayze thought. The gash was superficial, so the medic held a rag firmly against it, applying pressure and waiting for the bleeding to stop. "I am..." the battle priest started to say, and then with a thud, he collapsed onto the bed. A second medic approached, holding a large needle threaded with twine. With expert precision, he began to sew up the wound. The sight and the smell of the blood was overpowering, causing a rush, an uncontrollable urge. Quickly turning his head, Rayze breathed deeply, distracting himself with other thoughts.

He smiled as he thought about the plan he and Darla had come up with. They made a pretty good team, and their plan, even with all its flaws, had gone better than expected. The arrival of the demon had thrown things into a bit of disarray, causing them to improvise, but it had saved them from the problematic situation of having to kill Velander. Delusional and psychopathic, the prince would have plunged Aragoth into chaos and war. His death had been inevitable, but instead of it being a smooth operation, everything had gone to hell. The demon's arrival ironically had provided them with a solution, however. They had found themselves sharing a common cause with the elves and had allied with them to kill the demon. And they had emerged as heroes.

Rayze heard the banter outside. The sergeant and the rest of the squad had arrived a short while ago. They now sat, relaxing with their captain, drinking and laughing around a campfire. Rayze watched the flickering flames from the slight gap in the tent opening, listening intently for any mention of the Divinity Stone. There was nothing, at least for now. Instead, they all talked about their battle wounds. They all had various degrees of injuries, minor wounds that would heal soon enough. The fight the sergeant had stirred up had been staged, a show put on to distract the elves, while Brenan and Rayze had snuck out and escaped.

It had worked a treat. Darla had instructed the sergeant regarding how to stem the flow of blood before he bled out. She knew the exact position to aim for, stabbing him in a nonfatal spot that would still causse a lot of bleeding. Even her slice across the swordsman's wrist had been perfectly placed, ensuring she didn't hit an artery. Marek also had been in on the ruse, loading his repeater crossbow with blunt bolts. These bolts were nonlethal and used for incapacitating targets. Their tips, made from rounded hardened leather, would bruise and pack a wallop, though; the two crossbowmen could vouch for it. Rayze continued his eavesdropping, picking up everything due to his impeccable hearing. They teased and joked, laughing at each other's expense, but not once did they mention anything about the fake Divinity Stone.

Darla had successfully stolen the Divinity Stone. She would keep it safe while Rayze took the duplicate gem to Sethanon. It was a perfect copy they would use to dupe Malgorath, lure him out, and reveal his identity. It was a gamble, though, one that would put Rayze's life in peril. Even so, he wanted to do it; he was the best person for the job—or so he'd thought. Now he was questioning whether he should take on the demon prince himself or collaborate with Darla. For now he'd leave it up to destiny. Let the cards fall where they fell; let the dice roll where they rolled.

Darla had grown up into a beautiful young woman. She also was deadly, resourceful, loyal, and independent. Her parents would have been proud. Their families had been friends and, more important, allies. He knew her secret, her heritage, and regretted not telling her, but the timing hadn't been right. Then again, when was the timing ever right? He made a vow that when their paths crossed again, he would tell her and set things straight.

Deep in thought, he removed the ornate gold ring with the mountain and fangs engraved into it. An heirloom, it held powerful magic, masking his appearance and subduing his unquenchable hunger. His features immediately changed, his skin paling to a ghostly white as two elongated fangs grew. His irises also changed, the shimmering blue radiating outwards and encompassing the rest of his eyes—eyes that distinguished his race from any other. He needed to feed, replenish his strength. The drunken brawler would do; he would quench his appetite for blood. The battle priest was snoring loudly. The blood on the side of his neck had dried, the cut sealing and closing nicely. It was the perfect place to camouflage the bite amongst his other wounds. In a flash, he bore down on the man, his fangs tearing into his exposed neck.

The man began to stir and Rayze clamped his hand over his mouth. Groggy from the elixir, he began to struggle and convulse. Rayze continue to drink, quenching his thirst, his insatiable hunger. The convulsing slowed and then stopped, as the battle priest died upon the bed, drained of blood.

Blood dripped from his fangs onto his chin. He lifted the dead battle priest's wrist and wiped it off with the man's sleeve. He felt better, his hunger sated. As he looked at his stump, the bones regrew and the flesh and muscles reformed, sewing back together. Finally, the skin formed, covering his forearm like a pale white glove. Clenching his hand into a fist, he smiled. His hand and wrist were as good as new.

Fully healed, he walked back to the cot and put on his ring, masking his appearance. After readjusting his sword, he lay down. Called "Nightbringer," the sword was magical, an heirloom passed down from generation to generation. His skin resumed its tanned appearance; his fangs disappeared; and his eyes returned to their natural human form. He hated the deception, but it was necessary. The medics would wonder how Rayze's hand had grown back—a miracle, an act of God, they would claim; hell, some of them would even say it was a direct result of the battle priest's vomit.

Let them think that; let them be naïve and wonder about the mystery —Rayze alone would know the truth about who and what he was. Only those who recognised the royal insignia of House Valkryd on his ring would know. The house was an ancient one, with his surname being a name that instilled fear in most people. It revealed who and what he was. A vampire prince! A vampire prince who knew Darla's real name, history, and identity.

I would like to give a heartfelt thank you to my family and friends. I wouldn't have developed the love and passion that I have for fantasy and science fiction if it wasn't for them. Without their love and support, this endeavour would not have eventuated. Janet-Marie, you have been a shining star, guiding me and helping me throughout this venture. Your support, assistance and feedback have been invaluable. My editor Angela, thank you for all your hard work and the positive feedback that you provided. My cover designer Thea, your awesome magic and artistic talent helped to bring my manuscript to life. Thank you, Michelle for your artistic ability and helping me with my author photo (and not cracking the camera lens in the process...hehe).

Jeff, you are a godsend for easing my frustration and helping me out with my author webpage and the other IT stuff that I couldn't get a handle on. Fiona, Marion, Hannah, Mattie and Natalie, all of you listened, shared advice and helped to keep me motivated. My cats also should get a special mention for all the snuggle breaks that they provided me (even though it was partly due to procrastination and distraction half of the time). Bands like Shinedown, Godsmack, Pop Evil and Papa Roach (just to name a few) also deserve a mention for their awesome music, which I spent countless hours listening to, getting inspiration while I wrote the novel. Lastly, I would like to thank my fans. I hope you enjoyed reading the novel as much as I enjoyed writing it!

If you have 5 minutes to spare and have read *The Werewolf Thief* you would make this author very happy if you could write a short review.

* * *

Born and raised in Perth, Western Australia, this is Steven Wombell's first fantasy novel - *The Werewolf Thief*, which is Book 1 to his Divinity Stone series. Holding a Bachelor of Education, he is a passionate primary school teacher, who loves inspiring and passing on his knowledge to his students (especially when it comes to teaching narrative writing).

An enthusiastic lover of both fantasy and science-fiction, he always enjoyed writing this kind of material. Passionate about these genres he often gets inspiration through novels, movies, music and computer games. His other interests include cooking, Lego, cycling, travelling and volleyball. When he isn't writing or partaking in one of his interests, he can be found catching up with friends and family. They are extremely important to him, because without their love and support this novel would have never eventuated.